The Pole Vault Championship of the Entire Universe

The Pole Vault Championship of the Entire Universe

Conor Lastowka

For Carey & Austin

one

It was the last day of ninth grade and Kara Everglades was about to meet her dead grandfather.

He wasn't actually dead. That was just her parents' stance on the matter, and Kara never had any reason to doubt them. There were pictures of her at the funeral as a baby, an urn of ashes on the mantel, and a framed death certificate in the foyer that her father insisted everyone tap when they came in or out the front door. They even kept one of his fingers under a bell jar in the bathroom, as you would a relic of a sixteenth-century saint. Kara had trouble getting classmates to come over to play more than once.

In retrospect, it would be very obvious to Kara that her parents were overdoing it on the whole "your grandfather is absolutely, without a doubt, 100 percent dead" angle. Right now, however, she sat in the waiting room outside the principal's office hoping she wasn't going to miss the bus.

Meanwhile, the cool kids were already getting drunk in a field, the less cool kids were getting drunk in an inferior field, and the miscellaneous kids were huddled in something that was *technically* more of a drainage ditch than a field. The rumor was they intended to race a bunch of bullfrogs at some point in time.

Kara wouldn't have minded attending either of the first two gatherings. Unfortunately, the third was the only one she had received an invitation to. "No bullfrog? No problem!" an eager but sweaty sophomore had insisted, while his friends stood behind him making wincing faces that indicated he was going way off the rails by inviting amphibian-less underclassmen.

Just when things looked to be going south with the frog kids, a group that by no means did you *ever* want things to go south with, the PA system had crackled and a stern voice summoned Kara to the principal's office. The frog kids slunk away, their backpacks wriggling and dripping rather suspiciously.

Kara glanced around the office where she would be spending most of her summer. She had been hired as an assistant to Jefferson High School's principal. Kara hadn't expected to get the job when she applied, but it turned out that filing and light typing weren't how most of her peers wanted to spend their summer vacation, and she had been the only applicant. Kara tried to think of other ways she might have preferred to spend her summer: lounging at the pool, sneaking into R-rated movies, riding her bike… But every time she envisioned an activity, the mental image was interrupted by a group of greasy misfits chasing a few confused frogs across the scene. If the state of her social life was this dismal, perhaps she would be better off at the office job.

"Principal Dunbar will see you now," said Nancy, a sweatpants-wearing sixty-something secretary who looked more like a lunch lady than any of the high school's lunch ladies did. Nancy had actually been the one who conducted the job interview; outside of school assemblies and a few chance passings in the halls, Kara had never actually seen the principal.

Kara didn't even have time to gather her gym bag before the door to Principal Dunbar's office swung open and Dunbar himself stepped into the doorframe. He was a square-jawed man whose rigid posture made his six-foot-three height appear even more imposing. His haircut looked wildly expensive, and he sported a bespoke suit that would have fit right in on the cover of *GQ* or at a movie premiere, but tended to look very out of place when he was disciplining fourteen-year-old boys for throwing tater tots at each other.

"You're still here, Nancy?" Principal Dunbar said, flashing his secretary a winning grin. "You should head home, it'll be fall before you know it!"

Nancy tittered at the joke that she presumably heard at the end of every school year. Dunbar chuckled briefly, then strode over to Nancy's desk with a very serious expression on his face, reached into his pocket, and produced a small jewelry box, which he handed to his secretary.

"With my sincere thanks for another great year," Principal Dunbar said, taking Nancy's hand and pressing the box into it. "I couldn't do any of this without you."

Nancy's eyes went wide. She gasped when she opened the box, and Kara could see the glint of the diamond earrings from all the way across the room.

"Tell Jerry to come out to the club any time. I'm still waiting for that rematch on the links!" Principal Dunbar said, grinning again. "This time *he* can hit the hole in one!"

Obviously touched by the principal's generous gift, Nancy could only nod her head. She mouthed the words "thank you" as Principal Dunbar turned to face Kara.

"And you must be Kara," he said, beaming as he stepped toward her and offered an outstretched hand. "I hear you're one of the bright young stars on our track team."

Kara had joined the track team solely so she could eventually list it as an extracurricular activity on her college applications. Her crowning achievement freshman year had been a fourth-place finish in an exhibition JV long jump event. A stray dog had pooped in the landing area sand right after Kara had gone, and everyone else refused to jump and was therefore disqualified.

Kara reached out and gently returned the handshake. "Well, you know what they say: *Citius, Altius, Fortius.* Faster, higher, stronger."

"Ah, the Olympic motto," Principal Dunbar said, giving Kara's hand several approving, patriotic pumps. "I trust you'll be cheering on our athletes when the games kick off in Hawaii in a couple days?"

Kara only knew the motto because of the incessant commercials that had been running on TV for the past month and had no intention of watching other people compete in sports she barely enjoyed playing herself. "Of course, sir," she lied. "And who knows? Maybe you'll be rooting for me in the games four years from now." Kara quickly bit her lip to avoid giggling at the memory of the equipment manager futilely trying to get the dog to stop rolling around in his own poop before eventually calling off the triple jump as well.

"I used to run track myself," Principal Dunbar said. "Finished just a few seconds behind the great Carl Lewis at a meet once. Of course he was running the mile and I was running the hundred-meter dash!" Back at her desk, Nancy giggled at another joke she'd surely heard dozens of times. "It's great to finally meet you, Kara," Principal Dunbar said, assuming a more business-oriented tone. "Nancy tells me you were by far the most qualified applicant."

Kara resisted the urge to correct him. If diamond earrings were getting handed out for simple acts of secretarying, she didn't want to say anything that might scuttle her chance of a big-ticket reward. "Thank you, sir," she said instead. "I'm looking forward to the opportunity."

"Let's step into my office," Principal Dunbar said, gesturing toward the open door. "This won't take long, I know you've got a bus to catch! I just want to get you up to speed on how this place works so we can hit the ground running tomorrow."

Kara picked up her bag and stepped past the principal into his office. The room smelled of fine leather and pipe tobacco. On the desk were photos of the principal posing at a black-tie charity fundraiser with the local TV news anchor and taking part in a groundbreaking ceremony for a children's hospital with the governor. Just to show that he could play as hard as he worked, there was also a picture of the principal clowning around on a homecoming float with beloved Jefferson mascot Jeff the Jackrabbit. Framed diplomas and letters of commendation lined the wall. Clearly, Dunbar was a well-connected big shot, the kind of guy college admissions officers respected and possibly received regular bribes from. Kara had hitched her horse to the right wagon.

Principal Dunbar pulled the door closed behind him and immediately began sobbing. Kara turned to look at her new boss. Tears streamed down his already wet face as he reached into his pocket for a handkerchief.

"It's my father," Principal Dunbar managed to choke out as he dabbed at his eyes. "He passed away last night."

Kara's jaw dropped. Once in fourth grade, one of her classmates had lost both his parents in a car crash. Unsure of how best to console a victim of such a monumental tragedy, Kara had given him her pudding cup at snack time. He seemed cheered up by it, to such a disproportionate degree that Kara wondered if maybe she had given it to the wrong kid. Kara patted her pockets, hoping for a miracle, but there were no desserts to be found. She began to panic.

Principal Dunbar staggered over to his desk chair, collapsed into it, and laid his head down on his arms. "Boo hoo," he wailed. "Boo hoo hoo hoo." Kara did not know that grieving people actually uttered the syllables "boo hoo." She was in way over her head.

The principal raised his head up off his desk and looked at Kara with red eyes. "He would have loved you," the grown man who had met Kara less than ninety seconds ago assured her. The principal got up from his chair and slowly wobbled toward her. "I would be honored if you'd attend the funeral with me," he sputtered as he extended his trembling arms toward the terrified fifteen-year-old girl. "We don't have much family, so it will probably just be you and me there. I hope you'll be OK with doing a reading," he said in a quivering voice. Kara froze as she realized that Principal Dunbar was about to hug her.

The attempted embrace was mercifully cut short by the sound of the door opening. Kara turned and saw Nancy leaning in to the doorway. "I'm going to take off for the summer, sir," the secretary said. "I just wanted to say goodbye and thank you again for the earrings."

"No, thank you, *Nancy*," boomed a steadfast voice from behind Kara—confident, charismatic, and definitely not weeping like a baby. She turned back to the principal, and was amazed to see him sitting on the edge of his desk, looking relaxed and happy. His eyes were no longer red, and his face was not wet. The handkerchief was neatly tucked back into his pocket and the smell of leather in the room had somehow gotten stronger.

Principal Dunbar flashed Nancy a wide grin. "And I'm serious about sending Jerry by the club!" he instructed. "Something about him brings out the best in my golf game. He's my good luck charm, Nancy!"

Nancy chuckled and nodded as she withdrew her head from the doorframe. Kara heard the door click shut, and not a second later, Principal Dunbar was laid out on his desk again, blubbering and pulling at his hair.

"Boo hoo hoo!" he sobbed. Kara quickly scanned the room for additional exit routes and, in the process, noticed that there wasn't anything in the office that was actually made of leather.

"Where is that leather smell coming from?" Kara wondered aloud, sniffing the air as Principal Dunbar pounded the edge of the desk with his fist. "You're not permitted to smoke a pipe on school grounds either," she mused, moving to inspect one of the bookcases while the principal blew his nose into his handkerchief.

"Is this a scented candle?" Kara blurted as she spotted the telltale flickering flame inside a glass jar on the bookcase. She reached out and turned it around. "Fine Leather and Pipe Tobacco" the label read, with smaller script spelling out "The Trappings of Success Collection" just beneath it.

Kara blew the candle out. Quickly, what must have been the room's original musty odor filled the air again. It smelled like stale VapoRub and microwavable frozen entrees. Next to the bookshelf, a familiar logo on one of the principal's diplomas caught Kara's eye.

"You were presented an honorary degree by Burger King?" she asked in amazement. She leaned in closer to study it as Principal Dunbar wailed in the background.

"I just wanted to make my daddy happy!" the principal cried. "How was I to know they had a reputation as a diploma mill?" Kara continued to examine the diploma. "Bachelor's degree in advanced deliciousness," the embossed script read. "Congratulations on achieving *Summa Cum Whopper.*"

"I was a fool to think this idiotic Burger King degree was worth anything!" Principal Dunbar screamed from behind her. Kara turned just in time to see the principal lift one of the other frames off the wall and smash it in half over his knee.

"No, sir, *this* is the one that says Burger King on it," she said quietly, not wishing to upset the man further.

"Please don't mock me," the principal said, tossing the bottom half of the frame at Kara's feet before resting his forehead on the spot on the wall where it had been displayed. Kara looked down, and sure enough, the fast food chain's logo was on the second diploma as well.

"How many of these degrees are from Burger King?" she asked, surveying the room in amazement. Principal Dunbar made a gurgling noise as he tried to catch his breath.

Kara's curiosity was piqued. She wanted to get a closer look at the framed photos on the wall to see how many of the celebrities were being forced to pose with the principal at gunpoint or how many of the respectable-looking politicians were actually just several small dogs stuffed into a suit, but she didn't want to stay in the office any longer than she had to.

"Sir, if that's all you needed to talk about, I should probably get going," she offered hesitantly. "Bus to catch and all."

The principal turned around. He swayed back and forth for a moment before his eyes focused. He wiped his nose on the sleeve of his jacket and tried to scrunch his face into something faintly resembling the shiny smile he'd sported earlier.

"I'm so sorry. I don't grieve very well," Principal Dunbar managed to wheeze. "Thank God I'll have you here all summer as a shoulder to cry on, Kara. It's not going to be easy, but we'll get through this together. So, the funeral's at nine, what say I pick you up at 6:30 tomorrow? We can get breakfast beforehand."

Through the office window, Kara heard the distant sound of her school bus lurching into gear and pulling away.

two

Kara kicked a rock into the street, hoisted her gym bag onto her shoulder, and slowly started to walk home. A grown man who also happened to be her new boss had decided that she was the only person he could cry in front of, and was probably going to do it quite often over the next few months. And now she had missed the bus and had a four-mile walk ahead of her. Summer was off to a hell of a start.

The walk wasn't too big a deal, Kara told herself. After all, she had routinely covered longer distances during track season. Her attempt to look on the bright side proved futile, though, as all positive thoughts were quickly pushed out of her mind by the mental image of Principal Dunbar bawling and stacking up a sizeable pile of soggy handkerchiefs next to her as his father's coffin was lowered into the ground.

As she walked, Kara's mind raced trying to figure out an excuse to get her out of attending. "I overslept"? "I've been grounded for bad final exam grades"? "I also died"? Everything that came to mind seemed destined to set Principal Dunbar off on another crying jag.

Kara was so preoccupied with the dead-father dilemma that she didn't even notice the car slowing down next to her until the driver gave the horn a quick honk. She looked up and saw a shiny red convertible crawling along beside her. Kara panicked, fearing it might be Principal Dunbar about to pull a drive-by weeping.

The driver lowered the passenger window and waved at her. "Hello, Kara!" he shouted with a smile. Kara leaned down to look in the window. It was not a man she recognized. He looked to be in his late sixties, had a wild white beard, and wore a floral-print shirt. The tiny backseat was taken up by a large suitcase. It looked like he was on his way to or coming back from a vacation.

"Sorry, I'm not supposed to talk to strangers," Kara said, starting to walk again, this time at a brisker clip.

The car accelerated to match her pace. "I'm not a stranger!" the man in the car reassured her. "I'm your grandfather, Cornelius Everglades!"

"Nice try, sicko," Kara scoffed. "Do your research next time. My grandfather's dead."

"Dead?" The man in the car seemed shocked. "Is that what your parents told you?"

"Don't make me call the police," Kara hissed. She silently wondered if the police could also help her with her principal situation. Maybe she could accuse the man who claimed to be her grandfather of threatening to bomb the cemetery. It was needlessly elaborate, could easily scuttle her college hopes, and might ruin an innocent stranger's life, but at this point those all seemed like risks she was willing to take.

"I'm telling the truth!" the elderly man protested, slowly rolling along the road next to her. "Here, I'll tell you something that only I could know. Let's see... Oh, when your father was about eighteen months old, he was toddling around the house naked and his toy chest slammed shut on his wiener."

"Oh my God!" Kara said to the stranger who was providing unsolicited information about injuries sustained by her father's infant penis. She started to walk much faster.

The car sped up. "Is that not something he's ever told you?" the driver asked, chuckling nervously. "I sort of assumed that would be an embarrassing but beloved family story! I'd tease him about it all the time growing up. 'Oh, son, one of these days I'll be telling that tale to your prom date!' That sort of thing. He thought I was joking. When I actually did tell his prom date about it, she dumped him before the dance started, and that's why he was single and free to dance with your mother!"

Kara stopped in her tracks. Unlike the awful toy chest story, the story of how her parents met at the prom when her dad got dumped at the last minute actually *was* Everglades family lore.

"He always told me that his date ditched him because he tried to force himself on her in the car outside the dance," Kara told the driver.

"That's his cover story?" the man said, justifiably appalled. "It makes him sound like a degenerate!"

"Yeah, it's much worse," Kara said. "The real version is only mildly embarrassing. In fact it mostly just indicates a lack of judgment on *your* part."

"You mean me telling the story to his prom date or me letting him waddle around naked near a dangerous toy chest?" the driver asked.

"Both!"

"Well, that's something you can discuss with him later," the man said. Kara had no intention of ever breaching this subject with her father and, frankly, after her last two conversations, was considering never speaking to a man again. But the guy in the car had made a persuasive case for being her grandfather. As she took a closer look, Kara thought that under the beard there might actually be a faint resemblance to her dad.

"Did you miss the bus?" the man who claimed to be Cornelius Everglades asked. "Why don't you let me give you a ride home?"

"I'm not sure about that," Kara said, glancing around for potential witnesses. "At school they tell us not to accept rides from people we thought were dead for the past decade and a half."

"They do?" Cornelius replied. "That seems like an oddly specific safety tip."

"Some kid got hacked to pieces and thrown in a storm sewer when he got in a car with someone claiming to be his dead uncle a few years ago."

"Hm…" Cornelius mused. "I suppose that *is* the sort of thing that can drastically alter a lesson plan."

16

"I think I'll just walk the rest of the way home," Kara told him. "I'd like some time alone with my thoughts."

"Suit yourself—" Cornelius started to say, but his voice was drowned out by the loud motor of a pickup truck revving on the road behind him. Kara turned to look at it and was dismayed to see that the sweaty sophomore who had invited her to the frog race earlier in the day was behind the wheel.

Cornelius pulled his car over to the side of the road a few feet ahead of Kara, and the truck drove up to where the red sports car had been. Several kids sat in the back of the truck. Fishing poles and empty beer cans were strewn about. There were at least a dozen plastic buckets that were full of water, several of which frothed with activity just beneath the surface. Kara saw that the word "ribbit" was scrawled in the dirt on the rear windshield.

"Hey, Kara," said one of the kids in the back of the truck. He held a large butterfly net in one hand, and a giant, cartoonish wooden mallet in the other. "It's going to be a great race. You sure you don't want to *hop* in?" The other kids snickered at what Kara later realized had been a frog pun.

Another kid leered at her. "The frogs really respond well to ladies," he slurred. "It sure would be nice if you joined us." He tilted back a beer can that was obviously not his first of the day.

Kara scrunched up her face in disgust. Out of the corner of her eye, she noticed that Cornelius had parked the car and stepped outside to monitor the situation.

"He's right," said the kid with the mallet. "Sometimes if the frogs really like someone, they seek them out. At their home. At night. In fact, they just might   "

"Loose frog! Loose frog!" shouted the second kid. The boy who had been talking abruptly leapt to his feet in a panic. He bounced from foot to foot, obviously trying to avoid something that was now free in the bed of the truck as his friends started to shriek in terror. There were a few seconds of utter chaos before the boy with the mallet raised it up over his head with two hands, then quickly and repeatedly brought it down like he was playing the Test Your Strength game at a carnival.

"I think you should come with me before this gets ugly," a voice whispered in her ear. Kara jumped. She was so preoccupied with the weirdos in the truck that she hadn't noticed that the man claiming to be her grandfather had sidled up next to her. She glanced at Cornelius, then back at the truck, then back at Cornelius again. She forced herself to nod.

"Good decision," Cornelius said. He took off toward the sports car. After another moment of hesitation, Kara followed after him.

What the hell, Kara thought, as she hastened her pace toward the passenger side. *If he hacks me up and tosses the parts in a storm sewer, at least I won't have to go to my principal's dad's funeral.* As she opened the door and tossed her gym bag onto the suitcase in the backseat, Kara realized this was quite possibly the most depressing thought she'd ever had. She sat down and glanced at Cornelius as she pulled the door shut. He was leaning out the window, looking back at the truck.

"Watch out for frogs, Everglades!" shouted the first boy as the pickup truck peeled out and sped past them. "This summer they're gonna be everywhere!" He gave the mallet a menacing shake for emphasis.

Cornelius gave the frog kids the finger as they sped off toward an evening of competitive amphibian racing and whatever other unspeakable activities went along with such a pastime. Then he drew his head back into the car and turned to Kara.

"Are you OK?" he asked. Kara was slightly unnerved, but none of the boys had been close enough to get frog residue on her. She nodded, but before she could even mutter the words "I'm fine," her grandfather cranked the ignition.

"Then let's haul ass, baby!" he cackled, flooring the gas pedal. The sports car exploded off the shoulder and onto the road where it began to accelerate at a rate unlike anything Kara had experienced before.

Kara barely had time to process what was going on, let alone fumble in terror for her seatbelt, before she heard sirens. Cornelius glanced in the rearview mirror. "Well, dammit," he muttered. He slammed on the brakes and skidded the car over to the side of the road. Once they had come to a stop, a thoroughly jostled Kara reached out and quickly buckled her seatbelt. She looked out her window. They'd come maybe five hundred feet from where the frog racers had hassled her. In fact, the truck puttered past them again as Cornelius applied the parking brake. The boy in the back shook his mallet at her again, but in a slightly less menacing manner since there was now a cop around.

"Let me do all the talking," Cornelius said, reaching into his pockets and pulling out some papers. Kara had no intention of talking to the cop, though she wondered if she could maybe blink some sort of coded message at him to indicate her sewer-based fears.

Cornelius rolled down the window. "Hello, officer," he said with a smile as the cop approached the car. "What seems to be the trouble?"

"I had you clocked at one hundred and fifteen miles an hour," the cop replied, stone-faced.

"This seems like an odd spot for a speed trap," Cornelius replied, trying to sound friendly. "Wouldn't the taxpayers be better served with you out on the highway, busting the real offenders?"

"I'm here twice a day, sir," the policeman replied. "Protecting our most valuable resource: our children. This is a school zone."

"School zone, you say?" Cornelius sounded shocked. "You should put some signs up! How is a driver supposed to know there's a school nearby?"

There was a loud blast of music, and Kara, Cornelius, and the cop all turned to look. Ten feet from the passenger side of the car, on the other side of a fence, the high school marching band was gathered on the school's soccer field. The fifty or so students launched into a spirited version of "Louie Louie" as the drill team unfurled a giant banner spelling out "Welcome to Jefferson High School."

They're practicing already? Kara thought to herself. *At least I'm not having the lamest summer in school.* Just then, the song abruptly concluded, everyone set their instruments down, and two tuba players lugged a keg into the middle of the field. The drum major tapped it and started handing out beers to the kids who weren't already making out with each other. "Dammit," Kara muttered.

"Sir, the speed limit here is twenty-five miles an hour," the cop said, turning his attention back to Cornelius. "You were engaging in triple reckless driving in a school zone. In this state, that's technically a worse crime than genocide. In terms of points on your license, at least."

"Are you not going to do anything about those kids and their keg?" Cornelius asked.

"The Jefferson marching band runs a very successful annual fundraiser for families of police officers who died in the line of duty," replied the cop. "License and registration please, sir."

Cornelius sighed and reached into his pocket. "I was hoping it wouldn't come to this," he told the cop in a tone of voice that indicated he was in fact quite pleased it had come to this. He passed whatever he'd removed from his pocket over to the cop.

"As my passport clearly indicates, I am a diplomat," Cornelius continued. "You're well aware of the policy of diplomatic immunity, no?"

The cop turned the passport over in his hands. "Well, of course I am, but..."

"Well, if you'll kindly hand that back to me and let me go on my way, I'll forget about the police department's egregious xenophobia and we can avoid an international incident!"

"Where is this country?" the cop asked. "I've never even heard of Ha—"

"Typical Americans!" Cornelius shouted. "If it doesn't have an NFL franchise or it isn't the setting of a *CSI* spinoff, you can't point it out on a map!"

"Is that the Burger King logo?" the cop asked, leaning in closer to examine the document. Cornelius reached out and snatched his passport back through the window.

"If the next words out of your mouth aren't 'have a nice day, sir,' they had better be your badge number," Cornelius said. "I can have an embassy full of protestors outside the precinct before you get back from your donut break."

The policeman opened his mouth to protest, but then,

undoubtedly imagining an outraged euphonium player informing the chief that the Jefferson marching band was suspending its lucrative fundraiser in light of the scandal involving the diplomat's speeding ticket, reconsidered. "Have a nice day, sir," he said, before straightening up and hustling back to his car. Ten seconds later, the cop car was out of sight.

"I'm glad that worked," Cornelius said as he turned the key and pulled onto the road at a much more reasonable speed. "If he kept asking questions he might have found out that this is a stolen car."

Kara looked at her grandfather, mouth agape. "I don't think that stealing a car is the sort of thing that's protected by diplomatic immunity!" she eventually said.

"That's OK," Cornelius replied. "I'm not really a diplomat." Upon hearing this, Kara reflexively shrunk back toward the passenger door. Her mind started to race as she tried to decide which limb she wouldn't mind him hacking off first.

Noticing her tension, Cornelius chuckled reassuringly. "I'm sorry, I phrased that poorly." Kara relaxed. "It's just that the country I represent technically doesn't exist."

My left foot, Kara thought as she jerked back up against the door. *I can get around on a scooter if I manage to escape after just that.*

"Would you stop twitching around like that!" Cornelius shouted as he tightened his grip on the steering wheel. "It's very distracting when I'm trying to drive a stolen— an *unfamiliar* car! Look, the country doesn't exist according to those eggheads at the United Nations, but that doesn't mean it's not real!"

Kara relaxed about halfway. Cornelius looked over at her, attempting to beam something resembling a reassuring expression toward his granddaughter. Considering he was an admitted felon, claimed to be a diplomat from a potentially fictional country, and until only recently had been presumed quite dead, it was an admirable effort.

"Look," he said. "It's summer break! This is the most exciting time of year for kids like you! Let's have some fun! What do you say we put on some music?" Cornelius fiddled with the radio until it crackled to life. A classic rock station was blaring the festive opening notes of "Louie Louie."

Kara darted her hand out and switched the radio off almost instantaneously. "I'm not really in the mood," she said. She folded her arms and slumped against the seat back.

Cornelius drove the car in silence for a few seconds before speaking again. "I've got to say," he lamented, trying his best to sound hurt, "you don't seem too excited to see me."

"Excited?" Kara shouted, her sullenness shifting to outrage. "I've gone fifteen years without a single birthday card, or Christmas present, or even a disgusting hard candy that I pretend to like from you! And now you just show up, tell me you're not dead, and expect me to want to bounce up and down on your knee? Listen to your stories about Uncle Wiggily and Martin Van Buren? Fetch you poultices to help with your rheumatic elbow while you're planning your next move in 'Pinochle by Mail'?"

"Have you ever actually met someone over the age of sixty?" Cornelius asked.

"It's too little too late, Grandpa," Kara said, turning to look out her window.

"Look, I know I haven't been the Grandfather of the Year. That competition is rigged anyway. Corrupt sons of bitches... But look, never mind that! That's the old me, Kara," Cornelius said, lowering his voice to a somber, serious tone. "Going forward, things are going to be very different between you and me. You're my granddaughter, I love you, and I'm going to make up for a lot of lost time. Starting now!"

Cornelius gave the wheel a sharp left turn. The tires squealed as the car lurched across oncoming traffic and into a parking lot. Cornelius gave the wheel one more jerk and then slammed on the brakes. The car came to a stop in the drive-thru lane of a Mexican fast-food joint.

"May I take your order, please?" came a garbled voice from the intercom. Kara stared at Cornelius skeptically.

"Well, I didn't mean starting this exact instant!" he protested.

"Come on, I haven't eaten all day!"

"Chicken burrito?" the intercom attempted to confirm.

"No, dammit!" Cornelius yelled out the window. "Give us a minute!" He looked back at Kara. "Trust me," he told her. "I've got some news that you're going to find extremely exciting."

three

"Mom! Dad! I'm home!" Kara said as she flung the front door open and dumped her gym bag on the floor. "I made the A/B honor roll, Grandpa's alive, and Principal Dunbar wants me to come to his dad's funeral. I'll be in my room!"

Kara instinctively reached out and tapped the death certificate of the man who was still fumbling with the emergency brake of the car he'd stolen and started up the stairs. She had only taken a few steps when simultaneous shrieks of "WHAT?" came from the living room. Kara froze, rolled her eyes, turned around, and slowly walked back down to the main foyer.

Her mom and dad were standing in the entranceway to the living room with their arms crossed and worried expressions on their faces. Kara reached down to pet her corgi, Buster, who had waddled up next to her and was panting happily.

"Did you just say what I think you said?" Mrs. Everglades asked. Her father nodded emphatically to indicate his shared concern.

Kara avoided eye contact with both of them. "Uh, I think so," she said, suddenly very interested in the coat rack next to the door.

"A/*B* honor roll?" her mother shouted. "What did you get a 'B' in?"

"Never mind that!" her father said dismissively. "What's this other nonsense?" Kara looked at the still-open front door trying to find the words to describe her ride home from school, but her father continued before she could speak up.

"A funeral?" he bellowed. "What the hell's wrong with that guy! I'm calling the school!"

"Ask them if there was a mistake on her report card, dear," Mrs. Everglades said. "A 'B'? Honestly, Kara!"

Before Mr. Everglades's phone was halfway out of his pocket, Cornelius burst through the doorway, rooting through a paper fast-food bag. "I swear to God, if after all that they still got the order wrong," he muttered, brushing past Kara and her parents. Mr. and Mrs. Everglades's eyes went wide as the formerly dead grandfather made his way toward the kitchen. Buster barked at the intruder twice before losing interest.

Kara's mom looked like she might faint. "I thought you were kidding," Mr. Everglades murmured.

"But you accepted without question that my principal wanted me to come to his dad's funeral?" Kara asked, somewhat bewildered.

"Dammit!" Cornelius shouted from the kitchen. Kara's parents looked at each other, then slowly started to make their way down the hallway. Kara followed after them, Buster at her heels.

"Kara! You said you checked this bag!" Cornelius said through a mouth full of food. He held a burrito with a huge bite taken out of it.

"I did," Kara said, pushing past her parents so she could see what her grandfather was talking about. "I mean, I looked in the bag. It was obviously a burrito."

"A *chicken* burrito!" Cornelius said, waving it around in disgust. "I knew that idiot on the intercom couldn't understand me! Terrific, now I have to go back!"

"Dad?" Mr. Everglades finally spoke up. "Dad, what are you doing here?"

This was a tone of voice that Kara had never heard her father use. Gone was the furious man who was about to berate her principal. In his place was a nervous child addressing a parent. Cornelius, as if seeing Mr. and Mrs. Everglades for the first time, stopped waving the burrito around and took another huge bite.

"Franklin," he said, nodding at his son while chewing. "It's good to see you. Hope you're steering clear of any toy chests! And Marcy! It's been quite some ti— Good Lord, this burrito's terrible!" Cornelius made some exaggerated retching noises and coughed a few times. "Get your grandfather some water, will you, Kara?"

Kara started toward the cabinet that held the glasses, but her mother stopped her. "Stay where you are Kara," she said in an icy tone. "You don't have to do anything this... this *maniac* says!"

"The hell?" Cornelius said, indignant and insulted. "I'm choking on bad burrito here!" Apparently unable to control himself, he took another gigantic bite. As he chewed, he made a few more gagging noises, then snapped his fingers to get Kara's attention and pointed toward the cabinets. Kara walked over to them, pulled out a glass, and filled it with water from the dispenser on the fridge.

"I want you out of this house!" Kara's mother snapped at Cornelius. "Our daughter does not need bad influences like you in her life!"

"I'm a bad influence?" Cornelius said, spraying flecks of tortilla and salsa all over the table. "You've been lying to the kid for fifteen years! You told her I was dead!"

Mrs. Everglades looked too enraged to speak. Kara walked back to the table and handed her grandfather the water. He tilted back the glass and took a huge swig. "If Grandpa's not dead," Kara asked, "whose finger is that under the bell jar in the bathroom?"

Cornelius spit the water all over the table in shock, causing Mrs. Everglades to fume even more. "You told her my finger was in the bathroom?" he shouted while at the same time snapping and pointing for another glass of water. "What the hell is wrong with you people?"

Kara dutifully fetched more water while Cornelius chowed down on more of the apparently quite edible burrito. She handed her grandfather the glass, then walked to the bathroom, where she retrieved the bell jar that housed the mysterious severed finger. She returned to the kitchen and set it on the table, while her parents exchanged a nervous look.

"Jesus Christ," Cornelius said, smacking his lips and taking another bite of burrito as he eyed the bell jar. "This is some serious dedication. What did you do, pay off a morgue technician? Drug a hobo? Hit up an alley in Chinatown?" Kara was somewhat disturbed by how quickly these potential finger-procurement techniques sprang to her grandfather's mind, but she was more interested in hearing her parents' answer.

"Sausage," Mr. Everglades eventually said. He swallowed deeply before continuing. "Old, dried-up sausage and a bunch of raisins all mashed together."

Cornelius shook his head disapprovingly. "And I'm the maniac," he said. Kara took a closer look at the contents of the bell jar. Now that she knew what she was looking at, the "finger" was obviously just a tightly rolled mixture of old meat and raisins.

"What's the dog's name?" Cornelius asked. He set down what was left of the burrito and reached out to take the lid off the bell jar.

"Buster," Kara replied.

"Here, Buster!" Cornelius called. Buster waddled over to the table.

"No, Dad, don't..." Mr. Everglades started, but it was too late. Cornelius raised the "finger" up in the air, Buster sat down to beg, and Cornelius dropped it into the dog's open mouth. Buster chewed once or twice, licked his chops, then panted happily, hoping for more. Kara's parents looked horrified.

Cornelius sat back in his chair and smirked. "Now!" he said, sounding rather self-satisfied. "What do you say we set the record straight with my granddaughter about what really— Oh God, the dog's throwing up..."

Kara looked down at Buster, who had indeed thrown up all over the kitchen floor. "That finger must have been incredibly toxic," she said. "He eats his own poop almost every day and never does that." Buster lay down on the floor next to his pile of puke and started to turn green.

"I know how you feel, Buster," Cornelius said as he polished off the last bite of the burrito. "Consider yourself lucky you didn't have to choke this mistake down!" The last few words were difficult to make out, as his mouth was full of chunks of said mistake.

Kara's mother fumed, her father looked down at the floor, her grandfather licked his fingers, and her dog emitted a slow wheeze. Kara decided to seize the moment. "Why did you lie to me?" she asked, turning to face her parents.

"Excellent question!" Cornelius applauded. "I would love to hear the answer! A child has a right to know her grandfather."

"Not so fast, old man! Where have you been?" Kara said. "Why are you only showing up now?"

"Whoa, whoa!" Cornelius protested, suddenly on the defensive. "I am not the bad guy here!"

"Not the bad guy? You killed my dog!"

"Hey, he might not die!"

"Enough!" Mrs. Everglades shrieked. Mr. Everglades jumped a little and Kara and Cornelius snapped their attention toward the irritated woman.

Mrs. Everglades took a deep breath. "Kara," she started to explain, in a tone Kara recognized all too well. It was a tone that said "It is requiring great effort to speak calmly right now, for with every fiber of my being I am suppressing the vile harpy who lies within purely as a courtesy to you, the harpy's potential victim." Kara had heard her mom employ it in many situations: when she was on the phone with customer service representatives, when she was playing hardball with clients, while inquiring how a neighbor's sick relative was. Come to think of it, it was really her mother's only tone of voice.

"Your grandfather," Mrs. Everglades continued, "was not somebody we considered a good influence for a young girl. He had wild ideas and dangerous theories. Fortunately, right before you were born, as a direct result of these ideas and theories, it appeared that he'd never be allowed back in the country. And we thought we might be able to raise our daughter in peace. As a decent lady." She looked pointedly at Cornelius as she delivered this last jab.

"Looks like you thought wrong!" Cornelius cackled. He immediately backtracked. "Oh God, that sounded bad, didn't it? I didn't mean you were wrong that you could raise Kara in peace as a decent lady. I'm not here to do anything indecent. I meant about me never being allowed back into America. You were wrong about that." Cornelius looked from Kara's mom, to her dad, then to Kara. "Nothing indecent!" he announced to the room, a little too loudly.

"How did you get back into the country, dad?" Mr. Everglades asked, determined to move along before Cornelius dug himself any deeper. His voice was meek, but he sounded genuinely curious.

"That's a great question, son." Cornelius's eyes twinkled. "As it turns out, when they detain you at customs, if you make a big fuss and start shouting about how they're not letting you into the country, eventually they'll just give up and wave you through!" Cornelius sat back in his chair and beamed. Everyone else looked stunned.

Eventually, Mr. Everglades spoke up. He sounded incredulous. "You arrived at the airport... got detained by border security... and you just yelled at them until they let you through?"

"That's right!" Cornelius seemed to relish sharing his tale of triumph. "Just got real angry at everyone! Called them all sorts of names, flew into a rage, broke a few things. Made some various threats. I guess they just didn't want to deal with it anymore and told me to get out of there."

"That is wildly unsafe!" Kara's mother sounded horrified.

"I was frankly surprised that it worked myself," Cornelius conceded. "It was pretty much a Hail Mary."

"You've exposed gross incompetence at our borders!" Mrs. Everglades continued. "Our entire nation could be at risk if any of our enemies discover how easy it is to—"

"Yeah, yeah, yeah," Cornelius said, cutting her off with a dismissive wave of his hand. He didn't sound like he appreciated having his technique questioned, especially as a means of aiding and abetting terrorists. Especially abetting them.

Mr. Everglades cleared his throat. "Dad? Are you still living in... well, *on*... um, you know what I mean?"

"Yep!" Cornelius beamed. "And believe me, it's a great time to be there. Exciting things are happening." He gave Kara a knowing wink. She was about to open her mouth to ask what the hell he was talking about when Buster whimpered from the floor.

"See? Not dead!" Cornelius said proudly, as if he'd played a role in reviving the sick dog instead of being the primary cause of its current state. "Now, tell me, son. The mascot costume. Do you still have it?"

Ever since Cornelius arrived, Kara's father had looked like he had seen a ghost, or at least a particularly horrible traffic accident. But upon the mention of "the mascot costume" his face fell even further. Now he looked like he'd not only seen a ghost, but the naked ghost of an elderly relative, or he was being asked to identify the victim of a particularly horrible traffic incident, and it was an elderly, naked relative. His jaw quivered as he tried to find the words to respond to his father.

"The... the... the..." he sputtered.

"The damn mascot costume, boy," Cornelius barked. "Drag it out of the mothballs, I'm going to put it to use."

"We don't have that filthy costume anymore," Mrs. Everglades hissed, her voice sharp and final. "Franklin got rid of that awful thing when we got married."

Cornelius leaned back in his chair. He stared at Mrs. Everglades for a moment before turning back to his son. "Is this true, Franklin?" he asked with a raise of an eyebrow. Franklin avoided eye contact and started to scratch the back of his neck.

Mrs. Everglades spoke for her husband. "Of course it's true," she said, a hint of delight in her voice. If Cornelius was upset, then Kara's mom was happy. "I watched him march it out to the dumpster the day we returned from our honeymoon. There was no way I was going to live in a house with that filthy heap of rags."

Cornelius refused to look at Mrs. Everglades, opting to narrow his gaze at his son until he was staring at him through icy, narrow slits. "Three generations of Everglades wore that costume for Jefferson," Cornelius said. "Am I to understand that you just threw it in the garbage?"

Kara's eyes darted around the room trying to get a read on the situation. She had no idea what "the mascot costume" was or why it was such a sore subject, but she'd never seen her parents like this. Her dad was sweating and pale. His comfort level appeared similar to Buster's just after the dog had eaten the sausage finger. Mrs. Everglades, on the other hand, looked delighted. Her lips were pulled back into a ghastly little smile and she clapped her hands in excitement.

"If that's what you came back for, you may as well hit the road!" she cackled. Cornelius grumbled something under his breath and shook his head in disappointment. "If you could see the look on your face!" Mrs. Everglades continued. "Maybe you could go out to the dump and search for it! All these years decomposing next to the rest of the garbage may have improved its looks!"

Mrs. Everglades threw back her head and emitted a wheezing, nasal laugh. The sound of it made Kara glad that her mom so rarely displayed such unfettered joy. Kara thought that if a blind person had wandered into the kitchen at that moment, they would have totally believed it was the sound of two penguins having sex. Kara closed her eyes for a few seconds to test this theory before she started to worry that people would be able to tell what she was imagining. She popped her eyes back open, but nobody was paying any attention to her. Her mom was still laughing, her dad was still sweating, and her grandfather was slowly getting to his feet, a defeated man.

"He didn't even put up a fight about throwing it away!" Mrs. Everglades hooted. Cornelius started to shuffle toward the hallway. When he reached his son, he paused. Kara's dad looked down at his shoes. After a few seconds, Cornelius shook his head before continuing on.

"He said he never liked wearing the thing!" the taunts continued. "He said the tradition was stupid! He said he would have rather been a male cheerlea—"

But before Mrs. Everglades could deliver what certainly sounded like something that was shaping up to be a definitive backbreaking blow to any father/son relationship, her husband interrupted her.

"I never threw it out," Mr. Everglades said quietly. Cornelius froze in his tracks and Kara's mom ceased emitting the sound of amorous penguins. Kara's dad raised his gaze from the floor and took a deep breath before continuing. "I kept the costume. It's still in the basement."

The penguins' silence proved to be brief.

four

Kara crouched on the floor and gently scratched Buster's back. Death no longer appeared imminent for the family dog, but the threat of more barf loomed large, and Kara's petting was halfhearted, mostly due to the awkward posture she was maintaining in the event she needed to make a quick escape. After her father had gone down to the basement to retrieve the mysterious mascot costume, Kara had gradually moved Buster away from the pile of vomit. This involved tentatively gripping one of his hind paws between her thumb and first two fingers, then slowly dragging him across the floor, all the while ready to bolt if the dog showed any signs of a relapse.

Cornelius had returned to his seat at the table and sat there beaming. Kara liked to think that the look on his face was one of paternal pride, of renewed faith in his son. But she knew it was just as—if not more—likely one of victory over an old nemesis: her mom. The fact that Cornelius grinned wider and wider every time Mrs. Everglades shrieked a new epithet at her husband made Kara fairly certain it was the latter.

"Lied to! I've been lied to all these years!" Mrs. Everglades shouted into the basement from the top of the stairs. "My mother was right about you! She took me aside the night you proposed and warned me that one day you'd pull something exactly like this!" From across the room, Kara wondered how true this could possibly be. Pulling someone aside on the night they got engaged to caution them that one day their husband would reveal that he'd kept a contraband mascot costume squirreled away in the basement was the behavior of a severe psychotic or a horrible gypsy fortune teller. Either one would probably ruin the joyous moment. Kara hoped when that day came for her, her parents would simply pop a bottle of champagne.

"'Put it in the pre-nup!' she said. 'No costumes!' I thought she was being dramatic, but—" This latest harangue stopped mid-sentence. Kara glanced at Cornelius, then followed his gaze to her mother, who was slowly backing away from the basement stairs with her palms outstretched in front of her.

"Dammit, Franklin, do not bring that up here!" she yelled at her husband. "I am warning you! That thing is not coming into my kitchen."

Franklin emerged from the staircase, pulling a large, furry pile behind him. Ignoring his wife's threats, he began to drag it toward Kara and Cornelius.

Mrs. Everglades balled her hands into fists as she tried to concentrate and focus her rage. "You listen to me! Push it back down the stairs right now, I'll board up the basement, and we'll look into finding a new home! Franklin, I've had dreams where that thing—" Mrs. Everglades's last sentence abruptly ended with a stark cry of horror. "It brushed against my leg!" she screamed as she ran out of the kitchen. The door to the hallway bathroom slammed shut, water began to run, and the distant sound of Mrs. Everglades alternating between wailing and retching filled the air.

"I hid it behind some of the paneling in the basement," Mr. Everglades said, sounding somewhat proud of himself as he deposited the costume at his father's feet. "Moved some of the insulation out of the way. Figured there wouldn't be much of a difference, Lord knows this thing kept the heat in while you were wearing it, huh, Dad?"

Cornelius nodded. "It sure did, son. It sure did." Had Kara been looking at either her father or grandfather at that moment, she would have seen them smiling at each other with expressions that were almost recognizable as genuine warmth. But Kara's gaze was firmly locked on the mascot costume, because it was one of the most ghastly things she'd ever seen in her life. As her father propped it up against a chair, she tried to identify what she was looking at. The fur was faded and stained. Kara thought it might have been blue at one point, or maybe pink, but now it was a flat grey, the color of gruel served to orphans in a Dickens novel. It had a large pot belly with several tufts of fur missing that revealed a chicken-wire frame underneath. Both the feet and hands were oversized paws with long, yellowed claws that resembled infected toenails.

But the worst part was the head. The nostrils were way too big for the nose. The ears had been hacked off and only their fraying stumps remained. The mouth was a piece of fabric designed to look like a big grin, but at some point it had evidently fallen off and been hastily sewn back on. This now made the mouth look like it had been stitched shut, like the victim of a horror movie villain. The eyes were different colors: one bloodshot red and one blue. The blue one for some reason had a narrow reptilian pupil, and hung from a thread off the side of the head. What type of animal or creature this was supposed to be was anyone's guess. It looked like the mascot costume factory had gone out of business, then been looted, then taken over by cult members who assembled everything that remained into one ungodly idol to worship.

"Boy, this brings back some memories!" Mr. Everglades said, beaming.

"You got that right!" said Cornelius. He turned to Kara. "Kara, years ago your father stepped inside this suit for every Jefferson football game. And years before that, I was the mascot at Jefferson, just like my father before me. The Everglades were the longest-running mascot dynasty in the history of the school!"

Kara looked back at the costume and tried to figure out how to respond. There had to be something nice to say, but she still wasn't even sure what the damn thing was. She tried her hardest to concentrate but eventually started to worry that if she stared at the costume for too long, it would raise its arms and slowly start to lurch toward her. She jerked her head away and decided to go with the "that's so interesting" plan of attack.

"That's so *interesting!*" Kara said, still shaken by the mental image of the suit coming to life. "I had no idea that Jefferson's mascot used to be the, er…" Kara stole another glance at the suit out of the corner of her eye, then took a wild guess. "Used to be the hippo! When did they change it to the jackrabbit?"

"Dammit, it's always been the jackrabbit!" Cornelius said. "That's not a hippo, that's Jeff the Jackrabbit!"

"Holy shit, that thing is supposed to be a jackrabbit?" Kara blurted. She covered her mouth but it was too late. "I mean," she backtracked. "I think I see it now. Sure, there it is. I hadn't noticed the toenails."

Cornelius glared at her. "You're probably just confused because it doesn't look right at the present moment."

"Ah, sure," Kara replied. Phew! So she wasn't the only one that thought so. "Send it to be steam cleaned, reupholster the fur, replace the ears, get some normal looking eyes…"

"I meant because there's nobody in it, dammit!" Cornelius snapped. "Of course it looks weird just hanging there limp. You've got to have someone step inside and instill it with life!"

"You stop right there," hissed an icy voice. The three of them turned around to see that Kara's mother had reappeared in the kitchen. Her leg still glistened from her efforts to wash away any residual fibers or germs from her contact with Jeff the Jackrabbit. "Nobody is stepping inside that costume," she informed the rest of the family.

"Is that so?" Cornelius bellowed, puffing out his chest at the challenge. "Well I'd like to see you stop me."

"Actually, uh… I think that's a good idea, Dad." Cornelius and Kara turned to look at Mr. Everglades. Cornelius's eyes narrowed at his son's apparent betrayal. Franklin tried to explain. "For now at least! You see, something… Well, maybe you should just come over here and give the right leg a feel."

Cornelius walked over to his son and knelt down next to the jackrabbit costume. He reached out and rapped the right foot with his knuckles. Then he gradually moved up the leg a few inches at a time, testing as he went. Eventually he heard something of significance and gave the costume leg a tentative squeeze. There was a crackling sound from inside. Cornelius looked up at his son.

"Nest?" he asked.

"Nest," Mr. Everglades confirmed.

"Nest!" Mrs. Everglades shrieked. "A creature built a nest in that thing?"

"Maybe Mom's right, Dad," Kara suggested. "Maybe you ought to throw it out if vermin are nesting in it."

"Preposterous!" Cornelius scoffed. "Any good mascot costume is gonna get the occasional vermin nest in it. Used to happen all the time during the offseason. They're attracted to the darkness and the warmth. Not to mention the salt from all the dried sweat that they can lick to survive during the lean months! You just squeeze the nests up and out or kick them down into the foot. Whatever's easiest."

"There are still nests down there?" Kara asked, looking at the big, floppy jackrabbit feet in a combination of amazement and disgust. "You didn't get rid of them? Or find an extracurricular activity that didn't involve standing on piles of twigs and newspaper that a rat had assembled into a crude shelter?"

"You're making two major assumptions there that I've got to call you out on," Cornelius said, calmly raising his fingers to tick them off. "One, that it was a rat, which is frankly just *so* presumptuous. And two, that these nests were crude. The one or two we managed to squeeze up and out were anything but. In fact, they were—"

"OUT!" Mrs. Everglades shouted. "I want that costume out! I want the nests out! And I want the vermin out. That includes you!" She jabbed a trembling finger at Cornelius. Kara had never seen her mother so livid before. She seemed to be on the verge of vocal cord damage or popping a blood vessel. This was awesome.

"Honey, please," Mr. Everglades said. He dropped the Jeff the Jackrabbit costume and walked over to his wife as it slumped to the floor. As the body crumpled, the head slowly twisted around. It ended up between the two floppy feet, staring up at the ceiling with a vacant yet maniacal expression. It looked like the mascot was doing an extremely difficult yoga pose, or that its severed body parts had been ritualistically arranged by a serial killer, perhaps one who had performed the deed while wearing a similar costume.

"My father doesn't mean us any harm," Mr. Everglades continued, trying to reassure his hysterical wife. "And it's been so long since we've seen him. Let's allow him to leave on good terms, OK? Besides, we don't even know why he wants the costume."

"I thought you would never ask," Cornelius said, making no attempt to conceal the excitement in his voice. "I'm bringing it with me to the Olympics."

"The Olympics!" screeched Mrs. Everglades. "Ha! You'll never get within ten miles of the Olympics wearing that thing! They won't even let you bring it into Hawaii!"

"Well, I think you're wrong about that," Cornelius said with a mischievous tone. "And besides, I'm not going to be the one wearing it. Kara is." Cornelius turned to his dumbfounded granddaughter and winked.

Mrs. Everglades leapt into action with a speed that surprised everyone in the room. Before Kara could even process what her grandfather might be talking about, her mom had dashed over to the kitchen sink, and was rummaging in a cabinet beneath it. By the time Kara had prepared an intelligent follow-up question for her grandfather (the question was going to be "Uh, what?"), Mrs. Everglades was streaking back across the kitchen toward Jeff the Jackrabbit. And before any of them could react fast enough to stop her, she began shaking a can of WD-40 and flicking a long butane grill lighter.

"See you in hell, Jeff!" Mrs. Everglades cackled as she pressed the nozzle on the top of the WD-40 can. The immediate heat from the impromptu flamethrower made everyone leap back and cover their faces. Kara's mom laughed gleefully as she continued to direct the flames at Jeff, sweeping from side to side, making sure that every inch of the mascot costume was exposed to the handheld inferno.

After about ten seconds of crazed laughter, she paused for a moment. Kara heard her mom taking deep breaths over the roar of the blowtorch. Slowly, Kara lowered her hands from her face to take a look at what was left of the beloved Everglades family heirloom. But to her surprise, Jeff appeared unharmed.

Kara's mom was just as confused as Kara. She lifted her finger off the WD-40 nozzle and the fire immediately ceased. Mrs. Everglades looked over her shoulder at the cowering members of her family. Still determined, she turned back to the mascot costume, flicked the lighter, and pressed the nozzle again. The flamethrower reignited, and Kara's mom emitted some halfhearted crazed laughter which quickly petered out once she realized that the costume was just not catching.

"What the hell is wrong with this stuff?" Mrs. Everglades asked, letting the lighter go out as she examined the WD-40 can.

"Ha ha! You'll need more than flames to kill a jackrabbit, that's what we always used to say!" Cornelius smiled proudly as he strode over to the costume.

"Have you practiced that, honey?" Mr. Everglades asked his wife, sounding quite concerned.

Kara walked over to her grandfather, who was inspecting Jeff for damages. Finding none, he looked up at Kara's mom, who still stood staring at the can of lubricant, baffled. "Pure dasbestos!" Cornelius crowed. "This thing wouldn't burn if you sent it to Mercury!"

"Don't you mean asbestos?" Kara asked her grandfather.

"Nah, this was *das*bestos," Cornelius replied. "They brought in asbestos to replace it when some people got worried dasbestos was bad for your health."

"Asbestos was the *safer* alternative to this thing?" Kara asked, backing away in terror.

"Oh, don't be such a worrywart," Cornelius scoffed. "You know how crappy science was back then. They didn't even have computers. Some guy moves the wrong bead on his abacus and boom! The government makes you get rid of a perfectly good dasbestos mascot costume. Besides, your father and I wore it for years and we turned out fi—"

Here Cornelius's reassurances were interrupted by a severe coughing jag. He leaned forward and covered his mouth as he hacked and wheezed. His face turned red and he sounded like he was about to expel several internal organs. After about twenty seconds, the coughing finally slowed and Cornelius straightened back up.

"That was burrito heartburn," he said confidently, noticing Kara's horrified expression. He wiped some sweat from his forehead. "Look, the costume is as safe as can be!"

For the time being, Kara decided to ignore what terminal illnesses the costume might or might not cause in the long run. Right now, her mother was stymied. Mrs. Everglades stood there stunned, looking from the WD-40 to the mascot costume and back again. Soon she'd emerge from her stupor with a new idea of how to destroy it. Kara thought this might be her only chance.

"What did you mean about me wearing the costume at the Olympics?" she asked.

"Well, I meant just that!" Cornelius said. "If you're up for it, I'd like you to carry on the family tradition on the biggest athletic stage of them all! I've got two tickets, and the games start in two days. We can leave tonight!"

Kara looked down at the Jeff the Jackrabbit costume, taking another glimpse at the yellowed claws. Then she looked at her grandfather, the man she had thought was dead until a few hours ago. She looked back at the costume, trying to avoid staring into the horrible mismatched eyes. She looked at her grandfather. Who knew how many additional felonies he'd committed during his missing years? She looked at the costume, trying not to breathe in the potentially lethal material it was made out of. She looked at her grandfather, not sure she could trust a thing he said after so many years of deceit and half-truths. She looked back at the costume, suddenly realizing there was an odor of expired Worcestershire sauce wafting off of it.

"Would you stop looking back and forth between me and the costume!" Cornelius blurted.

Kara jumped. At that same moment, her phone buzzed in her pocket and a chime indicated an incoming text message. She pulled it out and looked at it. The message was from Principal Dunbar. "CAT DIED TONIGHT TOO. BEYOND DEVASTATED. BRING EXTRA TISSUES TOMORROW. WHY? WHY???"

She looked up from her phone and smiled at Cornelius. "I'll do it."

five

Meanwhile, roughly one hundred and forty-six million light years away from the living room where Kara's mom was currently flying into rabid histrionics, a spacecraft hovered, unsure of where to go next.

"I think… left. Take a left," said Zzarvon the Navigator. "Definitely a left. No wait, hang on." Zzarvon rotated the StarMap he was holding one hundred and eighty degrees. "I meant right. We should definitely go right."

Intergalactic StarBarge Commander 9-Krelblax buried his face in his tentacles. How had it come to this?

"You know what?" Zzarvon said, quickly sounding very uncertain again. "It may actually be left. Wait, where are we headed again?"

"We're headed to the Big Dipper, Zzarvon!" 9 Krelblax barked at him, not bothering to raise an eye antenna. "It's the most famous constellation there is, it shouldn't be that hard to remember! Dammit!"

"Right, right!" said Zzarvon, trying and failing to sound calm. "The Ol' Big Dipper. The Biiiiig Dipper. El Dipper Grande…" He studied the map intently for a few seconds. "Sir, this StarMap appears to only be in Latin, I'm having one hell of a time locating anything labeled the 'Big Dipper'…"

"It's the fucking Big Dipper!" shouted 9-Krelblax, finally giving in and spinning around in his commander's chair to face his navigator. "Look for the group of stars that looks like a dipper and navigate us to it!"

Zzarvon flinched at the outburst, and his tentacles that weren't holding the StarMap retracted back into his thorax. "Yes, sir! I'm sorry, sir!" The navigator scanned the StarMap, and smiled as soon as he located something that appeared promising. But just as quickly his face fell again. He looked back and forth between two spots on the StarMap.

"So the *Big* Dipper..." Zzarvon said uncertainly. "That would be *Ursa... Minor*?"

"*Major!*" snapped 9-Krelblax. "*Minor* is obviously the Little Dipper and *Major* is the Big Dipper!"

"Got it! I got it!"

"Regardless of the name, Zzarvon, one of those constellations is clearly bigger than the other on the StarMap!"

"Yeah but I thought it was sort of a trick question. You know, once you factor in the scale..."

"The scale? The *scale*?" 9-Krelblax was furious. "In what nebula does scale work that way? What kind of cracked StarMap cartographer would decide to use a scale that makes small objects look big and big objects look small? And furthermore, why the hell are you even using a printed StarMap? We've got a computer nav system that can calculate everything in a nanosecond, and the computer never holds the map upside-down!"

Zzarvon looked like he was about to cry. All four of his eyes watered, and the foot-long antennae stalks that jutted out of his head and supported his eyes quivered and drooped. In the center of his chest the light of his moodcore turned a gloomy greyish blue. He pretended to study the map, but it was obvious to Commander 9-Krelblax that this was a lost cause. With a sigh, he hoisted himself out of his chair, and oozed across the command bridge to where his navigator stood.

9-Krelblax extended a tentacle and patted Zzarvon on the back.

He took a quick look around the room to make sure nobody was watching, then after deep breath assumed a tone of voice that he hoped projected calmness and patience. "Listen, Zzarvon, I didn't mean to get upset with you just then. But you know how hard it has been for me, adjusting to this new mission. It's been hard for all of us. I just want everything to go smoothly so that when it's all over, we can get assigned some real, important work. Understand?"

Zzarvon sniffled and nodded. "Good," 9-Krelblax said. "Now why don't you let me have a look at that StarMap and maybe together we can figure out which way we need to go, huh?"

Zzarvon nodded some more as he wiped some moisture away from his eyes. Then he shifted the StarMap toward 9-Krelblax so they could look at it together. "Here's what I think we have to do," the navigator said. "So it looks like *Ursa Minor* is 599 light years away, and it's 799 light years to *Ursa Major*. And I'm not sure if we have any business in the Make It A Meal Deal Galaxy, but that appears to be just 100 light years extra. We may as well check it out because it's Free Delivery if you travel 2500 light years and up."

"You utter moron!" 9-Krelblax bellowed. "This isn't a StarMap, it's a takeout menu!" The commander snatched the "StarMap" away from his navigator and furiously scanned it from top to bottom. It was immediately obvious that it was from a deli in the vicinity of the star μ Cephei. There was a logo of a robot in an apron and chef's hat at the top of it. "Piled so high, they might even counteract μ Cephei's massive gravitational pull!" their motto proclaimed. Beneath was a list of sandwiches, salads, and sides that were available for pickup or delivery.

"*Ursa Minor* is just what they call a turkey club you idiot!" he yelled at Zzarvon. "*Ursa Major* means double meat on it! Look at these: the Taurus, that's chopped steak topped with Neptune's Onion Rings. Orion's Belt Loosener: five types of meat, for intergalactic-sized appetites only! Canis Major, that's marinated— wow, that one's actually dog. They have a dog sandwich..."

"Really?" asked Zzarvon. "Is that one eligible for Make It A Meal Deal?

9-Krelblax rolled up the menu and whacked Zzarvon's leftmost eye stalk with it. "How in the hell did you confuse this for a StarMap?" he shouted, delivering several more whacks for emphasis. Zzarvon flailed his tentacles in a fruitless effort to defend himself.

"I'm sorry!" he pleaded. "Delivery boys stick menus on our windshield every time we dock in a space port. We have so many of them now that sometimes one of them gets put in the wrong stack!"

9-Krelblax was furious. All four of his eyes bugged out and inside his chest his moodcore started to glow a bright orange. "You're getting paid to navigate a StarBarge from one corner of the universe to the other and you can't keep the official paperwork separate from the junk mail?" he shrieked. "Why are you even bringing these stupid flyers onto my ship in the first place?"

"Sometimes they have coupons," Zzarvon whimpered.

9-Krelblax took a deep breath. He trained three of his eyes on Zzarvon while the fourth slowly turned to survey the command bridge. Yes, a member of his crew had once again proven to be woefully incompetent, but at least this time there had been no civilian fatalities or, more importantly, damage to the StarBarge as a result. 9-Krelblax knew he had to be careful not to let matters that were so trivial in the long run overwhelm him. Reluctantly, he twisted his fourth eye back around until it was facing Zzarvon again. The intensity of his moodcore slowly faded. Wordlessly, he crumpled the takeout menu into a ball and tossed it away.

"Zzarvon, you are temporarily relieved of your duties as navigator until you can learn the difference between a StarMap and a list of sandwiches," said 9-Krelblax. "Please hand over your navigator pin."

His head hung in shame, Zzarvon reluctantly pulled the gold tri-circle navigator insignia pin off his chest and handed it to his commander.

9-Krelblax took the pin and placed it in his thorax pouch. "Thank you, Zzarvon," he said. "In the meantime, I will fire up the computer and try to figure out the route myself. Navigator dismissed."

"Since you just called me navigator, does that mean I'm technically the navigator again?" Zzarvon said eagerly, hoping he'd found a loophole to quick reinstatement.

"*Former* navigator dismissed!" 9-Krelblax shouted, his moodcore pulsing a furious ruby red. Zzarvon quickly oozed away to a remote corner of the bridge where he found a set of knobs to busy himself with. 9-Krelblax hoped they didn't control anything important.

The StarBarge commander sighed and glided off in the opposite direction, toward the navigation computer. As he oozed along the bridge, he looked down at the bright red glow emanating from his chest. Glowing this color this often wasn't good for a Larvilkian's health. He'd been trying to keep his emotions under control over the past few weeks, but the crew was certainly making it difficult.

9-Krelblax had lost count of how many times he'd been forced to reprimand his crew in the nine months since they unceremoniously departed their home planet of Larvilkian-B. Come to think of it, that was actually something a crew member should be keeping track of. 9-Krelblax looked around for somebody to reprimand, but Zzarvon was still the only crew member in sight. The former navigator stopped fiddling with the knobs just long enough to shoot 9-Krelblax a nervous grin and make an OK sign with a tentacle. 9-Krelblax thought he detected the outer ring of a massive, planet-sized explosion way off in the direction that Zzarvon had been facing, but feeling his moodcore start to flare up again, he took another deep breath and focused his attention back to the task at hand: heading to the Big Dipper so they could pick up some garbage.

Picking up garbage had been the primary objective of the StarBarge *Stupid Butt* ever since it left Larvilkian-B. It wasn't phrased as such, of course. Cruising around the universe picking up garbage was no job for the son of the planet president. No, 9-Krelblax had been tasked by his father with a "goodwill mission" that would "foster harmonious relations with our intergalactic brethren." So far he'd been able to haul in quite a bit of "goodwill," most of it either smelling terrible or glowing a wildly unnatural shade of radioactive yellow. Sadly, very few of the "intergalactic brethren" seemed interested in "harmonious relationships." Most of them were just groaning, or slowly rotting away, possibly due to the devastating effects of the radioactive yellow garbage that the *Stupid Butt* was usually at least several weeks late to pick up.

It was at these times that 9-Krelblax regretted the name of his ship most of all. If he were to land on a planet, apologize to the natives about the delay, then cruise off in a ship named the *Salvation* or the *Joybringer*, the natives might not have whined so much. Hell, even a ship named *Stinky's Trash Service* might have kept them quiet. But when the StarBarge *Stupid Butt* touched down, the natives' (at least the non-mutated ones) frustrations tended to boil over. The mutated ones had, by then, usually relocated to an underground duct system of some sort.

But 9-Krelblax wasn't the captain of the *Salvation* or *Stinky's Trash Service*. He was the captain of the *Stupid Butt*. It was a humiliating situation that was, sadly, 100 percent his own damn fault.

His father, the esteemed president of Larvilkian-B, had given him the ship when he finally graduated from the academy. His father brought him out to a giant StarCraft hangar, where the present sat with an enormous red bow tied around it. 9-Krelblax pulled on one end of the bow to untie it, and his face fell as he realized that what sat in front of him was not the sleek new StarCruiser he had been hoping for, but instead an industrial StarBarge.

9-Krelblax's father had also been disappointed, mainly by the fact that his son had been unable to discern the ship's make and model until he had removed a ribbon that, frankly, didn't cover much of the ship to begin with. This disappointment was quickly surpassed by a much deeper disappointment, as his son threw a tantrum that members of his father's staff still spoke of in hushed tones, and in much louder, substantially more mocking tones when the president left the room and they didn't have to keep their voices down.

As 9-Krelblax wailed and pounded the floor with his tentacles, his father tried to diffuse the situation, enthusiastically pointing out how *his* first vehicle had been a StarBarge just like this one when he was a young Larvilkian. 9-Krelblax was having none of it. As far as he was concerned, his social life was ruined. The gift may as well have come with a bumper sticker that said "Attention ladies: My lower tentacles don't extend past the two-inch mark."

It was in the midst of this fit that 9-Krelblax's father had asked his son what he wanted to name his new StarBarge, and 9-Krelblax had yelled the first thing that sprang into his sullen, pouting mind: "Stupid butt!" According to Larvilkian superstition, it was bad luck to go back on a StarCraft-naming instinct, so the unfortunate name was to be permanent. The outburst rendered the real birthday present, a gleaming new StarCruiser 9-Krelblax's dad revealed thirty seconds later, somewhat anticlimactic. 9-Krelblax named it the *Hell Comet*, drove drunk the first time he took it out, and totaled it by ramming it into the side of Larvilkian-B's nearest moon. "Planetwide disgrace!" the headlines screamed, along with "Seriously, how do you not see a moon coming?"

As it turns out, when you are the planet president's son, this is the exact type of thing that lands you on a "goodwill mission" to "foster harmonious relations with our intergalactic brethren" on a StarBarge that you yourself named the *Stupid Butt*.

9-Krelblax extended a tentacle and activated the navigation computer. The holoscreen lit up with a bright map of the nearby planets and stars. 9-Krelblax immediately noted the flashing icon of one of the nearest planets and a bold warning that said "AVOID—CURRENTLY EXPLODING." He glared back at Zzarvon once more, then called up the keyboard and typed in "*Ursa Major*."

The computer displayed a page for *Ursa Major*. This consisted of the constellation's StarMap coordinates, an icon that indicated there was an outstanding work order, and a couple bulleted "Fun Facts." "Looks like a big dipper!" read the first Fun Fact. The rest of the screen's real estate was taken up by ads for takeout restaurants in the area. 9-Krelblax narrowed his eyes at those before tapping the work order icon. The details filled the screen:

WORK ORDER #: 57-HVR2XP9
    SUBJECT: trash
    DETAILED DESCRIPTION: come get the trash
    SERVICE REQUEST DATE: trash

9-Krelblax leaned in closer to examine the SERVICE REQUEST DATE. He was pretty sure that in the online form you filled out to request a StarBarge pickup, this field supplied a little calendar where all you had to do was click the date you wanted. He wasn't sure how someone had managed to get the field to say "trash."

For a brief moment, 9-Krelblax felt the weight of every wrong decision he'd ever made settle on him. The entitlement, the laziness, the drunk driving, the rudeness; it all descended on him like a stark, black cloud of disappointment and failure. He was an underachiever who had besmirched his family's name, but despite being wildly undeserving of a second chance, he had been given one. Maybe, just maybe, if he swallowed his pride and worked hard enough at this humiliating, smelly assignment, he might be able to claw his way back to redemption.

He quickly brushed these feelings aside and tried to figure out if this improperly filled out date field was justifiable cause for voiding the entire work order and saving himself a trip across the galaxy.

But soon enough, the weighty sensation crept back into his mind, and he knew that this time he wouldn't be taking the easy way out. He turned and called across the bridge to his disgraced navigator. "Zzarvon! Summon all essential crew members to the bridge! I need to speak to them face-to-face."

Zzarvon saluted, then pressed a button on his communicator. "Attention," his voice boomed out over the *Stupid Butt*'s PA system. "This is Zzarvon the Navigator. All essential crew must report to the—"

9-Krelblax quickly fumbled for his own communicator. There was a squawk of feedback over the PA as he interrupted. "Zzarvon has actually been temporarily stripped of all navigation duties!" he blurted. "You should not address him as Zzarvon the Navigator, and more importantly, he is not to introduce himself as such until his duties are reinstated!" 9-Krelblax clicked his communicator off and smirked at Zzarvon.

Zzarvon looked back at his commander and slowly clicked his communicator back on. "Commander 9-Krelblax has instructed me to summon all crew members—"

Another burst of feedback. "All *essential* crew members! Just essential!" 9-Krelblax clicked his communicator back off.

Zzarvon slowly started to speak again. "Right. 9-Krelblax has instructed me to summon all essential crew members to the captain's chambers immediate—"

The loudest, shrillest feedback yet caused the former navigator to shoves tentacles into his ear openings. "To the *bridge!*" 9-Krelblax corrected.

"Do you want to make the announcement?" Zzarvon asked.

"Of course not," replied 9-Krelblax. "Such a lowly duty is beneath a commander of my stature." The navigation system beeped and 9-Krelblax turned one of his four eyes to the blinking screen. "REMINDER: GO GET THE TRASH" the screen flashed in bright red letters. 9-Krelblax swiped the alert away in disgust as Zzarvon clicked on his communicator one more time.

"Right. So, our esteemed commander 9-Krelblax has instructed me to summon..." he paused, to make sure he had everything right.

SQUAWK! "All essential crew members," 9-Krelblax said into his communicator. SQUAWK!

"To the..."

SCREECH! "To the command bridge." SCREECH!

"This has been an announcement from Zzarvon the..."

SQUAWK! "The *temporarily relieved-of-duty* navigator!" SCREECH!

"Thank you, Zzarvon," 9-Krelblax said as he clicked off his communicator. "I hope you understand how unprofessional it would be if I had to make such a mundane announcement myself. On a ship like this, one has to keep the chain of command firmly in place if one expects to get anything done."

Zzarvon nodded. Five minutes passed. Not a single Larvilkian appeared on the command bridge.

9-Krelblax's moodcore started to glow a deep orange again and after thirty more seconds he angrily clicked on his communicator. "Get your worthless tentacles down here!" he bellowed into the device. Moments later, the doors to the command bridge slid open with a hiss, and the essential crew members of the *Stupid Butt* quickly oozed through.

There were Lieutenant Ogrot, 3-Berak the Weapons Master, and Technician Class A Timblorx. Along with Zzarvon, they comprised his four-member essential crew. They were in fact, the *only* four members of his crew, but 9-Krelblax thought calling them an essential crew made him sound more important. They kept the *Stupid Butt* running like a well-oiled machine, at least when Technician Timblorx remembered to oil the ship and its various machines, which rarely actually happened.

"What the hell took you idiots so long?" 9-Krelblax barked as his staff slunk past him to join Zzarvon. "You were summoned five minutes ago!"

"Sorry, sir," Technician Timblorx said, staring remorsefully at the floor with three of his eyes. "We heard Zzarvon and assumed it wasn't important."

"You should really make those announcements yourself if you want people to pay attention," added Lieutenant Ogrot.

"I made like half the announcement myself because Zzarvon kept screwing it up!" yelled 9-Krelblax.

"Half an announcement is my new personal best!" Zzarvon announced. The rest of the essential crew murmured their congratulations to the navigator as 9-Krelblax felt his moodcore ramping back up to a brilliant ruby red.

"Silence!" the commander bellowed. His four essential crew members snapped to attention. 9-Krelblax stared them down for a few moments, then folded his tentacles behind his back and began to ooze back and forth in the closest approximation of dramatic pacing he could muster.

"There comes a time in every Larvilkian's lifespan," 9-Krelblax intoned solemnly, "when he must look at his holographic representation in the mirror-scope and ask 'Is this what I want?' After all, on average one can only expect to circulate the Tri-Sun three hundred and ninety-one times in one's life. Should we be content to spend that time puttering around the galaxy, hauling away other civilizations' trash? Or should we aspire to more? Should we aspire…" Commander 9-Krelblax stopped oozing and paused dramatically at a window to look out into the infinite void of space. "To greatness?"

His words hung in the air. At first the effect was dramatic, but as the silence lingered, 9-Krelblax began to grow suspicious. He rotated his leftmost eye to face behind him and saw that the essential crew members were all huddled around the takeout menu that Zzarvon had confused for a StarMap earlier.

"Is the Canis Major eligible for the Make It A Meal Deal?" whispered Ogrot.

"The menu's unclear about that," Zzarvon whispered back.

Furious, 9-Krelblax whipped his other three eyes around, his body quickly following. As he spun, the commander reached a tentacle inside his thorax pouch and produced a ray gun. He aimed it at the takeout menu and pulled the trigger. A green burst of electrified plasma shot out of the ray gun, traveled across the room, and disintegrated Weapons Master 3-Berak, the farthest Larvilkian from the menu by a good five feet, into a pile of dust.

9-Krelblax stared at the weapon. "Goddamn calibration on this thing is worthless!" he muttered. "Well, it serves him right for maintaining the weapons so poorly!"

"Actually, sir," Zzarvon hesitantly chimed in. "He'd only been weapons master for two days. We hired him after you also disintegrated the last weapons master."

"That was an accident!" 9-Krelblax said. "You all know that!"

"We know, sir," said Technician Timblorx. "It misfired when you were trying to disintegrate me."

"If you'd just keep the damn machines oiled I wouldn't—" 9-Krelblax felt his moodcore throbbing and took a deep breath to get his emotions under control. He looked at his men. "My point is—"

"We heard you!" said Lieutenant Ogrot. "Limited Tri-Sun cycles, picking up trash, that's how you want to spend your life. Very inspiring, sir."

"That's not what I was saying at all! What I was saying was, do you want to spend your days picking up trash, or do you want to try to achieve great—"

A loud whooshing noise interrupted him. 9-Krelblax looked down at the pile of dust that had been 3-Berak. A service bot had rolled onto the bridge. The lowly frisbee-shaped service bots did all the jobs the Larvilkians were too lazy to do. They were extremely busy. The service bot extended a hose and started to vacuum up the former weapons master.

"WHAT'S THAT, SIR?" Zzarvon yelled over the noise.

"I'LL WAIT UNTIL IT'S DONE!" 9-Krelblax replied.

The service bot continued vacuuming for nearly forty-five seconds before the dust was finally gone. As the sound died, 9-Krelblax spoke up again. "So, the question is, do you want to spend your days picking up trash, or do you—"

A blue light on top of the service bot turned on and it started to emit an even louder noise than the vacuuming. The bot extended a large, fluffy rotating appendage and began to buff the floor where the dust pile had been.

"WOULD YOU PLEASE DO THAT LATER?" 9-Krelblax shrieked at the service bot. The blue light turned off, the buffer retracted, and a chime sounded to indicate compliance. The service bot began to roll away.

9-Krelblax started up one more time, speaking quickly so he could avoid any more interruptions. "Do you want to pick up trash or to do you want to—"

There was a loud bang, followed by the sound of twisting metal. All four of the Larvilkians turned to look at the service bot, which had ground to a halt in front of the command bridge door and was now billowing clouds of black smoke.

"I've been meaning to oil that thing," Technician Timblorx said sheepishly as the service bot burst into flames. The surviving essential crew members casually inched away. Zzarvon stifled a cough.

Do you want to pick up trash or do you want to do something great with your life? 9-Krelblax thought to himself. But as he watched the command bridge doors slide open, and another rusty service bot start to creak its way toward the remains of the first one, he couldn't bring himself to say it.

Instead, he looked down at the floor, sighed, and then, without looking up, muttered, "Order me an Orion's Belt Loosener, would you, Zzarvon?"

six

Kara sat in the passenger seat of her no-longer-dead grandfather's stolen car as it sped through the summer night toward the airport. Every time she tried to tell herself that this wasn't actually happening, that it was all some kind of weird, possibly food-poisoning-induced dream, she remembered that her cheeks hurt. She hadn't stopped grinning since she left her parents' house.

There had been no time to pack, so Kara had hastily tossed a bunch of clothes and toiletries into her gym bag, which sat in the back seat. Next to it was a giant reusable canvas shopping bag that Jeff the Jackrabbit had been shoved into. Kara had purposely brought an absurdly large amount of clothes just so she wouldn't have room to pack any part of the dasbestos costume in her gym bag. One of Jeff's feet jutted out of the shopping bag, its yellowed claws reflecting the headlights of the passing cars.

Once she'd announced her intentions to accompany her grandfather to the Olympics, and thereby avoid a summer of close contact and funeral attendance with her emotionally unstable principal, the already tension-filled Everglades household had erupted into the type of chaos usually reserved for a murder trial where the murderer makes a kissy face at the victim's family after being acquitted on a technicality. Her mother immediately forbade her to leave the house; first for the rest of the evening, then for the entire summer, and finally for an indeterminate number of decades. Indeterminate because as Mrs. Everglades grew angrier, her screaming voice became less coherent. Eventually it began to sound less like a woman in her mid-forties and more like the noise the two penguins would make if they were being fed feet-first into a rusty paper shredder.

Once she realized that there was no point in reasoning with, or even attempting to understand, her mother, Kara had dejectedly shuffled upstairs to her bedroom. She looked at the same old bed she'd slept in for the past nine years. Glanced over the same old stuffed animals that greeted her every morning. Glared at the same old construction-site-style flip-numbers sign that said "1708 Days Without an Adventure." *Why did I ever put that up?* Kara wondered. *And why did I call and order extra numbers when it hit the one-thousand mark instead of just taking it down?*

Kara was in the midst of convincing herself that the encounter with the frog racers qualified as an adventure so she could turn the numbers back to zero when she realized she was crying. It had taken a lot of guts to step outside her comfort zone and cast her lot in with her grandfather. To get shot down immediately was beyond discouraging; it was devastating. She was wrong to try to have an adventure. Hell, she may as well order the extra numbers for the *ten*-thousand mark right now.

Just then her phone buzzed. Another text from Principal Dunbar. "GOT A REPLACEMENT CAT FROM THE POUND AND IT JUST DIED TOO. WHY???"

Kara typed out "that took less than an hour, how is that possible, please don't get another one" in reply. Then she thought better of it, deleted it, and typed out "so sorry for your loss, sir." She was about to hit send when she heard a knock at her door. Assuming it was her grandfather coming to say something along the lines of "Goodbye forever, guess the next time I see you will be at my *real* funeral," she shoved the phone back in her pocket, sniffled, and went to answer the door.

To Kara's surprise, it was her father.

She had no desire to talk to her parents at the moment, but something about Mr. Everglades's expression kept Kara from slamming the door. He looked as nervous as she felt dejected. Her father glanced over his shoulder to make sure his wife wasn't within earshot. This seemed unnecessary as Mrs. Everglades's incoherent ranting could still be heard echoing from the kitchen. Occasionally something would shatter.

"Can I talk to you?" Mr. Everglades asked.

"There's nothing to talk about," Kara replied, trying not to let her voice waver.

"Kara, you should give your father a chance." Mr. Everglades stepped to the side to reveal that Cornelius was standing behind him.

Kara looked at her smiling grandfather and sniffled. "Wait, who is she yelling at down there?"

"I dunno... Buster? Some leftovers in the fridge? Once she gets going like this she's sort of in her own little world," Mr. Everglades explained. "I'll just have to listen for when she starts sounding tired, then sneak back into the room and look appropriately chagrined. Can I come in?"

Kara glanced at Cornelius, who gave a nod of reassurance. She moved out of the doorway and let her father into her room. Before he had a chance to speak, Kara was looking down at the floor and apologizing.

"Look, Dad, it was a stupid idea. I know I have responsibilities that I agreed to and I can't just back out of those because something better came along. I was just about to text Principal Dunbar about his cat when you knock—"

"Honey, I think you should do it," her father interrupted.

Kara snapped her head up and locked eyes with her dad. "You what?"

"I think you should go with your grandfather," Mr. Everglades smiled. "It'll be exciting. You work so hard during the school year, and maybe that's because your mother and I push you too hard. Between schoolwork and track, you never have time for adventures. I think you deserve one."

Kara stared at her dad for a few seconds, then looked back at her grandfather, who smiled and winked from the hallway. Her face lit up and she embraced her father.

"Oh, Dad!" she exclaimed. "Thank you!"

"Why is the principal texting you about his cat?" Mr. Everglades asked as he gently returned the embrace.

"Never mind that," Kara said rather quickly. "But what am I going to tell him? He's been counting on me to work as his assistant for weeks now."

Kara's dad pulled away from the embrace and placed both of his hands on her shoulders. "Kara," he said in a reassuring voice. "You have the rest of your life to work. But you're only young once. Principal Dunbar may have graduated *Summa Cum Whopper*, but he doesn't get to control your summer. I'll call him tomorrow and tell him you got another opportunity that you couldn't pass up."

"You have no idea how much this means to me!" Kara said, pulling her father in even tighter.

"You're going to have a great time," Mr. Everglades said, gently patting her on the back with one hand. "And besides, it means a lot to me, too. Your mother really doesn't like having sex when you're in the house."

Kara pulled away from the embrace in a flash and grimaced like she'd just walked in on said act occurring.

Her father barreled on, oblivious to his daughter's immediately elevated level of discomfort. "Yeah, she's always been like that. Says your presence 'de-hornyizes' her."

Whatever horrors might have awaited me at the frog races could never compare to this, Kara thought. She looked to the doorway for help, but Cornelius was already backing away with both palms raised. He shook his head and mouthed "good luck" before turning and darting for the stairs.

"Now, I'm not familiar with that particular medical term, but I will assure you that sex with your mom is just out of the question if you're within a three-county area," Kara's dad continued.

I would rather be helping Principal Dunbar pick out a third cat, staying with him for as long as it took the thing to die, then going back to pick out a fourth, Kara thought.

"So, my point is," her father said, wrapping up his horrible soliloquy, "I'm in favor of your trip to Hawaii with your grandfather because it will provide me with the first opportunity for some serious action with your mom in a long, long time."

"Please, Dad," Kara said, taking a quick breath and hoping that she wouldn't join Buster on a "Members of the Everglades household who have vomited tonight" list. "You were doing fine with the 'you're only young once' talk."

"Long time," Mr. Everglades repeated, staring at an indeterminate point somewhere in the middle distance.

From downstairs came a noise that sounded like a Tasmanian devil undergoing a colonoscopy.

* * *

"Fourteen miles." Cornelius's voice snapped Kara back to the present. She looked over at her grandfather who pointed up at a highway sign: AIRPORT EXIT—14 MILES. Kara shook her head and made a vow to never think about the real reason she had been granted permission to go on this adventure again.

"I don't want to risk another encounter with airport security," Cornelius continued. "Yelling at them worked last time, but who knows when they'll wise up to that tactic. I need to look as upstanding as possible and, unfortunately, that means this sweet beard of mine needs a trim. Kara, I stashed a razor in the glove box, will you grab it for me? I'm just going to give myself a quick shave."

This isn't that odd of a request, Kara told herself. Her mom would often touch up her lipstick at a traffic light. *Besides, when you're driving to the airport in a car you freely admit is stolen, it's probably best to minimize how much attention you attract.* She opened the glove compartment.

"I don't see an electric razor." There were a few maps and a leather zipper case that she assumed contained the car's manual and registration, but nothing resembling the bulky Norelco that her father used.

"Do I look like a wuss?" Cornelius scoffed. "Unzip that black case, I do it the old fashioned way."

Kara reached in, pulled out the leather case, and unzipped it. Inside, there was a small wooden bowl with what looked like a piece of soap embedded in it, a bristly brush, and an imposing six-inch hunting knife with a handle made of some sort of tusk. Without taking his eyes off the road, Cornelius reached over and grabbed the bowl. He set it in his lap, then fumbled around underneath his seat until he pulled out a half-empty bottle of water. He poured a few splashes of water into the bowl, then threw the rest into the backseat without bothering to put the cap on. "Brush," he said to Kara, extending his right hand.

"I don't think this is a very good idea," Kara said hesitantly.

Cornelius sighed and impatiently started to root around in the kit, coming dangerously close to gripping the knife blade several times.

"OK, OK, here!" Kara relented, quickly handing him the brush.

"Do you mind taking the wheel?" Cornelius asked. Without waiting for a response, he took his other hand off the steering wheel, gripped the bowl, and started stirring the contents with the brush.

"I don't even have a driver's license!" Kara protested.

"You've really got to work up a good lather," Cornelius said, ignoring her as he furiously whipped the brush around in the bowl. The car started to drift to the right and Kara had no choice but to reach over her grandfather and start steering.

"Boar's bristles," Cornelius continued. "Don't use a brush made of anything else. Their stiffness is the key." Kara stared ahead in terror, gripping the wheel with white knuckles. The car shot past another highway sign: AIRPORT EXIT—7 MILES.

"How fast are we going?" Kara shrieked. "Didn't we just pass a sign that said fourteen miles?"

"You worry about keeping the car straight and I'll worry about the gas pedal," Cornelius said. He dropped the brush then dipped his fingers into the shaving bowl. Kara couldn't see the speedometer, but she was fairly certain she felt the car accelerate slightly as Cornelius defiantly smeared the later all over his face.

The stolen sports car careened down the highway as Kara desperately tried to keep it in one lane. Once Cornelius had lathered up to his satisfaction, he reached for the knife, then held it up admiringly. The edge was so sharp that Kara swore she could hear it humming.

"Now this part is going to be critical," Cornelius said as foam began to drip off of his chin. "You jerk the wheel or sideswipe another car and you'll be going to two funerals tomorrow."

"We must be going two hundred miles an hour!" Kara screamed. "If I… I mean, if *you* sideswipe a car we're *both* going to die!" Cornelius held up a finger to his lips to shush her. Then he tilted his head back and lifted the knife so that it was just underneath his right ear. Kara took a deep breath and turned her attention back to the highway.

Just then, a medium sized beetle flew into the windshield with a soft splat. This barely perceptible impact startled Cornelius and the knife sailed backwards out of his hand. It plunged into the headrest behind him and sank all the way through until the tip emerged out the back.

"Watch where you're going, dammit!" Cornelius yelled.

"The bug flew into us!" Kara shouted right back. "There was nothing I could do!"

"Well don't let it happen again! I get very jumpy when I'm holding something that sharp next to my jugular!"

"You *should* be jumpy! That thing went through the headrest like warm butter! It could probably slice through bone!"

Cornelius had turned around and was wrestling with the knife. Kara noted with amazement that he was still able to keep his foot on the gas pedal while he was doing this. Pulling the knife back out proved difficult, so eventually Cornelius gave up and pushed down on the tusk handle, like he was cutting a piece of birthday cake. The knife was so sharp that it easily glided through the rest of the headrest and came out the bottom.

He turned back around and pointed the knife at Kara. "No more surprises," he said sternly. Kara gulped and nodded, hoping that the next few moments would be free of shocking distractions, such as the car in front of them putting on its turn signal or an ad for a mattress dealer coming on the radio.

Cornelius lifted the knife to his ear again, and then with a few quick strokes, reduced his beard to a pile of trimmings on his lap. He turned back to Kara and grinned. With the beard removed, he looked at least a decade younger. His smile seemed less maniacal and more boyish. Kara thought it made the resemblance to her father even more pronounced. She felt her grip on the wheel relax, and she exhaled.

At that exact same moment the car hit an enormous pothole. The knife flew up out of Cornelius's hand again, pierced straight through the convertible's soft top, and sailed out into the night. The car lurched to the right. Kara froze. Cornelius seized the wheel and yanked it hard to the left. The car, which had obviously suffered at the very least a flat tire, and possibly cracked an axle, barely responded. Kara started to scream.

Cornelius slammed on the brakes as the car fishtailed across three lanes of traffic. Even with the brake pedal fully depressed, the speeding sports car had been going so fast that it would be a while before it could stop. Kara saw a sign rush by that said "AIRPORT EXIT—½ MILE." She barely had time to process it before Cornelius emitted a huge grunt of exertion and pulled the emergency brake up as far as he could manage.

Metal squealed, rubber burned, piles of recently shaved beard hair flew into the air. Somehow, Cornelius managed to keep the car from sailing off the road. It rounded the curve of the exit at something finally resembling a normal speed and wobbled out onto the airport road.

Cornelius was by now practically standing on the brake pedal, and eventually the car skidded to a halt next to a sign with a little airplane logo on it. It said "Cellphone/Shaving Lot." Kara looked over at the two dozen or so cars idling in the lot. A few people were answering phone calls from newly arrived passengers ready to be picked up. The vast majority of them were shaving.

"Well!" Cornelius snorted. "How was I supposed to know they had one of *these*!"

He released the emergency brake, revved the engine, and the car puttered off toward the airport as fast as it could manage, which to Kara's relief was not very. The vehicle tilted noticeably toward the passenger side and the front two wheels sounded like they were about to fall off. Fortunately, the terminal was only about a third of a mile down the road, and Cornelius eventually guided the car into the mostly empty departures area.

Cornelius pulled over to the curb in front of a skycap station. "That wasn't so bad, was it?" he asked Kara with a smile. He popped what was left of the emergency brake and pulled the keys out of the ignition.

Kara looked at the hole in the roof and then reached out and poked the sheared-off part of the headrest. "Is it legal to have a knife that sharp?" she asked.

"Don't ask me about my blade," Cornelius hissed. Kara had never encountered someone who referred to a knife as a "blade" before. Therefore, she had certainly never encountered anyone who demanded that you not ask questions about said "blade." She was, however, able to quickly determine that when encountering such a person, it was best not to point out that the blade in question was no longer technically in their possession. That might be the sort of thing that would make them start twitching, and the last thing you wanted someone who called a knife a "blade" to do was start twitching.

Fortunately, before anyone could start twitching, a light shone through the windshield. Cornelius and Kara both raised a hand to shield their eyes. A skycap was holding the flashlight and gesturing at them to keep moving.

"Grab your bags," Cornelius muttered. "I'll handle this." He opened the door and stepped out. Once the door slammed shut, Kara pulled her gym bag and the shopping bag with the mascot costume out of the backseat, then hopped out of the car herself.

"Move along," the skycap was saying to her grandfather. "You can't park here."

"Keep it," Cornelius said, and coolly tossed the skycap the keys as if he'd practiced the move many times.

The skycap deftly snatched the keys out of the air and propelled them back toward Cornelius in one motion. They hit him in the chest and fell to the ground. Cornelius looked down at the keys then back at the skycap, dumbfounded.

"No way, man," the skycap said, shaking his head and holding up his palms. "Absolutely not."

"What the hell do you mean, 'Absolutely not'?" Cornelius demanded. "I said 'keep it' and tossed you the keys. You keep the car, we've got a flight to catch!"

"This is like the fifth one today," the skycap said. He gestured to the curb in front of where Cornelius had parked. There were several sports cars, each one hastily parked at an odd angle. The skycap reached into his pocket and produced a wad of keychains. "People pull up in a hurry and just shrug and say 'Keep it!' and toss me the keys. You have any idea how big a burden it is to come into possession of four cars during a single shift? Any idea of the registration fees and taxes involved? Plus, I live forty minutes from here! Even if I were to drive one home, then take a car service back, that's like five, six hours to drive all of these cars to my apartment!"

"You don't have a roommate that could drive you back and forth?" Cornelius asked.

"I have a *wife*, thank you very much," the skycap snapped. "And she has better things to do than help me transport my unwanted cars. She's made that clear to me, *and* to our therapist. I honestly don't know how I'm going to explain these four new ones. I've already got her moving cars a dozen times a day so we don't get parking tickets."

"I never really thought I might be imposing a burden on the guy I flip the keys to,'" Cornelius said, somewhat remorsefully.

"Nobody does!" the skycap replied. He waved his flashlight at another car lingering at the curb a few yards behind them. "Everyone's in such a hurry to get to their damn flight. If you all would plan a bit better, you could take advantage of the airport's extremely reasonable long-term parking rates. How close did you cut it, if you don't mind me asking?"

Cornelius looked down at the ground and kicked the sidewalk with his heels. He muttered something unintelligible.

"I didn't catch that!" the skycap said, cupping his non-flashlight hand to his ear.

Cornelius raised his voice to barely a mumble. "Two and a half hours."

"Excuse me? Did you say two and a half hours?"

Cornelius nodded.

"You couldn't take the time to park your car and your flight isn't for two and a half hours?" The skycap puffed out his chest, indignant and emboldened.

"The flight actually isn't for three hours, we're just boarding in two and a half," Cornelius admitted.

"Why were you in such a hurry to get here if we're just going to sit around the airport for two hours?" Kara asked her grandfather. Cornelius kicked at her ankle to shut her up.

The skycap waved his arm along the length of the sleepy terminal. "This airport has like six gates! An hour early is reasonable, *maybe* an hour and fifteen minutes if it's a busy day, which it is obviously not."

"I thought because it was an international flight?" Cornelius offered. Kara raised her eyebrow, but fearing another kick, said nothing.

"Get back in the car and drive to the parking lot," the skycap said, shaking his head. "You'll be back here in ten minutes. I'll get them to hold the flight for you if they start boarding a couple hours early." He snorted in disgusted amusement and waved his flashlight at another car.

"Yeah, that's going to be a problem," Cornelius replied. "This thing is pretty much undrivable. I hit a pothole doing nearly two hundred."

The skycap stared at him, incredulous.

"What? I was shaving!"

"You were going to leave me a totaled car?" The skycap sighed in disgust. "That is some nerve. You think everyone has to play by your rules just because you're a big shot who owns an expensive sports car."

"It's actually stol—," Kara started to say, before Cornelius kicked her again, this time in the butt.

The skycap paid them no attention. He was waving his flashlight and ranting. "You jet off to your exotic destination and leave behind a big old mess. You stay long enough to get a tan and eat some animals you're not allowed to eat in the States. Then your handlers give you the all-clear once everyone back home is finished cleaning up after you, so you fly back and start making plans to do it all over again. Well, I can tell you it's not going to last. You can't just dump things at our feet when you want to go eat a goddamn panda. The working class are not your trash bin. I refuse to allow—"

The loud sound of screeching tires interrupted the lecture. Everyone looked to the street, where a large, gleaming SUV had come to a halt after narrowly missing Cornelius's car and partially hopping the curb. The driver got out, obviously in a hurry, and slammed his door shut. Two stunningly attractive women emerged from the backseat wearing outfits so skimpy they essentially negated the need for a pre-flight security screening.

"Keep it," the driver said, tossing the keys in the general direction of the stupefied skycap. He slung an arm around the hips of both his companions, threw back his head, and laughed uproariously as they marched off to the terminal without a second thought. Wherever they were headed, they seemed to be a trio destined to eat some goddamn panda. The SUV's enormous rims were still spinning as the keys fell to the ground.

The skycap looked down at the keys for a solid ten seconds. Finally he looked up at Cornelius. "I will help you push your car to the long-term parking lot," he said in a flat voice.

"Great!" Cornelius replied. "Hop in, Kara, we've got plenty of time. Bring the bags, he can carry them on the way back."

The skycap slumped his shoulders, clicked his flashlight off, and walked around to the back of the car. Kara felt a slight twinge of pity for the man, then shrugged and tossed her bags back into the car. She hopped into the passenger seat and slammed the door shut. A few seconds later Cornelius sat down in the driver's seat.

"OK! I'm putting her in neutral!" he yelled out the window. Cornelius started the car and shifted it out of park. The skycap leaned into the bumper, and slowly, the stolen convertible began to roll forward. Cornelius leaned back and smiled. "This is actually kind of luxurious!" he said as he slipped his hands behind his head. "It's like a rickshaw you don't have to pretend to feel guilty about!"

Kara had never experienced this much excitement at the airport. On family trips the closest thing she'd ever had to drama was the time her father had worked up the nerve to ask a flight attendant for the full can of soda. He'd then been unable to decide if he still wanted a cup of ice or not and left to go take deep breaths in the lavatory. If traveling with her grandfather had started off like *this*, who knew what they were in for once they finally reached their destination? Their destination…

"Grandpa," Kara said, turning to face Cornelius. "You told that guy we were here early to catch an international flight. But that's not true. The Olympics are in Hawaii."

Cornelius looked over at her. He was trying to contain his excitement, but his eyes were dancing. "I knew you were a sharp one, Kara. The thing about that is, we're— Hey! Let's pick up the pace back there!" Cornelius stuck his hand out the window and banged on the side of the car. "Some of us have a plane to catch!" he shouted back at the skycap, who had taken a break and was leaning on the trunk of the car trying to catch his breath. Without lifting his head, the poor skycap gave them a thumbs-up and began to push forward again.

Cornelius turned back to Kara again, no longer able to keep a wide grin from spreading across his face. "I forgot to give you your boarding passes," he said. Cornelius brought his palms together, gave them a quick rub, and then spread them apart with a flourish. Two pieces of paper had appeared in his right hand.

It's obviously just a dopey magic trick, Kara told herself. *Like pulling a quarter out of your ear, that's what grandfathers do.* But was she really that certain? Cornelius's past was so mysterious, his sudden reappearance so interesting. Was it possible that he really *was* magic? Was it possible that—

"It's just a dopey magic trick," Cornelius said, cutting off Kara's train of thought. "They were in my sleeve." He waved the papers impatiently. "Take the damn passes."

Kara reached out and took the boarding passes. She fanned them out and examined them. "Yep, says right here, 'DESTINATION: HAWAII.' The fiftieth state, definitely part of America. But wait, this first pass says London?" She held the passes out to show Cornelius. "Why are we flying all the way to London before we go to Hawaii?"

"Well, the thing is," Cornelius said, squirming in his seat with glee. "That pass doesn't say 'DESTINATION: HAWAII.' Those aren't uppercase *i*'s. Those are lowercase *l*'s."

Kara looked at the boarding pass again. Written in what appeared to be all-caps, it was impossible to differentiate HAWAII with two uppercase *i*'s from HAWAll with two lowercase *l*'s. "HAWAll?" she asked. "We're going to HAWAll?" She looked over at Cornelius. "Where the hell is HAWAll?"

Cornelius winked. "Let the games begin."

seven

Commander 9-Krelblax stared out the window of the *Stupid Butt* as he poked at his Orion's Belt Loosener with a tentacle. He'd only managed to take a few bites of the sandwich before he lost his appetite. The five types of meat had gone cold, juice from the pickles had soaked through the bread, and the unfortunately named Betelgeuse sauce had begun to congeal.

This did not stop the crew from eyeing it hungrily. Zzarvon, Ogrot, and Timblorx had wolfed down their meal deals almost instantaneously. A Larvilkian wolfing down a sandwich was not a pretty sight. It involved secreting a vile-smelling mucus that quickly broke the sandwich down into a viscous slurry that was evidently impossible to ingest without making revolting slurping noises. 9-Krelblax had actually thought his sandwich was pretty tasty until his crew made such a disgusting show out of eating their own. The worst part was, Larvilkians were perfectly capable of eating a sandwich normally, making only polite noises and emitting a mucus that actually smelled somewhat pleasant. Sadly, his crew always insisted on wolfing.

Eventually Zzarvon broke the silence. "Sir, are you going to finish that? We'd be happy to take it off your tentacles if you aren't."

9-Krelblax turned to look at his navigator. Zzarvon shrugged. "Just saying. No reason to let a perfectly good sandwich go to waste."

9-Krelblax scowled at his navigator with his first eye. *Utterly useless*, he thought. He trained his second eye on Lieutenant Ogrot, who was dabbing digestive fluid off of his mouth with a napkin. *What a clown.* He swiveled his third eye to Timblorx. The technician emitted a loud burp. *Disgusting.* His anger mounting, 9-Krelblax focused his fourth eye on an unfamiliar figure.

"I could always dash back to the deli and get more grub if you guys are still hungry," the figure said.

"Why is the delivery boy still here?" 9-Krelblax shouted. "He dropped off the sandwiches twenty-five minutes ago!"

"Zzarvon said if I stuck around he was going to get two service bots to fight," the obviously chemically impaired delivery boy mumbled. "That sounded pretty bad ass."

"We have active work orders to attend to!" 9-Krelblax screamed. "Get the hell out of here!"

"I haven't been paid yet," the delivery boy announced.

His moodcore pulsing, 9-Krelblax reached into his thorax pouch. He produced an assortment of universal currency coins and flung them across the command bridge. They bounced off the delivery boy's chest and landed at his feet.

The delivery boy looked down at the coins then back at 9-Krelblax. "No tip?" he asked.

Fuming, 9-Krelblax reached into his thorax pouch, produced a few more coins, and hurled them at the delivery boy.

The delivery boy looked down at the coins for a bit longer, then back up at 9-Krelblax. "We actually don't accept universal currency coins anymore," the delivery boy informed him. "Only Andromedan virtu-credits."

9-Krelblax's moodcore glowed so brightly that the crew members had to shield their eyes. "Why didn't you mention that in the first place?" he demanded.

"I told Zzarvon, like, three times."

Zzarvon shrugged as the delivery boy produced a small payment device and offered it to 9-Krelblax. 9-Krelblax took the device, signed on the line authorizing the virtu-credit transfer and shoved it back at the delivery boy.

"No tip?" he asked.

The ship's computer, mistaking 9-Krelblax's suddenly brilliant moodcore for the rays of a nearby sun, closed the auto-blinds on the command bridge's windows. The commander took the payment device from the delivery boy, furiously authorized a token tip amount, and thrust it back at him.

Satisfied, the delivery boy pocketed the device. He shuffled off toward the exit. The doors whooshed open, and just as he was about to step through, the delivery boy turned back around. "Wait, is the service bot fight not happening, or...?"

"Get the hell off my ship before I disintegrate you!" 9-Krelblax shouted. The delivery boy made a hasty departure and the doors whooshed closed behind him. 9-Krelblax closed all four of his eyes, took a deep breath, and tried to calm himself. It must have had the desired effect because after a few seconds, he heard the sound of the auto-blinds opening again. His moodcore must have cooled down.

"So, sir?" Zzarvon spoke up. "The sandwich?"

9-Krelblax popped open a single, twitching eye. Without looking at his crew, he picked up his mostly uneaten Orion's Belt Loosener and oozed over to a refuse port. He shoved the sandwich in and hit the "JETTISON CONTENTS" button. The port sealed with a hiss, there was a quick whirring sound, and then the sandwich shot up a tube toward the void of space, where it promptly got stuck about two feet into its journey.

9-Krelblax reached out a tentacle and hit the JETTISON button again. The sandwich stayed put. He repeatedly jammed the button a few dozen times like a little kid in an elevator, but it had no effect. "Would someone, namely Technician Timblorx, care to explain to me why we can't get something as simple as a refuse port to function properly on this stupid ship?" 9-Krelblax roared. He popped his three remaining eyes open and spun them around to stare at his crew. All three remaining essential crew members of the *Stupid Butt* were bent over, picking universal currency coins off the ground.

The ship's auto-blinds snapped shut again.

"Attention on the bridge!" 9-Krelblax bellowed. Zzarvon, Ogrot, and Timblorx dropped the coins they were gathering and immediately straightened up to look at their commander. 9-Krelblax stared back at his crew. He clasped several of his tentacles behind his back and began to pace-ooze back and forth while he collected his thoughts. Finally he spoke up.

"It's time for a change. It's time to claim our rightful place in the galaxy. That's certainly not going to happen by picking up other planets' garbage. That's not what I was meant to do. That's not what any of us were meant to do." 9-Krelblax's tone had started off grave, but he was quickly getting worked up.

"We are Larvilkians, dammit! We were the first race to ever develop the ray gun! When the Piltrixians of Ribercon-C invented the hyperwarp, *Larvilkians* were the first race to invade them and steal it. Out of the entire galaxy, *we* were the first race to harness the power of a wormhole to redirect a comet, and *we* were the first race to ever relocate to a new planet because of catastrophic damage to our original planet caused by an errantly redirected comet!"

9-Krelblax looked at his crew. His jingoistic rhetoric had done the trick. Each of their moodcores was glowing a patriotic shade of green. He continued.

"Yet, despite all of these accomplishments, what are we best known for? Being the suckers who will come and haul off your garbage! Now admittedly part of that is due to the extremely catchy jingle that runs in all of our radio ads—DO NOT hum it, Zzarvon!" Zzarvon looked disappointed. "But on the whole, Larvilkians have done a very poor job of building our reputation in non-garbage areas. But that's going to change. We're going to start earning admiration. We're going to start demanding respect. And you know where that change is going to start?"

9-Krelblax scanned his crew, waiting for an answer. Eventually Ogrot spoke up. "On the *Stupid Butt*?"

"You know what, just say 'on this ship,' OK?" 9-Krelblax said.

"Well, it's named the *Stupid Butt*—"

"I know what the ship is named!" 9-Krelblax shouted. He quickly calmed himself, not wanting to lose his momentum, and walked over to a window. "But you're right. It starts with the attitude of everyone on this ship. When I look out into the vastness of space, I shouldn't think to myself, 'Where am I going to pick up trash today?' I should think to myself, 'I am 9-Krelblax of Larvilkian-B, son of the planet president and future heir to the presidency!'"

"I thought that planet president was a democratically elected position?" Zzarvon said.

"Uh, sure it is!" 9-Krelblax said, shifting all four of his eyes from side to side. "Absolutely! Those bi-annual elections definitely aren't shams!"

The crew exchanged a look. 9-Krelblax kept talking. "Lieutenant Ogrot. You are the first person in your family to serve in the Larvilkian Fleet!"

"First person to serve in the Larvilkian Fleet *without being dishonorably discharged*," Ogrot corrected. "Yet!"

"I keep telling you, you need to stop adding 'Yet' when you say that." 9-Krelblax sighed and turned his eyes to Timblorx. "Now, talk about a Larvilkian who's brimming with potential! Sure, you're hauling garbage for now, Timblorx. But let's not forget that you had the highest scores in your class at the academy!"

"Technically, all of my high scores were in garbage-hauling electives. I failed my other classes. Ogrot's father was dishonorably discharged for fixing my transcript."

"Again, there is just no need to bring up information like that when we're focusing on the positive." 9-Krelblax made a mental note to actually look at a résumé or two the next time he was hiring a crew.

"And that brings us to Zzarvon." 9-Krelblax paused. He eyed his former navigator up and down. Zzarvon grinned, eager to hear whatever it was he should feel positive about.

"So, you see," 9-Krelblax continued, "we all have so much to offer." Zzarvon looked confused, but 9-Krelblax kept talking. "Now, do you want to do something besides pick up trash?"

"Yeah!" the crew cheered.

9-Krelblax thrust several triumphant tentacles into the air. "Who wants to show the universe what Larvilkians are really made of?" he asked.

"We do!" the crew announced in unison.

"Zzarvon! Call up the Big Dipper on the navigation system!"

"Yes, sir!" Zzarvon oozed over to the computer and tapped a few buttons with his tentacles. 9-Krelblax followed him over, watching the activity on the holoscreen with four wide eyes. He'd never given a speech like that before. By the end, he had started to believe what he was saying. It was an odd sensation. He kind of wished his father had been able to see it.

"Here's the Big Dipper," Zzarvon said. He waved a tentacle and the star system filled the holoscreen. 9-Krelblax studied it.

"Are there any life forms near that part of the universe?" he asked.

"Well, this system looks promising." Zzarvon pressed a few keys and a map zoomed into view. "Eight planets, over one hundred moons."

"Call up the planets." 9-Krelblax leaned in to examine the display. Zzarvon tapped away and a hyper-realistic rendering of the system and its planets filled the screen.

"Oh wow," Zzarvon said. "Unbelievable! One of the planets… You're never going to believe this, sir. They have a planet called Uranus!"

9-Krelblax was stunned. "Who the hell would name a planet that?" he asked. "Do you think the people who live there have any idea what that means?" Zzarvon shook his head in disbelief. The Uranus was the name of the largest ethnic cleansing in Larvilkian history. Perpetrated by the Piltrixians of Ribercon-C only one hundred and ninety Tri-Sun cycles ago, the tragedy's wounds were still fresh for the Larvilkians who had lost family and loved ones.

Of course, the Uranus involved a mere fraction of deaths compared to the number of Piltrixians the Larvilkians had murdered in order to steal their hyperwarp technology. In fact, the intergalactic court of law had called the Uranus "completely justified," "100 percent provoked," and "maybe even something the rest of us should have lent a hand with." This did not stop the Larvilkians from feeling like victims. The event was spoken of only in hushed tones, and every year a solemn ceremony was held for the three Larvilkians who had perished.

Zzarvon wiped away a tear. "Ura— I'm sorry, I can't even say it. *The planet* is uninhabited," he blubbered.

"Never forget," 9-Krelblax said, patting his suspended navigator on the back. "What about that big one with the spot?"

Zzarvon pinched the holoscreen to zoom in on the largest of the planets. "That's Jupiter. According to our database, it's home to a hyper-intelligent mist."

"Not interested." 9-Krelblax waved a dismissive tentacle. "Nobody cares if you prove your superiority to a mist."

"Well, this one looks like it might be our best bet then," Zzarvon said, zooming back out and centering on the small blue and green planet near the sun. "Earth. The dominant life form appears to be the 'human.' They're unaware of our existence. In fact, they think they're the only intelligent life in the entire universe. And hey! Get a load of this: A bunch of them speak English!"

Most Larvilkians opted to study English to fulfill their language requirement in high school. As far as they were concerned, it was a dead language, unspoken for millennia throughout the universe. Piltrixian was the other language the school system offered. Learning it would have been much more practical, allowing them to foster more harmonious relations with their closest galactic neighbor, but Larvilkians thought the Piltrixian accent made them sound like dorks.

"Perfect! Lieutenant Ogrot! Let's have a look at these Earth humans!"

"Right away, sir!" Lieutenant Ogrot replied. There were a few bleeps and bloops, and then another holoscreen materialized a few feet in front of 9-Krelblax.

"This is a random selection of footage," Ogrot explained. "If you see something you're interested in we can hone in on it."

9-Krelblax nodded and stared at the projection. There were several images being displayed concurrently: a majestic panorama of a vast forest, footage from a traffic camera mounted at an intersection, a baby deer taking its first steps, and grainy video of a man running on a treadmill.

"More like this one," 9-Krelblax said pointing to the treadmill video. Ogrot pressed a few buttons and the treadmill popped up larger, surrounded by several other videos of humans engaged in various activities. 9-Krelblax studied it intently. After a few seconds of running normally, the man on the treadmill stepped on his shoelace, tripped, and hit his head on the control console. His body shot off the treadmill and he slumped to the floor, apparently unconscious. The humans in the other videos were similarly experiencing other humiliations: being humped by dogs, falling into pools, lighting themselves on fire when they tried to blow out candles on birthday cakes.

"None of this works," 9-Krelblax said in disgust. "It's just morons injuring other morons! It does our reputation no good to humiliate a bunch of idiots. We've got to wow the Earth on its biggest stage, show them that their highest achievements are nothing compared to our innate Larvilkian superiority! Show me their best and brightest."

"Sorry, sir," Ogrot replied. "I thought the 'most popular' list would be a good place to start. Give me one second." The holographic field flickered as thousands of video thumbnails rushed past. They began to filter out one by one until only a few were left. The remaining few enlarged and 9-Krelblax leaned in to study them. There was footage of mountain climbers with ice in their beards smiling on top of a summit, hunters standing next to impressive trophy animals, and scientists gathered around bubbling lab equipment.

"Keep them coming," 9-Krelblax instructed. "Moments with more participants." More videos populated the holoscreen. This time there was footage of beautiful people wearing fancy clothes on a red carpet, important-looking speakers at podiums in front of crowds of thousands, orchestras performing at packed concert halls. 9-Krelblax watched intently until one particular moment caught his attention.

"What's happening here?" he asked, pointing at a projection of a man tossing a ball through a circle. "A competition of some sort?"

Lieutenant Ogrot called up the video's metadata. "Yes, sir. That appears to be the sport of 'basketball.' This particular moment is evidently one of the 'Top Ten Epic Buzzer Beaters.'"

"Look at the people observing him," 9-Krelblax marveled, pointing at the fans in the stands. "So captivated by a simple physical act. More like this!"

More videos of sports highlights rushed into view. Everywhere 9-Krelblax looked there were throngs of cheering fans applauding athletes. His moodcore started to glow an excited shade of blue.

"And everywhere on Earth, they are this besotted by the same simple physical feats?" he asked.

"Not exactly, sir," Lieutenant Ogrot replied. "Many of these sports only enjoy regional popularity. The one in the upper left, 'baseball,' that is mainly watched by people in the Americas and Asia. The one on the slick surface with the curved sticks, on the other hand, has a fanatical following in Canada and Europe."

"What about this one?" 9-Krelblax said, gesturing with a tentacle. "Surely this activity has captivated the entire planet. Look at the delicate finesse required, the concentration! Those players must walk the Earth as gods!"

"That appears to be something called 'cricket,' sir." Ogrot replied. "Apparently nobody understands it and you're liable to get beat up if you go around talking about how much you like it."

This does us no good, 9-Krelblax thought to himself. How could the people of a planet be so divided? On Larvilkian-B there was one sport that everyone enjoyed: Paddyroy. In Paddyroy, an unfortunate participant was selected to dress up like a Piltrixian of Ribercon-C. Then, Larvilkians chased him through the streets pelting him with fruits and vegetables. Nobody really understood how the rules worked, but the day of the championship was a planetwide holiday.

"We can't just show up and impress 'Canada,'" 9-Krelblax sneered. "We must prove our superiority to the entire planet! Are there no events that unite the entire Earth?"

Ogrot tapped a few buttons. A video of a clown getting kicked in the crotch by a young boy popped up on the display.

"Try harder, Lieutenant," 9-Krelblax muttered.

"I'm looking!" Ogrot pleaded. "It's harder than you'd think. But I may have something." The lieutenant hit a few more buttons, and the writhing clown disappeared. He was replaced by the words "Citius, Altius, Fortius" written in dignified script. Each of 9-Krelblax's eyes went wide.

A rousing, horn-based call to arms began to play over the holoscreen's sound system. 9-Krelblax felt a surge of patriotism, and instinctively looked around for a Piltrixian to pelt with fruit. Seeing nobody but Zzarvon grinning like an idiot, he gestured for Ogrot to keep this footage coming.

Videos rushed across the viewing field. Some of them black-and-white and grainy, some in sharp full color, they obviously spanned many generations. An endless variety of competitions seemed to be taking place. Humans marched with flags, hugged loved ones in the stands, and broke down crying when presented with shiny medals in stadiums filled with thousands more humans who went wild for every moment.

"What am I seeing?" 9-Krelblax asked without taking any of his eyes off the projections.

"This is something called the 'Olympics,'" Ogrot informed his commander. "A giant athletic festival where human athletes participate in every type of sport. Swimming, running, gymnastics, basketball..."

"Cricket?" 9-Krelblax asked hopefully.

"No, sir. And really, I can't emphasize enough that you should not go around Earth proclaiming that you are interested in playing, watching, or discussing cricket. You'll disgrace our entire planet."

9-Krelblax felt a twinge of disappointment but forced himself to focus on the positive. "So, these Olympics... the entire planet participates?"

"For the most part, sir. A few of the crappier countries are currently banned."

"What did they do? Party a little too hard at the last one?" 9-Krelblax chuckled. "Sneak in an athlete who hadn't filled out his entry form properly?"

"Massive human-rights violations within their borders, actually. But it's probably safe to say that citizens of those places would lack the necessary vitamins in their diet and/or appendages to compete on a world-class level. Apart from them, the Olympics are the best representation of the planet as a whole as I could find."

"And it's all positive achievements? Things that these humans are proud of?" 9-Krelblax asked. "Nobody falls on their face or gets humped by an animal?"

"That happens occasionally. The former more than the latter. But for some reason, humans tend not to focus on the failures during this event. Of course, as soon as the Olympics are over, they go back to watching their fellow Earthlings fall down and kick each other in the genitals. For these three weeks, however, humans are quite proud of what their fellow man is able to accomplish."

"As they should be!" 9-Krelblax marveled. "Competing on the ultimate stage, proving your superiority to the whole world! It demonstrates the value of hard work, dedication, and sacrifice! Seeing what other humans can accomplish if they dedicate themselves to a seemingly impossible goal should inspire everyone on the planet!" He turned to face his crew. "So let's go down there and humiliate them for our own personal gain!"

There were shouts of approval from the crew. As they rushed into action, 9-Krelblax's moodcore glowed a deep, satisfied blue. These Earth humans thought they were pretty great. But as soon as the *Stupid Butt* landed at the Olympics and humiliated their athletes, the entire planet would be forced to acknowledge the Larvilkians' all-around superiority, and word would quickly spread through the galaxy. It would essentially be the exact opposite of what happened every time the Larvilkians landed on a planet and loaded seventeen thousand tons of dirty diapers onto their ship for a relatively token sum of money.

9-Krelblax was so excited about his plan that he decided to bury the hatchet with Zzarvon. "If you would be so kind, *Navigator* Zzarvon," he said, winking his first and third eyes. "Set a course for planet Earth!" He produced the confiscated navigator's pin from his thorax pouch and tossed it to Zzarvon.

"Yes, sir!" Zzarvon excitedly reached out and caught the pin with one tentacle while tapping the navigation computer with another. The navigator's elation lasted only a moment, however. His face quickly fell as red text appeared on the screen.

"What's the matter?" 9-Krelblax asked. He felt his moodcore dimming preemptively. He knew the plan had seemed too perfect.

"I'm sorry, sir," Zzarvon said. He turned to face his commander, looking chagrined. "I'm afraid that we're too late." Zzarvon pointed at the screen and 9-Krelblax hurriedly oozed over for a look.

Zzarvon was right. Displayed on the navigation console was a calendar app with text that said "Olympics Closing Ceremony." Next to it was intergalactic date notation that indicated the games had ended a long time ago.

"Damn my luck!" 9-Krelblax bellowed, his moodcore flaring up in frustration. The fantasy of returning to Larvilkian-B to announce the planet's new reputation as a respected athletic powerhouse was quickly buried under seventeen thousand tons of mental diapers.

But then Zzarvon piped up. "There is something we could try..." 9-Krelblax looked up at his navigator. Zzarvon sounded tentative, but at this point in time, 9-Krelblax was willing to listen to any solution if it meant they didn't have to throw in the towel and go pick up more garbage.

"It's still an experimental feature," Zzarvon continued, sounding unsure of himself. "But technically, if I were to overclock the ship's hyperwarp, it could create a wormhole that might allow us to travel back in time."

"We could go back all the way to the start of the Olympics?" 9-Krelblax asked.

"I don't know if anyone's ever pulled off that long of a jump," Zzarvon said. "That would be a pretty big wormhole. I've only heard of this being used to jump back a day or two, maybe a week tops. This would be uncharted territory."

"Hm...I'm not sure that we should risk it..."

"You could always think it over while we go and pick up a load of garbage?" Zzarvon suggested.

"Lieutenant Ogrot!" 9-Krelblax shouted. "Issue an immediate directive to all crew members: Brace yourselves for overclocked hyperwarp. This is not a drill, we are cranking this sucker way past anything we've ever done before!"

Lieutenant Ogrot slithered over to the navigation console as fast as he could manage. "Hang on! Overclocked hyperwarp? Why would we do that?"

"It's our only chance to get to the Olympics," Zzarvon explained, pointing a tentacle at the calendar. "We missed them. We've got to use the hyperwarp to create a wormhole so we can travel back in time."

Lieutenant Ogrot sighed. "We *could* travel back in time through a wormhole..." Zzarvon smiled as he reached out a tentacle and started to twist the hyperwarp dial into the red. Ogrot smacked the navigator's tentacle away and continued his sentence. "Or we could *not* do that and enter the *next* Olympics that begins in two days! Look!"

Ogrot pointed at the calendar app. "The Olympics take place every four years! Yes, the last one ended three years and three hundred sixty-three days ago. But the next one begins in less than fifty hours in a place called Hawaii! Just go there!" As he oozed away from the navigation console, the lieutenant sighed the sigh of a Larvilkian who was starting to understand the appeal of a neat and tidy dishonorable discharge.

"That's actually a much better idea," Zzarvon said. "Overclocking the hyperwarp to that level would have almost certainly imploded the ship. Actually, because of the way wormholes twist time, it could have retroactively imploded the ship before we had even activated the hyperwarp!"

"You're saying that there's a chance this entire ship might still implode because actions we didn't even take might still reverberate into the past because of the wormhole caused by those actions, even though we didn't take them?" 9-Krelblax's moodcore, confused what color to glow, opted to just send out a few searing bursts of pain into the commander's abdomen.

"I think so?" Zzarvon said. "To be honest, I really only skimmed a post on a forum about this whole overclocking thing."

"Well, how do you suggest we go about not getting imploded by a wormhole we never even activated?" 9-Krelblax asked, already regretting his decision to reinstate his navigator. Zzarvon thought about this for a few seconds, then slowly began to extend a tentacle across the command console. His wide, uncertain eyes still locked with 9-Krelblax's, he grasped the hyperwarp knob and gradually began to twist it into the red.

"No! No! Not a viable solution!" This time it was 9-Krelblax's turn to smack Zzarvon's tentacle away. "From now on, no more suggestions where immediate death is an almost certain outcome. And *absolutely* no more suggestions where even *considering* the action could bring about immediate death."

This wormhole business had 9-Krelblax worried. Zzarvon almost exclusively made bad decisions. If their lives were now at risk because of bad decisions that he hadn't actually *made* yet, they were probably doomed. On the other hand, the fact that they were still alive at this moment meant that Zzarvon hadn't actually considered making the bad decision that would kill them in the future. But did that mean that Zzarvon hadn't considered it yet, or had just not *made the decision* to consider it yet?

A second set of stabbing pains from his moodcore was enough of an excuse for 9-Krelblax to stop trying to comprehend the horrible implications his idiot navigator half-reading a post on some forum might have on the universe.

"Let's just head to Earth," 9-Krelblax said, trying to sound calm. "You know what? I'll stay here and observe you. It's good to refamiliarize myself with some of the ship's more basic procedures." *Just in case our navigator happens to get lured into an airlock and I accidentally jettison it*, he thought.

"Yes, sir!" Zzarvon said. He leaned forward so that his mouth was just a few inches from the console. "Computer! Navigate... to... Earth..." Zzarvon spoke crisply, enunciating every syllable.

There was a pleasant chime from the navigation console and then a friendly robotic voice replied. "Destination set as: Earth. Beginning navigation in ten seconds unless override is issued."

Zzarvon sat back in his chair and smiled at 9-Krelblax. "And we are on our way!"

9-Krelblax looked from his navigator to the console and back again. He thought about all the times Zzarvon had managed to screw up his duties as navigator. The time they'd overshot their destination by over one hundred thousand light years because Zzarvon had mistaken a smudge on the windshield for the Triangulum Galaxy. Or the incident when Zzarvon misread a work order for the Crab Nebula and took them to a private moon owned by a farmer named Nab Crebula, who was none too pleased that the *Stupid Butt* had crushed half of his space-llama herd upon landing.

Most shameful of all was the time that Zzarvon had directed the ship into a black hole, thinking they could use it as a shortcut to shave off a few minutes on the way to a hauling job. The ship ended up getting trapped in a nether-dimension for over a week. Ogrot had sneezed while some natives were helpfully trying to give them directions. Evidently, immune systems in the nether-dimension were not prepared for whatever it was that Ogrot had splattered on them, and bodies started dropping almost immediately. By the time the *Stupid Butt* made its hasty getaway, cities were burning and the few remaining survivors had divided into warring death cults. 9-Krelblax filed paperwork saying the trip had encountered a "brief, uneventful delay."

9-Krelblax blinked his eyes, trying to comprehend what he'd just seen. How had Zzarvon made mistakes of such a titanic caliber if the system was basically idiot proof? "It says there that it will take forty-six minutes to get to Earth," 9-Krelblax said in disbelief. Typically, forty-six minutes was roughly how long it took Zzarvon to remember his password to reactivate the navigation computer from screensaver mode. There had never been a voyage on the *Stupid Butt* that took less than ten times that long to complete.

"Whoa! Forty-six minutes? What the hell?" Zzarvon looked concerned. He leaned forward to inspect the console. Immediately, he rolled his eyes and chuckled to himself. "Of course! Forgot to activate the hyperwarp."

At the mention of the hyperwarp, 9-Krelblax's moodcore emitted a piercing yellow glow of terror. Zzarvon shielded his eyes. "Don't worry, sir," he said. "Keeping it purely within the manufacturer's recommended levels. No chance of activating a wormhole."

There was a sudden loud bang. Fearing that it was the first sound in a chain reaction culminating in the ship's implosion, 9-Krelblax's tentacles and eyes reflexively retracted into his body. When no further sounds followed, 9-Krelblax slowly raised one of his eye antennae and rotated it in the direction of the sound.

"Sorry about that!" Technician Timblorx shouted from across the bridge. "Just used some compressed air to try and dislodge your sandwich, sir! It's wedged in there real good but I managed to get half of it!" Timblorx pointed a satisfied tentacle at a window, and sure enough, the jettisoned remains of half the Belt Buster were drifting aimlessly through space.

Feeling an unhealthy mix of foolish and furious, 9-Krelblax popped his tentacles and antennae back out to their normal lengths. He turned back to Zzarvon. "How long is the trip actually going to take if we use hyperwarp?" he asked.

"We just arrived," Zzarvon said with a smile. "I'm glad you reminded me to use hyperwarp this time. That could save us a lot of time going forward. I should put a reminder by the hyperwarp dial. Do you see a sticky note anywhere?" The navigator rummaged around his console, looking for something to write a reminder on as 9-Krelblax swallowed hard, trying to contain yet another moodcore flare up.

Outside, the blue-green sphere of Earth hovered in the distance. *It looks peaceful*, 9-Krelblax thought. Down there, the humans were going about their day secure in the belief that they were the highest form of life in all existence. They had explored the stars and conquered the atom, all in the entitled spirit of manifest destiny. After all, they believed they were made in God's own image. Greatness was humanity's birthright, their reason for being, the force that kept them firmly in place at the center of their known universe.

Their minds were going to be so blown when the *Stupid Butt* landed and totally proved how much more awesome the Larvilkians were at everything.

There was just one more thing to do before initiating a planet-approach procedure. "Zzarvon!" 9-Krelblax barked. The navigator abandoned his search for a sticky note and snapped to attention.

"Yes, sir!"

"Start a LightYearLink with my father. There's been a change of plans. He needs to know that his son is about to wow the galax— No! Zzarvon, no! Do *not* look up his number in your desk planner!" Zzarvon froze. He was clutching a sloppy collection of notepaper that had been shoved into a three-ring binder. "Use the ship's computer," 9-Krelblax sighed. "It's so much more efficient. We *just* proved that."

"Right!" Zzarvon dropped the planner and turned back to his console. "Initiate LYL with your father..." he thought aloud. He paused, then looked at his commander with uncertain eyes. "Your father..." he repeated, obviously stalling for time. "And that would be..." Zzarvon thought for a few more seconds then took a stab at it. "8-Krelblax?"

"9-Krelblax Senior! *President* 9-Krelblax Senior. You don't know the name of the president of your planet?"

"It's hard to remember!" Zzarvon protested.

"It's *my* name!" 9-Krelblax jabbed several tentacles at different parts of his body. "It is exactly the same name as the person you are currently interacting with! It should be scientifically impossible for there to be a name that you are more aware of at the current moment."

Zzarvon nodded in assent, then turned his attention back to his console. He tapped a few keys and swiped away a notification window. Then Zzarvon squinted intently at a screen that, to 9-Krelblax's eyes, contained a disproportionately small amount of information compared to how long Zzarvon was taking to study it. Eventually the navigator turned back to his commander and delivered his report. "We only have one 9-Krelblax in our system. How do we know if that's you or your dad?"

"Why would I be in our own LYL directory? I'm *here*. There is never a need to contact me via LightYearLink." Annoyed, 9-Krelblax began to count off the reasons this was a stupid question on his tentacles. "I'm reachable over the ship's general intercom and over the private intercom that only essential crew members have access to. You can walk into my personal space and speak directly to me. You can shout across the bridge if the news is urgent and I am within earshot. God forbid, you can even speak to me through the bathroom door if the situation is particularly dire. Nobody would have ever, at any time, had any reason to put me in our LYL system."

"Right," said Zzarvon. "It was a stupid question." He tapped the initiate-call button. 9-Krelblax's communicator buzzed.

"Goddammit," 9-Krelblax muttered. Merely initiating a LightYearLink was wildly expensive. He'd planned to reverse the charges to his father. Accidentally calling himself had just exhausted half of next month's food budget. He hit the ignore button on his communicator.

"You know what?" 9-Krelblax snapped at Zzarvon. "Lieutenant Ogrot can handle this task. Ogrot!" The lieutenant oozed over to Zzarvon's console as quickly as he could manage.

"Send an email to my father, Planet President *9-Krelblax Senior.*" 9-Krelblax emphasized his father's name as he turned his back on Zzarvon to face Lieutenant Ogrot. "Inform him that we will not be picking up the Big Dipper's garbage due to the fact that we're going to be too busy wowing an entire galaxy."

Lieutenant Ogrot took studious notes. "No garbage... Too busy wowing... Do you want me to say an entire galaxy? Technically we're just going to be wowing the people on one planet."

"Say galaxy," 9-Krelblax ordered.

Lieutenant Ogrot thought about this for a few seconds. "Do you maybe just want me to just say 'wowing an entire planet'? Wowing an entire planet is still pretty good."

"Look: Let's say I'm onstage doing stand-up comedy. Zzarvon is the only person in the theater. I tell a joke that makes him laugh... I dunno, the one about the Piltrixian and the space-llama farmer's daughter. You couldn't deny that I made the whole theater laugh, right?"

"Oh, hey, we still owe that space-llama farmer for half of his herd," Ogrot remembered. "He sent us a summons last week."

"Would your act have one of those ventriloquist dummies?" Zzarvon asked. "Those things terrify me! If you were using one of those I wouldn't be laughing."

9-Krelblax ignored both crew members. "Humans are the only advanced life forms in this galaxy. So if we wow them, we wow every advanced life form in the whole galaxy. It's 100 percent true. Technically."

"Don't forget about Jupiter," Zzarvon reminded him. "The mist."

"Fuck the mist!" 9-Krelblax scoffed, not bothering to turn around. "Nobody cares about impressing a mist! 'Wowing an entire galaxy,' that's the message. Send the email."

"Oh, man," Zzarvon said. "I wouldn't say things like that about the mist while we're in this galaxy. It may be non-corporeal, but its collective hive-sense is quite strong. It definitely just heard you. You don't want to piss off the mist."

"Send the email!" 9-Krelblax said even louder. Lieutenant Ogrot saluted then busied himself with his communicator. 9-Krelblax continued shouting orders. "Technician Timblorx! There's been a change of plans. We won't need any garbage bags today! Zzarvon! In ten minutes, initiate atmos— What the hell is that?"

"What, sir?" Zzarvon asked.

"Listen!" 9-Krelblax held up a tentacle. After a few seconds, there was a faint pinging sound. 9-Krelblax pointed at Zzarvon. "Did you hear that?" Zzarvon nodded. A few seconds later there was another faint ping, and then another. It seemed to be emanating out of nowhere.

"What is that noise?" 9-Krelblax asked.

"My guess is that it's the mist's way of getting revenge for your insult," Zzarvon said. "By making a little pinging noise every so often."

"*That's* its revenge?" 9-Krelblax snorted. "I thought you said it was hyperintelligent!"

"I dunno… I think a pinging noise is pretty good for a mist! Especially one all the way out there on Jupiter!"

"Well, it's mildly irritating," 9-Krelblax said. "And I wish it would stop."

"Maybe you should apologize," Zzarvon suggested.

"I'm not apologizing to a mist!" 9-Krelblax hissed. The next ping was slightly louder. Zzarvon looked nervous. 9-Krelblax rolled his eyes.

"Fine." 9-Krelblax spoke up as he addressed the void. "I'm very sorry I insulted you, mist. I'm sure you're very nice. We should get together for beers after you put in a couple billion more years of evolution. Now please leave us alone!"

9-Krelblax held his breath and glanced around the ship. The pinging appeared to have stopped. The mist must have accepted his apology. 9-Krelblax smiled and picked up his orders right where he'd left off. "Zzarvon! In ten minutes, initiate atmospheric re-entry procedure. We're going to Earth, men!"

"Yes, sir!" Zzarvon replied.

9-Krelblax slithered back over to the holoscreens. Images and videos of the Olympic games continued to rush past. Humans who had pushed themselves to previously unimagined limits. Spectators who had traveled from all around the globe to unite in celebration of their fellow man. A contagious spirit of sportsmanship, camaraderie, and peace.

If this was the best that Earth had to offer, it was a pretty lame planet.

But just then, 9-Krelblax spotted something out of the corner of his second eye. His smirk disappeared. He waved a tentacle at a small video, and it quickly enlarged, filling the entire holoscreen.

It was black-and-white footage of a bygone Olympics. Compared to some of the other footage he'd seen, the athletes looked smaller, less powerful. But that wasn't what 9-Krelblax had noticed. It was the precision and organization of these particular games. A lockstep sense of timing and order. The overpowering sense that what you were seeing was the human race at its pinnacle. Now, this! *This* was a well-oiled machine!

And at the center of it was a man.

He was not an attractive man. Even to a Larvilkian who had seen his first human just a few minutes earlier, this was extremely apparent. Yet 9-Krelblax still felt drawn to him. And he was evidently not the only one. The video showed the greatest athletes on Earth standing before him minutes after their ultimate triumphs, hoping to receive a brief signal of his approval. Entire stadiums waited for his signal, then burst into unified exultations. When 9-Krelblax watched the man address the Olympic spectators, roaring and bellowing with rightful pride in the event he was hosting, he could have sworn that he felt his physical presence. The holoscreen exuded his ugly, sweaty energy.

9-Krelblax waved a tentacle to call up the video's metadata. "The Games of the XI Olympiad," the info box read. "1936. Berlin, Germany."

The Larvilkian commander's moodcore glowed a deep purple. Perhaps there was someone on Earth who was worthy of his respect after all.

eight

The airplane soared majestically above the clouds. It raced away from the ever-fainter orange and pink rays of the setting sun, toward a blue-black night dotted by the faintest pinpricks of stars. The giant machine was a concert of thousands of tiny feats of engineering and countless man-hours working together to produce something that 99 percent of humans who had ever walked the earth would rightly consider a miracle.

Kara would have been able to appreciate it a lot more if she wasn't so concerned that her grandfather had been sucked out of the toilet.

Cornelius had booked it for the bathroom as soon as the captain turned off the seatbelt sign. That was nearly half an hour ago. Kara wasn't a natural worrier, but as time passed, she began to imagine elaborate scenarios about what could be taking Cornelius so long. They started off fairly mundane, if not disgusting. But once she had the image in her head of the toilet malfunctioning and opening up a small but extremely pressurized hole that was capable of sucking out a grown man, it was difficult to shake it.

In the meantime, a number of increasingly irritated passengers were lining up in the aisle. They had begun to mutter after about ten minutes, grumble loudly after fifteen, and after twenty held an election to determine a mob leader. The man they chose appeared to be either quite angry, in dire need of using the lavatory, or an unholy combination of both. He glared up and down the plane as if looking for clues about the occupier.

Kara casually pulled the shopping bag that held the mascot costume out from under the seat in front of her. Jack's head had been a tight fit, requiring a few swift kicks before it was properly stowed, and it was now sporting various dents that were all mostly lateral moves in terms of ghoulishness. Kara transferred the bag to Cornelius's seat and tried to position the protruding head so that the mob wouldn't be able to tell that the culprit had been sitting next to her.

The ruse appeared to work, as the elected leader of the aisle mob resumed pounding on the bathroom door.

Hoping to remain as inconspicuous as possible while sitting next to a hideous giant rabbit head, Kara busied herself with the in-flight magazine, *Seat Back Vistas (Brought to you by Microsoft® Bing)*. It was even more dreadful than it sounded. The first article Kara turned to was a travelogue about how to spend "Three Perfect Days in Western New Jersey." The author spent most of the first day on the phone with the airline trying to retrieve his lost baggage. He'd gotten arrested on the morning of day two and the rest of the article was filled with *lorem ipsum* placeholder text.

Next, there was an interview with a Division III college football backup punter, a photo essay about a factory that makes those little plastic discs that keep the pizza box from touching the pizza, and a scathing editorial about burlap. By then, Kara was not particularly shocked when she turned to the Sudoku puzzle and discovered it had already been filled out with numbers that appeared to be written in blood. A peek at the answers page revealed not a single number was in the right box.

She was about to cast the magazine aside in disgust when the drink cart came to a stop next to her. "Can I get you anything to drink, hon?" the flight attendant asked without even bothering to look at Kara.

"Ginger ale?" Kara replied. Still looking straight ahead, the flight attendant smiled an empty smile at nobody in particular as she grabbed a can and began pouring.

"And for you, sir— OH MY GOD!" The flight attendant recoiled in horror as she noticed Jeff the Jackrabbit's misshapen head for the first time. Packets of pretzels spilled all over the man on the other side of the aisle.

"My grandfather's carry-on!" Kara chuckled nervously.

The flight attendant gathered herself. "You're going to need to stow that... hippo?"

"Jackrabbit," Kara corrected.

"Whatever it is, it needs to be stowed," the flight attendant said as she handed Kara her soda and wheeled the drink cart off. Kara pushed the shopping bag onto the floor and kicked it back under the seat in front of her. As she did, she glanced back toward the bathroom, where to her dismay, the rabble had noticed the startled flight attendant. They were looking her way and pointing. Not sure what else to do, Kara lowered her head back into the magazine.

The rest of *Seat Back Vistas* proved just as dismal. There was a stylized infographic about all the Hollywood films where asparagus had appeared onscreen. It analyzed the amount of screen time the vegetable had received, which star had eaten the most cumulative asparagus, and films that actually depicted asparagus being eaten as opposed to the ones that just implied it. Some person who had read the magazine before Kara had circled and underlined parts of the infographic that interested them, and had even ripped out one corner section for unfathomable reasons.

After that, there was an article about a dog who had successfully landed a plane with nearly two hundred passengers on board. The author treated it as more of a humorous human-interest piece, rather than the terrifying, life-endangering breach of safety protocol that it actually was. That was followed by a "Flight Attendant of the Month" profile. The lucky flight attendant had been asked a series of stock questions: favorite place to travel, window or aisle seat, craziest thing you ever saw someone try to carry on. It was kind of charming, except that evidently something terrible had happened to the unfortunate woman just before the magazine went to press and every mention of her name was followed by the parenthetical statement (NOW DECEASED).

SBV(BTYBM®B): *Where would you fly if you had your own private jet?*

Mary Forsythe (NOW DECEASED): *I'd love to surprise my parents! I'd pick them up, and fly them to their favorite vacation spot, St. Thomas in the Virgin Islands. They'd be so excited!*

Kara wondered if the safety-procedure card might prove a bit more entertaining, but just then something on the next page caught her attention. Several local tourism boards had taken out ads to try to lure visitors to their destination. Attractive ads for Iceland, Brazil, and New Zealand took up three of the four quadrants of the page. In the fourth, there was a small ad for a lawyer who guaranteed you a huge cash settlement if you had been unfortunate enough to come down with a disease that Kara had never heard of. "Call before it claims your power of speech!" the ad encouraged. Below that, there was an ad for a 1-900 sex-chat line that promised "the hottest, most racist dirty talk you've ever experienced!" And below that, in tiny letters, were the words "VISIT HAWAII."

Kara leaned in to study this last ad closer. Compared to the other tourism ads on the page, it was minimalist and uninviting. Kara recognized the typeface as Arial, the required font for all her high school writing assignments. It worked well for book reports, but looked terrible in an ad. Underneath the words VISIT HAWAII there was a bulleted list:

- *Drugs = Legal!*
- *Hookers = Legal!!*
- *Gambling = Legal!!!*
- *All this plus the Olympics!!!! Book your trip to HAWAII today!!!!!*

Next to the bulleted list was a clip art image of a hula girl in a grass skirt, and the iconic five ring logo of the Olympic games. Kara examined the word HAWAII. After close to a minute of intent study, she decided that there *might* be a slight difference in the kerning of the last two letters that could possibly tip off the trained eye of a typeface expert that they weren't actually uppercase *i*'s. To 99.99 percent of the magazine's readership, though, it would read as the name of the Aloha State.

There was a sudden commotion behind her, and Kara reluctantly pulled herself away from the magazine. She braced herself for a confrontation and slowly turned around. The flight attendant who had served her the ginger ale had continued to push the drink cart down the aisle and now found her way blocked by the unruly mob in front of the bathroom. A heated exchange had developed between the flight attendant and the mob leader, who was now shifting his weight from foot to foot and shamelessly squeezing his genitals through his pants pocket in an effort to hold it in.

With his other hand, the leader was gesturing back and forth from the bathroom to Kara's seat. Kara deftly avoided eye contact whenever he looked in her direction. The flight attendant loudly informed the crowd that gathering in the aisle was strictly forbidden, and that they were required by law to take their seats. Ignoring her, the mob leader reached out and banged on the lavatory door again.

Evidently sensing that she was outnumbered, the flight attendant backed up the drink cart to give the mob some space. Then, without any warning, she quickly pushed it forward again, ramming into the leader and sending him careening back into the assembled rabble. The flight attendant leaned her whole weight into the cart, and the mob roared in confusion as they were shoved to the back of the plane.

As soon as the drink cart was past the lavatory door, the overhead indicator light switched from red "occupied" to green "vacant" and Cornelius burst out the door and into the aisle. He didn't even glance at the mob, whose confusion quickly shifted to outrage as they noticed him scampering away. The drink cart took up the entire aisle, blocking any of the furious passengers from chasing the man who had wronged them. Hands shot past the flight attendant like a zombie horde trying to get in through a hastily boarded-up door, but the drink cart proved impenetrable. In seconds, Cornelius settled in next to Kara, grinning as he buckled his seatbelt.

Kara stared at her grandfather. She was relieved that he wasn't currently plummeting to Earth, frozen after passing through the aircraft's plumbing system, but this relief was overshadowed by irritation. She was tired of being kept in the dark about where he'd come from, where and what HAWAll was, and what he had been doing in the bathroom for the better part of an hour.

"Grandpa, what the hell just happened?"

"I let the drink cart run interference on the bathroom mob so I could have a clear path back to my seat," Cornelius informed her. "One of the oldest tricks in the book." He reached out and stabbed at the touchscreen on the seat back in front of him until the in-flight entertainment channel turned on.

Kara immediately reached out a finger and powered it back down. "I thought you'd been sucked out of a toilet vacuum!"

Cornelius raised his eyebrows as his mouth dropped open in surprise. Then he threw back his head and laughed uproariously.

"A toilet vacuum!" he guffawed. "That is spectacular!" Cornelius wiped a tear away from his eye. "Oh my dear, sometimes I forget how much you have to learn about the world!" He laughed for a bit longer then abruptly stopped. He reached out and jabbed various areas of the touchscreen until it turned on again.

Just as quickly, Kara tapped it back off. An elderly woman sitting in front of Cornelius turned around to wordlessly glare at whoever kept poking her seat. Cornelius averted his eyes and pointed a finger at his granddaughter. The woman directed her sour expression at Kara, then turned back around and began hiss-whispering to the person seated next to her.

Kara ignored the betrayal. "How is that the oldest trick in the book?" she asked. "How often do you have mobs gather outside the bathroom that need to have 'interference' run on them? What on earth were you doing in there?"

"Kara, do you know what jet lag is?" Cornelius asked. He continued without waiting for a response. "Without getting into the hard science, it is the equivalent of having all the energy and excitement in your body replaced with the liquid that pools at the bottom of a garbage bag. The 'experts' tout a bunch of snake oil to alleviate the effects of jet lag: melatonin, exercise, coffee at night, fasting. But there's only one solution guaranteed to work every time. And that is a power nap in the can as soon as the airplane takes off."

Kara stared at her grandfather for a few more seconds until she realized that this was all the explanation he was going to offer. "You were sleeping in the bathroom?" she asked.

"That's right," Cornelius said.

"You ran back there as soon as the plane took off, locked the door, and fell asleep?"

"Uh, yeah," Cornelius said with a touch of irritation. "I don't know what's so hard to understand about that. It's not rocket science. I didn't run up to the cockpit and seize the controls like that hero dog did. I just made a pillow out of some toilet paper, stretched out, and caught some z's."

"Why didn't you just fall asleep in your seat?" Kara asked.

"Are you kidding me? It's better than first class in there! These seats offer no lumbar support, and the person in front of you is always reclining their seat and slamming into your knees."

"The first thing you did when you sat down was jab a plastic wedge into the seat in front of you so the person in it would be unable to recline," Kara reminded her grandfather. "You said 'Let the buyer beware!' when I asked you if that was legal or ethical, and when I asked what you meant by *that,* you dashed off to the bathroom!"

On cue, the old woman in front of Cornelius attempted to lean back in her seat. There were a few tentative pushes, then some full body slams to try to get the backrest to recline a few centimeters. Cornelius's plastic wedge held tight and the seat didn't budge, leaving his legroom free of encroachment. The woman looked back over the seat again, this time appearing far more irritated. Cornelius gestured toward Kara with his head. She sneered at Kara, then turned around and rang the flight attendant call button.

"Besides," Cornelius continued. "There's always a racket out here.

Screaming babies, chatty neighbors. Not to mention the angry aisle mobs that seem to pop up on these longer flights. You drift off for even a second and they're liable to drag you out of your seat and shove a barf bag down your throat!"

"That mob only formed because you locked them out of the bathroom while you were napping! They turned on you because you intentionally inconvenienced them!"

"Hey, I've got a lot to do once we land," Cornelius said. "I can't afford to be operating at anything less than 100 percent."

Just then a flight attendant appeared in the aisle. "Did someone ring the call bell?" she asked.

The woman in the row ahead started to speak up, but Cornelius was quicker. "Yeah, that was me. You skipped me on the drink service, I'll need a Bloody Mary, four vodkas." The flight attendant nodded politely and reached up to reset the call button. She was off to retrieve Cornelius's beverage before the woman one row up could protest.

"Four vodkas is operating at 100 percent?" Kara asked skeptically.

"Crap, did I say four?" Cornelius asked. He reached up to hit the call button, but the irritated woman in front of him was faster. She jammed the button and the bell dinged again. The flight attendant turned around and doubled back down the aisle.

The woman from one row up raised a finger, but Cornelius once again intercepted the flight attendant. "I meant to say five vodkas," he said. "With a chaser of Jack." The flight attendant smiled, nodded, and reset the call button.

"You do realize that when she brings you your drinks, she's going to have to wheel the cart back down here and the mob is going to follow her right to you?" Kara asked.

Cornelius offered no reply. He merely smirked and held up three fingers. Then two. Then one.

"Oh God, he went right in the aisle!" came a hysterical voice from behind them.

Kara swiveled her head around. The flight attendant was quickly pulling the drink cart back to the front of the plane. The aisle mob was dispersing just as fast. And lying in the aisle, looking defeated and quite wet in the crotch, was the former mob leader. Unable to use the bathroom, he'd finally reached the breaking point and wet his pants in the aisle.

"Grab some toilet paper and clean it up!" someone yelled. Another passenger darted through the finally unimpeded lavatory door. He popped his head back out a few seconds later.

"There's none left!" he replied in a panic. "Someone mashed all of it into a giant wad!" The man brandished the enormous clump of toilet paper for his fellow passengers to see. After a few seconds, he shrugged and tossed it like a football to someone sitting a few rows away. They tossed it back, and a game of catch broke out. The soggy, forgotten mob leader whimpered from the floor of the plane.

Cornelius winked at Kara. His casual demeanor seemed warranted. Half the mob was distracted by the puddle of urine quickly flowing down the aisle and the other half was waving for the toilet paper ball. Meanwhile, the woman one row up reached up and repeatedly jammed the call button.

The flight attendant wheeled the cart past Kara and Cornelius and came to a stop at the row in front of them. The flight attendant looked quite irritated. "Ma'am, the call button is not a toy!" she informed the woman as she reached up and smacked the button to dismiss the call signal.

"But he—"

The flight attendant cut the woman off before she could get out another word. "Ma'am, please stop making a scene! If you're not going to cooperate, we'll have to restrain you!" The woman shrunk down into her seat. The flight attendant stared daggers at her for a few seconds then pushed the cart back to Cornelius.

"Sorry about all that, sir," she said, flashing Cornelius a broad smile. "Some passengers…"

"I know how it is," Cornelius said with a roll of his eyes.

The flight attendant cracked a can of Bloody Mary mix, poured it into a cup of ice, and handed it to Cornelius. Then she fumbled around inside the drink cart and eventually produced five small bottles of vodka and one of Jack Daniels. She handed them over as well.

"Those will be on the house of course," the flight attendant said with a smile. "Because of the disturbance," she added, lowering her voice to a sinister growl and pointedly glaring at the woman one row up.

"If I'd have known that, I would have asked for seven!" Cornelius chuckled. The flight attendant humored him with a polite titter.

"Seriously, can I have two more?" Cornelius asked. The flight attendant thought about it for a second, then shrugged and tossed two more bottles of vodka into Cornelius's lap. Then she rolled the cart up to the front of the plane, where she secured it and got on the intercom.

"Flight attendants, we have a two-fourteen in the right aisle next to the lavatory," she announced. "That is a two-fourteen next to the lavatory. Requesting sedation kit and assistance."

"I never understand why they don't just use the other bathroom," Cornelius said as he twisted open a vodka and poured it into the Bloody Mary mix. "Guess they get so blinded with rage that they forget here's always, like, at least three on an international flight. At a minimum."

"Where are you taking me?" Kara blurted. She thrust the in-flight magazine into her grandfather's lap and pointed to the tiny HAWAII ad. Cornelius took a sip of his drink and looked down at it.

"Well, look at that! There it is, out in the wild!" Cornelius held up the magazine for a closer look. "Designed the ad myself!" he said with a proud smirk.

"So you're not just the diplomat, you're also the graphic designer for the tourism board of..." Kara paused as she realized she had no idea how to pronounce HAWAII. "Huh-WALL? HA-wail? HUH-wai-ee?"

"Break it down," Cornelius said. "It's pronounced exactly how it's written."

"It most certainly isn't," Kara replied.

Cornelius ignored her. "It's Huh-WALL. You were right the first time. And I'm designing tourism ads for them because, well... I'm the president!"

"Of course." Kara made no effort to disguise her skepticism. "I hear that's one of the primary duties of any president. In history class they told us that Clinton used to fire up Photoshop and make a few *Visit Niagara Falls* ads in between the budget meeting and the State of the Union. William Henry Harrison designed an ad each of the thirty-two days he was in office! And on the day Kennedy got shot he laid out an ad for Lincoln, Nebraska, and on the day Lincoln got shot he launched a campaign for Cape Kennedy!"

"Are you done?" Cornelius asked.

"I have no idea what's going on!"

Cornelius smiled and unscrewed the top of another bottle of vodka. He poured it into his half-empty Bloody Mary and gave it a quick stir.

"You seem to know your presidents pretty well, Kara," he said, pausing dramatically to take a sip. "But I think it's time for an entirely different sort of history lesson."

Kara stared back at him with a mix of blankness and fury.

"HAWAll," Cornelius added. "The history lesson is about HAWAll."

"I understood what you were implying," Kara said.

"Well, you were just sort of staring at me…"

"You want permission to tell your story? I don't think you need it from me. After all, you're the *president*." Sarcasm dripped from the last word.

"I just thought… Look. OK. I'll tell you everything you need to know about HAWAll. But you ruined a darn good segue there."

"*I* ruined it?"

"I'm just going to start telling it," Cornelius said with a sigh. "Kids these days…"

nine

I had just returned to the States from a tour of duty in Vietnam. The war was nearing its end and public opinion had turned against it. This made it really hard to adjust to life back home. People wouldn't look me in the eye, drivers in passing cars would call me "baby killer." The very first parade I marched in, a girl who couldn't have been older than eight walked up to me and spat in my face.

I should clarify that I was in a mascot costume during all of this. Yes, despite having a college degree, a good job at the factory, and a brand new family, I had signed on to a USO show where I had dressed in a bald eagle costume to entertain the troops in Vietnam. I guess I needed to fill a hole that had been empty since I took off the Jeff suit for the last time.

The shows went very poorly, mainly because I'd designed the costume myself. It turns out that dressing as a mascot and making a mascot costume are two very different things. My Egbert the Eagle made ol' Jeff the Jackrabbit look like the Phillie Phanatic. The feathers kept coming off in patches, and you could tell that the beak was obviously made of a Pringles can. At the first USO performance I had this whole routine planned where I came out with a Viet Cong flag. I'd make a big show out of it, wave it around, get the crowd to boo. Then, for the grand finale, I'd pretend to wipe my butt with it.

The crowd turned on me immediately. When a bunch of enlisted men who are risking their lives get promised entertainment, they're thinking Bob Hope, Sinatra, Ann-Margret. When I came out instead, in a costume that had really taken a beating on the flight over, the boos were deafening. And that was before I started waving around the flag of the people who were killing their friends.

In retrospect, I probably should have made sure that my display of the flag did not look as "celebratory" or as "reverent" as the *Army Times* later described it. I thought it was perfectly clear that when I saluted it, I did so mockingly, and when I lit the American flag on fire, it was clearly an ironic commentary. Maybe I should have gone straight to the butt-wiping, I dunno... But of course, hindsight is twenty-twenty and all that. You can't beat yourself up over an honest mistake.

Anyway, long story short, I'm back from Vietnam, the eight-year-old spits in my face during the parade, and I think to myself: *This is no way to live.* Dressing up in a homemade eagle costume and having epithets hurled at you was no life for a grown man with a wife and young son. So I made a homemade *tiger* costume.

That went almost as poorly. But I was learning! I converted the garage into a makeshift workshop. I made a frog suit, then a wild boar, and then a crazy furball of a creature that I just called Yippie. The first time I wore that one to a football game, a five-year-old sucking on a giant lollipop punched me in the crotch within five minutes. But listen to this: it was only *a glancing blow,* not full-on testicle contact! I knew I was onto something.

I came home that night with a renewed sense of purpose only to find that your grandmother had left me a Dear John letter. Said she was taking our son and heading to the big city to get a fresh start. I was distraught—even more so after I realized that she forgot to take your father with her!

So I was left to raise a growing boy all by myself. Well, I shouldn't say by myself... I had some very special help from a few furry friends! Now, I didn't know the first thing about parenting, but I saw how your dad responded to those puppets on *Sesame Street*. He thought they were just as real as the people on the show. If he thought Egbert the Eagle was a real creature who lived with us, well, that was just as good as having another adult to help raise him! Who needed his mother when I had Yippie?

Now, the Muppets already had the learning thing covered. Counting, the ABCs, manners, all that garbage. So, I figured, where do I need the most help? That's right: discipline. Every time your dad did something wrong, I'd send him down into the basement. One of the mascots would appear soon after, ready to yell at him, punish him, spank him. Spanking was The Frog's department. I never gave that one a name, just called him The Frog. More sinister that way. It was your classic good cop/bad cop scenario! I told him that I was afraid the noise that the furnace made, so I couldn't go down there with him. That really helped, him knowing that I was powerless to stop these giant animals that lived below us. It made them the ultimate authority and kept him from resenting me when one of the mascots grounded him.

Soon I came to realize that these mascot suits weren't just good for laying down the law. They were also a good way to get out of conversations I didn't want to have! As your dad got older and started asking why he didn't have a mommy like the other kids at school, I realized I was going to have to tell him the truth. That was going to be awkward as hell. So I sent him to the basement and had Yippie explain it to him. One year when I didn't have enough money for birthday presents, I had Egbert inform him that his birthday was cancelled that year. I also took that opportunity to explain to him that Santa wasn't real. Figured I'd kill two birds with one stone.

Oh, speaking of birds! One time your dad left his bike in the yard when it rained and The Frog was really laying into him down there, yelling at him about responsibility, threatening him, breaking stuff, pulling out the toy chest and staring at him silently as he slammed the lid shut over and over again, when it dawned on me: We'd never had the birds and the bees discussion! Talk about something I wish I could have pawned off on your grandmother! So I had The Frog shift gears abruptly and teach him all about sex. It was going really well, he was demonstrating all the moves and everything until one of the frog eyes fell off and your father fainted.

So that left me with quite the dilemma: who should be there when he regained consciousness? The way I saw it, both sides had their pluses and minuses. If I took off the costume I—

* * *

"Why are you looking at me like that, Kara?"

Kara was staring at her grandfather in slack-jawed horror. "That was abuse!" she finally managed to exclaim. "You were an abusive parent who warped your only child!"

"Nonsense!" Cornelius scoffed. He twisted open another bottle of vodka and poured it into his cup. "One, it was a different time. Stuff like this was going on in every suburb in America."

"In every suburb in America, parents were sending their children into the basement to get spanked by a sinister frog mascot? I'm sorry, I must have missed the episode of *The Wonder Years* where they covered that."

"Two," Cornelius continued, ignoring her. "Look at how your father turned out. Tried out for Jeff the Jackrabbit the first week of high school and proudly wore the costume all four years. In fact, by the time he graduated, he refused to relinquish the costume! He took it home and the school had to buy a brand new one. If he'd been 'warped' by my 'parenting style' do you really think there's a chance he'd have done any of that?"

"He had Stockholm syndrome about mascots! He was twisted into caring about the terrifying basement-dwellers that haunted his childhood! You raised a disturbed child!"

"Anyone who has successfully raised a kid who didn't grow up to kill a bunch of neighborhood pets or shoot up a post office, raise their hand," Cornelius said.

"That's a low, low bar!" Kara protested.

"Anybody who's raised a child who didn't go around setting the neighbors' cats on fire, raise their hand!" Cornelius repeated with a touch of irritation. He hoisted his drink into the air for emphasis and stared at Kara. She sighed and looked down at her feet. "I thought so," Cornelius smirked. He took another sip of his drink. "Now where were we?"

"I *thought* you were telling me where you were taking me," Kara replied.

"Ah yes. Don't worry, I'm getting there."

* * *

So anyway, I saw how your father responded to these mascots. They were real to him. And that knowledge kept me going when it would have been so easy to just pack it in and get a normal job. It made me double down on my efforts to become a professional mascot. Now in the spring of 1986—I remember it specifically because that was the summer that a bunch of neighbors' pets went missing—your father was thirteen years old. Don't look at me like that, it wasn't him. Believe me, The Frog spent hours interrogating the hell out of him in the basement that summer. If he had done it, The Frog would have gotten him to crack.

So one hot summer night, your father was down in the basement talking to Egbert. He'd started to spend more and more time down there. One of the mascots would get done chewing him out and he'd just stay down there, sniffling and spilling his guts. I guess he found it easier to talk to them than me. Talk about irony, huh? I would tune him out for the most part, but that night he said something that caught my attention. He said, "When I go off to college, will you still be able to watch me?" I'll tell you, I nearly choked on the beer that I'd rigged the costume to allow me to drink while I was inside it. College! He was only five years away and I hadn't saved a penny.

It wasn't for lack of effort! It's just that in terms of mascot jobs in town, there were two tiers: Jeff the Jackrabbit and everyone else. Jeff already had the biggest stage in town, the high school football games. So if you were opening a car dealership or throwing your kid a birthday party, you wanted Jeff there, not Egbert or Yippie or The Frog. Definitely not The Frog. Word had gotten out about The Frog.

103

I tried undercutting Jeff's appearance fees. But it turned out the pimply kid who was currently wearing the jackrabbit suit was just doing it so he'd have something to put on his college application and wasn't charging a dime. Then I tried positioning myself as the high-end mascot, charging five thousand bucks per appearance. There are idiots out there who think because something is the most expensive, that makes it the best. But then the pimply kid found out about it and started charging *six* thousand. He was always one step ahead!

Once the pimply kid started making that kind of money, he was quick to hire some muscle. One night his goons snuck into our house and put Egbert's head in your dad's bed, Godfather style. I woke up the next morning to your father screaming. He thought The Frog had done it, but I knew better. It was time to leave town. The writing was on the wall. The pimply kid's goons literally wrote on the wall: LEAVE TOWN. I knew it was red paint, but your dad thought it was Egbert's blood. That pimply kid had some great ideas about intimidation, I'll give him that. If we'd been able to put our heads together on disciplinary methods, who knows, your dad might have been president by now. But as it stood, my days as a mascot in the Jefferson School District were finished.

I tried to look on the bright side: here was a chance to strike out for the big leagues, really find a place where I could earn enough money for us to live comfortably. But I couldn't bring myself to uproot your father right as he started high school. Boys at that age act tough, but they're really very vulnerable; you don't want to do anything to make those years harder for them. So I stocked the cupboard with a six month supply of canned beef stew and left him home alone.

I had to make sure he'd behave while I was gone, so one day I told him that while I was out running errands I had seen The Frog purchasing a gun. Figured that ought to keep him in line. But he mouthed off, said that The Frog couldn't leave the basement or his psychic powers would be sapped. By this time it was honestly hard to keep track of the web of lies I'd constructed about the universe of the basement mascots, so it was easiest just to buy a gun and have The Frog be loading it in silence the next time I sent your dad down there.

I was in a cab to the airport before he regained consciousness. I've never been good at goodbyes.

To help narrow down where to move, I had made a list of all the places where a mascot might thrive. It needed to be a place where sports were a way of life. A place where the quarterback dates the head cheerleader and the football coach is more powerful than the mayor. A place where entire communities come together on Friday nights under the lights to support the high school team. A place where a lone star like me could shine brightly. A place people don't mess with. A place where everything… where everything just seems *bigger*.

So I bought a ticket to England. I was in the air for no more than five minutes when I realized I'd forgotten to consider Texas as one of my options. In retrospect that would have been a much more logical choice. But England was where I had cast my lot and now there was no turning back!

I landed at Heathrow on a foggy September day. It was my first time out of the country since my ill-fated USO trip to Vietnam. All I had with me were my costumes and a vague promise to the State Department that I wouldn't incite any more international incidents. I had every intention of keeping my costumes.

While I waited in line for a taxi, I happened to notice that the two men in front of me were having a conversation about soccer. I leaned in to see if I could pick up any leads. They were discussing a team named Arsenal, and it was obvious that it meant a great deal to them. They were brothers, and had been going to Arsenal matches with their father since before either of them could walk. They spoke of memories of triumphant victories and devastating losses. After a few minutes of eavesdropping I heard their voices start to catch, and I noticed for the first time that they both had tears in their eyes. I soon gathered that they were returning from their father's funeral.

One man reminded his brother about the old man's superstition of keeping the same seat on the couch while Arsenal was winning. The other smiled, and told a story about the time they'd surprised him with front-row seats to a tournament match. Their father had fallen to his knees when he realized it wasn't a joke. At one point, one of the brothers revealed to the other that his wife was pregnant with their first child, a son. He could barely choke out the words through the sobs, but he said he had been planning to tell their father that he was going to be a grandfather at the next Arsenal match they attended together. Now he would be scattering his father's ashes at the midfield line instead. By this point, both brothers were weeping openly, and before they parted ways, they hugged and told each other "I love you."

Arsenal fans seemed like pussies, so when I got in a cab I asked the driver who Arsenal's biggest rival was. He said it was a team called Chelsea. Sounded good to me. Hopefully their fans were more in control of their emotions. People go to a sporting event to have fun and be entertained by a professional mascot, not to sob on each other's shoulders and lament that an unborn child will never know his grandfather.

I explained to my driver that I was in the mascot business, and wanted to rent a flat right next to Chelsea's stadium. I was brimming with confidence and even though I didn't have a job, I was already envisioning waking up, putting on my costume, and strolling across the street to the stadium, accidentally tripping any Arsenal fans carrying urns I might happen to encounter.

London cabbies know the city like the back of their hand, and so this guy had just the place in mind. The building had a great view into Stamford Bridge, the Chelsea stadium, and even better, the driver played darts with the building's super, so he got me an insider's deal on my lease. The paint was peeling, the shower dripped, and a shiny plaque mounted to the front of the building commemorated its historical status as the site where Jack the Ripper was said to have contracted the strain of syphilis that eventually caused the madness that led to his killing spree. But none of that mattered. I was home.

I'll never forget that first night. For over an hour, I stood staring out the kitchen window, transfixed by the stadium lights. I didn't completely understand the rules of the game, but as I watched those little kids run around chasing that ball and sucking on orange slices on the sidelines, I knew that I was destined to be the next Chelsea mascot.

That stadium of course, was not Stamford Bridge and those nine-year-olds were definitely not the Chelsea Football Club. Turns out the cab driver was *also* a die-hard Arsenal supporter. He hated Chelsea so much that he was willing to go to elaborate lengths to prank a complete stranger who just wanted to *work* for the team.

When you're unemployed in a foreign country, renting an apartment in the building whose unsanitary conditions may have led to the most famous serial-killer rampage in history, hoping you don't have to pawn one of your mascot heads in order to send money home so that the child you abandoned can eat, you have two options. One, you can grit your teeth and do what by God needs to be done. Or two, you can make getting revenge on the stranger who wronged you your all-consuming obsession.

In the heat of the moment, Plan B seemed like the way to go. The next morning, Egbert the Eagle was waiting outside the gates of Arsenal's stadium when the owner's Rolls Royce pulled in. My plan was to tap on the window, then kill him in cold blood. I figured that would balance the scales a bit. After all, I had been tricked into signing a six-month lease. But I chickened out and when he rolled down the window, I instead asked him if there were any mascot jobs available. He said no. So the next day I threw myself in front of the car and threatened to sue him unless he gave me a job. Which he did. Idiot was probably worried I was crazy and would kill him if he didn't.

The way I saw it, what better way to get revenge on the horrible Arsenal fans than to infiltrate their ranks, gain their trust, and delight them as the official team mascot for an extended period of time before revealing that I had been a Chelsea fan all along? I mean, imagine those two brothers were about to scatter their father's ashes at midfield when all of a sudden the Arsenal Eagle rips off his jersey to reveal a Chelsea one underneath and has to be escorted off the field, all the while yelling that everything about their beloved franchise is a lie. They'd probably be telling that one to a therapist for years! God, sports are great…

So I had the job. I was getting paid to be a mascot for a franchise that many Europeans and South Americans considered an important professional sports team. There was one thing I hadn't counted on: the hooligans. You know, those rowdy fans who show up at a soccer match just so they can turn it into a drunken race riot? Sounds awesome, I know. But it turns out that there's one thing that's even more fun than shattering a bottle on someone's head while shouting ethnic slurs at them and, sadly, that's beating up the mascot.

My first day on the job, I showed up eager to get to work. Egbert had been freshly steam cleaned, I had several new physical-comedy bits ready to debut, and I'd been doing an upper-body strengthening routine so that my agility while in costume was at an all-new level. I was ready to rock.

Someone knocked me unconscious with a whiskey bottle before I even left the dressing room.

To this day, I don't know who did it. Nobody but team employees and reporters were allowed in the dressing room, so it was either someone I worked with or an ultra-ambitious hooligan who'd forged a press credential. I regained consciousness at halftime and was able to stagger out to the field and perform a routine that mostly consisted of me holding up a hand to indicate that I would need just a few more seconds. The crowd pelted me with garbage, a few drunk fans rushed the field and tackled me, I threw up inside Egbert's head, and the debut was widely considered to be a success.

The next game, I was more vigilant in the locker room. I berated the towel boy, spied on the trainer while he was in the can, berated the towel boy some more. I thought I had solved the problem when I discovered an empty whiskey bottle in the captain's locker, but upon discovering three more in a forward's locker and as many as eight or nine in the goalkeeper's, I realized that these so-called athletes were more or less plowed all the time. Typical Arsenal. I started to berate the towel boy for enabling such behavior, but before I could really lay into him, I heard the game starting.

Within ten seconds of taking the field, a fan shot me with one of those non-lethal beanbags that cops fire into riots. No idea where he got one of those, but it didn't bode well for anyone who was in the business of stopping drunken riots. When I came to, someone yelled "He's not dead!" and then dozens of people started kicking me. I managed to crawl off while they were distracted after Arsenal somehow scored a goal, and was about to do my patented "handcuff the referee then pull his pants down" routine when another group of hooligans came out of the stands and started to shock/beat me with some sort of experimental electrified crowbar they had been working on.

Not a single one of the next five games went as well as that one.

The owner loved it. When the hooligans were focused on harming me, normal fans felt more comfortable coming to the stadium. There was a dramatic decrease in trampling deaths and, more importantly, a slight uptick in concession sales. Of course, it usually wasn't long before those regular fans saw how much fun the hooligans were having and decided to hurl blunt objects at me too.

So it was hard work, but ice-cold revenge usually is. There's a reason you have to "carry out" revenge and not just "do it on a whim when you've got a free half hour." Plus, I was making decent money to send back home to your father, which, I occasionally had to remind myself, had actually been the primary goal here. Your dad was a trooper, I'll tell you. I was so proud the day I got his letter telling me that he'd gotten the gig as the Jefferson mascot. I wrote back to him and told him that I had no idea who he was or why he was writing to me or where I was currently writing from. They weren't so good at diagnosing massive concussions in those days.

I was dressing up as an increasingly filthy homemade eagle and regularly getting pummeled by drunks. But all good things have to come to an end. For me it was when the team planned a special pregame show on Easter Sunday. They made me carry a cross into the stadium, and the hooligans lined up and hurled stones at me and shouted stuff. At one point I looked around and I noticed the team hadn't even bothered to put up the goals. I don't think they were ever planning to play that day, they just wanted to crucify a mascot. Fortunately, the guy with the non-lethal beanbag gun got overexcited and shot me with a knockout blow to the head before they could start nailing me up.

When I came to in the hospital, the first face I saw was the owner. He'd been keeping a steady vigil at my bedside. My first words were unsteady, but I managed to mutter the team's motto, "*Victoria Concordia Crescit.*" I could tell he was on the verge of tears. Then I explained to him that even though I loved him, and I loved Arsenal (lies), I needed to find a less violent crowd to perform in front of. I feared that if I stayed with the team, I might never make it home to one day see my son don his own costume.

He smiled and nodded and patted my hand, then informed me that if I quit, he would immediately invalidate my visa, then simultaneously have me deported while suing to recover back wages. Panicked, I hit the call button for the nurse, but when she arrived, she had a shaved head, was sporting an Arsenal jersey, and was toting what looked like a non-lethal beanbag gun. I don't think the hooligan who owned it realized it was non-lethal; he seemed really confused that I kept surviving. Fortunately, I'd also been hitting the morphine button pretty hard while I spilled my guts to the owner, and I drifted off just a few seconds later.

When the hospital discharged me, I was terrified and slightly addicted to morphine. I was essentially a prisoner of the team. I could keep showing up to games and letting the hooligans knock me senseless, or I could abandon everything I'd worked for and get sent back home without a penny.

* * *

Cornelius paused and glanced at Kara. She was staring at him, riveted. Any irritation she'd previously felt about being kept in the dark had been forgotten in light of hearing about his dramatic mascot exploits. Cornelius opened another bottle of vodka and poured it into his increasingly booze-forward Bloody Mary.

"So what did you do?" Kara finally asked.

"Oh? Interested in what comes next? I bet you didn't think your old grandfather had lived such an exciting life, huh?" Cornelius smirked. He was starting to feel a little drunk and more than a little self-righteous.

"Of course I didn't," Kara replied. "I thought you were dead. You could have spent the past thirty years filing papers at the DMV and that would have been more interesting than being dead."

Cornelius ignored her and leaned in closer. "You want a drink?" he whispered, waggling his eyebrows and flashing an impish grin.

"I'm fifteen!" Kara replied, out of habit more than any genuine principle. It was the first time anyone, let alone an adult, had offered her a drink and it felt like a trap. Kara suddenly realized how surreal it was that while she was thirty thousand feet in the air, all of her classmates were just now stumbling home from the after-school field parties she hadn't been invited to, pretending they were just really tired and trying not to puke on the family dog.

"Didn't you see the ad?" Cornelius asked. "Drugs are legal in HAWAll, and that includes booze. If there's no drinking age in your final destination, you're allowed to drink on the plane!"

"It said that hookers were legal too," Kara replied. "I'm not going to get a hooker just because it's not against the law."

"That's good," Cornelius said, suddenly serious. "We don't actually have any hookers at the moment. But if any ever show up they *are* completely legal, so that's technically not false advertising! It even says that at the bottom of the ad." Cornelius pulled out the magazine and ran his finger along the bottom right corner. Kara squinted and leaned in until it was about two inches from her face. Even then, she could barely make out an asterisk and the fine print "Technically not false advertising."

Kara wondered if there had ever been a case described by an advertiser as "technically not false advertising" that did not consist of 100 percent pure false advertising. But she pushed the thought from her mind. She was more intrigued by something else her grandfather had said.

"Wait. You said *we* don't have any hookers."

"At the moment!" Cornelius corrected.

"I meant the 'we' part! You still haven't explained how you came to be 'president' of HAWAll."

Cornelius winked. "You want me to finish my story?" Kara

nodded emphatically. Cornelius smiled, then reached for one of the remaining bottles of vodka. He wiggled it between his thumb and forefinger and looked at Kara. "What do you say? he asked.

Kara bit her lower lip and thought the matter over. "You won't tell Mom and Dad?" she finally asked.

"They told you I was dead! The fuck do I owe them?" Cornelius scoffed, a little too loudly. The profanity sparked loud clucks of distaste from the elderly woman in front of Cornelius. Kara could hear her loudly whispering to the person in the seat next to her. Eventually, a tiny bald man who looked even older than the woman he was traveling with popped his head up over the seat.

The man was extremely nervous. He licked his lips and took a deep breath. "My wife was wondering if you could…" There was a rustling followed by inaudible but emphatic directions being given by the man's wife.

"I know dear, I'm getting to it!" the husband said. It wasn't obvious whether he was more uncomfortable addressing Cornelius or his wife. He licked his lips again and swallowed. "She was hoping that, if it were possible, you might refrain from using such vulgar language?"

"Tell that crone to put a sock in it!" Cornelius snapped at him. The man recoiled and shrank back to the safety of his own seat. Cornelius wasn't done. "And, hey, granny? Good luck not getting jetlagged when you can't recline your seat all night!" When a finger immediately shot up and dinged the call button, Cornelius looked at Kara expectantly.

Kara nodded her understanding, then reached up and hit the button again to turn it off. Cornelius smiled, then handed her the bottle of vodka. Kara took it, unscrewed the lid, then clinked it against the bottle her grandfather was offering. She raised it to her lips, tilted it back, and almost retched up her entire digestive system plus several other organs completely unrelated to the process of ingesting liquids.

"Yeah, that's about how my first sip of booze went, too," Cornelius said as he poured his own bottle into what was now a vodka with a splash of Bloody Mary mix. "It gets better. Trust me."

Kara coughed and sputtered. At least this had happened here, amongst family, and not in a field surrounded by her peers. God forbid her inexperience with alcohol had somehow altered the outcome of a frog race. If that had happened, she might still be on a plane to another country, but out of concern for her own safety.

"Just take it slow," Cornelius offered after he was sure she was okay. "It's meant to be savored." Kara nodded and took a smaller, more tentative sip, barely wetting her lips. It burned her throat, but she was prepared for the sensation this time. Once she realized she wasn't about to puke out anything vital, she took another sip, sat back in her seat, and let her grandfather resume his story.

* * *

What's the old saying? If you can't beat 'em, join 'em? I figured that was my best shot at endearing myself to the Arsenal fans and sparing myself another hospital trip or deportation. So one night there was a big fan rally, and I decided to attend it, really show that I was one of the guys.

Turned out that the "rally" involved driving over to the home of the guy who dressed as the mascot for Chelsea, dragging him out into the street, and then kicking the shit out of him. I mean, you run track, Kara, you understand how sports work. So we put a royal beating on him, all took turns, cheering each other on the entire time. For the first time since I'd moved to England, I really felt like I was part of something. Our guys were slapping me on the back, tossing me beers, laughing at my impression of how the guy's kids were crying when a hooligan slammed him in the back of the head with a garbage can.

It wasn't until the next morning that I realized I should have shown up in costume. The hooligans had no idea that their team's mascot was alongside them the whole time! I tried to rectify my mistake. I called into the hooligan phone tree and suggested that we go beat up the Newcastle mascot. I figured that this time, I'd show up as Egbert, we'd beat up another innocent man for no reason, and I'd get all the credit for it since it was my idea. Only problem was, the cops had started sniffing around and the hooligans were wary.

The Arsenal hooligans all went way back. They'd known each other since their youth-league soccer days. They didn't play, mind you. They just went to their classmates' games as nine-year-olds and beat up the dads who had come to watch the other team. They celebrated at each other's weddings, mourned at the funerals, and assaulted a surprisingly high number of attendees at the annual charity gala they hosted, up until it was classified as a terrorist event by the Thatcher administration.

The point is, now that the police were involved, they were instantly suspicious of the new guy who had joined them to assault the Chelsea mascot. An outsider shows up and the next day the cops come a-calling? That just screams narc. I was screwed. If I showed up to a game as Egbert, they'd beat me up out of principle. If I showed up as myself, they'd beat me up out of a slightly different principle. There was a decent chance that if I just sat at home in my apartment, the hooligans would get bored and start going door-to-door beating up random people. If I was lucky, they'd get to me after beating up a hundred, maybe a thousand innocent people. If I was unlucky, I'd be one of the first doors they kicked in.

I needed a friend. An advocate. An ally. And I found one in William Fitzpatrick.

Fitz ran the most popular pirate radio station in London. Well, I should say it was the most popular pirate radio station *to listen to* in London. He actually broadcast from a small, undisclosed island that was far enough off the coast of England to qualify as international waters. None of the equipment he had was legal in the UK, but it didn't matter. He also didn't have to abide by anyone else's standards and practices. He broadcast whatever the hell he wanted to.

I'm sure that doesn't sound like a big deal to you, because you grew up with the internet. If you want to listen to profanity-laden music now, all it takes is a click. You want to call someone a dipshit, tap tap tap, post it to their Facebook wall, "You're a dipshit." It wasn't that easy in the eighties. But precisely *because* it was difficult, our entertainment was a lot more creative.

Take Fitz's two most popular pirate radio shows for instance: *The Profanity-Laden Music Hour* and *You're a Dipshit*. I got keyed into them that night I spent hanging out with the hooligans. The punk rock he'd play on *TPLMH* was great, but *You're a Dipshit* was my favorite. It pioneered some bold innovations with the talk radio format. Pretty much he'd spend a while laying out his case that a particular target was a dipshit, then in the second half, people would call in and talk about dipshits of their own. Then there were recurring segments like "What an Asshole" and "Fuck *This* Guy!"

He didn't have the biggest audience, but his listeners were passionate. The kind of fans who would do anything for you. The hooligans loved him. Mostly this was just because the station was illegal, so they considered it their duty to support it. Fitz could read cookie recipes out of a cookbook or let his dog pant into the microphone and the hooligans would tune in out of solidarity. He actually stopped broadcasting *Rover Coast to Coast* after just three episodes because some hooligans thought the pup was telling them that it wanted them to bomb a hospital. Fitz got tired of them calling in during *You're a Dipshit* and asking to speak to his dog for further instructions, so he pulled the plug. They bombed a hospital anyway, but it was after a big Arsenal victory, so it was hard to prove Rover's program was responsible. Fitz reported the next day that Rover was licking his butt on the floor next to him, so his conscience appeared to be clear.

As I sat penned up in my apartment, realizing the influence this station had over the hooligans, it became clear to me that I had to get Fitz to evangelize my cause. If he told the hooligans to stop beating me up, they'd listen to him. And if he directed their rage toward finding that cabbie who had tricked me initially, or those two loser brothers with the dead dad, all the better. I mean, even I could acknowledge that they needed *some* sort of release valve on all that aggression.

The question was how to make my case. I couldn't just call in while he was reading cookie recipes and interrupt with non-cookie related material. I'd find myself being mocked on the next *You're a Dipshit* if I tried that. I had heard it happen. I needed to find the perfect show for me to make my case. I brewed a big pot of coffee, poured myself a cup, and vowed to listen to the pirate channel until I found it.

I sat through a lot of radio shows. Fitz had something for everyone. The most highbrow show was *The Investment Aria Cavalcade*, where Fitz would give stock tips by singing opera. But there was also *Sounds Plausible* where you'd call in and tell Fitz your crazy conspiracy theories and he would agree with you and encourage you to pursue whatever course of action you thought was just. On *Lucky Numbers,* Fitz was going through all the numbers in order and analyzing how lucky each one felt to him. The episode I heard was a special where the whole show was dedicated to 11,416. It was "not very" lucky, Fitz concluded at the end of the hour.

I'd been listening for twenty-nine consecutive hours by the time a show called *Snow Job* came on. On that one, Fitz would pretend to be all seven of the seven dwarfs, and he'd have these lengthy conversations with himself that mainly centered on dirty things the dwarves wanted to do to Snow White. I was pinching myself to keep from nodding off at this point, but here was Fitz assuming seven different personalities, arguing with himself, maintaining a long-running fiction where Dopey had a camera in the bathroom and Bashful secretly found Sneezy's sneezing erotic. In retrospect, it was quite obvious that Fitz's broadcasts were nothing but the rantings of a sleep-deprived madman. But when I heard those dwarfs arguing about who got to sleep with one of Snow White's bras that had fallen out of the laundry basket, I knew what I needed to do.

I was exhausted, but *You're a Dipshit* was up next. If I called in and said that I thought the hooligans who beat up Egbert at Arsenal games were dipshits, nobody would pay attention. But if several different people, all with different voices and personalities called in, everyone would think there was some sort of critical mass, a grassroots movement out there that was too big to ignore. So I dialed in and when Fitz picked up, I spoke with my best elderly British matron voice.

"Mmmm-yes, I truly feel that the hooligans who beat up the Arsenal mascot are… Oh, I don't normally swear, but… well, they're just dipshits!"

Then I hung up and immediately dialed back in as a working stiff from Liverpool. "Oy guvna! I agree with the elderly matron! Leave that Egbert bloke alone!"

Then a Manchester teenager: "G'day mate! Put down the billabong next time you're headed to the socceroo! Egbert's never hurt a swagman, ya wallaby!"

Then a refined London gentleman: "Heep how kemosabe. No make-um war with paleface mascot. Hi-yi-yi-yi, hi-yi-yi-yi!"

* * *

Kara stared in horror for what seemed like the twentieth time that day. Cornelius was caught up in the moment, and his refined London gentleman was currently performing a tomahawk chop motion. Eventually he noticed his granddaughter looking at him and quickly stopped chopping.

"Like I said, I had been up for about a day and a half by that time. It was hard to get the specific dialects down exactly."

"Those weren't even close!" Kara said. "You sounded like a bunch of banned cartoon characters from the thirties!"

"I'll ignore that," Cornelius said sipping his drink. "The point is, somehow Fitz knew that all the different callers were actually just me."

"Because your impressions were all uniquely terrible but still somehow managed to sound like the same person was doing them?"

"No!" Suddenly, Cornelius found himself on the defensive. "No! That wasn't it at all."

"Well if it wasn't your 'Manchester teen' who wanted to throw another shrimp on the barbie, what was it?" Kara asked, smirking.

"Caller ID."

"Caller ID?"

"Yes, smarty pants. The switchboard at the pirate radio station had caller ID. Fitz could tell that everyone defending the mascot was really coming from the same phone number." For some reason, Cornelius decided it was his turn to smirk.

"Oh…" Kara waited for the other shoe to drop. Her grandfather was acting smug, and for the life of her, she couldn't tell what part of this idiotic story he thought made himself look good.

"Bet you didn't see that coming, did you?" Cornelius crowed. "He had all that expensive, illegal radio equipment, of course he had caller ID!"

"So even if your impressions had been world class…"

"The quality of the impressions is not on trial here," Cornelius snapped, irritated again.

"He would have still figured you out." After Kara finished her sentence, she stroked her chin and thought for a second. "That's really not an impressive story. It makes you look dumb. Him having caller ID is a pretty basic thing to overlook when you were planning your scheme."

"Would a dumb guy have thought to call up the operator and ask her to run a trace on the call-in number for *You're a Dipshit*? Because that's what I did. 'G'day Matilda, I'm gonna run some down under numerals by you and you boomerang a location back to me faster than a kiwi who just spotted the dingo's shadow.'"

"Why were you still talking like an Austral—" Kara stopped short. "Like a teenager from Manchester?" she corrected, rolling her eyes.

"True impressionists can sometimes get locked into a character without even realizing it," Cornelius informed her. "I wouldn't expect you to understand."

* * *

So, anyway, it took a bit more explaining, but I finally got her to do a reverse lookup on the phone number. She was concerned about privacy laws, or some nonsense, but I got really angry and told her that my wife had just given birth and the baby was having trouble breathing. I think she was confused about why I suddenly stopped talking like a Manchester teen, but she still coughed up the address.

Well, not necessarily the address. The coordinates.

Forty-five minutes later, I was cruising down the Thames toward the North Sea in a rented speedboat. The guys at the marina tried to pull some heavy-handed stuff like "asking if I knew how to operate a high-speed watercraft," but I played the choking newborn card again and that shut the door on that line of inquiry. All you had to do was leave a credit card and ID as collateral. The only ID I had was my passport, which gave me pause for a few seconds. Little did I know the next time I set foot on the mainland it would have expired.

Now, by this time, it had been nearly two days since I'd slept. So, yes, I nodded off at the helm a few times. But that's much less of a big deal in a boat than it is in a car. You drift off in a car and right away you're jarred awake by those grooves they put in the side of the road. Makes it really difficult to get the restorative sleep that one obviously needs if they're in that position in the first place. But as long as you've got your boat pointed in the right general direction, you can pass out for a good fifteen-, twenty-minute power nap.

The only thing about the journey that wasn't relaxing were all the dolphins I kept hitting. I'll tell you, you hit one of those things and you honestly think you've hit a large swimming child. It's unnerving. You learn to just keep moving after it happens a couple times, but in the beginning I was stopping almost every other thud just to make sure. A lot of people say dolphins' intelligence is second to ours. Then explain why they never get out of the way when a speedboat going seventy miles an hour suddenly swerves at them while they're minding their own business.

Eventually, all landmarks disappeared and I was left with a solid horizon of ocean. I had to trust that my bearing was accurate as I sped along toward what I hoped was my destination. Things really aren't well marked out there. I thought there would at least be some clear indicator that I had entered international waters. At least a sign on a buoy saying that it was OK to gamble or bang hookers. But every sign I saw just had the same stupid warning about endangered dolphin breeding habitats so I figured I still had a ways to go.

Just when I was starting to wonder if I was actually hallucinating while still lying unconscious in my hospital bed, I finally saw it: a faint shimmer on the horizon that quickly solidified and emerged into view. It was Fitz's island.

It was a quiet, unassuming little place, undeveloped and rustic. But I knew that its appeal lay not in its aesthetic beauty, but in the freedom it represented. That's something worth keeping in mind,

Kara, on this journey and as you go through life as a whole. But especially on this journey. What is truly worth more: white sandy beaches or the ability to live without Big Brother breathing down your neck? Do we care that the environment isn't exactly what we consider "paradise," or is the reassurance that we are living the life of a self-actualized person all the good weather we need? Is it such a big deal if your sleeping surface is damp and rusty and devoid of pillows if it means that the thought police aren't mounting you with a shock collar and blasting your neck with electricity every time you consider dissension?

* * *

Kara actually thought that America had done a decent job of finding a happy medium for its citizens somewhere between "government-mandated shock collars" and "damp, rusty, pillowless beds," but she also sensed that her grandfather's story was nearing its end, if not necessarily a point, and didn't feel like interrupting.

* * *

After I docked the boat, it didn't take long to locate the radio tower. Fitz hadn't done much with the island in terms of making it a tourist destination, so it was really the only thing to see. There was a rickety shack with a giant antenna jutting out of the roof. It was so powerful that it was actually giving off sparks of electricity as Fitz broadcast. Gulls would fly past it and it would fry them like a bug zapper. They'd fall into the sea, already blackened and smoldering while a caller on *You're a Dipshit* barked some drivel about how much he hated his neighbor who wouldn't mow his lawn. That is the true power of a free press right there!

I was eager to embrace the freedom of international waters myself, but it turns out that most things that are illegal back on the mainland tend to involve other people. There's unfortunately very few crimes you can commit on your own. I settled for a quick public urination. It was just OK. Felt good to deal tyranny a blow, but was also unsatisfying since nobody was there to watch. If there *had* been someone there, though, I could have forced them to watch, and it wouldn't have been a crime. I felt like one of the founding fathers, but not one of the good ones. One of the ones that never got to be president, like Madison, or Monroe, or the third Roosevelt brother.

* * *

"Those first two you mentioned *were* president," Kara corrected. "And the Roosevelts weren't founding fathers, and they didn't have a *third* brother, because they weren't brothers themselves! But they both *were* presidents!"

"Grover Cleveland, I think his name was," Cornelius said, not listening. "What a shame. Always a bridesmaid, never a bride."

"The only thing that Grover Cleveland is famous for is the number of times that he *was* president!" Kara replied in spite of herself.

Cornelius ignored her. "I still donate to his campaign every four years. He's the right man for the job. So where was I?"

"Urinating in public," Kara sighed.

Cornelius pursed his lips, his eyes searching. "Can you be more specific?" he finally asked.

"Urinating in public on the private island where Fitz was broadcasting his pirate radio station!"

"Oh, right, of course!"

* * *

I was standing tall, feeling free and independent, basking in the warmth of true self-actualization. So I marched up to that radio tower, got on my knees, and begged a man I'd never met to please, please help me.

Fitz was in the middle of a call when I crawled through the door of his studio. I'll never forget the exact words of the guy he was talking to: "I think this is it, I'm tying a noose, I don't want to go on living." I yelled out, "Fitz, this is more important! I really need help with my mascot career!" Fitz slowly turned around in his chair, and for the first time in the history of his station, he was speechless. The guy on the phone started getting hysterical, but then abruptly stopped. I

121

didn't feel bad, he was completely off topic: he wasn't talking opera *or* stock tips. Plus, if Fitz had been able to afford someone to screen the calls, noose guy never would have gotten through in the first place.

I was on my knees, clasping my hands, but all Fitz could do was stare at me. I kept saying "Please, help me," but after a few minutes it got a little weird so I stood up. It turns out that I was the first human being Fitz had seen since he moved to the island. It had been nearly a decade, and that much isolation isn't good for anybody.

I gathered that that at some point over the past few years, Fitz believed he had died, and he'd been assigned the task of running the radio station as some kind of purgatorial challenge. Fitz thought he had to keep talking to people and playing music, and if he failed he'd have to spend an eternity in hell. He started weeping and asking me if this meant he'd passed the test and got to go to heaven. I didn't really understand what he was talking about, and frankly I didn't try that hard. I was the one who needed help, not him. Well, me and that caller who hung himself.

Eventually, I assured Fitz that yes, I was God, and sure, why not, he could go to heaven. I've got a few years under my belt, Kara, and if I had to offer you one piece of advice, it would be to always say yes when a lunatic asks you if you are God. Best case scenario, you find yourself a willing servant. Worst case, you tell him that it is your will that he find a different seat on the city bus and leave you alone.

With Fitz it seemed to be more of the former. Whatever I desired, he told me, he'd be willing to do. I told him to get on the horn and put out an edict to all the hooligans: quit beating up the Arsenal mascot. Fitz just nodded, and said, "Thy will be done." I asked him if he could tack on another message about maybe tossing Egbert some spare change the next time the hooligans saw him. Fitz said absolutely. I was going to ask if he could actually specify that paper money was vastly preferable, but I was still getting used to the whole "being God" thing and didn't want to press my luck.

What happened next was incredible. Fitz took the mic and announced that he had something special to say. Then he told his listeners that he was disgusted by the violent acts being perpetrated against Arsenal's mascot. He told them that inside of Egbert, there was a man who breathed and bled and loved just like they did. Any true fan, not just of Arsenal, but of soccer in general, would treat this symbol of the team with honor and respect. I caught Fitz's eye and rubbed my thumb on my index and middle fingers, and he added that maybe the fans should help me out with some ka-ching if they had any lying around.

The phone lines lit up. One hooligan after another called in to tearfully renounce their violent ways. They apologized and begged my forgiveness. Fitz handled the whole thing like a complete professional. He kept it light, knew when to let them speak, and when to interject and move the conversation along. More than anything, it was obvious that he had control. These people were in the palm of his hand, and here he was evangelizing my cause. I was in awe of his ability to diffuse, cajole, entertain, and manipulate without it being obvious that he was doing so or showing the faintest hint of effort. I watched him do all this and I felt my burdens lift off my shoulders. I had struggled and suffered, but at long last, this saint of a man had shown me kindness. Finally, I had an ally.

So, I waited until Fitz cut to commercial, whacked him over the head with a microphone, dragged him into my boat, pushed it out to sea, declared the island a new country, and deemed myself its undisputed ruler.

* * *

"So, to answer your question, Kara, that is where I'm taking you. The glorious island micronation of HAWAll, ruled over by yours truly, the benevolent President Cornelius Everglades." Cornelius smiled, unscrewed the top of the miniature bottle of whiskey, raised it in a cheers motion, and downed it in one gulp.

"I have several questions," Kara replied.

Cornelius rolled his eyes. "I knew it. Here comes the third degree."

"When you pushed Fitz out to sea, he probably died, right?" Kara asked. Throughout the story she'd been carefully cataloging her follow-up questions in terms of what she was most incredulous about. She could not believe that in the last fifteen seconds of the story, the number-one spot had been claimed by an attempted murder.

"He didn't die," Cornelius replied with a weary sigh, as if he'd grown tired of reassuring people of this fact.

"How do you know that?" Kara asked.

"The hold on my credit card for the boat deposit got released eight weeks later. They're not going to do that unless the boat makes it back to the marina. Pirates aren't going to return a crummy little rental speedboat, and neither is anyone who discovers it floating around with a dead guy in it. I got the deposit returned, so I just put two and two together. Obviously Fitz somehow made it back to the marina after an admittedly hellish ordeal at sea. Next question," he said, evidently considering the matter put to rest.

"Why did you strand him at sea?" Kara asked. "He was trying to help you!"

"Fitz didn't dream big, Kara," Cornelius said. "Pirate radio only took advantage of a small fraction of what the island had to offer. It was unjust to let him squander that potential on drive-time drivel. Under my leadership, HAWAIl has established a new paradigm in sovereignty, redefining what freedom means and offering a tourism experience unlike any other nation on Earth."

"Uh-huh. And how much of that paradigm involves tricking those tourists into thinking they're going to Hawaii?"

"I'm disappointed you would accuse me of such a thing, Kara," Cornelius said, trying to sound hurt. "Deceit has never been my intention."

"Well then why did you name your country HAWAIl?"

"You'll see when you get there," Cornelius assured her. "When you're strolling along the shoreline, the ocean seems to whisper 'HAWAIl' at you. The island really named itself."

"And after it whispers its name at you," Kara asked, "does it whisper, 'Oh, by the way, the last two letters of my name are lowercase so when it's written it's indistinguishable from a major tourist destination?'"

"Sometimes at low tide, yes!" Cornelius snapped back at her.

"Well, what about this ad?" Kara said. She pulled out the in-flight magazine and thrust it at her grandfather. "You claim you're not trying to trick people into thinking they're booking a ticket to Hawaii, but there's a picture of a hula dancer in a grass skirt and coconut bra right there."

"That is just one of the many types of tourists we'd love to have visit the country," Cornelius said with a dismissive wave of his hand. "We're advertising to many diverse demographics."

"Is that right? Who else are you trying to 'attract' to your country? What are the pictures in the other ads you are running? "

"Well, there's a surfer. A ukulele player. King Moholaiko of Maui."

"Who is King Moholaiko of Maui? You're running a picture of a specific Hawaiian guy in the ads for your country because you're trying to attract the 'demographic' of people that are him?"

"The king and his family are of course always welcome to visit HAWAIl, something many other countries have not gone out of their way to make clear. To be honest, it seems kind of racist to me." Cornelius puffed out his chest at his humanitarian gesture.

Kara stared at her father's father. She wasn't sure what to say. Twelve hours ago, she thought he was dead. Now she was soaring through the air toward a country he claimed to rule over, listening to him spout obvious lies about his attempts to lure unsuspecting tourists there. Kara hoped that "tourists" was the right word. As she became less and less convinced that her grandfather was not an entry-level supervillain, "victims" seemed like it was quickly making a case for itself. She wondered if that was the type of thing you should alert a flight attendant about.

Next to her, Cornelius fidgeted with the empty whiskey bottle. His shoulders slumped and he slowly let his chest deflate.

"OK!" he eventually blurted. "You're right! It's all intentional deception! Do you have any idea how hard it is to get people to visit a brand new country that they've never heard of? Everyone just wants to go someplace that they've 'heard is nice' or they 'know they'll come back safely from' or that 'impartial third parties have assured them is real.' It's impossible! Especially when those bastards at the UN keep voting not to admit me! I swear they just want me to show up at the hearings so they can humiliate me."

"You've appeared before the UN?" Kara asked. That was a rational-sounding act. Kara relaxed a bit, figuring that your average supervillain tended to skip "petitioning international governing bodies for recognition" in favor of something like "threatening to blow up Neptune."

"Yes, I've appeared before the UN," Cornelius sighed. "You didn't think that I came back to the States just to get the mascot costume, did you? I give it about five years between appearances. By then there's usually been enough turnover at the front desk that I can talk my way in without anyone recognizing me. The UN may be corrupt and impotent, but unfortunately for guys like me, there aren't that many other players in the 'country acknowledging' game. Their seal of approval is still pretty damn valuable."

"How come you never visited me during any of those other times you've been back?"

"Because the delegate from Finland never left the keys to his sports car sitting on the sink in the men's room before! Duh!"

"Grandpa, when you're being interrogated by the United Nations, do you usually fold as quickly as you did with me just now?"

"For your information, my sassy granddaughter, I usually haven't had six drinks before I address the general assembly."

"That's probably a good idea!"

"Yeah, I usually put away eight or nine. All those translators creep me out! Those elitists from Rwanda and Sudan and Haiti think they're so high and mighty. 'Oooh, we're big-shot countries in the United Nations, every tourist wants to visit us! Let's ignore tiny countries who aren't as fortunate and blessed as we are!'" Cornelius spat in disgust against the seat back in front of him.

"And that is *not* a good idea!" Kara fished an airsickness bag out of the pocket in front of her and wiped off the loogie before it could dribble down too far. "You've already made a bunch of enemies up here, in case you don't remember."

Cornelius ignored her, his wild eyes darting around the cabin. "Stupid UN," he grumbled. "They may not recognize HAWAII as a country yet. But let's just say I have something planned that's going to force them to acknowledge me..." He trailed off cryptically, chuckling under his breath.

My God, he really is a supervillain, Kara thought. She pictured waves crashing against the rocky coast of HAWAIl, while a gleaming, solid gold castle in the shape of a skull rose up from the center of the island. "Grandpa?" she asked. "Are you plotting to blow up the UN?"

Cornelius looked taken aback. "Blow up the...? What? No, of course not!"

"Are you going to hijack a commercial airliner?"

Now it was Cornelius's turn to scold. "Of course not!" he shushed, glancing around the cabin. "And keep it down!"

"Well, what are you going to blow up or terrorize?" Kara asked. She hoped it wouldn't come to either, but she couldn't think of an attention-getting scheme that didn't. It seemed to her like most of the hot upstart countries were relying on "atrocities" as their top strategy for building their country's brand.

"Nothing!" Cornelius hissed. "I just rigged it so that HAWAIl is hosting the Olympics! There's no event more international. Once the eyes of the world are on HAWAIl, there will be no way for the UN to deny us our full rights as an independent country!"

"How did you 'rig it' so HAWAIl is hosting the Olympics?"

"Eh, I just filled out the online form and paid the fifty dollar application fee."

This was way less sinister and way, way less impressive than Kara had imagined. "The application fee to host the Olympics is only fifty dollars?" she asked.

"Yeah, they keep it low so the shitty countries can afford it." Cornelius waved a dismissive hand. "They want everyone to think they have a shot, but obviously the International Olympic Committee prefers to go to nice places. When an application came in for 'Hawaii' it was like red meat to them. Who would turn down a paid vacation in paradise? They just don't realize that all the contracts they emailed me say HAWAIl and not all-caps Hawaii. And believe me, those babies will hold up in court!"

Kara opened her mouth to reply but realized that parts of her brain were still processing everything she'd seen and heard since the plane had taken off. Her grandfather had made someone pee in the aisle, she'd learned that her father had spent his childhood living in fear of a giant frog, and now she was headed to a "sort of" country that was somehow hosting the Olympics. Words failed her.

Her grandfather didn't notice. "Of course, if this doesn't work I'll probably have to blow up a plane!" he quipped. Cornelius chuckled, winked, then promptly reclined his seat into the knees of the passenger behind him and passed out.

There was a loud ding from the row in front of them.

ten

Moholaiko relaxed on the brilliant white sand of Maui's Makena Beach. To his right, a succulent roast pig turned on a spit. To his left, a beautiful woman offered him a daiquiri served inside a hollowed-out pineapple while an even more beautiful woman fanned him with a giant palm leaf. Behind him, scores of friends and relatives strummed ukuleles and sang and feasted. In front of him, the ocean stretched as far as the eye could see.

It was good to be king.

Moho was the reigning king of Maui, one of eight kings who made up a secret cabal of Hawaiian rulers. The royal families had lorded over Hawaii in a loose alliance ever since the islands were first populated. Despite publicly appearing to cede power when Hawaii became an American territory, they continued to rule behind the scenes. The business-suit-wearing members of the official government represented Hawaii back on the mainland, and tried to convince the world that Hawaii was a thriving, modern-day destination, with more to it than mai tais, luaus, babes in grass skirts, leis, and surfers.

Moho didn't know why they bothered. All of those things were awesome. As far as he was concerned, the Hawaiian state flag should just be a picture of him drinking a mai tai at a luau while a babe in a grass skirt placed a lei around his neck while both of them surfed a monster wave. The idea had been voted down seven to one every single time he brought it up.

Moho didn't let this discourage him. He was living the good life. He reaped Maui's untold riches while the public face of the government did all the real work. The existence of the kings was only whispered about by the citizens, who mostly dismissed it as a rumor, so there was no danger of revolt or overthrow. Barring an utter catastrophe, there was no conceivable way that King Moho wouldn't spend the rest of his life basking in Pacific Island luxury.

So it was to his great dismay that an alien spaceship currently appeared to be materializing out of thin air thirty feet from where he lay sprawled on the beach.

As the *Stupid Butt*'s cloaking device finished deactivating and the giant StarBarge slowly began to extend its landing gear, King Moho propped himself up on his elbows. He reached out for the daiquiri being offered to him, took a sip, and glanced to his rear. He had the unsettling feeling that this was a "get to your feet" type of situation and wanted to survey the mood of his entourage.

The volleyball game had screeched to a halt. The ball rolled away as the players stared at the spaceship. A man was frozen mid-limbo in a contorted position that looked like it had probably already caused him permanent back damage. The beautiful woman who had been fanning the king clutched her palm leaf in terror, and the guy manning the spit had ceased turning it and was gawking slack-jawed. Moho sniffed twice. The pig's rump was starting to burn. The king leapt into action.

He pointed at the guy manning the spit and then made a cranking motion. The chagrined worker resumed cranking and the pig began to turn again. Then he turned to the woman with the palm leaf and waved his arm up and down. She looked mortified and resumed fanning. Then Moho turned halfway around and spread his arms wide in a "what the hell, people?" gesture. Immediately, the ukulele music resumed, one of the volleyball players picked up and served the ball, and the limbo participant was moved out of the way by several friends, his back still bent at a nearly ninety-degree angle.

Maui's relaxed island rhythms had just experienced their longest recorded halt under King Moho's reign, but now as they resumed the vibe was more laid back than ever. This crisis averted, the king turned his attention back to the gigantic alien shuttlecraft that was currently extending something from its hull that Moho very much hoped was not a death ray. Getting vaporized before the succulent pig was finished roasting would be unacceptable.

The potential death ray was rapidly telescoping out of the front of the spaceship. After a dozen feet or so, it tapered to a fine point and began to sway back and forth, canvassing the beach party. King Moho felt a deep surge of relief when it passed over him, only to watch it immediately snap back toward him and cease its movement. There was a humming sound from the ship, and the bright green dot of a laser sight appeared on the king's substantial bare stomach.

King Moholaiko looked down at his belly, then back up at the spaceship. Trying to remain inconspicuous, he tilted his head twice toward the babe who was fanning him. The green light slowly traced a path toward the woman until it came to a halt in the center of her forehead. Moho gave a conspiratorial nod.

There was a loud crackle and a burst of feedback as a speaker mounted on the outside of the spaceship clicked on. Then Zzarvon's voice boomed out over the beach. "Attention Earthling of the planet Earth! The green light means you have been identified by the LeaderTron 7000 as the leader of this tribe of Earth people! With LeaderTron 7000, saying 'Take Me To Your Leader' is a thing of the past. Available at Trillig's Bot Repair and other fine stores."

There was another crackle from the speaker. Then Zzarvon spoke again, this time sounding like he was further away from the PA system's microphone. "What?" he said to a voice that the mic was not picking up. "Sir, we have to say it… Yes we do, it's in our contract… They gave us a promotional system for free, but in exchange we have to read that every time we use it… It definitely is… You were upset that I'd let those StarPirates on the ship because they were posing as plumbers and they stole all the copper out of your executive bathroom so you signed it without reading it so I'd get out of your sight… Sir, what are you doing… Hey, put that down— OW!"

Moho leaned forward as the noise of a short scuffle blared out of the speaker, followed by what sounded like the microphone being dropped. Moments later, the same voice began to speak again, this time sounding somewhat rushed and subdued. "So anyway," it said, "you are clearly the supreme, exalted leader of these people, everyone respects and fears you, etcetera, etcetera, and we have chosen to share the ultimate secret of the universe with you."

"I'm the leader!" King Moho blurted, unable to resist the flattery and allure of a mysterious secret. He flailed his arms as he struggled to his feet. "King Moholaiko of Maui," he panted. "These idiots wouldn't understand your secrets, they're just here for the party." The woman who had been fanning him briefly looked offended, but then shrugged and turned to rejoin the party. The king looked down at the daiquiri in a pineapple he held in his hand. He quickly moved it behind his back, but one of the parasol garnishes poked him in the butt. He yelped and dropped the drink to the ground, where it spilled freezing slush all over his feet.

"You're the leader?" the voice asked.

"That's right," King Moho replied.

"The ultimate secret of the universe is that you actually suck compared to us! Prepare to be humiliated by 9-Krelblax of Larvilkian-B!"

"Dammit!" King Moholaiko cursed the alien treachery while looking around for something to throw at them. The only things within his immediate reach were hollowed out pineapples that had contained daiquiris earlier in the day. The king bent down to pick one up, but that effort, on the heels of the previous struggle to stand, exhausted him. He slumped down into the same reclining position he had been in when the aliens first appeared.

Meanwhile, a section of the *Stupid Butt* was dissolving, revealing a large doorway in its place. Beneath it, a glowing ramp leading down to the sand materialized out of thin air. A hush fell over the beach, punctuated every so often by creaks and wheezes from the ramp generator, which was desperately in need of an oiling. Then, after what seemed like forever, the silhouette of 9-Krelblax appeared in the doorway.

"King Moholaiko and his fellow Earthlings!" the commander boomed as he stepped into view, his moodcore glowing an intimidating dark blue. "We have traveled across the universe to humiliate the human race! Gaze upon your superiors and tremble!" 9-Krelblax's next sentence was pre-empted by a loud whoosh as the unjettisoned half of the Orion's Belt Loosener finally shot out of the refuse port, struck his second and third eye, and splattered against the side of the *Stupid Butt.* "Ow! Dammit!" the commander howled as his middle eyes knocked into his side eyes. His four antennae swayed and the eyes began clicking and clacking against each other like one of those desk toys in an executive's office.

As his moodcore flushed a deep crimson, 9-Krelblax retracted his eye stalks halfway. Once they were steadied, he re-extended them. 9-Krelblax decided his best course was to pretend that nothing had happened, proceed with the original plan, and disintegrate responsible parties once he was back on board his ship. He slithered forward.

"I know that our existence is difficult to grasp," 9-Krelblax continued. "You may be intimidated, scared, even terrified!"

"Pig's done!" yelled the guy manning the spit. Several Hawaiians grabbed paper plates and began to form a line. King Moholaiko shot them an envious glance and fidgeted.

"Is this humiliation going to take long?" he asked 9-Krelblax.

"Silence!" the Larvilkian commander shouted. He pulled his ray gun out of his thorax pouch and fired an electrified plasma shot at the pig. It hit the apple in the pig's mouth like an arrow in a William Tell fever dream and the swine disintegrated in a burst of delicious-smelling green fire. There was a loud chorus of boos from the gathered Hawaiians.

9-Krelblax tried to shout over the unruly picnickers. "Even though you are no doubt quaking in fear, I assure you that we Larvilkians have come to your planet in peace! We want nothing more than to compete in the Olympic games you are hosting. As a goodwill gesture, and to hopefully win your respect before crushing your spirit, our navigator, Zzarvon, has dressed himself in the style of one of your most admired Earthlings."

9-Krelblax stepped to one side of the ramp and gestured back at the doorway. Zzarvon stepped through, smiling broadly. He had swept three of his eye antennae down across his forehead in a surprisingly accurate approximation of Adolf Hitler's haircut, and had smeared a small rectangle of motor oil where he figured a mustache belonged on his face. A cut-out paper swastika was taped over his chest, turning his moodcore into a DIY Nazi batsignal. The navigator shot a tentacle to the sky in a goofy imitation of the fuhrer's signature salute.

There was a more subdued smattering of boos from the crowd, many of whom seemed more concerned about whether the various side dishes people had brought to the luau could now prove substantial enough to serve as an entire lunch. 9-Krelblax looked around confused. Zzarvon shrugged, saluted one more time, and oozed back onto the ship.

9-Krelblax cleared his throat and resumed speaking as he slid down the ramp and onto the sand. "Anyways, please direct us to the nearest Olympic event so that our galactic superiority can be proven as soon as possible." He folded his tentacles and waited for King Moholaiko to provide him with the information he requested.

King Moho looked longingly at the last vapors of his beloved pig and sighed. There would be no afternoon roast. They would have to wait until the mid-afternoon roast, which fortunately was just now being carried toward the spit by four burly Hawaiians. The king's stomach rumbled, but he forced himself back to his feet and shuffled toward the alien leader.

"What the hell is going on?" King Moho asked, snapping his fingers. A lovely young woman rushed up and handed him a new pineapple. The king took a long sip through a curly straw, then continued. "You show up dressed as Hitler and vaporize our pig? That's two strikes, buddy!"

9-Krelblax's moodcore cycled through a series of confused colors. "I don't understand," he stammered. "We thought that Hitler was a revered Olympic hero?"

"Hitler is one of the most evil humans who ever existed!" Moho countered. "Your pal in there better be changing his outfit, or else he's gonna bring down the whole good-time island vibe we got going here!"

9-Krelblax pondered this. "We must have missed that detail. We just thought he ran an efficient Olympics. One of the most evil Earthlings ever, you say?"

King Moho nodded vigorously. "He killed millions of people!"

9-Krelblax pondered this a bit more. "I can't help but point out that your friends seemed to boo a lot louder when I shot the pig than when someone dressed as a mass murderer showed up..."

"In their defense, those atrocities are like, at least seventy years old by now. And that pig was looking particularly succulent. Daiquiri?" the king offered.

"No, thank you," 9-Krelblax replied. "Maybe after. Can't dull my senses before our physical triumph in the Olympics."

King Moho chuckled. "You keep talking about the Olympics, chief. I think your navigator got a little distracted putting on his makeup and steered your spaceship in the wrong direction."

9-Krelblax knew this was all too real a possibility. "Zzarvon! Get your excretion unit out here!" he shrieked.

King Moho laughed harder. He was tipsy from day-drinking pineapple-sized rum drinks and feeling a little bold. "Olympics! Ha! You see any Olympics here?" The king started to sweep his arm across the expanse of beach, but halfway between the fire twirlers and the hula dancers he stopped. His smile faded, he blushed, and he leaned forward and took a long sip of his daiquiri.

"Ah, your facial moodcore betrays you, Earthling!" 9-Krelblax said, pointing at King Moho's flushed cheeks. The Larvilkian leader sensed he had a chance to regain the upper hand. "Our triumph over the Earthlings will not be staved off by mere deception. Ah, Zzarvon, there you are." Zzarvon slithered to a halt behind his commander.

"I couldn't get the mustache off," Zzarvon whispered. "I don't think I should have put that stuff on my face—it really itches."

"Never mind that, Zzarvon," 9-Krelblax said, his own glowing moodcore betraying the calm exterior he was trying to project. "The Earthling king was just explaining to us how the Olympics aren't actually taking place here."

"I don't understand," Zzarvon said. "We picked up news feeds from all over the world! Every media outlet was reporting that the Olympics were about to start in Hawaii."

"Well, there you go!" King Moholaiko sputtered. "I just rule over Maui! Hawaii's a big place, there's like six islands! I can't be expected to know what's going on on all of them."

"There's actually eight islands," Zzarvon corrected.

"Exactly my point!" Moho said. "Who can even keep track? And don't even get me started on all the atolls! They must be holding the Olympics on one of the other islands."

"Zzarvon!" 9-Krelblax barked. "Go check with the other seven islands. And make it snappy!" 9-Krelblax feared that for every second they weren't competing against Earthlings, there were athletic triumphs going unsecured.

"Yes, sir! I'll use the hyperwarp!" Zzarvon oozed up the ramp in a hurry and seconds later, the *Stupid Butt* disappeared in a flash of light.

"How long will it take him to hyperwarp to the other seven islands?" King Moholaiko asked, fidgeting with his pineapple.

"They say they aren't hosting them either," Zzarvon replied, gliding back down the ramp of the just-reappeared *Stupid Butt*.

"You traveled to all seven that quickly?" King Moho asked in disbelief.

"I had the hyperwarp pretty seriously cranked," Zzarvon explained. "I think I may have visited several of the islands simultaneously. Actually, the first time I came back to Maui, another *Stupid Butt* was still here so I had to slow down a bit."

"What did we discuss about overdoing it on the hyperwarp?" 9-Krelblax hissed. Zzarvon just smiled and formed an A-OK with one of his tentacles.

"You didn't land at Kalaupapa, did you?" King Moho asked, taking a precautionary step away from the two Larvilkians.

"The leper colony?" Zzarvon shook his head no. "Of course not. Steered very clear."

"So, let me get this straight," the king asked. "In your research into planet Earth, you came across the fact that there was a leper colony on a remote corner of one of Hawaii's smaller islands, but you somehow managed to discover *who* Hitler was *without* learning that he was bad?"

"SILENCE!" 9-Krelblax commanded. Zzarvon and King Moho jumped. The commander clearly meant business.

9-Krelblax folded two of his tentacles behind his back in a contemplative gesture while stroking his ray gun with another. He leaned his antennae forward until his eyes were just a few inches from King Moho's face.

"I know you're not being honest with me," the Larvilkian commander sneered. "But we have ways of making people talk. And let me tell you, we're not afraid to use them."

King Moho's face fell and his eyes went wide. 9-Krelblax could smell blood in the water, but just for fun decided to lay the intimidation on even thicker.

"That's right," he continued. "It's not the most comfortable process. We probe pretty deep. You probably won't be walking straight for a few days afterwards. But man, is it fun for us! Everyone on board is going to want a turn!"

"Alright!" King Moho pleaded. He fell to his knees and clasped his hands as he beseeched 9-Krelblax. "I'll tell you everything! Just please, please, don't give me an anal probe!"

Now it was 9-Krelblax's turn to blanch. "Whoa, whoa, keep it down!" he said, rotating three of his eyes to see if anyone had heard. "Nobody's going to give you a... Nobody's going to do that to you! Where the hell did you get that idea?"

"It's a thing aliens do to people they abduct!" the king said, his voice catching as he took several deep breaths. "Everyone knows that!"

"It most definitely is not!" 9-Krelblax shot back.

"Well, then what the hell is your 'way of making people talk' that 'probes deep' and leaves you 'not walking straight'?" King Moho asked.

"We have a mild truth serum that's usually pretty good at uncovering any information you're trying to keep from us. The only unfortunate side effect, which we have scientists working to eliminate, is that it can sometimes trigger mild vertigo for a period of up to forty-eight hours!" 9-Krelblax put a thoughtful tentacle to the side of his head. "But now that I think about it, a lot of times abductees end up divulging whatever we need during the 'vague sinister threats' stage. This *undeserved* butt probe reputation might explain a lot of that."

King Moho got to his feet, still sniffling, but grateful that he was not going to be subjected to an unwanted medical procedure. "There's no Olympics here. We never even filled out an application! But one day, these suits from the International Olympic Committee show up. They say they're on some sort of 'host city candidate exploratory mission' to see if our facilities could accommodate the Olympics. I didn't know what they were talking about, but I'd had a few mai tais, and a roast pig was just about ready, so I invited them to stay for the luau and party. That's our standard procedure with visitors," the king added pointedly. "Hospitality is part of the aloha spirit. Guests usually don't evaporate the main course."

"Look, nobody was paying attention to us!" 9-Krelblax muttered.

King Moho shook his head with a mixture of pity and contempt before continuing his story. "So these IOC guys get liquored up and start telling us how great it is to be here. How all the other potential hosts they checked out wanted to show off boring stuff like their traffic management plan and infrastructure upgrades and security strategy, while we just wanted to party. They kept saying how they'd check out the stadiums 'first thing in the morning,' but it was clear that these guys were not going to be in good shape when they woke up, and plus, we still had no idea what the hell they were talking about. At one point, my buddy Steve remembered that he might have sent in an application to host the Olympics, but then it turned out it had just been a letter to *Penthouse*.

"After a couple days, we started to get tired of them and tried to pull the whole 'we're running out of pineapples and pigs' move. You know, 'Gee, look at the time, guess the party's wrapping up, everyone should go home.' That's when they pulled out the suitcases full of cash. I guess every other host candidate had given them these bribes, and now they were offering them to us in order to buy more supplies to keep the party going. So, we did what anyone would do when presented with a several suitcases full of obviously dirty money."

"You turned them over to the international authorities?" Zzarvon offered.

"We accepted them without even counting the dough," King Moho corrected. "We partied our asses off! Sure, every now and then one of them would wind up in the conga line behind you and start slurring something about how we needed to make sure 'The Games' would have a rigid anti-terrorism framework in place or how they could only cover up the first thirty construction worker deaths. When buzzkills like that happened, we'd politely suggest that that particular IOC member might like to visit to one of Hawaii's five other islands."

"*Seven* other islands," Zzarvon corrected. 9-Krelblax jabbed his navigator with a tentacle.

"Who cares!" King Moho said. "The IOC sure didn't. They tossed their dirty money around no matter if they ended up on Oahu or Kahoolawe. Every island got a piece of it. Even some of the damn atolls! They just kept handing us these suitcases! Half the time we didn't even know what the bribe was supposed to be for. It was like they had a pathological need to give us money under the table. And they insisted that we actually do it under a literal table! One time there wasn't a table nearby and we had to cut down a thousand-year-old banyan tree and carve it into a makeshift one before they'd hand over the dough."

"They sound incompetent," Zzarvon said. The irony caused 9-Krelblax's moodcore to shine bright yellow, and he bit the closest thing he had to a tongue.

"It was something more than that," the king nodded. "One night, after too many daiquiris, I told them point blank, 'We never asked to host the Olympics. None of this stuff is getting built.' The IOC took that to mean that we were playing hardball. They passed us so many suitcases the next day that we had to put an extra leaf in the table!"

"Wait. Did that throttle the rate they were able to pass the suitcases or simply allow for bigger suitcases?" Zzarvon asked.

"I was hungover; it made sense at the time," the king said, not actually answering the question. "Soon after that, we realized that the IOC's first priority was to have a good time. Putting on the world's preeminent athletic competition was a distant second. The longer they drew out their 'negotiations,' the longer they could stay here. In fact, some of them never left! That guy taking steel drum lessons over there is the vice president of the finance and development committee!"

King Moho pointed at a doughy man with a white stomach and a sunburned neck. A steel drum was strapped around his waist and he was drunkenly banging on it with no discernible rhythm. He noticed the trio was staring at him, stopped playing, and waved.

"Gonna be a great games, King!" the vice president of the finance and development committee shouted, swaying on his feet. "Tell Cornelius I'm looking forward to cutting the ribbon on that natatorium any day now!" He resumed banging out something that might have been Harry Belafonte, or perhaps some sort of polka, while his instructor looked on, chagrined.

"What the hell is a natatorium anyways? And does anyone at this party look like a 'Cornelius'?" King Moho wondered aloud. He turned back to the Larvilkians. "Even now, they still don't get it. It's like there's somebody else out there telling them that everything is coming along just fine."

"So are you hosting the Olympics or not?" Zzarvon asked, scratching his head in confusion.

9-Krelblax's moodcore flared bright red and he smacked his navigator's closest antennae. "Silence, Zzarvon! I need to think!"

"Would you like me to fetch the RitaLink?" Zzarvon asked.

"No!" 9-Krelblax blurted. "Er, that is to say, I don't think it will be necessary this time, Zzarvon." The RitaLink was a rounded metal rod about six inches long that served as a concentration-aiding device. It electrically stimulated nerve endings that helped Larvilkians focus. It was very effective, but the necessary nerve endings were contained in a small orifice that was located about halfway down a Larvilkian's back. It wasn't anywhere near any of their actual butts, but after the vehement denials of anal probing a few minutes earlier, 9-Krelblax figured it would do their credibility no good to whip out an actual probe and start shoving it up butt-like places.

9-Krelblax folded his tentacles and pondered the situation while King Moho and Zzarvon awaited his decision. The drawn out, uncomfortable silence was too much for Zzarvon to take, and eventually he decided to make small talk.

"So…" Larvilkians were terrible at small talk. "Oahu? Kahoolawe? You've sure got some goofy-sounding places down here!"

"You spacemen are ones to talk!" King Moho chuckled. "Say, did you happen to swing by Uranus on the way here?"

"Please, no jokes," Zzarvon said, his voice immediately turning solemn. "The Uranus is the biggest tragedy in the history of our planet. By comparison, it makes your planet's 'Holocaust' look like a good thing."

"You already thought the Holocaust was a good thing!" King Moho shouted. "You slithered down that ramp dressed as its primary architect!"

"Wait… That was the same Hitler? Oh, man, that explains a lot!"

"Will both of you please shut up!" 9-Krelblax bellowed. King Moho and Zzarvon both jumped back a step. 9-Krelblax instinctively reached back to scratch at his RitaLink hole, but caught himself and pulled the tentacle away just in time.

9-Krelblax thought out loud, trying to make sense of the matter. "The Olympics aren't here. That much is clear. But the rest of the world thinks they are in Hawaii. So there's been a breakdown in communication somewhere. Zzarvon!"

"Yes, sir!" the navigator saluted.

"What was the name of that infamous communications mishap with the Piltrixians of Ribercon-C?" 9-Krelblax had never paid much attention in history class. He figured that the saying was right: that those who focus too much on history are doomed to repeat it. His grades in history had been almost as bad as his grades in popular quotations class.

"Ah yes," Zzarvon said, holding a tentacle respectfully over his moodcore. "That would be the Telegram of Piltrixian Aggression. They sent us an ultimatum that consisted of just one word: War. But it turned out that because of a barely perceptible difference between two letters in our alphabets, 'War' in our language looks the same as 'We would be delighted to share our hyperwarp technology with you, no need for bloodshed, and by the way, would you like to get together for dinner next weekend?' in theirs. Since the many deaths that followed, auto-translation has been a recommended procedure anytime we engage in written communications with a non-Larvilkian system."

"And we of course employ this recommendation on the *Stupid Butt*?" 9-Krelblax asked, tensing as he awaited the answer.

"We do not, sir," Zzarvon admitted. "The translation plugin makes web pages load like, a half second slower. It doesn't sound like a lot, but man! Believe me, you notice it."

"Does that hurt?" King Moholaiko asked as 9-Krelblax's moodcore flared up a brilliant volcanic red.

"No," 9-Krelblax lied. He turned all four of his eyes to his navigator. "If you could be so kind as to call up a holoscreen and see if the official literature about the Olympics looks any different in Larvilkian," he seethed.

"Yes, sir," Zzarvon said.

He reached for his communicator, and pressed a sequence of buttons. There was a pleasant chime, and then a beam of light extended from the communicator and widened into a brilliant holoscreen that hovered in between Zzarvon and 9-Krelblax.

"Wowee!" exclaimed King Moho. "Would you look at that!"

9-Krelblax chuckled. He had forgotten how impressive Larvilkian technology could seem to the backwards rubes on other planets. "Do they not have these on Earth?" he asked, winking his rightmost eye at Zzarvon.

"It's so big!" King Moho gasped.

"This is actually last year's model," 9-Krelblax said, feigning modesty. "I don't know how we're still creaking along with this hunk of junk."

"And so incredibly succulent!"

"The hell? Succulent?" 9-Krelblax wheeled two eyes around. King Moho had his back to the Larvilkians and their holoscreen, and was instead gazing at the mid-afternoon roast pig as a smiling chef carved the first tender slice and handed it to a reveler.

"Pay attention, shirtless one!" 9-Krelblax shouted. King Moho whirled around and wiped a strand of drool from the corner of his mouth.

"Sorry," he said. He stole one more longing glancing over his shoulder at the pig.

"Now, sir," Zzarvon said, fiddling with the communicator. "This is a duplicate of my workstation screen. Front and center is the homepage for the Olympics. Here it is in its native English." The holoscreen displayed a large banner headline that said "COUNTDOWN TO THE HAWAII OLYMPICS!" Zzarvon pressed a few buttons on his communicator and made a circular gesture with a tentacle. The Olympics page flashed white and then reappeared translated into Larvilkian.

"Shield your eyes, Earthling," 9-Krelblax cautioned.

"Shield my eyes? You just told me to pay attention!"

"Yes, but the Larvilkian alphabet is ten thousand times more advanced than your simple twenty-six character one. Just one glance and it could very well blind you with its sheer complexity!"

"Is that the winky tongue-out emoji?" King Moho asked, pointing at the holoscreen.

"Sorry! Sorry! That's just an IM from Technician Timblorx." Zzarvon hit a sequence of buttons on his communicator and the chat window minimized, leaving the translated Olympics homepage front and center.

9-Krelblax leaned his antennae toward the holoscreen and studied it for clues. Zzarvon did the same from the other side of the semi-transparent display. 9-Krelblax thought he spied something noteworthy in the top left corner and began to scan side to side with his leftmost eye. Zzarvon began to scan the same area with his right eye. At the same time, 9-Krelblax's right two eyes traced the rings of the Olympic logos for any differences. Zzarvon followed suit.

"Could you *please* not imitate me!" 9-Krelblax shouted, pulling all his eyes back from the holoscreen. "It's like looking into an idiotic mirror!"

"Phew!" Zzarvon sighed, also pulling back. "No problem! That was like trying to rub your head and pat your moodcore at the same time!"

"I need both of you to be quiet while I examine this," 9-Krelblax insisted. He leaned in again, and his eyes went wide as he began a deep inspection of the holoscreen. Each eye stalk scanned in a different direction, one moving up and down, one side to side, one diagonally, and the final one rotating in ever expanding circles. After about a minute, his moodcore flushed a bright, tired pink; after another, beads of sweat began to break out all over his body. The Larvilkian commander concentrated so hard that he began to tremble. Eventually, he could bear the effort no longer and pulled back from the holoscreen, shaking and gasping for breath.

"Are you OK, sir?" Zzarvon asked, oozing to his commander's side.

"I'll be fine," 9-Krelblax panted. "It's just... the strain on your... I'll be fine..." He waved a tentacle at Zzarvon and the navigator gave him some air.

"There doesn't seem to be any differences," Zzarvon said.

9-Krelblax was still struggling to catch his breath. "I... know..." he wheezed. "I think... I may... need... to lie..."

"Except for the spelling of Hawaii," Zzarvon continued. "It's so weird that in Larvilkian we'd write it like 'huh-wall.'"

Years later, 9-Krelblax would still swear to anyone who would listen that his moodcore had glowed such a bright red that it evaporated the beads of sweat on his skin into wisps of vapor. The commander raised each of his eyes individually and, with great effort, stared at his navigator.

"Huh-wall?" 9-Krelblax asked.

"Yes, Huh-wall. Says it right there. And there and there and there." Zzarvon gestured at four different points on the holoscreen with various tentacles. "I'm surprised you didn't notice it, sir. It leapt out at me right away."

Forgetting his exhaustion for a moment, 9-Krelblax oozed as fast as he could back to the holoscreen and began to strike it with all his tentacles. "Why didn't you say anything, you intergalactic moron?" he shouted. His flailing tentacles went right through the holoscreen with no noticeable effect.

"Sir, that's really not... You shouldn't..." Zzarvon stammered as 9-Krelblax continued to attempt his futile rampage. "Sir, you can't tear apart a holoscreen; it doesn't actually exist in any material form. I'm pretty sure it can burn your tentacles if they breach the plane of the screen for too long."

9-Krelblax took a deep breath and blew into the hovering display, thinking that might cause it to disperse like a cloud of smoke, but, other than a barely perceptible ripple, this also had no effect.

"Careful there, Niner," King Moho cautioned. "It's bad luck if an alien passes out from hyperventilating in the middle of a luau."

"It's not a mistranslation of Hawaii, you nitwit!" 9-Krelblax shrieked. "It's a completely different place! That's why nobody here is ready for the Olympics. It's because they're not in Hawaii; they're in HAWAll!"

"Well, that explains it," King Moho shrugged. "No idea where that place is. I've never even heard of it. Maybe it's one of those new countries that splits off when there's a huge war and nobody pays attention because they just assume it's going to collapse into turmoil and rename itself again in a few years? Kinda like a restaurant that opens in your neighborhood that nobody's going to from day one?"

9-Krelblax glared at the king then back to his navigator. "Zzarvon, if you would kindly... Zzarvon! ZZARVON!"

Zzarvon startled and looked up from his communicator. "What? Sorry! I was just texting Technician Timblorx. He wants to know what all the shouting is about." Zzarvon looked at 9-Krelblax for a few seconds. "What *is* all the shouting about?" he eventually asked. "I kinda zoned out."

"We are going to HAWAII for the Olympics, you addled son of a Piltrixian!" 9-Krelblax shouted.

"Right! Of course!" Zzarvon paused again and absently fiddled with his communicator. "How do we get there?"

9-Krelblax very briefly felt the familiar stabbing pain in his moodcore before everything went dark. The next thing he knew, he was throttling Zzarvon's antennae with some tentacles while slapping him across the face with another and shouting "Navigator! You! Are! The! Navigator!" over and over again.

"Whoa, Niner! Whoa!" King Moho was saying. Uncertain if a Larvilkian was safe for a human to touch, the king made no actual attempt to separate the two aliens, despite Zzarvon gurgling out a choked plea for help. 9-Krelblax got in a couple more satisfying slaps before relaxing his grips around Zzarvon's antennae, then dropping them altogether. Zzarvon cowered and retracted his eyes into his body.

9-Krelblax took a step back as he composed himself. "I'm sorry, Zzarvon," he said. "I don't know what came over me. My moodcore overheated and I must have blacked out for a second."

"That's OK, sir," Zzarvon said, cautiously re-extending two of his eyes.

The Larvilkian commander turned from his navigator to look at his ship. 9-Krelblax told himself that this had been a momentary setback. A mere hiccup. A bump in the road en route to the inevitable songs that would be sung of the Larvilkians triumph over the entire planet Earth. The brilliant Hawaiian sun shimmered off the *Stupid Butt*'s chrome, glistening everywhere except for the streak of grease where the Orion's Belt Loosener had struck the side of the ship and slowly slid down to the beach below, where a seagull stood pecking at it next to several more dead or dying seagulls.

"Guess those birds are allergic to something in your sandwich, sir," Zzarvon said, oozing up next to 9-Krelblax. "I thought the Betelgeuse sauce tasted a bit off. Ooh, maybe if we complain they'll give us a free drink next time!"

9-Krelblax winced at the brief stabbing moodcore pain and continued to stare at the ship as he addressed his navigator. "Zzarvon. Set a course for HAWAll. It's time to win the Olympics."

"So I guess that wraps things up here," King Moho said, inching away from the two Larvilkians. "I'll just be heading back to the luau then!"

"I think you should come with us," 9-Krelblax suggested, in a tone that indicated it was definitely not just a suggestion. "It could prove advantageous. If the other Earthlings fear that we might capture more of their high-ranking government officials, it could affect their concentration while 'hurdling' or 'putting the shot.'"

"Brilliant strategy, sir," Zzarvon said. "And if that doesn't work, we can always jam probes up their asses!" Zzarvon nudged 9-Krelblax with a tentacle and winked with two of his eyes.

"No, that's… dammit, Zzarvon!" 9-Krelblax turned to King Moho, who looked quite pale for a guy who spent every waking hour basking in the sun. "We don't jam things up people's asses. He's kidding."

"Or am I?" Zzarvon said, winking again.

King Moho looked like he was about to faint.

"Seriously, get on the ship," 9-Krelblax instructed, shaking all four of his eyes in disgust. He reached for his ray gun, pointed it at King Moho, and gestured toward the *Stupid Butt*'s ramp.

"I should probably put on a shirt," King Moho finally managed to stammer. "And can we bring the pig?"

"We only have time for one," 9-Krelblax replied.

Thirty seconds later, the *Stupid Butt* blasted off, now carrying with it a bewildered, shirtless Hawaiian king and one succulent-as-hell roast pig.

eleven

Right about the time that mankind first learned it was not alone in the universe—a moment that would be regarded by historians and philosophers as the most spiritually transcendent in all of recorded history—Kara Everglades was barfing off the side of a speedboat. So far, it was the highlight of her day.

Kara wasn't sure if the speedboat or her first taste of alcohol was responsible for her nausea. She hoped it was the former. Unless the frog-racing kids were concealing some monumental earning power, speedboats did not figure to play a big role in future after-school activities. But not being able to hold her liquor would mean the death of her social life before it even began.

Of course, her current social life wasn't exactly the stuff of MTV reality shows, or even PBS antique-appraising shows. She was currently spending the first day of her summer break on a boat where the other passengers were her grandfather, the unfortunate elderly couple who had been seated in front of them on the flight to London, a gaunt African man who was lying under a towel, potentially dead, and someone who appeared to be his coach who seemed unconcerned about that fact.

The speedboat raced head-on into a wave and lifted off into the air before crashing down with a huge splash. Kara's stomach lurched, and she leaned back over the side and let fly what little remained in her stomach. Once she had finished, she took a few deep breaths and wiped at her mouth with the back of her hand. Under most circumstances, she would have worried she was making a bad first impression on her fellow passengers. As it stood, that was impossible.

The older African man was too busy yukking it up with her grandfather as they took turns endangering everyone's lives at the helm of the boat. The potentially dead man was in no position to judge anyone given that he was potentially dead. And she would have gladly accepted a *bad* first impression from the elderly couple, as opposed to the *terrible* first impression she'd actually already made.

The old man looked down at a slip of paper he held in his hand. He squinted as if looking for something that he hadn't noticed any of the previous three dozen times Kara had seen him examine it. Then he lowered the paper and looked around at his surroundings, which were currently whizzing by at ninety miles per hour. Kara was no mind reader, but she assumed that his confusion was due to Hawaii being a lot greyer, colder, and more "consisting of nothing but expansive stretches of ocean instead of tropical islands" than he was expecting.

Also, Kara guessed that almost dying in a plane crash hadn't been on his itinerary either.

* * *

Hours earlier, when they had filed off the plane at Heathrow, a still-drunk Cornelius had been unable to resist one last dig at the couple. When the husband pulled down an ancient looking leather satchel from the overhead compartment, Cornelius had heckled him. "What's the matter, buddy? One old bag wasn't enough?" Then he pointed at the man's wife for emphasis, snickered, and rang the flight attendant call button, presumably to ask for more booze. Kara smacked the button off and whisked him off the plane.

A few minutes later, they had sat down for breakfast at an airport food court when Cornelius spotted the couple again. Kara pleaded with her grandfather to not say anything, and he promised he wouldn't, but then, as soon as she took a bite of her yogurt, he hurled a bran muffin at them. He missed the woman, but the muffin landed in her bowl of oatmeal, and she ended up throwing away what wasn't already scattered all over the floor.

After breakfast, Kara and Cornelius marched off to their connecting flight's gate, which was evidently located in a part of the airport called Terminal X. The airport underwent distinct changes as they approached the terminal. The modern decor and pleasing ambience of the main terminal gave way to stained carpeting and flickering florescent lights. Some bathrooms were marked out of order, others just had the yellow-and-black nuclear symbol hastily painted on their doors.

Soon, the concourse descended into further disrepair. Sunlight streamed in through holes in the ceiling where tiles had crashed to the floor. Moss and lichen grew on the walls. Instead of familiar airport chain restaurants, there was a man in an eyepatch selling a basket full of eggs that were much too large to be chicken eggs. Kara almost tripped on a gigantic snake that was stretched out across a non-functioning moving walkway. There was a sizeable lump halfway down its body, and whatever the snake had recently ingested was still writhing inside.

"Grandpa, where the hell are we?" Kara asked her grandfather as she took a few hasty steps away from the snake. "Is this a safe place to be?"

"Not with price gouging like that going on," Cornelius said, clucking his tongue and staring back at the creepy guy with the basket. "Eyepatch Pete used to sell those eggs for half that much. Guess everything's about the money these days. You sold out, Pete!" he shouted back at the salesman. Pete slowly raised the arm that wasn't holding his basket and pointed it at Cornelius. He opened his mouth to speak but instead of words, a large brown moth fluttered out.

"A *brown* moth!" Cornelius exclaimed. "He must be really worked up. Jesse must have eaten something he had his eye on himself."

"Jesse?" Kara asked.

"Sure!" Cornelius prodded the side of the snake with his right foot. "Hungry fella, that Jesse!"

Kara looked down, then nodded in understanding while taking another precautionary step back. "Grandpa, have you spent a lot of time in Terminal X?" she asked.

"Well, Kara," Cornelius said, chuckling. He paused, and his smile quickly fell as he glanced back at where they'd come from. "I've spent enough time here to know when someone isn't wanted!" He shouted the last four words, and Kara turned around to see the elderly man and woman tentatively making their way down another of Terminal X's non-functioning moving walkways. The woman glared at them while her husband lowered his gaze to avoid eye contact.

"Intruders. I've never seen anybody else in this terminal besides Pete and Jesse," Cornelius confided to Kara. "They must be up to no good."

"Or maybe they're also going to the Olympics? You know, that giant event that the whole world attends?" Kara suggested. "When we were getting off the plane, I saw that the old guy had a bunch of Olympic logo pins on his suitcase."

But Cornelius didn't hear her. He was already striding off toward Eyepatch Pete, brandishing a twenty-dollar bill. Pete, sensing a potential sale, emitted a low croaking noise that lured the moth back into his mouth. He swallowed once, then raised his basket of eggs for Cornelius to inspect. Cornelius looked it over for a few seconds, then hefted two large green eggs out of it and dropped the twenty in the basket. He hustled back to where Kara was standing, while Eyepatch Pete produced a fancy-looking handbag from inside his trenchcoat and slipped the twenty into it.

"Is that a Louis Vuitton handbag he's got there?" Kara asked Cornelius.

"Knockoff," Cornelius replied. "He used to sell those, but airport security put a stop to that. It was a blessing in disguise, though: the eggs evidently have a much higher profit margin. Here, take one." When Kara hesitated, Cornelius grabbed her wrist and pushed an egg into her palm. About the size of a softball, the egg seemed to shimmer between its original green color and a light blue, depending on how the light hit it.

"On the count of three, let fly at those two idiots," Cornelius instructed.

"Let fly?" Kara asked. "You mean throw this at them?"

"Just like you're egging a house. It's not that hard, Kara. One…"

Kara looked up at the elderly couple. The walkway had suddenly started moving, and they were struggling to go back the way they'd come. Kara wasn't sure why they were going against the flow until she looked a bit farther down the walkway's path and noticed that it ended in a giant crater.

"One of Pete's traps," Cornelius said, not taking his eye off the couple. "He's a clever guy. And faster than you'd think. Two…"

"I'm not egging that poor couple!"

"Is the hand the egg is in starting to tingle?" Cornelius asked.

Kara hadn't really noticed, but now that her grandfather mentioned it, there was a very unpleasant tingling sensation. "Is the egg doing that?" she asked, her voice rising in panic.

"Trust me, you don't want to hold on and find out! Three!" Cornelius reared back and let the egg fly. Sensing no other choice, Kara did the same. Her throw was well short of the couple, and landed in the pit at the end of the walkway. But Cornelius's was on target, and looked certain to be a direct hit until the walkway stopped moving as abruptly as it had started. The old man and his wife had built up quite the head of steam while they were struggling against it, and they went flying off the end of the walkway, out of the egg's path.

Which was fortunate, because when the egg shattered against the terminal wall, whatever was inside it began to eat away at the plaster, like a vial of acid in a comic book. The terrified couple scrambled to crawl away from the green plumes of smoke caused by the reaction.

"Dammit!" Cornelius grumbled. "Pete did that on purpose! I hate Terminal X. Terminal Question Mark was so much nicer." Kara stared at the old couple, who had collapsed amidst their luggage in a heap on the floor. The woman's voice was one long unintelligible shriek, but she could make out the husband saying "I'm sorry!" repeatedly.

"Did mine not go off?" Kara asked. "I don't see any smoke coming out of the pit."

"If I know Pete, I'd wager that pit doesn't have a bottom," Cornelius said. "Now come on, we've got a connection to make."

They continued through the rubble of Terminal X until eventually Kara spotted their gate. She was delighted that it appeared to be in much better shape than the rest of the terminal. The sign identifying it as Gate 1 was shiny and gleaming, and a friendly airline employee standing next to the doorway to the jet bridge smiled and waved. Kara breathed a deep sigh of relief and reached for her boarding pass as she quickened her pace. The sooner they got out of here the better.

Then she felt Cornelius's hand grab her shoulder. "Don't take another step," he whispered in her ear. Kara froze.

"What's the matter?" she asked, scanning the area for threats without moving her head.

"Pete," Cornelius replied. "I'll be damned if it isn't another one of his traps." He pointed at the jet bridge doorway. "See that door? Painted on."

"How can you tell?" Kara asked, still not moving a muscle.

"You spend enough time flying out of Terminal X and you learn to recognize his craftsmanship," Cornelius replied. "Watch." Cornelius stepped in front of Kara and fished a packet of airplane pretzels out of his pocket. He tore the packet open, shook a few into his right hand, and flung them at the jet bridge. Sure enough, the pretzels bounced right off of the supposedly open doorway and clattered to the floor. Milliseconds later, a large net fell from the ceiling and landed on top of the scattered pretzels.

"Plus," Cornelius said, "that gate attendant is clearly just a scarecrow." Kara took another look and was alarmed by how obvious it was that the smiling employee wasn't a real person. It was clearly just an old feedsack stuffed with rags and garbage, with a Picasso-esque face painted on the front. A creaky pulley system automatically raised and lowered a stick with a glove, which Kara had mistaken for a waving arm seconds earlier.

"I didn't… I guess I…" Kara stammered.

"That's OK," Cornelius said, patting her on the shoulder. "Pete's a crafty guy. It takes a trained eye." As he said that, the makeshift pulley system emitted a shower of sparks as the gears ground together. The stick arm snapped in half, and the garbage scarecrow toppled backward onto the floor. "We should probably keep moving though. I'm sure Pete will be here any minute. He knows he's got to beat Jesse to the traps, even if he's already full. That snake's got a hell of an appetite."

"Should we warn those two old people?" Kara asked, still looking back at Pete's cunning trap as Cornelius led her away.

"About what? It's going to be at least ten minutes until Pete gets that net rearmed. If they can't hobble their osteoporotic bones this far by then, they deserve the grim fate that awaits them."

"And what do you think that fate is?" Kara asked, not sure if she wanted to know the answer.

"He thinks if he eats someone's eyes, it will give him sight back in his dead eye," Cornelius said, as casually as if he were remarking on the weather. Kara's face went white. "Of course, that might just be Pete talking a big game. We had been drinking for hours by the time he told me that. He was saying a lot of weird things by that point."

Kara stopped in her tracks. "What?" Cornelius asked, turning to face her. "My flight was delayed and I had some time to kill. What was I supposed to do, slog all the way back to Terminal A? With the moving walkways out of order?"

Cornelius shook his head and grumbled something about millennials as he continued off toward the real Gate 1. Kara debated leaving the elderly couple a note, but figured it wasn't in her best interest to stray too far on her own in Terminal X. She took one last look at the garbage scarecrow, then hurried after her grandfather.

By the time they reached the real Gate 1, Kara's feet were sore and her left shoulder was aching from carrying her gym bag. Cornelius, on the other hand, only seemed to gain more energy as their journey progressed through the increasingly derelict terminal, despite the fact that he was carrying Jeff in addition to his own suitcase. When they finally reached the empty ticket counter, he was bouncing from one foot to the other in excitement. "Hello!" Cornelius called out, raising a large cloud of dust as he slapped his hand on the counter. "Anybody here? Come on, our flight's supposed to leave in half an hour!"

Kara dropped her bag to the ground and slumped over in the first chair she saw. There was a loud squeal from the seat cushion below her and she rocketed to her feet. Turning around, she saw a pair of beady eyes blinking back at her from a gnawed hole in the cushion.

"Catch!" Cornelius instructed without turning around. He reached into his pocket and produced a small bottle, which he then tossed over his shoulder. Kara pulled her eyes away from the creature in the chair just in time to snatch the bottle before it hit the ground.

"What is this for?" Kara asked as she studied the unlabeled bottle.

"Antidote," Cornelius replied. "Hellooooo! Frequent flier here!"

"Antidote for what?" Kara asked, scooting away from the chair as whatever was inside narrowed its eyes at her.

"One of those things bit you, didn't it?" Cornelius asked.

"No," Kara replied. "I just sat on it."

"Then, dear Lord, don't swallow a drop of that!" Cornelius lunged for the bottle and plucked it from Kara's hands. "Drinking the antidote when you haven't been exposed to the venom is a million times worse than the venom itself!"

"Well, maybe you should have all the facts before you go handing out toxic medicine!" Kara shot back. But Cornelius didn't hear her because the gate agent had finally appeared. He was slowly inching out from behind a shadowy row of chairs, shielding his eyes against the light that streamed in through the holes in the ceiling. Strings of greasy hair fell across his face as he hunched his gaunt frame toward the counter, clutching his hands together and emitting guttural wheezings with every step. What must have at one point been an airline uniform was now just a collection of greasy, tattered rags that barely clung to his bony limbs.

When the agent reached the counter, he deposited a handful of small objects into a pile on the counter. Kara leaned in for a closer look, saw that it was a collection of dead insects, and quickly leaned back out.

"I am the gatekeeper," the agent croaked, looking up at Kara and Cornelius with eyes that threatened to bulge all the way out of the hollow sockets of his skull. "What is your business with—hang on a second." The agent tapped a computer touch screen to wake it up, then scanned a yellowed ID badge that was attached to his waist with a retractable lanyard. "Got to mark this gate as staffed, otherwise it automatically gets flagged as delayed and then there's like a mountain of paperwork to fill out once it takes—sorry, sorry, you don't care about any of that. What was I saying? Oh yeah... I am the gatekeeper! What is your business with JetStream Airlines, a regional carrier of United?"

Cornelius appeared relieved that the spiel was over and handed the agent their boarding passes. The agent snatched them, and greedily licked his lips as his eyes darted back and forth from Cornelius to Kara.

"Travelers, you seek a place of ruin and dismay," the agent intoned. "Turn back or else walk amongst the damned! Beware! Bewa—" The agent noticed something and stopped short. "Oh, you're traveling to HAWAII." He chuckled, embarrassed. "I got confused, I thought this was the flight to Detroit! That one's flying out of here in an hour. Sorry about that!"

"No biggie," Cornelius said, inching his way toward the jetway. "We'll just be boarding now if that's OK."

"Halt!" the attendant hissed before lapsing into a rhythmic chant:

"Listen carefully, I implore you,
There are still two who trod before you,
A hero's status they attain,
As many moons do wax and wane!"

"What the hell does that mean?" Cornelius asked.

"You guys are JetStream Platinum Elite Silver status members," the attendant explained. "The other two people on the flight are JetStream Platinum Elite Gold status. That's forty segments annually instead of twenty. It means they get to board before you."

"Goddammit," Cornelius muttered.

"Thy wait will not be long," the attendant informed them. "For your rivals crest the horizon as we speak!"

The attendant pointed a bony finger over Cornelius's shoulder, and, despite having a very good idea who the JetStream Platinum Elite Gold status members were going to be, Kara turned to look. Sure enough, the elderly man and woman they'd harassed on the plane, thrown muffins at during breakfast, and nearly dissolved or at least scalded with whatever toxic goo was in the mystery eggs were coming into view as they rounded the burnt-out husk of a Cinnabon. The woman's lips were pursed tightly as she walked at a fast clip a good three feet in front of her husband, who lagged behind muttering apologies as he dragged their collective luggage. Kara noticed that there was straw and feathers sticking to the man's jacket and scalp that had not been there before he entered Terminal X.

Kara moved out of the way to let the couple approach the counter, but Cornelius stood his ground and the woman had to sidestep him and awkwardly lean in to speak to the attendant. The woman shot Cornelius a vicious look, but he feigned a sudden deep interest in a JetStream Airlines credit card brochure that he'd picked up off the counter and refused to make eye contact. Kara noted that the front of the brochure advertised that cardholders "receive a free alcoholic beverage on every flight" and also that they "enjoy a 78 percent higher chance of surviving a plane crash than non-cardholders." Kara didn't know how that last perk was possible or ethical, but it seemed like the sort of advantage that might make the card's outrageous 26 percent interest rate a bit more bearable.

The woman snapped her fingers at her husband, who fumbled in his pockets for a few seconds before producing his phone, which he handed to his wife. She called up his boarding pass, then did the same on her own phone before handing both of them to the gate attendant to scan. The gate attendant's eyes went wide as he plucked the phones from her hand. The glow from their screens lit his face up with a blue light that made him look even more ghastly than before. The attendant pulled his lips back in what was probably a smile, and a string of drool began to descend from the corner of his mouth.

"They're so… beautiful…" the attendant hissed. "Such power you must possess to wield such a treasure. I knew such power once, but not all are suited to bear the burden it imposes. A dark force enveloped me, and—" The agent wailed in pain. "Take them back! I feel its presence seizing control once again!" The agent quickly scanned the phones and handed them back to the woman. There were two dings, and then the agent extended a trembling arm toward the jetway. The elderly couple darted past him, careful not to brush against the rags that dangled almost all the way down to the floor.

Cornelius sneered at the couple as they moved out of sight, but Kara kept her attention on the gate agent. "What happened when the darkness enveloped you?" she asked.

"Used way more data than my plan allotted," the agent replied, still trembling. "Huge overage charge."

"How long have you been lurking here in Terminal X?" Kara asked.

"That depends. What stage of the unceasing celestial cycle does the outside world now find itself in?" the gatekeeper asked.

"Uh, it's June 26th," Kara replied. Then, just to be certain, she added, "2020."

"Oh, thank God," the agent sighed as he dragged a filthy arm across his brow. "My three-day shift is up tomorrow."

"You've only been here two days?" Kara asked, stunned.

"One," the agent corrected. "I called in sick the first day. Who can blame me, right?" The agent looked down at his raggedy uniform as if noticing it for the first time. He looked back up, now looking more "slightly embarrassed" and less like "something whose home you would describe as a 'lair' and when it left that lair you'd describe that action as 'emerging.'"

"I guess this place kind of takes its toll on you," the agent said sheepishly. "To be honest, I don't know how Eyepatch Pete keeps up such a sunny disposition considering how much time he spends here. Anyway, have a great flight! And, sir?" the agent pointed at the credit card brochure that Cornelius was still holding. "I strongly recommend getting one of those credit cards. *Strongly*."

The agent scanned their boarding passes and waved them onto the jetway. Kara and Cornelius made their way down a ramp, out a doorway, across the tarmac, and onto the smallest plane Kara had ever seen. Outside the cockpit door, there was a jump seat for a flight attendant and then just two rows of bench seats. Once again, Cornelius and Kara were assigned seats behind the elderly couple. Overhead space was non-existent; instead there were two lopsided shelves for baggage, one of which was already taken up by a first aid kit that bore a label that read "FOR JETSTREAM VISA CARD HOLDERS **ONLY!**" The word "only" had been underlined several times for emphasis.

The elderly man was struggling to lift his wife's bag up onto the other shelf. Before Kara could make a move to help him, she felt Cornelius leaning over her. He shoved his suitcase forward onto the empty shelf, followed by Jeff the Jackrabbit. Then Cornelius grabbed Kara's track bag off her shoulder and wedged it in between the others. Finally, without a word, he slid past Kara into his seat and slammed the window shade shut.

The befuddled old man looked at the shelf and back down at his wife's bag. "Just shove it up there, Henry!" his wife screeched at him. With great effort, Henry finally managed to hoist the bag, but there was no way it was going to fit. Unsure what to do, Kara hovered behind him, her hands raised halfway toward the bag in a stance that she hoped gave the appearance of being about to help.

Unfortunately for Henry, the flight attendant was having none of it. "Sir! Sir!" Her irritated tone sounded as if she were chastising a disobedient dog named "Sir" that she'd just caught eating out of the cat's litter box. "I'm afraid you'll have to check that, sir," she informed him as she elbowed her way past Kara. "The baggage shelves are full."

She snatched the bag from Henry as his wife shot him a withering glare. "This one, too," the flight attendant snapped. She grabbed the pin-covered satchel that Kara had noted on the first flight.

"Please be careful with that," Henry whimpered. "It's got pins from every Olympics from the past sixty years on it." His expression brightened a bit. "Pin trading is a big pastime in the Olympic Village.

I left just enough room for this year's designs! Once we get back, I'll have to start looking for a new bag!"

"We'll take good care of it, *sir*." This time the word was punctuated as if the dog being addressed had developed an erection while gorging on the litter-box buffet. Henry's lip quivered as the bag slid from his grasp. From his seat, Cornelius let out a loud snore.

The flight attendant walked back toward the airplane door. "Two late bags!" she bellowed. "If anyone's down there, see if you can find some room in the wheel compartment or something!" She tossed the bags out the door and slammed it shut before they hit the ground.

Kara slid into the seat next to her grandfather as Henry and his wife took the two seats in front of them. The intercom crackled and the pilot spoke up.

"This is JetStream Flight 2178 to HAWAII. You have a lot of choices when you fly, and we just thought we'd remind you of that. A lot of choices..." The captain paused to let his statement sink in. "Anyways, I sincerely hope you've got one of our JetStream Visa cards. Let's fly, bitches!"

The plane pulled away from the gate and began to taxi to the runway. The flight attendant stood at the front of the plane and launched into what Kara assumed was her safety speech. "Due to the delay caused by the customers who thought checked baggage requirements did not apply to them, there will be no beverage service." Her lecture concluded, she then opened the lavatory door, stepped inside, and pulled it shut. A light above the door came on indicating she had locked it.

Kara overheard Henry's wife hissing something at him in a panic. Henry was trying to calm her down. "I'm sure that's just how the locals pronounce it, dear. Please, let's try to enjoy ourselves!"

Kara elbowed Cornelius in the ribs. He woke with a start. "Huh? What? I've got one, I've got one!" Cornelius reached into his pocket, pulled out a crumpled Visa card application, and tossed it into the aisle.

"Grandpa!" Kara shout-whispered at him. Cornelius blinked a few times trying to figure out where he was. Kara didn't feel like waiting to let him get his bearings. "You've been so rude to those people! The Olympics are going to be super awkward if we keep running into them and you haven't apologized!"

"Wuzzat?" Cornelius mumbled. "Lemme take a nap in the bathroom and think it over."

"The flight attendant already locked herself in there," Kara informed him.

"Is that so? Well, I like her style. A real pro!"

"Just apologize!"

Cornelius raised up out of his seat to get a look at the couple. Henry fidgeted, not knowing what to do while separated from his beloved bag, while his wife fumed in icy silence.

"Do you really think they'd accept it if I said I'm sorry?" Cornelius asked, sitting back down and turning to face Kara.

"Yes! It certainly couldn't hurt!"

Cornelius thought about it for a moment longer. "You're probably right, Kara," he said eventually. "An apology just might solve everything."

Instead of apologizing, however, Cornelius managed to trick the poor couple into thinking the plane was going to crash and they were all going to die in a watery grave.

This was accomplished by shouting, "The plane is going to crash! We're all going to die in a watery grave!" It was made all the more convincing by the fact that the plane began plummeting toward the ocean. Had Henry and his wife known that there was no runway on HAWAII and they were in fact in an amphibious plane, they might have shrugged it off as a silly prank. Minus this tidbit of information, they began to weep and blubber incoherent prayers, acts of desperation that continued well after the plane had made a routine splash landing and Cornelius was calmly retrieving his bags.

* * *

And that was why Henry's wife was currently glaring at Kara from the other side of the boat.

There was a loud thump from the bow, followed by an even louder burst of laughter. Kara turned to see the African coach slapping Cornelius on the back. "Got one!" her grandfather crowed from the helm. It was hard to tell as they whizzed by at ninety miles an hour, but Kara was fairly certain that the grey lump she saw floating to the surface used to be a dolphin.

"Echolocate *that!*" Cornelius yelled over his shoulder, to uproarious laughter from his new pal, who was gesturing that he wanted a turn at the wheel. Cornelius reluctantly turned it over, and in doing so seemed to notice Kara for the first time since they'd boarded the boat and sped off from the seaplane. He beckoned her to the bow. Moving very deliberately, Kara got to her feet. Giving the potentially dead man under the blanket a wide berth, she inched her way to the front of the boat.

"Kara, I want you to meet President for Life Makepeace of The Principality of Warland." Cornelius said, gesturing at the man steering the boat. President for Life Makepeace turned, smiled at Kara, and gave her a nod hello before turning his attention back to the sea.

"Warland?" Kara asked.

"I know, I know." Cornelius shook his head. "My friend Makepeace here and I are in the same boat. He rules a country in Eastern Africa that the rest of the world refuses to acknowledge, or at least cut in on lucrative trade deals. He named his country Warland because he thought it would intimidate the other countries into recognizing him." Cornelius cupped a hand around his mouth and lowered his voice. "A little on the nose if you ask me. Sounds desperate. I told him, 'You can't just talk the talk, you've got to walk the walk! Perform a couple of public ethnic cleansings, then you establish yourself as the go-to country for someone looking to commit a genocide!'"

"That sounds like terrible advice," Kara said. "You could be tried as a party to war crimes."

Cornelius looked away and made the blah blah blah gesture with his hand. Kara wondered if it was the first time that gesture had ever been used to dismiss the notion that maybe a government should not be ritually executing entire populations.

"So just to clarify what this means..." Kara repeated the hand motion back to her grandfather. "You're saying that Warlanders are not genocidal maniacs?" she asked. This seemed like good information to know if you were going to be hanging out with someone for the duration of a major international sporting event.

"What *is* a genocidal maniac?" Cornelius asked. "I mean really, in the scheme of things? It's sort of like being a writer. Anybody can just wake up one day and decide that they're going to start calling themselves one. You don't actually have to anything published."

"But his name is Makepeace!"

"Yeah, I think he had kind of a 'Boy Named Sue' thing going on growing up. But I'm not here to play psychologist. Hey, you look kinda green," Cornelius remarked.

"I've been barfing the entire boat ride!" Kara snapped. "You and President for Life Makepeace have been driving this thing at like ninety miles an hour!"

"Knots, Kara. You measure a boat's speed in knots," Cornelius said. "And I'm sorry about that. We can usually get this puppy going way faster. It really shouldn't take this long to get to HAWAII from the drop zone. I blame the flags of convenience!"

Cornelius pointed to the stern of the boat, where a length of rope with six large flags attached ran up a twenty-foot pole. The colorful flags flapped and fluttered and clearly made the boat way less aerodynamic. Kara did not recognize any of the countries that the flags represented, but considering where they were headed, and who else was on board, this didn't surprise her.

"Wind resistance really slows us down," Cornelius muttered. "But it's worth it for the tax breaks. And the tariff breaks. And the smuggling breaks."

President for Life Makepeace swerved the boat toward some sort of marine life and was rewarded with a hefty thump. He cackled loudly as Kara steadied herself against the side of the boat. She closed her eyes and breathed through her nose, hoping that the need to puke would subside.

Against her better judgment, Kara wondered how Principal Dunbar was holding up. A vision of him weeping next to an open casket swept over her. In between frantic attempts to text Kara messages of despair, the principal was wiping away tears and dabbing his runny nose using his dead cat as a handkerchief. Kara opened her eyes. She would take her chances with the wannabe warlord.

"What is a flag of convenience?" she asked, wondering what this latest bit of knowledge might one day make *her* a party to.

"When you own a boat, you have to register it," Cornelius explained. "You can do this in the country that you're actually from, and pay taxes and abide by its cigarette-importing laws like an idiot… Or you can get a flag of convenience! You register it in a less restrictive country, then everyone on the ocean thinks you're from that country and you can do whatever you want."

Cornelius began to tick the flags off from top to bottom. "Let's see, I've got Panama, Liberia, the Marshall Islands. Then there's Austria-Hungary and the United Arab Republic. I should probably take those two down, they technically haven't existed for a combined century and a half. And then there's…"

"That's the Jolly Roger," Kara finished his thought. "The skull and crossbones. That's a pirate flag."

"Technically, it's the proud colors of Warland," Cornelius said. "Like I said, they do things pretty on the nose down there. Anyway, I figured if one flag of convenience provided tax breaks and shelter from various crimes, two flags would provide twice the benefits! Then the Marshall Islands was having a limited time offer, and it sort of escalated from there. Anyway, you're now riding on the most convenient ship on the seven seas!"

"But if you fly six flags, it's obvious that you don't come from any of those countries," Kara countered. "It's like a cop asking you for your ID and you handing over driver's licenses from half the states."

"Say, that's a hell of an idea!" Cornelius said, his eyes widening. "And while he's sorting through them, you gun the motor and leave him in a pile of plastic! That's the old Everglades family outside-the-box thinking. But honestly, kiddo, you've got to balance it out with common sense. Next time you get on a boat, take a Dramamine so you won't get seasick. The smell of your barf probably attracted that dolphin we hit, you know."

"I didn't have any Dramamine!" Kara protested.

"Well, you didn't ask!" Cornelius countered.

"Not only did I not know we were getting on a boat today, but I've never even been on a boat! I didn't know seasickness pills were a thing!"

"Well, it's a moot point," Cornelius said, trying to sound responsible. "I wouldn't have given them to you even if you'd asked. Booze and pills don't mix, and you've been drinking, Kara."

"So have you, Grandpa! You've had much more to drink than me!"

Cornelius pondered this. "I guess you're right," he said. "Well, it didn't seem to do me any harm! Would you like one now?"

"Of course I would!" Kara said. "I've been miserable this entire time!" Cornelius reached into his pocket and pulled out a small medicine bottle. He shook two pills out and handed them to Kara, who grabbed them and swallowed them dry. They stuck in her throat and left a gross, artificial taste in her mouth, but it was at least better than residual puke.

"Bleah," Kara muttered. "Disgusting. How long do they take to kick in?"

"It doesn't matter," Cornelius replied. "We're already here."

Kara bit her tongue and fumed as she felt President for Life Makepeace reduce the boat's speed. She took a deep breath, counted to ten, and, as Cornelius swept his hand across the horizon, she watched HAWAII come into view.

Ever since the first caveman went out on a hunt and did not die horribly, thereupon learning that life was not, in fact, one unceasing string of negative events, hope has been a uniquely human condition. And, shortly after that caveman returned to his cave expecting his cavewife and cavebaby to greet him and instead found a saber-toothed tiger snacking on their bloody remains, disappointment has gone hand in hand with hope.

In the millennia that followed, humans have experienced countless disappointments of varying degrees: from "I didn't get everything I wanted for Christmas" to "huh, I guess the plague still *isn't* cured"; from "the ice cream parlor was out of strawberry" to "that mushroom cloud in the direction of my village doesn't look so good"; from "a saber-toothed tiger ate my entire family" to "a saber-toothed tiger ate *most* of my family but left my annoying wiener of a son, and, no, I didn't bring you back a wheel, Thag Jr., do you have any idea how much Ugg the Inventor is charging for those damn things?"

And yet, in all those years of the earth spinning around the sun, as hopes were dashed left and right, as dreams went unfulfilled, as dorky offspring survived instead of the cool ones, the ones who would eat wooly mammoth steaks medium rare without scrunching up their nose at them, it's unlikely anyone has ever felt as profound a disappointment as Kara now felt upon seeing her grandfather's "country" for the first time.

That is, until Henry turned around and caught *his* first glimpse of HAWAll a few moments later and immediately surpassed her in that department.

HAWAll was a platform. A thick, gross slab of a platform, maybe half the size of a football field, balanced forty feet or so up in the air on two thick, cylindrical cement pillars. It looked like someone had turned a condemned nuclear power plant upside down, with the floor supported by the cooling towers. The side of the platform they were approaching was covered in patches of rust and algae. Kara was willing to bet that HAWAll was probably the only country in the world where the greatest threat to its infrastructure was barnacles.

If boats were sentient and a boat needed a medical procedure that wasn't legal in the boat country it resided in, it would cross the border into a boat country where unlicensed boat doctors would strap them to something resembling HAWAll to perform the surgery.

HAWAll looked like the kind of structure that, if it were fenced off and abandoned in a remote lot in your neighborhood, parents would warn their children not to play on it. The kids, whose childhoods would have already been plagued by nightmares about the structure, even if they'd never actually seen it in person, would beg their parents to stop bringing it up. Later, on the cusp of adolescence, they would band together to destroy it, then reunite as adults to destroy it again.

If there had been a dog in the boat, it would have raised its hackles and barked at HAWAll. Hell, Kara almost barked at HAWAll.

Cornelius, on the other hand, beamed with pride. He looked like an old man meeting his grandchild for the first time, an expression that Kara distinctly remembered not seeing the previous day when that specific event had actually occurred. Choppy waves frothed around the sides of the pillars, and the occasional seagull playfully dipped under the country and emerged out the other side, as Cornelius smiled the smile of a man who was at long last returning home.

"Welcome to HAWAll, Kara," he said, gently placing an arm around his granddaughter's shoulders. Kara processed things in horrified silence for a few more seconds before she spoke.

"So... HAWAll is underwater? It's a submerged country of the future?" Kara asked, trying to sound hopeful. "There's some sort of compression chamber that extends down into the sea from the center of that platform and then there's a series of tunnels connecting all the spherical living quarters to each other? There's desalinization and greenhouses and government-mandated vitamin supplements to make up for the lack of sunlight?"

Cornelius snorted. "What? Of course not! Who'd want to live like that? All those idiotic dolphins peeking in through your windows all day long..."

Kara mentally grasped at a few straws. A utopian sky community. That must be it. "So then you've conquered the middle atmosphere? This is some sort of launching pad to deliver food and oxygen tanks to the group of people you've got residing in a part of the sky we'd previously thought uninhabitable?"

"Is that Dramamine sitting right?" Cornelius asked. He pulled his arm off Kara's shoulder and looked at her with concern. "What the hell are you talking about? This is HAWAll. You're looking at it. Ruled over by yours truly for over three decades."

Kara's jaw dropped again. Meanwhile, one of the seagulls that had been swooping under the country got a little too close to another seagull that had been swooping in the opposite direction. There were several loud squawks as the birds tussled, snapping and clawing at one another, until one plummeted dead into the frothy water below.

Cornelius watched it fall with grim determination. Then he turned to address the other people on the boat. "OK, folks, we are nearing our destination, the glorious micronation of HAWAII! In a few minutes, President for Life Makepeace is going to drop anchor next to the entrance ladder. That ladder is your only gateway in and out of the country, so I hope you're physically able to perform a forty-foot climb and not scared of heights."

Henry tentatively raised his hand, but Cornelius ignored him. "Now, as you may have heard, the seagulls that live under the platform are quite numerous, and possessing no natural predators out here, they've grown quite arrogant and aggressive. Not to mention it's nesting season, so they're more riled up than usual. Fortunately, I've got that under control."

Cornelius smiled and winked at Kara, then bent over to lift up a bench cushion, revealing a storage container underneath. He pulled out a few life jackets, tossed them overboard one by one, then reached in and grabbed an imposing-looking shotgun. Henry lowered his hand.

"I fire this thing," Cornelius said, cocking the enormous gun. "And those birds disperse. It's just about the only thing they fear. They take off and that is your signal to start climbing. Anything drops? You keep climbing. Anyone falls? You keep climbing. The middle twenty feet is key, folks. When they see you in that stretch of ladder, that's when they really think you're going after their eggs. You've got a window of about ninety to a hundred and twenty seconds before they return, but if they come back early, what do you do?"

Cornelius pointed at Henry. "I... I keep climbing?" Henry managed to stammer.

"Wrong!" Cornelius shouted. "You hold on for dear life and endure them tearing at your clothes and flesh. They are small birds in the scheme of things, so they don't have large appetites. A couple bites of your meat will temporarily satiate them. They tend to go for the back of your neck, and the midriff flab you expose when you reach for the next rung. Do *not* flail or swat at them in an attempt to defend yourself; just keep gripping the ladder." He described the horrific acts with the rote nonchalance of a flight attendant delivering a safety speech he'd already given thousands of times. "Once they're done feasting, you'll hopefully have enough strength left to finish the climb. Of course, like I said, it is nesting season, so they'll be tearing more off of you to regurgitate to their young, so it's really best that you get out of that middle twenty feet as fast as possible."

Henry's wife nudged him hard in the ribs and gestured with her head toward Cornelius. Henry rubbed his side and then tentatively spoke up. "My wife wants to know if this is the part of the trip where you give us our leis?"

Cornelius threw back his head and laughed. "Leis!" he roared. "That's fantastic! It's going to be a great Olympics if you keep cracking everyone up like that." Cornelius wiped a tear away from his right eye. "Leis…" he chuckled.

Then his face went deadly serious as he raised the shotgun straight up into the air and fired a deafening blast. Hundreds of terrified, angry seagulls squawked as they streamed out from underneath the country of HAWAIl in a grey-white cloud. The boat pulled up alongside a long, metal ladder. President for Life Makepeace of Warland hastily tied a length of rope to the bottom rung, then shot Cornelius a thumbs-up.

"Anyone who wants to see the goddamn Summer Olympics had better get climbing!" Cornelius shouted. Kara had scaled a half dozen rungs before she even realized what she was doing.

twelve

The dwindling rays of a glorious sunset tickled the coast of Maui. The revelers who had packed Makena Beach were now full, happy, and more than a little tipsy. They now faced the hardest decision they had encountered all day. Some opted to retire to their luxurious cabanas for a night of passionate lovemaking on king size beds adorned with crisp linen sheets before being lulled to sleep by the sound of lapping waves. Others, tempted by the massive bonfire that was being constructed and the rumors of a dessert pig so succulent that it would make the earlier pigs taste like remaindered shoe leather, managed to find a second wind. If only a camera were able to capture the sound of steel drums and slack key guitar, the scene would have made a perfect postcard.

Meanwhile, halfway across the world on HAWAII, the president was attempting to charge tourists ten dollars for an uncapped, half-empty bottle of water.

"It looks like there's something floating in there," Henry told Cornelius. He pointed at the bottle, where there was indeed some sort of object, maybe an insect, floating on the surface.

"Your wife looks awfully thirsty," Cornelius replied, not bothering to mask his disinterest. Henry's wife elbowed him in the ribs and pointed at the water bottle. Henry sighed and reached for his wallet. He fished out a ten dollar bill and held it out for Cornelius.

Cornelius sucked in some air through his teeth and winced. "Ooh… Did you not get your currency exchanged back in the airport?" Henry looked baffled. He nervously shook his head as his wife glared at him.

"Well, don't worry! We can do that for you right here!" Henry brightened at Cornelius's suddenly friendly tone, as if forgetting that he was hoping for the chance to buy eleven ounces of beetle-enhanced H_2O.

"Kara!" Cornelius called. Kara looked up at her grandfather. Ever since she'd determined that the vicious seagulls tended to avoid the rusting northernmost edge of HAWAll, she'd been dangling her legs off the side and watching the ocean as she tried to catch her breath. Her track workouts kept her in pretty good shape, but she was still feeling winded from the sprint-climb up the ladder fifteen minutes ago. She had no idea how the elderly couple, let alone the evidently not-dead Warlander, had survived it.

Well, at least the elderly couple had survived it. The jury was still out on the Warlander. As Kara rose to her feet and walked over to her grandfather, she glanced in the man's direction. He was still lying in the spot where Cornelius had rolled him after he finished his climb up the ladder. The man was rail thin, bordering on gaunt, and his breaths came in irregular gasps. He clearly needed medical attention.

"There's a metal box marked 'Change' in the governor's mansion," Cornelius shouted across the island. "Can you grab it and bring it here?"

Kara looked around for the governor's mansion. On the west side of the country there was a small enclosure, about the size of a tollbooth. Painted in broad strokes on its side were the words "KEEP OUT – GOVERNOR ONLY." It was the only notable feature on the otherwise flat platform. Kara walked over to the structure and poked her head in.

Inside, there was a small desk with a vast array of ancient-looking radio equipment on it. A college-dorm-sized refrigerator was next to it, and the change box she'd been sent to retrieve sat on top of the fridge. There was a rickety bookcase that appeared to be doubling as a clothes dresser; an office-style water cooler with several half-filled plastic bottles next to it; a pool skimmer with a long, retractable handle; and a sling hammock strung up between two corners. The only decoration in the stark room was a whiteboard, which had some writing on it.

CONTINGENCY PLAN:
    1. BETRAY MAKEPEACE
    2. INVADE WARLAND
    3. REPEAT WITH ESTONIA?

Kara walked over to the board, picked up the rag that hung over the corner of it, and erased the first two bullet points. She had no idea what circumstances might trigger the contingency plan, but guessed that the man being betrayed in Step One stumbling upon it might be high up on the list. For a few seconds she debated erasing the third point, but decided to leave it. It added a sense of mystery.

Kara had hoped to find a first aid kid or maybe some of those cool "CLEAR!" paddles in the governor's mansion to help the struggling Warlander. But seeing nothing of the sort, she retrieved the metal change box, walked back out onto the platform, and made her way over to where her grandfather stood.

"Ah, thank you, Kara!" Cornelius said. "I guess our friend Henry here didn't realize he needed to change out his US dollars for HAWAIl dollars. Fortunately, the government is happy to provide that service for its guests!" He beamed a smile at Henry and his wife.

"We thought there would be more palm trees," Henry said to Kara, sounding polite and hopelessly naïve. "Maybe that's on one of the other islands?"

"Hand over the money," Cornelius said, suddenly all business. Henry opened his wallet and handed Cornelius five crisp twenty dollar bills.

"One hundred US dollars!" Cornelius announced as he handed

Kara the money. "The current exchange rate is two to one, so Kara, if you'd be so kind, please issue fifty HAWAIl dollars to our friend here."

Kara opened the change box. Inside, there was a thick wad of cash that was rubber banded together. Kara slid the rubber band off and rifled through the stack.

"Grandpa, this is just American money as well," she said. She peeled off a few Hamiltons and Jacksons and showed them to her grandfather.

"With one difference!" Cornelius winked. "The president himself has handwritten 'HAWAIl' on the back of each bill!"

"Why does the president live in a building called the governor's mansion?" Kara asked.

"Because I'm both!" Cornelius snapped. "It's my country and if I want to be president *and* governor, I can be both!"

"None of these bills have HAWAIl written on them," Kara said, turning them over in her hand.

"Well I've been very busy!" Cornelius snapped again. "I don't know if you've heard, but a lot of work goes into hosting the Olympics. Just give me a ten and two twenties!" Kara handed her grandfather a well worn ten along with two of Henry's original twenties. Cornelius pulled a black sharpie out of his pocket and gestured for Kara to spin around. She did, and Cornelius pressed the bills onto her back so he could write on them. He hastily scrawled something on each bill then announced, "There we go!"

Cornelius held up the bills for Kara to see, and sure enough he'd written "HAWAIl" in big, black marker strokes on the back of each of them. He passed the two twenties back to Henry and pocketed the ten. "For the water," he informed everyone.

Henry looked at the HAWAIl currency and the half-empty bottle of bug water that he was slowly coming to realize had cost him sixty dollars. Eventually he gave up on trying to do the mental math and hopefully asked, "You mentioned the Olympics? Because I've been to every one since..."

Cornelius turned his back and walked away from the unfortunate man, motioning for Kara to come with him. Kara snapped the lid of the cash box closed, shrugged Henry an apology, and followed.

Cornelius handed Kara the marker as they walked. "Maybe you can take care of marking up the rest of that currency when you've got a moment, Kara? We're going to have the eyes of the entire world on us once the Olympics start, we've got to make sure we're running a tight ship!" Kara nodded.

"And let me know how much cash we've got in there," Cornelius added. "I may have to print up a few thousand more dollars before the games start."

"Print up?" Kara asked. "What do you mean print up?"

"What the hell do you think I mean?" Cornelius asked. "Print some more money. I've got a setup in the governor's mansion. Countries print their own money. It's called a mint. It's completely legal."

"I didn't claim that it wasn't," Kara said. "But since you defensively brought it up, it really doesn't seem like it is! If your currency is just American money with HAWAII written on it, then you aren't printing money. You're counterfeiting US dollars."

Cornelius grinned and did a big 'Whoosh!' gesture over his head. "Kara! You're talking in circles, it's making me dizzy here! I may need to lie down. Like that guy, he's got the right idea." Cornelius pointed to the gaunt Warlander who lay motionless a few feet away.

"He doesn't 'have the right idea,' Grandpa," Kara protested. "I think he needs medical attention, he seems really sick. Where did President for Life Makepeace take the boat?"

"President for Life Makepeace is serving as shuttle driver for the many guests and dignitaries who will be visiting the Olympic games," Cornelius informed her. "He had another pickup scheduled. And I'd be a bit more respectful of our friend here. Not only is he not 'sick' or 'dying,' he's actually one of the top athletes in the world. He's here to compete in the marathon event."

"That guy?" Kara blurted, unable to restrain herself. "That guy is going to run twenty-six point two miles? He looks like someone they were throwing benefit concerts for in the '80s." A stiff gust of wind blew the runner over onto his stomach. He groaned, struggled to flip himself back over, then gave up, opting to wait for the next gust of wind to do it for him.

"President for Life Makepeace has been personally supervising his training," Cornelius said. "Limiting his diet to three hundred calories per day. Have you ever seen marathon runners? They're not your muscled-up bodybuilder types. They're lean and mean!"

"They got that way because they are running fifteen four-minute miles a day for training, not the other way around! Nobody excels at extreme distance running because they're malnourished!"

"Eye of the beholder," Cornelius winked. "You say tomayto, I say tomahto. Some people say Hawaii, some say HAWAll."

"Nobody says HAWAll!" Kara spread her arms and gestured at the country. "Nobody does until you've tricked them into coming here and explained what the name of the country is, and they then repeat it back to you in disbelief! The only way you might use it in a sentence is if you were pleading to someone over the phone 'The madman calls it HAWAll, please do whatever he says, but in the very likely instance that I never leave this platform—'"

"Country," Cornelius corrected.

"'In the very likely instance that I never leave this *platform*,'" Kara continued. "'Please put our infant daughter on the line, for though I know in my heart she's too young to remember anything, maybe hearing "I love you" one last time will implant itself somewhere in her subconscious!' That's the only way someone would ever say HAWAll!"

"You seem upset," Cornelius said.

"You're damn right I'm upset!" Kara shouted back. "This is my summer vacation and I'm spending it on a platform!"

"Country," Cornelius corrected.

"This isn't a country, Grandpa! It's an abandoned pier with a feral bird problem."

"And that's exactly why I brought you here, Kara." Cornelius smiled. "Come and stroll to the south end with me." There was a mischievous twinkle in his eye that Kara couldn't help be intrigued by. Cornelius walked off and after a few steps Kara hurried after him.

"I find the south end of HAWAll to be the best for contemplation," Cornelius said as they strolled to the edge of the platform. "I believe there's an ancient seafarer's saying: 'To think, look north. To guess, look east. To waste time, look west. But to *know*, look south.' I've spent countless hours here staring out at the sea, searching for answers to life's biggest questions. Why are we here? What awaits us next? When do seagulls sleep? What's the most effective way to poison them in order to make my escape? Is there perhaps some sort of sound frequency that would drive them away without causing permanent damage to human ears?"

"This is the west end of HAWAII," Kara remarked. "Not the south end. The sun sets in the west. See?" She pointed up at the sun and traced the path it had made across the sky that day. "East to west."

"So it is," Cornelius remarked. "No wonder I never solved any of those problems."

"How many years did you waste trying to figure out how to escape the seagulls?" Kara asked.

"Well, they weren't technically wasted," Cornelius said. "It's not like I could have gone anywhere. You know, because of the seagulls. But one day, as I stared southward into a glorious orange and purple sunset, I came to a realization: the government was to blame for all of my problems."

Kara looked skeptical.

Cornelius chuckled. "I know, it sounds crazy. Isolated loner decides that elected officials and judges are conspiring to keep him down."

Kara waited for a "but" that was not forthcoming.

"So, I decided that if I formed my own country, where *I* was the entire government, that would fix everything!"

"Simple as that!" Kara said, heavy on the sarcasm.

"One would think!" Cornelius said, oblivious. "I certainly did. There's the Big Four things a country needs if it's going to be taken seriously: constitution, currency, national anthem, and flag. It sounds so easy, I thought it would be like getting a permit to dig in your backyard. You show up at the United Nations, prove to them you have all four of those—

"Where is the HAWAII flag, by the way?" Kara asked.

"Look, I've been focused on the big picture, I haven't had time to do every little thing! Besides, those bigwigs at the UN are as elitist as you could imagine. They think just because a country has existed for centuries or has a population of over twenty million, that makes it more legitimate than one that doesn't even have a flag."

"Why didn't you just make a flag?" Kara asked. "The flag of Poland is just two stripes, and one of them is white. It must have taken them thirty seconds."

"What color is the other stripe?" Cornelius asked.

"Red."

"Dammit! That was the only idea I came up with this entire time!" Cornelius paused, then lifted a hopeful finger into the air. "Wait, is the red one on the top or bottom?"

"Bottom," Kara replied.

"Dammit!" Cornelius spit off the side of the country in disgust. Mistaking the loogie for food, a blur of seagulls swooped out from underneath the platform. One lucky bird snatched it out of the air before it had descended more than a few feet.

"I can help you come up with a new design?" Kara offered, nervously backing up a few feet from the edge.

"I appreciate the offer, Kara," Cornelius said. "But I learned it would take more to gain the acceptance of those diplomatic pricks up in that ivory tower. Turns out that in order for the UN to recognize you as a country, you've got to prove that you have the capacity to enter into diplomatic relations with other member states. Of course, no states want to do that unless the UN recognizes you as a country. So you can see how that becomes a bit of a catch-22 for an upstart country like HAWAll."

Kara thought she knew where this was going. "But if you tricked the governing body of the premiere international athletic event on the planet into letting you host it…"

"Then everyone would have to acknowledge HAWAll!" Cornelius grinned and patted Kara on the shoulder. "If it's in the record books that, say, Canada won the gold medal in the hundred-meter dash in the HAWAll Olympics, there's no denying that HAWAll is a valid, independent country! And then I'll show them. Then I'll show them all…"

Kara opted to ignore her grandfather's ominous trail-off and instead pondered his plan as she stared westward. It made sense in a twisted way. If countries refused to acknowledge your diplomatic efforts, or if you were too busy thinking of insane schemes to actually make any diplomatic efforts, then tricking them was the next best way to get them to recognize you. But one thing still didn't make any sense to her.

"Why me, Grandpa?" Kara asked. "Why did you come get me? After all, you made it this far on your own." Kara swept her arm across the dismal landscape of HAWAll. As she did, a hunk of rust fell off the eastern side of the country into the ocean, prompting a brief but deafening series of squawks from the seagulls that lurked below the platform. To the north, Henry and his elderly wife huddled together, unsure of where they were and whether they were going to be allowed to leave. Everyone on the platform pretended not to hear the starving marathon runner's stomach rumbling.

Kara restarted her sentence. "After all, you did this all on your own, without anyone else serving as a party to any of these deeds. Let's be clear about that. But getting your granddaughter to prance around in a mascot costume seems like a pretty trivial concern in the scheme of things."

"Kara, I didn't bring you here to have you wear a mascot costume," Cornelius said. He stepped to the edge of the platform, folded his hands behind his back, and turned around to face his granddaughter. "I brought you here to win a gold medal for the United States of America."

Kara's jaw dropped. Suddenly things made sense to her. Not everything. Not a majority of things. But some things, and under the circumstances that seemed like the best she could hope for.

"Although I'm still gonna need you to wear the mascot costume in the opening ceremony," Cornelius added. "Olympic by-law, you have to have a mascot for the games to count."

"That seems unnecessarily arbitrary," Kara said.

"Yeah, but it almost fucked 'em in Atlanta in '96," Cornelius chuckled. "They forgot about the mascot until like, two days before the games were going to start. How the hell do you think something like Izzy ever got approved? They were in a panic! Some guy just drew something on a napkin in the can right before the final meeting."

"They'd be a stickler for the mascot requirement but not notice that they had been tricked into holding their billion dollar competition on a… What the hell is this place, Grandpa?"

"It's called a Maunsell Fort," Cornelius said. "England built 'em in World War II to protect their shipping barges from Nazi subs."

"Cool!" Kara took another look around the structure, trying to observe it through the lens of history. She smiled as she envisioned the heroic British Navy warding off the forces of evil from the same ground she now stood on. Perhaps having the Everglades family name tied to such a place wasn't such a depressing thing after all. Maybe it was actually something worth being proud of? She began to fantasize about being asked to cut the ribbon at the new Everglades Wing of the National World War II Museum in New Orleans.

"It nearly cost us the war," Cornelius said. "It was the quickest and largest mass defection in Royal Navy history. Everyone who was stationed here was eventually tried for treason. Half of the soldiers went over to the Nazis, the other half joined the seagulls. Now, I'm not convinced that those two camps weren't in league together, and here's why…"

Kara's uplifting vision was quickly replaced by one of Cornelius parading outside said museum waving a sign. It had a picture of a seagull with a rectangular Hitler mustache lifting one wing in a Nazi salute. "SEAGULLS = NAZIS" the sign said. "WAKE UP, SHEEPLE." Cornelius had not planned the lettering ahead of time and the PLE of SHEEPLE started on its own line. Kara was amazed by the clarity of the vision. She could even smell security guard's cologne as he tackled her grandfather from behind. When she snapped to, she was amazed that Cornelius was still talking.

"My point is, that would be one heck of a coincidence," Cornelius was saying. "Anyway, after that deep shame, England was more than happy to forget about this place. It was in international waters, so they just washed their hands of it and left it here to rot. Of course, I may have a few details wrong: that was in the BC era of HAWAIl's history."

Cornelius raised his eyebrows expectantly, but Kara knew full well what he wanted her to ask and why, and she refused to take the bait.

"That means Before Cornelius," Cornelius added. He sounded a touch irritated that a joke he'd undoubtedly been planning for more than a decade had gone over so poorly the first time he trotted it out.

Kara continued ignoring him and opted to point out what she had identified as the biggest hole in a scheme full of them. "Grandpa, I hate to break it to you, but I just ran track so I could put it on my college applications. I didn't even place at regionals. Olympians are elite athletes who have spent their entire lives working to hone and maximize their body's potential. That guy excepted."

Kara pointed at the Warlander who was currently licking a patch of HAWAIl, possibly hoping to extract trace amounts of the vital minerals his body was so sorely lacking.

She continued, trying not to imagine what her grandfather's country might taste like. "But as soon as the athletes from countries other than Warland show up, I'm toast!"

A dark cloud swept over Cornelius's face so quickly that Kara took a frightened step back. In the thirty or so hours she'd known the man, she'd seen him frustrated, angry, and disgusted. And that was just as he'd choked down the wrong burrito order. But this new look was the only time she'd been scared of him. It was a look of disappointment.

Cornelius shook his head and spoke softly. "I thought better of you, Kara." He folded his hands behind his back and began to pace back and forth, his tone quickly growing more emphatic. "I thought the Everglades spirit burned within you. We are a family of fighters, of believers! Defying the odds is in our blood! When people count us out, we thank them for the motivation, then crush them! When the deck is stacked against us, we tell the dealer to restack the deck so it's even more against us, then we crush the dealer! And when a can is too big to fit into the recycling bin, we crush it! And if it's still too big to fit, we throw it in the garbage and pretend we didn't know we were supposed to be recycling!"

Cornelius raised his voice to a shout and he thrust a defiant fist to the sky. "The Everglades don't give up before the competition begins. The Everglades *know they've won* before the competition begins! And that especially applies in this case because no other countries are going to show up, so there won't be any competition."

"No competition?" Kara repeated, still trying to process the motivational speech's abrupt shift in tone.

"Oh yeah, nobody's coming," Cornelius said matter-of-factly. "I mean, come on! Look at this place! You saw what it took to get here. We do the opening ceremony, then your event, and boom! We're outta here! All the real athletes are still going to be arguing with their cab drivers about how to get to the stadium from the Maui airport by the time we're in front of the UN's Country-Acknowledging Committee."

"So you never intended for your Olympics to be anything other than awarding one medal?" Kara asked.

"Even if I'd wanted to get more than one, it didn't make any financial sense," Cornelius exclaimed. "Do you have any idea how much Olympic medals cost? And the folks who are selling them are all 'sentimental value' this, and 'I had always hoped to leave it to my grandchildren' that. I'd tell them, 'Look ma'am, maybe if you'd chosen a better career path than "triple jumper," you'd be able to afford to keep your medal AND live in a nursing home with better security. Now hand it over and I'll plug your IV machine back in.'"

"Well, if you only have one medal, what are you going to do about the marathon runner from Warland?" Kara asked.

"To hell with him," Cornelius muttered. "Made-up countries like Warland winning medals does me no good in the eyes of the UN. Besides, what's a marathon take, three hours? Even if he physically *could* run the whole thing, we'll be long gone by that time."

"But won't he be upset?" Kara asked.

"What's he going to do?" Cornelius asked. "Starve at me?"

"I think he's actually doing that right now," Kara said. She looked over at the runner. The effort of licking the patch of platform appeared to have exhausted him. He lay on his back in the world's saddest food coma.

"You're getting distracted, Kara," Cornelius lectured. "We've got to stick to the plan. As soon as I award you your medal, the Olympics is in the books as an official event. That means I've diplomatically engaged with another country, and yours truly can finally establish HAWAll as the go-to nation for cheap online medications with no prescriptions needed!"

"Selling pills?" Kara asked, raising an eyebrow. "That's your endgame?"

"It's one of many endgames!" Cornelius shot back. "I've got lots of plans. That's just the first endgame that popped into my head!"

"What are some of the other endgames?" Kara asked.

"I've got an endgame for you," Cornelius replied. "It's called stop saying endgame and run the damn hundred-meters tomorrow so we can actually enter the endgame."

"Did you just lose that endgame by saying endgame?" Kara asked. "Or are we starting now?" Cornelius refused to respond. He glared at the horizon through pursed lips for a few seconds before Kara realized that he was actually trying to suppress a smile. He fought the losing battle for a few moments longer until a grin spread over his face. He slung an arm around Kara's shoulders and pulled her in for a side hug.

"That's my granddaughter!" Cornelius beamed. "An Everglades through and through!"

Kara felt the hair on her arms stand up at that pronouncement. The Everglades name suddenly carried much more weight than it had before the bell rang on the last day of school, and almost all that weight was weird or potentially illegal. And yet, she had little doubt that she was going to have the most original *How I Spent My Summer Vacation* essay when school started again in the fall. It sounded like, if she could manage to trot out an unopposed hundred-meter dash, she might even have an Olympic gold medal to show off. This was, of course, assuming that Principal Dunbar didn't chain himself to the school doors in despair, or that she didn't have a sudden crisis of conscience and return the medal to the presumably senile triple jumper it sounded like her grandfather had swindled.

"That was a pretty good motivational speech about our family, huh?" Cornelius asked, pulling his arm off her shoulder and ruffling her hair. "I wish I'd planned it a little better though. It would have been nice to have the HAWAll national anthem playing in the background."

"How does the national anthem go?" Kara asked.

"It's actually right after the flag on my to do list," Cornelius said. "Now come on, I've got a crate of saltines in the mansion, we can sell sleeves of them to the old shrew and her husband for fifteen HAWAll dollars a piece!"

Cornelius took a few steps toward the governor's mansion and motioned for Kara to follow. She took another look around HAWAll. When you thought of the platform less as a standalone nation and more as a rusty offshore holding company that you'd be allowed to leave in twenty-four hours, it didn't seem so bad. Plus, she planned on refusing to compete in the Olympics unless she got to sleep in the governor's mansion hammock. She hustled to catch up with her grandfather.

"I'm sorry I blew up back there, Grandpa," Kara said. "It's just been a wild few days. And you know what? I think this place kinda got to me. It's got a very strange vibe. It's like if Alcatraz were just one cell and it didn't have a roof."

"I understand completely, Kara," Cornelius said. "HAWAll can have that effect on you. To be honest, I think it's why Fitz went crazy."

"And why all those British soldiers betrayed their country," Kara added.

"And why all those British soldiers betrayed their country, yes. HAWAll is a strange place, Kara! Heck, I may be the first person who ever spent time here and *didn't* go crazy!"

And with that statement, the man who had run a decades-long con in order to host the Olympics so that the United Nations would be forced to acknowledge the micronation he'd established on an abandoned military fort in the middle of the ocean so that he could sell cheap drugs online threw back his head and began to laugh.

thirteen

The *Stupid Butt* soared across the American heartland at an excruciatingly slow six hundred miles an hour. The crew was relying on the standard propulsion system because 9-Krelblax had issued an executive order banning any use of the hyperwarp soon after they took off.

In an effort to impress King Moho, Zzarvon had attempted to hyperwarp them to HAWAll in record time. He had pushed the hyperwarp into a range where the entire journey should have been over in a blink of an eye. However, Zzarvon's main navigating tentacle was covered in roast-pig grease and slipped. Instead of immediately transporting them to HAWAll, the hyperwarp opened a wormhole that had a variety of unintended consequences.

There were now just seven Hawaiian islands. Whatever effect the overclocked hyperwarp had on the fabric of the universe had caused Niihau to sink into the ocean. King Moho assured them that it wasn't a big deal, that nobody really hung out there, and their king was kind of an asshole, but 9-Krelblax was pretty sure that Moho was just happy that there was one less island for him to remember.

Also, the wormhole opened a sister wormhole in a galaxy in another dimension. The remains of the Orion's Belt Loosener were sucked through, along with one of the seagulls that had died from consuming it. These were the only two material objects in this galaxy, and they soon began to orbit one another, their gravitational pulls competing to attract microscopic space dust. Trillions of years later, the sandwich and the seagull had formed two massive, life-sustaining planets, who eventually wiped each other out over a religious disagreement over whether the seagull or the sandwich came through the wormhole first. 9-Krelblax and Zzarvon had unknowingly become gods.

And, most importantly, they now had a second roast pig.

The hyperwarp wormhole had encountered one of the duplicate *Stupid Butt's* that Zzarvon had seen when he was fact-finding on the other Hawaiian islands. For a split second, the ship had merged directly on top of the parallel ship, the result being that all life forms within the immediate vicinity of the hyperwarp found themselves standing next to their exact duplicate.

There had been a lecture in the academy about what to do if you encountered a version of yourself from another dimension. Lots of steps to follow to ensure you wouldn't tear apart the weakened fabric of space-time. It was the one lecture that the professor had implored the students to, for the love of all they held dear, please not miss. 9-Krelblax skipped it to watch some upperclassmen get a service bot drunk in the dorm basement, because, honestly, what were the odds?

9-Krelblax had drawn his ray gun and vaporized his parallel self immediately, reality-imploding consequences be damned. He disintegrated the second King Moho before it had a chance to ask the first one for a sip of his daiquiri. The sudden commotion startled Lieutenant Ogrot, and as he instinctively recoiled, one of his tentacles brushed up against his duplicate's side. Occupying the same physical space as a version of yourself from another dimension was evidently the sort of thing that 9-Krelblax's professor had been concerned about and it did not end well for Lieutenant Ogrot. There was a horrible high-pitched screech and a pungent smell of burning ooze as his tentacle fused to his duplicate's side and began to draw the two Larvilkians' bodies into each other. Lieutenant Ogrot briefly locked four terrified eyes with himself before a searing white flash of light erased them both from existence.

9-Krelblax barely even noticed. He was about to live out his ultimate fantasy: He had turned his gun on Zzarvon.

A few hours later, 9-Krelblax's moodcore still glowed an erotically charged shade of turquoise-purple. It had surged the moment before he pulled the trigger to disintegrate the second Zzarvon, and now it was embarrassingly not going away. He had unfolded one of the real Zzarvon's idiotic takeout menus and was holding it over his moodcore in an effort to hide his arousal, but Zzarvon and King Moho seemed to take no notice. Unfazed by the annihilation of their crewmate, they were too busy trying to see if they could tell the difference between the original roast pig and the duplicate one that the wormhole had created.

"I dunno," Zzarvon mumbled through a mouthful of digestive slurry as he wolfed down a chunk of the original. "This one's definitely more succulent, but I feel like the second one has a smokier flavor."

"The duplicate has crispier skin," King Moho said, slicing off a piece of the second pig. "It's more of a Sunday evening pig. Here, try it." He tossed the slice to Zzarvon. Despite their newfound camaraderie, the king was reluctant to actually touch a Larvilkian. He hoped Zzarvon hadn't noticed that he was taking all his meat from the opposite side of the pig.

Zzarvon shoved the slice into his orifice and contemplated the texture as it was broken down. "Yeah, I can definitely see where you're coming from about Sunday evening. Much crispier. I think the spice rub is different too."

"They're the exact same pig!" 9-Krelblax shouted. To his relief, his irritation made his moodcore lower in intensity to a semi-aroused, semi-angered state. He crumpled up the takeout menu and tossed it aside. "The second one is the same pig, just from another timeline. It wasn't prepared with a different blend of spices, and it's certainly not any crispier!"

"With all due respect, how would you know, sir?" Zzarvon asked, pulling off another hunk of original pig. "You haven't tried any of the extra crispy."

It was true. After his trigger-happy disposal of the sentient duplicates, 9-Krelblax had refrained from vaporizing the second pig. He saw no harm since it wasn't alive. But there had seemed something very wrong to him about eating the same animal twice. He had kept an eye on King Moho and Zzarvon as they devoured it, looking for any signs of upset stomachs or sudden mutations that might cause the universe to implode. There had been no signs of either, and eventually 9-Krelblax helped himself to some loin, though he was careful to stick to the original.

"When you two have a free moment, we should go over our Olympic strategy," 9-Krelblax said, hoping his voice implied that the free moment should occur immediately.

"Original! No, no... doppelganger!" Zzarvon exclaimed. 9-Krelblax glared at his navigator and saw that he had all four of his eyes closed. King Moho had arranged morsels of pig in front of Zzarvon in a blind taste test.

"You were right the first time!" King Moho said, tossing a piece up in the air and catching it in his mouth.

"Damn!" Zzarvon said, popping his eyes open. "Are you sure? It was so crispy! Hey, I just had an idea: we open a restaurant where we sell hyperwarp-cloned pigs. We could call it *Porkelgangers*. Imagine how much we could save on food costs!" King Moho pointed a rib bone at Zzarvon and nodded emphatically.

"Will you stop eating the pig and its unholy double from another dimension and get over here!" 9-Krelblax shouted, brandishing his ray gun. Zzarvon and King Moho jumped. The memory of how quickly 9-Krelblax had evaporated their duplicates was still fresh in their minds. Their unspoken shared assumption was that 9-Krelblax had probably only been about 60 percent certain he was disintegrating the duplicates and not the originals. Human and Larvilkian dropped their hunks of pork to the serving trays and slunk over to the commander.

"Zzarvon, because of your navigational incompetence, we will be arriving in HAWAII twenty Earth hours later than should have been necessary. We will use this abundance of spare time to prepare our competition strategy so that our domination of the Earth athletes will be efficient and thorough. Call up a holoscreen with Olympic information so that King Moho can provide us with insider tips!"

Zzarvon initiated a holoscreen from his communicator while King Moho licked residual grease off his fingers. "I'm not sure how much help I'm going to be on this one, Niner," he informed 9-Krelblax. "I was never really that into sports you can't play with a drink in your hand."

"Nonsense!" 9-Krelblax said. "Your finest athletes are celebrated as planetwide heroes! Why, every Earthling child must harbor a fantasy of one day competing in the... Zzarvon, what is this event?" 9-Krelblax waved a tentacle at the holoscreen, which was full of videos showing equestrians, fencers, and swimmers.

"The modern pentathlon, sir," Zzarvon said.

"The modern pentathlon!" 9-Krelblax said in admiration, tapping two tentacles together as he eyed the holoscreen. "Mastery of water, beast, and sabre! Songs must be sung of their epic feats! Of course, they've never had to face off against a Larvilkian!" 9-Krelblax winked his first and third eyes at Zzarvon.

"Modern pentathlon?" King Moho said. "What the hell is that? I've never even heard of the *regular* pentathlon." King Moho gawked at the holoscreen in disbelieving horror. "They were just jumping over fences on a horse, why are they shooting guns now? And now they're swimming? Are you sure this is a real Olympic event? It looks like some kids messing around at summer camp!"

9-Krelblax turned his two most irritated-looking eyes toward Zzarvon. "It's real!" the navigator protested. "It's been historically dominated by the Swedes." 9-Krelblax added a third irritated eye to the mix. "Look, there's like a hundred more events," Zzarvon assured him. "We'll find one that is more popular."

Zzarvon waved a tentacle and the modern pentathlon footage disappeared. He made a scrolling motion with another tentacle until he found something more promising. He poked the air and the holoscreen filled with footage of men and women in shorts and tank tops, running, jumping, and throwing things.

"Perhaps the decathlon will be more suited to Larvilkian

domination," Zzarvon suggested. "After all, it's got twice as many events!"

9-Krelblax studied a scrolling ticker of text at the bottom of the holoscreen. "Every four years the winner of the decathlon is proclaimed the World's Greatest Athlete!" he read. He smiled and glanced at the king. "Gaze upon your legendary heroes of sport, King Moho. Their accomplishments inspire and unite an entire planet. Whose downfall will demoralize you the most when a Larvilkian trounces their records?"

King Moho leaned in to look at the holoscreen. "The world's greatest athlete? Really? I don't see anybody dunking…" He looked confused for a minute, then his face brightened. "Oh, it's that guy!"

9-Krelblax knowingly prodded Zzarvon in the side. "Your childhood idol, I assume? Did you have his poster on your wall? Pretend to be him on the school playground?"

"I think he was on this reality show where you got five bucks for every worm you ate. He lost because he puked on that chick from *Real Housewives*. He must have really needed the money. Oh, I recognize that guy, too. He got shot in the groin behind a strip club a few years ago."

Zzarvon quickly waved the decathlon footage off the screen before 9-Krelblax could hurt him. "Are there any Olympic athletes that you've actually heard of?" 9-Krelblax said, half asking King Moho, half directing it as a threat to Zzarvon.

"Hell yeah," King Moho said. "Those gymnast girls? Simone Biles, Kerri Strug, that smirking chick. They kick ass for the USA every year!" The king beamed with pride.

"Zzarvon! Gymnastics!" 9-Krelblax barked. Zzarvon flailed some tentacles and the holoscreen displayed a shot of a teenage girl standing at the edge of a gym mat.

"This pixie is your champion?" 9-Krelblax howled. "How tiny and delicate! What is her event, scampering between rows of Earth flowers? Why, I'd be afraid I might—" 9-Krelblax stopped midsentence as the gymnast on the holoscreen took a deep breath, then sprinted forward and launched into a series of handsprings and cartwheels capped off by a jaw-dropping double flip with a corkscrew twist. She flawlessly stuck the landing, saluted the judges, and ran off the floor to the rapturous applause of thousands of people as casually as if she'd just stepped outside to check her mailbox.

"Let's maybe avoid competing in the gymnastics events," 9-Krelblax said. He sounded terrified. Zzarvon's moodcore had gone white; he gulped and nodded in agreement.

"Holoscreen off!" 9-Krelblax shouted. He turned his back as it blipped out of sight and oozed over to the table where the roast pigs sat. He picked up a hunk of pork from the porkelganger and fiddled with it absentmindedly. "Dominating all three hundred events was admittedly an ambitious goal," he mused. "It's likely that the Earthlings would have pleaded for mercy after we crushed them in two hundred events anyway."

"Very true, sir," Zzarvon replied. "Nobody would consider it a failure if you only win two hundred gold medals. The average Earthling only wins .000000857 of them in their lifetime."

"That's very true," 9-Krelblax said. "But we still must practice! We can't afford to be rusty! I will not settle for simple victory when domination is within our grasp. King Moho! You will serve as my head trainer!"

King Moho shrugged. "Whatever you say, Niner. I haven't done much working out over the past few years, but I've shouted my fair share of encouragement from a beach blanket." Moho grabbed an empty garbage bag and nonchalantly rolled it out on the commander's chair as a protective sanitary layer. He plopped into the chair, wheeled it over to the pigs, and grabbed a slab of original belly. "If you wanna turn people's heads, there's no better place to start than the hundred-meter dash. They call the winner of that one the 'Fastest Man Alive.' It's a big deal, he almost always gets to endorse a chain of sandwich shops or something."

"I've chased my share of Piltrixians through the streets," 9-Krelblax said. "I wouldn't deem that a fair test of my abilities, though. I found their cowardice exhausting and usually ended up letting them escape in disgust."

"Well, this should be a piece of cake, then," King Moho said.

"What's the 'world' record?" 9-Krelblax asked. He snickered at the quaintness of the term.

Zzarvon pulled out his communicator, and tapped a few buttons. "9.58 seconds," he announced.

"Any longer than two thirds of that will be most shameful," 9-Krelblax said. "Mark off the course."

Zzarvon tapped the communicator again. In front of 9-Krelblax the floor of the *Stupid Butt* began to glow, illuminating a hundred-meter long path.

"Zzarvon, does that communication dealie keep time?" King Moho asked.

Zzarvon smiled and nodded as he patted his communicator.

"OK, Niner. We're aiming for six point four seconds," King Moho instructed.

9-Krelblax nodded, bent at his closest approximation of a waist, and touched several tentacles to the ground in a sprinter's starting position.

King Moho counted him off. "On your mark, get set, go!"

9-Krelblax thrust-oozed forward as fast as he could. His tentacles pumped forward, his lungs burned, and his moodcore shone a brilliant, victorious yellow. The last time 9-Krelblax had run at anything close to a full sprint was after he'd crashed the *Hell Comet* into the moon during its inaugural flight and tried to flee the scene. This didn't work, because the scene was the moon and you can't just flee on foot from the moon. The Larvilkian commander began to worry that he might be a little out of shape. But just as started to think that he could go no further, all four of his eyes snapped into tunnel vision. His moodcore glowed a bright, resilient orange. He was in the zone.

Then Zzarvon yelled, "Stop!" and 9-Krelblax collapsed to the ground, panting in exhaustion. It felt like someone had taken sandpaper to his lungs and his eyes welled with tears, but he told himself that it was all the price of excellence. He rolled over onto his back, and through deep, gasping breaths managed to croak out the words "How... did I... do?"

"Eight point seven," the answer came back from Zzarvon.

9-Krelblax exhaled in triumph and his moodcore glowed a deeply satisfied green. Though it wasn't the utter annihilation of the world record he'd hoped for, his first effort had still been greater than any Earth human had ever achieved. He envisioned choking back tears as he was awarded the Olympic gold medal, then choking back more tears as he presented his father with the medal back on Larvilkian-B. He imagined his father looking down at the medal, then back at his son, and it was becoming clear that he too was making an effort to choke back tears. 9-Krelblax had to choke back tears thinking about all these people choking back tears. Winning this race was going to be the greatest moment of his life.

"Eight point seven *meters* in twenty-four *seconds*," Zzarvon continued. "You made it almost one tenth of the way, sir. Not bad for your first attempt."

9-Krelblax's overworked moodcore gave off another stabbing pain as it shifted to a mortified pink. He raised two antennae and glanced around the room. The vast majority of the illuminated length of track still stretched forward. Behind him, there was the sad little stretch that he had actually covered. The lighting was dimmed by the trail of slime he had left behind.

"So I didn't get the world record?" 9-Krelblax said, holding out hope that he was still delirious from achieving an unprecedented feat of athleticism.

"You were on pace for nearly a five-minute hundred-meters!" Zzarvon crowed. "They run *miles* in way less time! The distance you managed to 'run' isn't even the world record in the long jump!"

"The long jump!" King Moho guffawed as he ripped a hunk of pork off the porkelganger. "They could use you to mark the spot! You gotta be careful though, I've heard that dogs sometimes see that sand pit and decide to do their business in there."

9-Krelblax lay on the ground trying not to hyperventilate. His seething rage was tempered only by the fact that he felt he might suffer a massive moodcore rupture if he even slightly exerted himself by berating Zzarvon and the King of Maui. He heard his commander's chair sliding across the deck of the *Stupid Butt* and was dismayed when King Moho's shirtless torso suddenly loomed over him.

The king smiled before biting off a hunk of pork from the bone he was gnawing on. "I dunno, Niner," he said. "Sprinting may not be your event! I don't know what they are or why you're chasing them through the streets, but I think I'd put my money on the Piltrixians!"

9-Krelblax raised his three strongest tentacles in a feeble attempt to issue King Moho a slap, but the effort exhausted him and the appendages fell back to the ground.

"Don't worry, sir!" Zzarvon chimed in. "I bet you could still dominate the four non-running events in the modern pentathlon!"

9-Krelblax was slapping Zzarvon with all three of his formerly exhausted tentacles before he realized he had regained his strength. The navigator yelped as he shielded his antennae from the blows.

"Whoa! Float like a butterfly, sting like a bee, Niner!" King Moho cheered from his chair and shadowboxed in an imitation of 9-Krelblax. "You've got some fists of fury there! Maybe Olympic boxing is the way to go?"

9-Krelblax stopped his slapping barrage at these encouraging words. Zzarvon opened a hopeful eye halfway. 9-Krelblax nodded at him. "Call it up," he said, trying and failing to disguise his heavy breathing.

Zzarvon put a few steps in between himself and his assailant while he pulled out his communicator and turned the holoscreen back on. 9-Krelblax's eyes immediately went wide as he stared in horror at the footage.

"Son of a Piltrixian!" he blurted. "Look at that footwork, at that upper body strength! The steely focus! They're wrecking machines, raw intimidation personified! They'd tear me tentacle from tentacle!"

"Whoops! Still footage of the female gymnasts!" Zzarvon apologized, tapping on his communicator. "That was a four-foot-nine Chinese girl."

"Keep her away from me!" 9-Krelblax whimpered.

"Maybe it's best if you don't show him the real boxers," King Moho cautioned Zzarvon. "They're substantially more intimidating than eighty-pound teens. A medalist from the last Olympics just got arrested for beating up one of his pet bears."

"Take all my universal currency!" 9-Krelblax wailed as he blindly thrust a tentacle full of coins over his shoulder. Zzarvon quietly shut the holoscreen down again and oozed over to 9-Krelblax. He slung a comforting tentacle around his leader and patted him on the back. Eventually 9-Krelblax stopped quivering and glanced around the command bridge. Seeing no more intimidating balance-beam specialists looming, he straightened up and assumed a more traditional captain's demeanor.

"Ahem! Well, high-level athletic training is known to be stressful," 9-Krelblax informed everyone. "Some even say the mental toll overshadows the physical. In fact, I've heard that complete psychological breakdowns like that are healthy. They show that you're exerting yourself, not slacking off and phoning in your workouts."

"You've been training for five minutes, sir. Want to take a break?" Zzarvon asked.

"Oh God, yes!" 9-Krelblax gasped. In between bouts of rage and terror, he'd forgotten how tired he was. He walked over to his commander's chair and motioned for King Moho to get up, which the king did reluctantly after grabbing an entire shank of pork.

9-Krelblax was about to collapse into his chair when there was a whoosh as the hallway doors slid open. Both Larvilkians and the King of Maui turned toward them just in time to see two Technician Timblorxes burst through onto the bridge.

"I'm not sure what happened!" the Timblorx on the left exclaimed.

"I was in the bathroom when all of a sudden this duplicate blipped into existence!" said the one on the right.

"Were you messing with any settings on the hyperwarp?" both technicians said in unison with more than a hint of accusation in their tones.

With the speed of a Wild West trick-shot artist, 9-Krelblax drew his ray gun, pointed it towards the Timblorxes, and pulled the trigger. There was no erotic pulsing of his moodcore this time, just a brilliant green blast of pure electrified plasma. The Timblorx on the right emitted a brief, high-pitched whine that didn't even have time to build to a proper scream before he was rendered into dust. All that was left behind was a piece of paper, which fluttered to the floor.

"What the hell is that?" 9-Krelblax asked, pointing to the floor with his ray gun.

The remaining Timblorx bent over to pick it up. "Uh, it's a takeout menu, sir. He must have been reading it on the toilet. I mean, *I*! *I* must have been reading it on the toilet!" The technician fiddled with the menu and chuckled, his eyes darting around the room.

"I'm the real Tamblirx," he added, the mispronunciation reassuring nobody. "Not the duplicate."

9-Krelblax noticed that the technician's second and fourth eyes now appeared to be permanently crossed and his first eye stalk was drooping. It gave him a very unsettling, unpredictable look. The commander glanced at Zzarvon, then King Moho to see if they had noticed. Both of them shrugged and made "What are you gonna do?" faces. 9-Krelblax sighed and holstered his ray gun. "Whatever," he muttered. "It's not like he could do any worse of a job. Get back to work Tamblirx."

"The technician's name was Timblorx," Zzarvon corrected.

"The technician's name *is* Tamblirx!" the technician re-corrected, kind of. "I'm right here, just as I always have been!" His two crossed eyes rolled back and forth like googly eyes on a hand puppet. Nobody said anything, perhaps fearing the duplicate was about to lunge for their brains or moodcores.

"So had the plan been that we were about to order delivery?" Tamblirx asked. "Is that why he was reading this in the bathroom? Because if we are, I'd like one of the Orion's—"

"Go fix something, you impudent clone of a buffoon!" 9-Krelblax shouted. Tamblirx dropped the menu, saluted an empty spot five feet to the right of 9-Krelblax, and oozed back through the doors just before they whooshed closed.

9-Krelblax brushed Moho's garbage bag away and slumped into his commander's chair. He pulled out his communicator and glanced at the clock on the screen. Nineteen and a half hours to go. He sighed, stowed the communicator and looked up at Zzarvon.

"What event is next on the list, Zzarvon?" he asked. The navigator's face lit up as he powered the holoscreen back on.

"Well, sir, this one looks like a lot of fun. Now it's called handball, but I don't see your lack of hands as being *too* big of a disadvantage. Wait, no, actually that's a *severe* disadvantage. Yeah, that one's going to be unplayable. Hang on!"

9-Krelblax tuned out Zzarvon's sputtered ramblings as the navigator scrolled through footage on the holoscreen. He massaged the Larvilkian equivalent of his temples with two tentacles while reaching another out toward the pigs. He pulled off a large chunk of pork, shoved it into his orifice, and was halfway through digesting it before he realized he'd accidentally grabbed it from the porkelganger.

It was definitely crispier.

fourteen

Kara woke up feeling so relaxed that she assumed she must still be dreaming. There was no way she should be this comfortable after spending a night in her grandfather's old hammock. Her back felt as if she'd had a massage, and her mind, typically a groggy mess when she was forced to wake up for school or track meets, was free of cobwebs. Kara squeezed her eyes shut tight and smiled a contented smile as she stretched her whole body like a cat. In the light of a brand new day, her grandfather's crazy scheme actually seemed like it might be kind of fun. Hell, it could even be an adventure! She vowed to be more optimistic going forward, to not give her grandfather such a hard time, and to happily participate in whatever the day had in store. But that could certainly wait five more minutes, Kara thought to herself as she yawned and settled back in for a quick snooze.

"That must be the hooker," she heard someone whisper.

Kara's eyes shot open and her entire body tensed, immediately undoing whatever positive effects the night's sleep had had on her physical and mental well-being. Her only hope for salvation was that whoever had spoken was talking about someone else. Hopefully Henry's wife.

"She looks kinda young," a second voice whispered back.

It could still be Henry's wife, Kara thought. *Maybe these guys are like a hundred years old.*

"How the hell are you supposed to do it in a hammock?" the second voice continued.

Kara toppled out of said hammock, immediately confirming the worries of the second voice and intriguing the owner of the first.

"I'll take that as a personal challenge!" crowed a stranger in a tank top and backwards baseball cap. Kara figured he was maybe five or six years older than her, probably in college. He pushed his friend to the side and strode forward while pulling some cash out of his pocket. "How much does forty get me?"

"I'm not a hooker," Kara informed him, pushing herself up into a sitting position. She shot a hopeful glance through the doorway of the governor's mansion for any sign of her grandfather.

"Ah, I see how this works," the college kid said with a wink. He fished another bill out of his pocket. "Sixty it is."

"I'm fifteen!" Kara said, hoping that would end the discussion.

"Oh man…" The college kid's face fell. "Does that cost extra? Because I'll be honest, I didn't know we were going to have to change our money when we got here and sixty HAWAIl dollars is all I have on me."

"Get the hell out of my room!" Kara yelled at the strangers. "I haven't even brushed my teeth yet!"

"Whoa!" the college dude in the backwards cap said, taking a few steps back. "I thought for half a hundo there'd at least be some hygienic standards. I dunno, Mac, maybe we should go put this money towards some weed instead." Mac nodded and the two of them hustled out the door. Kara glared at them while simultaneously marveling that "morning breath" had been a bigger dealbreaker than "being three years underage."

Her back now felt as stiff as one would expect after a night in a hammock and one of her knees was sore from the tumble onto the ground. *No big deal*, Kara thought as she limped out the doorway and onto the exposed platform of HAWAIl. *All I have to do today is win an Olympic gold medal.* Kara tried not to think about her other responsibility. The one that came before that.

The Olympic opening ceremony had long ago ceased to have anything to do with the athletic competition it preceded. It had morphed into an exercise in one-upmanship and gross excess on par with a Hollywood blockbuster, or perhaps the nightmares of a military dictator after he'd committed an atrocity that was particularly weighing on his mind. Before the last Winter Olympics, a rumor had circulated around Kara's middle school that in order to top the sheer scale and spectacle of the previous Olympics' ceremony, the host country was actually going to throw someone into the mouth of an erupting volcano. It turned out not to be true. Instead there was just some shit with people on trampolines.

If Cornelius had anything like that planned, there was no evidence of it on the rusty metal surface of HAWAll. The platform remained unadorned aside from some old parking cones and a tarp that had appeared in the middle of the night. There was a lump underneath the tarp that was suspiciously marathoner shaped. Kara wondered if maybe her grandfather had laid it down to kindly provide the Warlander with a rudimentary blanket, but she knew in her heart the guy had probably just been in the way.

President for Life Makepeace sat near the southern edge of HAWAll. He was holding the pool skimmer backwards and had tied a length of string to its end in order to use it as a fishing pole. He looked content, despite the fact that his activity had roused the ire of an increasing number of seagulls who swarmed around the fishing line, trying to figure out if it was something they could kill.

Cornelius stood in the center of the country having a visibly heated exchange with the two college students who had mistaken Kara for a prostitute. It occurred to Kara that they must have been the "dignitaries" that Makepeace had picked up on his second speedboat run. Middle fingers were being waved around, crotches were being grabbed, middle fingers were being pointed at crotches. Kara noted with equal parts dismay and intrigue that her grandfather was holding a megaphone.

On the eastern side of the platform, Henry and his wife sat huddled together, trying to warm themselves in the early morning sun. Even from a distance, Kara could tell that they were shivering. She ducked back into the governor's mansion, grabbed a bottle of water and a sleeve of saltines and walked over to them. She kept her distance from her grandfather, but was able to make out a few shouted phrases. "This is bullshit!" "We're going to sue!" "My dad's kind of a lawyer!" "Technically not false advertising!" "Fine, I'll buy some damn saltines!"

Kara knelt down next to Henry and rested a hand on his shoulder as she offered the water and crackers. Henry's wife snatched the sleeve of crackers out of her hand and tore it open, then began greedily shoving handfuls of crackers into her mouth like a chipmunk hoarding seeds. Henry accepted the bottle of water and looked up at Kara with dazed, unfocused eyes.

"Pins?" he asked in a dazed, faraway voice. The unfortunate man's face was somehow smeared with black soot and some unruly grey stubble had sprouted up overnight. "Do you want to trade pins? I have a rare Hodori tiger one from Seoul. The embossing on the javelin he's throwing is the wrong color. Only one hundred were produced." To Kara he sounded like somebody in a grainy videotape who was informing his parents that his kidnappers were now his real family.

"That sounds very interesting, sir," Kara humored him. "Were you two up all night? Why don't you drink some of that water, then try to take a quick nap. I don't think you're going to be stuck here much longer."

"Pin trading is a big pastime in the Olympic Village," Henry intoned as if he hadn't heard her. Meanwhile, his wife had shoved so many saltines into her mouth that they had absorbed all the saliva and formed a thick cracker paste. She began to cough and Kara worried that she might choke. She pulled the bottle of water away from Henry with very little resistance, and tried to push it into his wife's hands while swapping out the crackers.

Henry's wife made some sort of snarling noise that was muffled by the dozen or so crackers she'd shoved into her mouth and pulled away from Kara. Little bits of cracker paste flew out of her mouth. Some landed on the platform, some stuck to the side of Henry's face, and a few flew out over the side of HAWAll where they were snatched up by a cloud of seagulls that seemed to materialize out of nowhere. There were far more gulls than the few crumbs of expelled saltines warranted, and the birds who were unable to grab any food made agitated noises.

Kara set the bottle of water down next to Henry's wife and slowly backed away from the cacophony. She wasn't sure what she would do if the gulls set upon the helpless couple. She thought there was a decent chance that in three seconds they'd be reduced to skeletons like a B-movie explorer encountering a school of piranhas. Kara would be helpless. That wouldn't be enough time to even unlock her phone, let alone take a video.

Once she'd put some distance between herself and the birds, Kara turned and walked over to her grandfather and the two college kids. The guy in the backwards cap was still arguing with Cornelius while the other one angrily munched on an expensive packet of saltines. Her grandfather looked relieved when he noticed Kara approaching. He took a step toward her and slung a proud arm around her shoulders.

"Allow me to interrupt you, gentlemen," Cornelius said. "This is my granddaughter, Kara. She'll be pulling double duty today, competing for the United States in track and field and also serving as the Olympic mascot!" Cornelius beamed, but the two college kids didn't look impressed.

"We've met," Kara informed her grandfather. "They thought I was a hooker."

"We only thought that because this con man put up fliers all around our campus advertising how many hookers there were in his country!" yelled Backwards Cap.

"For the sake of accuracy," Cornelius said, holding up a correcting finger. "I didn't put those fliers up myself. I paid students to do it."

"We were those students!" Backwards Cap shouted. "We put up hundreds of fliers! And you 'paid' us in credits that we could use for hookers!"

"And if any show up, you'll be able to conduct that transaction without fear of violating any laws," Cornelius said. He thought for a moment, then added, "Provided your credits haven't expired."

"What's this about an Olympic mascot?" the one named Mac asked.

"We're hosting the Olympics here," Cornelius informed him.

"Kind of," Kara added. "Wait, you didn't know that?" She was flabbergasted. Mac shook his head. "You came all the way out here for the prostitutes?"

"And all the 'legal drugs,'" Backwards Cap said, his voice thick with sarcasm.

"Technically not false advertising," Cornelius responded automatically.

"If you weren't misled into coming here for the Olympics, it probably would have been cheaper and easier to just go to Nevada," Kara informed him.

"Our Nevada hooker credits expired!" Backwards Cap wailed. "The week before spring break!"

"Maybe you should get a job that pays you in something other than hooker credits?" Kara suggested, trying to sound polite.

"Show me a hooker-flier company that pays in anything else!" Backwards Cap retorted.

Kara thought that there might be a few misconceptions these guys held about the US economic system that she could theoretically clear up pretty quickly, but she'd had just about enough hooker talk for the day and decided to change the subject. She tapped the megaphone in Cornelius's hand while the two fuming college kids shuffled off. "Looks like you're ready to direct the opening ceremony, Grandpa!" Kara said.

"What, this?" Cornelius looked down at the megaphone and shook his head. "No, this is just for crowd control. In case there's a riot."

"That's a possibility?" Kara asked, looking around at the people gathered on HAWAIl. It hadn't occurred to her until right now that they were in fact outnumbered by people who were all quite unhappy. Things could get ugly if everyone collectively decided to get violent. "You really think that you might have to subdue the riot through the megaphone?"

"*Subdue* the riot?" Cornelius asked, looking as if she'd just suggested he take a shower in order to dry off. "No, no, this is to *direct* a riot, to seize control of the masses! Everyone listens to the guy with the loudest voice. With one of these puppies you can control a riot like a conductor with a baton. Just with more looting TVs from pawn shops and less telling the goddamn piccolos to *rallentando*." For a moment Cornelius stared into the distance and flexed his grip on the megaphone, apparently seething from what Kara hoped was an ancient grudge. Then he snapped back to the moment. "I just figured the Olympics are gonna wrap up in like twenty, thirty minutes, and then if everyone is in the mood we could possibly have a little riot? I dunno, maybe hop in the boat and take over another micronation with less legitimate claims of statehood?" He tilted his head toward President for Life Makepeace who was still fishing happily.

Kara ignored the suggestion. "It's really only going to take twenty or thirty minutes?" she asked. "What do you have planned for the ceremony?"

"Can you juggle fire?" Cornelius asked. Kara shook her head no. "Remember that the costume is made of dasbestos," Cornelius reminded her. "Fire is the least of your worries when you're wearing it."

"I'm not juggling fire!" Kara informed him.

"Well, then, yes, it's going to clock in closer to the twenty-minute side of things," Cornelius said, not bothering to mask his disappointment. "You walk out dressed as Jeff to get things started. Then you go and take that off and we do the parade of nations. Meaning you walk out again not in costume and we play the Star Spangled Banner. Then we'll introduce the hundred-meter dash event, you compete and win, we do a quick medal ceremony, badda bing, badda boom, everyone goes home happy. Unless people are up for an after party?" He waggled the megaphone suggestively.

"No leading riots! And no taking over other micronations until you've got your first one up and running," Kara insisted. "*Legitimately.*"

"Awww," Cornelius muttered. He looked down at his feet and kicked at the rusty surface of his country like a five-year-old.

"Hey!" Kara snapped her fingers until Cornelius looked up at her. "This is no time to sulk! And be careful what you wish for in terms of riots, because I think unless you give them a little bit of razzle dazzle, there's a very strong chance that these people you swindled will decide to throw one of their own!"

Cornelius stuck out his lower lip in a very ungrandfatherly pout, but it appeared she had his attention.

"Everyone here has either been misled, lied to, or thought they were going to die on their journey here," Kara continued. "I bet a couple of them would classify this as a hostage situation. I know this is all about your noble end goal of being a page-one Google result for prescriptionless meds, but just try to look at it from their perspective. They came here to see a show."

"Or to bang hookers," Cornelius corrected.

"Or to… Yeah, okay," Kara said. At least he was listening. "Anyway, just try to make a token effort to impress them. They should be able to go home with one good memory about their time here. Do it as a favor to me."

Cornelius took a deep breath and straightened his posture. He nodded grimly as he glanced around his country and the huddled masses he'd lured there. "You're right, Kara," he said in a resigned tone. "I've been very selfish. Thank you for the pep talk. I think I've got just the thing to send these folks home happy."

Kara smiled.

"Half-off all saltines during the opening ceremony!" Cornelius announced.

Kara stopped smiling. "Why don't you think about it a little longer, Grandpa?" she advised as she started off toward the governor's mansion. "I'm going to go get dressed." She left Cornelius to brainstorm and walked back to the shelter where she had spent the night.

The shopping bag with the Jeff the Jackrabbit costume sat on the floor of the governor's mansion underneath the whiteboard. The loose reptilian eye dangled over the side of the bag and appeared to stare at Kara as she approached it. She told herself that it was just a costume, that physical items becoming possessed by evil essences was only something that happened in the movies. She'd put it on, parade around the platform for a minute or two, just long enough to validate this sham Olympics in the eyes of the certifying board, then take it off before she breathed in too much dasbestos. Or before a hibernating rat bit her foot. Or before she too absorbed the evil essence, was forever bonded with it as one, and the fillings in her teeth started picking up instructions about who to kill.

"Just a costume," Kara said to herself out loud. She stepped forward and reached her hand out to pick up the bag. At that moment, Jeff's dangling blue reptilian eye winked at her.

fifteen

There was a sudden, powerful scent of laboratory chemicals, followed by the immediate sensation that a tiny janitor was power washing her nose with acid from somewhere inside her sinuses. Kara instinctively gasped, which caused her to inhale more of the chemicals, which caused her entire throat to burn, which made her flail around for air until she fell out of the hammock and landed facedown on the floor. And that is how Kara Everglades regained consciousness.

"Jesus!" Cornelius shouted, jumping out of the way as Kara toppled to the ground. "It's alright! They're just smelling salts, they'll wear off in a second. Hey! Relax, dammit!"

The panicky, shouted demands did not have the calming effect that her grandfather intended, and Kara continued to thrash around on her stomach. Eventually Cornelius reached out, grabbed Kara by both shoulders and flipped her over so she was lying on her back.

"Open your eyes!" he commanded. Kara popped her eyes open. They were teary from the smelling salts, but she could make out the blurry form of her grandfather. "You're going to be fine. Just take a slow breath and follow my hand." He started to move his hand back and forth from left to right. Kara did as he said. Her first breath was tentative, but when it didn't burn, she took another, then another, each one deeper than the last until she was breathing relatively normally.

"You fainted," Cornelius informed her. "What happened here?"

"The eye…" Kara panted. "Jeff's eye… It winked at me… Evil essence… Must do bidding… Must kill…"

"What happened *here*, to my whiteboard, I meant," Cornelius said. "Did you erase my contingency plan?"

Kara had thought that her deranged mutterings might get more of a response, but as she lay there, any sinister urges the eye might have implanted proved fleeting, and she was left less with a desire to do evil bidding and more of a general thirstiness.

"Months of strategy down the drain," Cornelius sighed.

"The eye winked at me!" Kara repeated.

"Uh, yeah!" Cornelius said. "It's supposed to. It's like one of those stickers that looks like it's moving when you tilt it back and forth. Or a baseball card where it looks like the guy is swinging the bat? The school didn't have much in the budget for mascot repairs so it was pretty much on us to do them ourselves. When the original eye needed fixing, I thought it might be something that the kids were into. There was some general panic and a few kids that didn't speak for a week or two after they saw it, but nobody fainted, Kara."

Kara blinked a few more times, but her vision remained oddly clouded. "I think I hit my head when I fainted," she said, starting to panic again. "I can't see clearly."

"Don't worry," Cornelius said. "That's just the mesh. It takes a little getting used to."

It took a moment before the word "mesh" registered with Kara, but when it finally did, the effect made the smelling salts seem like a scented candle at an overpriced home-decor store. Her entire body tensed the way it did when she was anticipating a dentist's drill. "Mesh? What do you mean mesh?" she asked, even though deep down she already knew the answer. "I'm in it, aren't I?" It came out as a hoarse whisper.

Kara shifted her eyes' focus and suddenly it was clear to her that there was a mesh screen between her and the outside world. She raised her right hand up in front of her field of vision, but all she saw was the matted fur of a mascot paw. A scream died in her throat. Then she had the grim realization that it wasn't the first thing to die inside the costume and she let loose for real.

"Yeah, I came in to see what was taking you so long and you were just lying here on the floor," Cornelius said, as casually as if he were describing finding a dime on the ground. "I figured that since you were already limp, it'd save us both some hassle if I just wedged you into the Jeff costume while you were out cold."

"Oh God, oh God, oh God!" Kara scrambled to her feet and began patting her costumed body, all the way up to her bulbous mascot head. With a layer of the Jeff costume over her hands and another layer covering the rest of her body, the tactile feedback was an odd, disassociated sensation. She was touching herself, but not really. "It feels like I'm stuck inside a dead body!" she cried. "I'm buried alive in a furry coffin!"

"Now that's hardly a fair comparison," Cornelius said. He appeared poised to continue defending the costume, but just then Kara emitted a high pitched shriek and started hopping up and down.

"I think something bit my foot!" she yelped.

"Dammit, now that's impossib—" Cornelius stopped midsentence. "Wait, left foot or right foot?"

"Left!"

"Nope!" Cornelius shook his head. "Impossible. I dangled a saltine over both leg chutes before I suited you up. Three varmints came charging out of the right one, but there wasn't a peep from the left leg. There was a weak sort of wheeze, but no peeps. But anything that wasn't strong enough to emerge and seize the cracker definitely wasn't in any sort of shape to take on an intruder like your foot. No, you probably just squashed it and maybe jabbed your foot on a bone that poked through its hide."

Kara, not comforted by this reassurance, squirmed around, trying to find a zipper or a seam to free herself from the costume. Cornelius watched her shimmy around for a little while, a large grin slowly inching its way onto his face. After a little while longer, he clapped his hands and announced, "Look at those antics! That capering! Kara, you're a natural!"

Kara froze. If she positioned herself just so, the only points of contact she had with the costume were where the head balanced on her shoulders. Any time she moved even slightly, the combination of sharp, cold chicken wire and the warm, scratchy fiberglass-like material that she guessed was dasbestos scraped against her skin.

"Don't stop now!" Cornelius said. "You were doing great! That was pretty much every move in a mascot's repertoire right there. Tripping on the big feet while you're jumping around is where most rookies hit the wall, but you're like a ballet dancer! Just learn a few advanced routines like 'pie in the manager's face' or 'cut the brakes on the other team's bus during halftime' and you could really go places in the mascot world!"

Kara ignored the compliments and looked down at her feet. Jeff's hideous yellow toenails—talons, really—stared back at her. She wiggled them and was gripped by the sudden knowledge that the toenails were fashioned out of human bones. She couldn't prove it, and her grandfather would never admit it, but deep down, she knew it was true.

"Those toenails are fashioned out of human bones, you know," Cornelius said. "Oh, don't look at me like that. It was a fellow mascot who wanted his remains preserved in a costume so he could go on entertaining even after he died."

"How'd you know what I was looking at you like?" Kara asked. Her voice echoed back at her from the spacious interior of Jeff's head.

"You learn," Cornelius said with a wink. "Now come on, we've got an opening ceremony to throw. And we're already late because you passed out. I'm glad I had these smelling salts in my desk, we can't afford to lose any more time if we want to—" Cornelius stopped short. Kara could see that he was examining something he held in his hand. "Huh. 'To operate, remove from packaging *and crack*.' You know what? I never even activated this thing!" Cornelius threw back his head and laughed.

"So that burning, chemically, medicinal smell that woke me up is just what the inside of the costume naturally smells like?" Kara asked, suddenly panicked again.

"I don't recall it having a particularly objectionable odor," Cornelius said. "Then again, those years are a bit hazy. The years immediately following it too. But the years leading up to when I stepped into that costume are as clear as day, and you'd think that if 'medicinal smell' was one of the many reasons those moms lobbied Congress to ban dasbestos, it'd be something I'd remember. Frankly, it seems like small potatoes compared to everything else that was on that list. Now scoot!"

Cornelius gestured toward the door, and Kara, thinking that the sooner she paraded around HAWAll as Jeff, the sooner she could escape the costume's confines, started to trudge toward it.

"Hey," Cornelius said, stopping Kara's progress with an outstretched palm. "Put some spring in your step, missy. This is the Olympics after all." Then he stepped out the door of the governor's mansion into the fresh HAWAll air.

Kara watched him march onto the rusty platform of his country through the mesh eyeholes of the family mascot costume. If you'd told her right then that her week was about to get monumentally, exponentially stranger than what she'd already experienced, she probably would have fainted again. As it was, she took a deep breath, immediately regretted it, then stepped out onto the main surface of HAWAll.

Well, cavorted really. Kara Everglades/Jeff the Jackrabbit *cavorted* onto the main surface of HAWAll.

sixteen

"Ladies and gentlemen! It is my esteemed pleasure to welcome you, one and all, to the HAWAll Olympics! We are gathered here today to witness the finest athletes in the world. *Citius! Altius! For fuck's sake, people! Pay attention, dammit!*"

So far the Olympics were off to a hell of a start.

Cornelius stopped his welcoming speech and stood in the center of HAWAll, his hands on his hips. Kara bounded up behind him in the Jeff costume. She'd quickly figured out that trying to shift your weight around inside the costume in order to minimize how much of it actually touched your body pretty much approximated the effect of the mascot capering around playfully to an external viewer. But now her grandfather was gesturing for her to dial it down until he got everyone's attention.

Henry and his wife were still huddled together, their bodies on HAWAll but their minds undoubtedly in some sort of happy place they'd constructed as a coping mechanism. President for Life Makepeace had abandoned his fishing endeavors, and was now napping next to his makeshift rod. The marathon runner had wriggled out of the tarp that had covered him earlier and was once again licking the surface of the country for sustenance. The two college hooker-seekers were entirely focused on observing him do it. As Kara watched, the one in the backwards cap, perhaps thinking this was some sort of Warlandian method of getting high, got down on his hands and knees, and also started licking with surprising gusto. Nobody was paying attention to Cornelius.

Cornelius shook his head in disappointment, then cupped a hand to his mouth and shouted "It's a ship! We're saved!" in an affected voice that, to Kara, sounded very much like her grandfather cupping a hand to his mouth trying to affect a voice. But it got the job done.

Henry and his wife leapt to their feet, scanning the horizon for their salvation. The two college students stood at notice as well, perhaps thinking that while this new boat remained in international waters there might be an opportunity to pay money in exchange for sex. President for Life Makepeace sat up, yawned, stretched, and smiled. The marathon runner collapsed in an exhausted heap mid-lick. Five out of six ain't bad, Kara figured.

"Now that I have your attention," Cornelius said. "Let's get this party started! Ladies and gentlemen, here to welcome you to the HAWAll Olympics, is our official mascot... Jeff!"

Cornelius motioned Kara forward, and she skipped past him into the center of the island. She spun in a circle, pointed finger guns at everyone on the island, then started to raise the roof. She hadn't really had time to plan what she was going to do, and assumed that it would come naturally once she was in the moment. However, without music, it seemed very unnatural to just be out there pointing and thrusting. And Kara was quickly realizing that she didn't have many moves left in her repertoire.

Kara wasn't sure if she'd never gone to school dances because she couldn't dance, or if she'd never learned to dance because she'd never attended a school dance. It dawned on her that the answer was that neither of those had ever really been options because she was evidently the kind of person who voluntarily puts on a fifty-year-old mascot costume at least partially made of human remains. The realization terrified her, and she started doing jumping jacks in a frenzied panic.

"What the hell are you doing?" Cornelius hissed out of the corner of his mouth. "Stop exercising! It isn't entertaining!"

But at least one person on the island would beg to differ. Backwards Cap stared at Kara/Jeff with wide, rapt eyes. "Mac!" he whispered. "I think licking the ground really worked! I'm tripping balls!"

"Your tongue is bleeding," Mac replied. But nevertheless he gave the surface of HAWAll a quick downward glance.

"What do you want me to do instead?" Kara asked her grandfather. "What will fulfill the letter of the law in a quick and efficient manner?"

Cornelius pondered this. "Go caper in front of the runner. We need to make sure everyone here is a potential witness." Kara was somewhat comforted by the fact that at this point in her grandfather's scheme they were determined to *gain* witnesses instead of *eliminate* them. She gave an A-OK from inside her paw and pranced off toward the marathoner.

The two college kids saw her coming and took a few steps back, leaving the sickly marathon runner alone on his back. Kara came to a stop near his feet, then leaned over him and waved. Then she waved a little longer. Finally, she reached out with one of her feet and scraped Jeff's human-bone foot talons across the surface of HAWAll. It produced an ungodly sound, and Kara felt the hair on her arms stand on end. Then she realized that it wasn't actually her hair that was standing on end, but rather the fur of the mascot costume. She didn't have time to start shrieking in terror at the apparent symbiotic bond she was developing with the Jeff suit because right then the marathon runner's eyes flew open and he started shrieking in terror himself.

The man's cries were unintelligible but his actions were less ambiguous. With ninja-like reflexes, he propped himself onto his hands and feet and crabwalked about ten feet away from Kara. Without taking his eyes off her or stopping screaming, he vaulted to his feet and sprinted to the farthest edge of HAWAll. Kara was worried that the hysterical distance runner might actually run over the edge, look down, then wave bye-bye to everyone like a cartoon character, but he apparently exhausted everything in his tank just before he reached the end of solid land and collapsed in a slightly differently aligned heap than he had been laying in before.

Kara shrugged. *Well, he's certainly aware of the mascot,* she thought as she headed back to her grandfather. As she made her way over, President for Life Makepeace approached from the other end of the country.

"A thousand pardons I beg of you, fellow president!" Makepeace boomed to Cornelius, sporting a bright grin. "I apologize for my countryman. Though he is a tremendous athlete, strong as ox, he has a tremendous fear of this type of animal." He gestured at Kara, who came to a stop next to them and stood there with her hands on her hips. She was done capering.

"Well," Cornelius said, throwing a friendly arm around Makepeace. "That's understandable. You forget that to some people, the jackra—"

"Yes, terrible fear of hippo!" Makepeace continued.

"Dammit," Cornelius muttered.

"I told you!" Kara exclaimed, though the costume muffled her shout. Cornelius dropped his arm from Makepeace's shoulder and quickly identified a nearby patch of rust that needed his attention.

"Ever since hippo kill his brother, he very scared of them!" Makepeace continued, shaking his head at the somber memory.

"That's terrible," Kara tried to articulate through the mesh. "Are they a big problem in Warland? I've heard that they're actually the most deadly animal in Africa."

"Was not in Warland," Makepeace corrected. "Not in Africa at all. Toronto. The zoo. His brother jumped into hippo exhibit."

"Why would he do that?" Kara asked. She realized the absurdity of hearing such a grim tale from inside a giant bunny costume, but she was intrigued by the sordid details of what would drive a perfectly sane man to undertake such a wanton, rash, self-destructive act.

"Your grandfather dare him to," Makepeace said. Kara did not detect any accusation in Makepeace's tone; rather, he seemed to find the circumstances of his countryman's death rather amusing.

"We were there for International Micronation Conference," Makepeace continued. "Many good networking opportunities.

Runner Goodluck, he so stricken with grief about his brother, he break his diet! I say, 'You have Olympics coming up!' But he would not listen! Start eating ice cream and cheeseburger. Look at how many pounds he pack on!"

Makepeace gestured to the side of HAWAll where Goodluck the distance runner had collapsed. He scanned his index finger back and forth for a while until it came to a stop. Kara squinted at where Makepeace was pointing but couldn't see Goodluck. Then the wind slightly shifted, and seemingly out of nowhere one of the runner's bony arms fluttered up into the air like a birthday streamer.

"He can be hard to see from certain angles," President for Life Makepeace conceded as the wind stopped and the arm fell back to the ground. Even though she knew he was lying there, Kara still had trouble identifying the form of the rail-thin runner.

"I think that Jeff *the Jackrabbit* has more than served his purpose," Cornelius announced as he drifted back over. "Why don't we start the Parade of Nations in five minutes?"

Kara nodded. So far, being in the suit hadn't imbued her with an urge to go on a killing spree, but some part of her *had* started to wonder if maybe killing sprees weren't all that bad of a thing. You know, when you really thought about it? Come on. At least just go on a generic spree, and if it happens to turn into a killing spree, then—

"I'm not going on a killing spree!" Kara announced in defiance to the costume, not realizing she was speaking aloud.

"What did she just say?" President for Life Makepeace asked, sounding alarmed.

"Nothing!" Cornelius snapped. "Go change, Kara, you're holding everyone up." He gave Kara a shove from behind and she stumbled off toward the governor's mansion, talons clacking, trying to ignore the faint, taunting voice buck-buck-buckawking like a chicken that she could have sworn was coming from her fillings.

Kara pried Jeff's head off of her shoulders as soon as she entered the shelter. As she drew her first breath, her eyes began to water and her throat stung, but any thoughts of sprees or revenge on those who had wronged her immediately disappeared. Kara realized that even just fifteen minutes of breathing inside the dasbestos prison was enough to make the healthy fresh air of HAWAll seem harsh and toxic, and she threw the head to the ground in disgust. It rolled to a corner, the reptilian eye sticker slowly winking shut as it came to a stop.

She hastily climbed out of the costume, and kicked it into the corner next to the head. Right now, she wanted access to one of the body-wash stations they had in Jefferson's science classrooms in case of chemical burns, or maybe a hose the size of the one the keepers at the Toronto zoo would have been using to bathe the hippos the morning they discovered Goodluck's dead brother. But she had to settle for one of the bottles of water that Cornelius hadn't yet gouged someone for. She unscrewed the cap, poured it over her head, and immediately regretted doing so. Before, she had been itchy from the dasbestos and warding off madness. Now she was itchy from the dasbestos, warding off madness, and slightly damp.

Kara threw the bottle down next to the Jeff costume and rifled through her gym bag. She pulled out her track uniform, running shoes, and socks. She glanced out the door of the mansion to make sure nobody was watching, then quickly turned her back, took off her pants and slipped into running shorts. She had her shirt halfway off when a bone-chilling thought occurred to her. Her arms still raised over her head, she turned to look at the costume, just in time to see the reptilian eye snap shut again, like a kid at a sleepover when an adult comes in to see if they're still awake.

Great, Kara thought as she turned her back again and hustled out of her shirt and into her running tank top. *The costume's a psychotic evil presence* and *a perv.*

Not letting herself wonder how much Jeff had seen, she laced up her shoes and wandered back out the door onto HAWAll for the second, and hopefully final, time that day.

Cornelius waved her over to him, looking impatient. Kara felt underdressed and a tad chilly, but was just as eager to get the sham Olympics over with. She hustled across HAWAll to her grandfather.

"I'm not going to lie," Cornelius said. "A little part of me is sorry to see you out of the costume, Kara. You did the family proud. But I'm sure there will be more opportunities for you to wear it in the future!"

"If any part of our trip home takes us over the Mariana Trench, I'm dropping that thing in," Kara replied.

"I'll take that as a 'we'll see,'" Cornelius said with a smile. "And our route goes nowhere near there."

Cornelius put two fingers in his mouth and blew a loud whistle. Then he spoke into the megaphone. "Attention, sports fans! The opening ceremony is now continuing. The finest athletes on the planet will now parade in front of the entire world in a spirit of camaraderie, sportsmanship, and international unity." He clicked the megaphone off with a burst of static before reconsidering, flipping it back on, and adding "Viewing is mandatory if you ever want to get home, you jackals!"

This got the attention of the two college students and Henry and his wife. Cornelius turned to Makepeace and gave him a thumbs-up. Then he announced into the megaphone, "Our first contestant, participating in the marathon event, from the soon-to-be-recognized micronation of Warland... Mr. Goodluck!"

At the mention of his name, Goodluck made a feeble effort to roll over and get to his feet. He slowly raised himself to a knee, then wobbled for a few seconds. Kara crossed her fingers that the wind didn't pick up; at that moment, it might have blown him all the way back to England. Eventually the runner tottered to his feet, and raised a shaky hand as a greeting. The spectators gave him a tepid round of applause, even though Kara could tell that at least half the people on the island were resisting the urge to shout, "Look out for that hippo!"

Makepeace sidled up to Cornelius and whispered, "He need to start event now. Need to keep momentum going. I don't know if he can get up again today."

Cornelius nodded, then raised the megaphone. "By my estimate, the marathon distance equals six hundred and forty-seven laps around the circumference of HAWAII. On your mark, get set, go!"

At the go signal, Goodluck became a different person. The tentative look of someone who might be carried off by the wind like a plastic bag in a pretentious film was replaced by the steel-eyed confidence of a veteran competitor who was fairly certain there weren't any hippos in the immediate vicinity. He breathed deeply, pumped his arms, and launched into a loping, fluid gait around the edge of the platform.

"Looking good!" Cornelius shouted. "Attaboy! You can do it! OH GOD, DON'T STEP THERE!"

Goodluck fortunately was able to adjust his footfall on the fly and narrowly missed stepping into a part of the country that was actually just a rusty hole.

"Should we put up a warning sign or tape that area off?" Kara asked. "He'd probably break his leg if he stepped in it."

"Marathon runners are used to stuff like this," Cornelius said, waving the megaphone dismissively. "There's always a couple of obstacles on the course for them to avoid. Not to mention avoiding all those bulls running everywhere."

"That's not a marathon," Kara said. "You're thinking of Pamplona."

"I'm often thinking of Pamplona," Cornelius suddenly sounded far off and wistful. "Of a bottle of red wine and the lover I shared it with." Cornelius looked out to sea, took a deep breath, and when he turned back to Kara he was his normal self again. "Not really a place I'd associate with bulls, though," he said with a confused smile.

Kara would have liked to delve deeper into what sort of life experience could cause a person to be so utterly wrong about something, but before she could engage her grandfather, Goodluck he emitted a titanic burst of flatulence and a dark stain appeared on the back of his running shorts. He had not made it more than half a lap around HAWAll. Kara's jaw nearly hit the platform, but Cornelius didn't seem to notice that anything was amiss.

"You're up next," he said, turning to Kara. "You ready?"

"Did you not see that?" Kara asked, pointing at Goodluck, who continued to navigate the border of HAWAll with remarkable speed considering he had just expelled a substantial percentage of his body weight. "He just shit his pants!"

"Ah yes," Cornelius replied. "Runner's diarrhea. One of the many risks of putting your body through the stress of a marathon. I thought as a fellow athlete you'd be more understanding about such matters, Kara."

"Runner's diarrhea? He's run maybe two hundred feet! I think that's just diarrhea!"

"Well, he *was* licking the ground a lot," Cornelius admitted. "That probably wasn't the healthiest thing to do."

Kara continued to follow the marathoner's progress. The incident did not appear to have slowed him down, but if this had happened on lap one, Kara hoped that Cornelius's claim that they would be long gone by the time Goodluck finished was accurate. She didn't want to know what his body would be expelling if he was still alive after six hundred more laps.

Cornelius did not seem concerned. "You're up next," he repeated. Then he pulled out his phone, tapped a few buttons, and dramatically announced into the megaphone, "The athletes from the United States of America!" Then Cornelius held the phone up to the megaphone and an MP3 began to play across HAWAll. It was the Star Spangled Banner being barked by dogs. It was simultaneously tinny, blown out, and possibly the most disrespectful thing Kara had ever heard. Cornelius beamed and leaned in to make another announcement.

"Competing in the hundred-meter dash... Kara Everglades!" He motioned Kara forward as a shrill, yappy little dog, maybe a chihuahua, took over on the "whose broad stripes and bright stars" line. Kara took a few steps, then looked back at her grandfather. Cornelius made an exaggerated waving motion, pointed at the spectators/captives who were being forced to watch, then stage-whispered "don't slip in it!" as he tilted his head toward Goodluck. Kara shuddered, then started to walk and wave like a beauty pageant contestant as a large-sounding hound began to howl the notes of "the rockets' red glare."

Henry and his wife kept a disinterested distance, but Backwards Cap looked very intrigued by the makeshift parade. He popped up from the surface of the country and wandered over to Cornelius. Kara kept walking and waving as she tried to hear what he had to say over the din of the potentially treasonous dogs.

"So wait... Are the Olympics actually happening?" Backwards

Cap asked. Cornelius kept the anthem playing into the megaphone but nodded to the kid dismissively as if to say, "Of course."

"Whoa," Backwards Cap said. "I thought this was all just a scam. I honestly thought you'd lured us out here to harvest our organs or something."

Kara wanted to interrupt her runway walk to yell back "Don't give him any ideas!" but it wasn't necessary. The college student had already moved on. If he'd spent the past few hours living in fear that he might leave the island with one less kidney than he'd arrived with, it appeared not to have caused too much permanent psychological damage. Now he just wanted to gamble.

"It's in the ad," Backwards Cap was insisting. "'Gambling legal.' We can't do any of the other awesome crap that you promised us, but if there's a sporting event happening, I want to bet on it. And you better not tell me that's not an option."

Kara's almost felt her heart go out to the poor degenerate as she braced for him to receive more disappointing news. But then Cornelius surprised her.

"Sounds good," he said. "How much would you like to bet?"

The college student pondered this for a moment. "Uh… Fifty… No! A hundred bucks!"

"The minimum bet is ten thousand dollars," Cornelius said as a chorus of crazy canines howled an extended final note of "home of the brave." "I'll take Kara in the hundred-meter dash, and the HAWAII sportsbook will offer you twenty-five-to-one odds on the field."

Backwards Cap did some quick mental math. This took him a while. "So that means…"

"If anybody besides Kara wins, I pay you a quarter of a million dollars," Cornelius explained. "If Kara wins, I'll garnish the money you owe me out of your student loans."

Backwards Cap's eyes went wide at the prospect of such a fast, easy payday. He took a glance at Kara, who couldn't even drive yet, standing there in a Jefferson track uniform that had been handed down to freshmen athletes for over a decade. His mind undoubtedly racing with images of the muscular, near-superhuman women he'd seen sprinting to victory in previous Olympics, he blurted, "You've got a deal!" He stuck his hand out and Cornelius gave it a formal, single-pump handshake.

"So, who are the other athletes in the field?" Backwards Cap asked.

"This concludes the parade of participants in the HAWAll Olympics," Cornelius's voice boomed out of the megaphone. "The hundred-meter dash will commence momentarily."

"What the shit?" Backwards Cap shouted. "She's running unopposed?"

"Do some research next time," Cornelius smirked. "By the way, that ten thousand is in HAWAll dollars. You better hope for a favorable exchange rate!"

The unfortunate idiot's face fell and Kara almost felt bad for him until she remembered that she'd nearly had to fend him off with a sleeve of saltines when he mistook her for a hooker. He shuffled off to no doubt inform his friend that he'd mortgaged what little future he possessed at the start of their vacation.

"Alright!" Cornelius said to Kara, clapping his hands together in glee. "That may mean a first class upgrade for the ride home! Are you ready to go?"

"I'm ready, Grandpa. But I thought you promised you had something special for these people? So far you've swindled one of them out of his life savings and treated the other three to an African with diarrhea."

"In my day, that could have been a successful touring act!" Cornelius said. "But I don't forget a promise. I think they're going to like what I've got cooked up. And more importantly, *you're* going to like it, Kara."

Kara smiled. His methods might be uncouth, probably illegal, perhaps even the sort of thing that might necessitate a name change and relocation to South America later in life, but if there was one thing about her grandfather she had faith in, it was his ability to surprise.

Cornelius's eyes twinkled as he raised the megaphone to his lips. Decades of scheming and betrayal and mascot costumes were about to culminate. For a few seconds, Kara got lost in the moment. Being mistaken for a hooker was a distant memory. Making her dog barf was water under the bridge. Tricking the elderly couple into thinking they were dying was ancient history. The runner's diarrhea was— Actually, remembering the runner's diarrhea took Kara right out of forgiveness mode. She smiled a thin, formal smile as she stood next to her grandfather and readied herself for a perfunctory hundred meters.

"Ladies and gentlemen," Cornelius's voice boomed. "I would like to officially proclaim the HAWAll Olympics... underway!" He spread his arms to the sky, and for a moment Kara half expected a squad of fighter planes to fly over in formation. It would have been insane, but underestimating her grandfather was a dangerous game, one for fools, people who didn't dream big, or kind but unfortunate elderly couples. But the horizon remained free of spectacle. Not even a rogue firework or skywriter appeared.

"Pretty sweet, pops!" Backwards Cap shouted, flipping Cornelius a middle finger. Henry looked like he was about to cry. On the border of the country, Goodluck rushed past, somehow managing not to slip on whatever he'd left behind on his first lap. Kara realized she'd been holding her breath and exhaled in disappointment. She cast her grandfather a reproachful look. It had been stupid to trust someone whose end goal was as shallow as building a pill empire. Kara lowered her head. She would participate in the Olympics, but she wouldn't show the games any respect. Hopefully by the time she started, she could think of a better form of protest than imitating Goodluck's first lap. But at least she had that as a fallback plan.

And a fallback plan it would fortunately remain, because that was when the Larvilkian StarBarge *Stupid Butt* deactivated its cloaking device and materialized out of thin air ten feet above the surface of HAWAll.

Henry's wife shrieked. The college kids whooped in appreciation. Kara's eyes went wide and she turned to Cornelius, who was looking up at the ship, slack-jawed.

"Grandpa, is this...?" Kara asked.

"No," Cornelius gulped. "This… this isn't me." Kara didn't think it was possible, but Cornelius being caught off guard was even more unsettling than Cornelius being in complete control.

The ship hovered motionlessly as the doorway began to dissolve away. A few seconds later, the still unoiled ramp generator emitted a cough of black smoke as it sputtered to life and a glowing ramp appeared. There was a pause as everyone on the island waited to see what would happen next. Other than the wheezing and grinding generator, the only sound was Goodluck's footsteps as he continued his race around the perimeter of HAWAll. Kara noticed with dismay that every now and then there was a step that sounded squishier than the others.

"Grandpa," she eventually whispered. "If this isn't you… What was your plan to impress these people?"

"I was going to show them my thumb trick," Cornelius whispered out of the side of his mouth, not taking his eyes off the *Stupid Butt*. He held up his right hand and waggled his thumb back and forth. "See? It's double jointed. It can kinda move around like…" Cornelius maneuvered his thumb in a manner that, to Kara, looked way beyond unimpressive.

"That's how you were going to wow them?" she hissed. "By doing this?" Kara held up her own thumb and clicked it back and forth in an exact mimic of Cornelius's movements.

"Well of course *you're* not impressed by it. Double-jointedness is hereditary! But these people have probably never seen anything like it!"

Kara never got a chance to protest, which was good because she had about two dozen bullet points that she felt would systematically destroy her grandfather's argument that a slightly bendy thumb was a good trick, and it probably would have taken the rest of the day and made use of the whiteboard in the governor's mansion.

"Contestants in the Earth Olympic Games!" an unseen voice boomed out of the ship's PA system. "We have traveled to your planet across vast galaxies and we demand your attention!" The platform went still again. At that moment, though they were of all different backgrounds and assembled together only because of dishonesty and treachery, every person on HAWAIl realized that they were now bound together for the ages. They simultaneously felt microscopically insignificant and yet boundlessly alive. More than one person on the island would later recall that they had shed a tear of joyful fear as they awaited whatever communication, whatever wisdom, these otherworldly beings were about to bestow upon them.

"OK, be honest," crackled the voice over the *Stupid Butt's* PA. "What do you guys think about Hitler?"

seventeen

"It sounds like they're booing," Zzarvon informed 9-Krelblax.

"I can hear that, you idiot!" 9-Krelblax shouted over the boos from down on HAWAll.

"I told you guys," King Moho said. "Way to make an entrance."

9-Krelblax narrowed three of his eyes at the king, who was lazing in the commander's chair, sucking the juices off a glistening rib bone. The picked-over carcasses of both the original pig and the clone sat congealing behind him. They had served as breakfast, lunch, and two dinners over the course of the journey to HAWAll, and now the sight of them made 9-Krelblax feel ill. Zzarvon and King Moho couldn't seem to get enough though, and had at one point lamented that the malfunctioning hyperwarp hadn't resulted in a second clone. One of the pigs was snoutless, as the new Technician Tamblirx had absconded with its nose, claiming he needed it "for repairs."

"We had to make sure you weren't betraying us," 9-Krelblax told the king. "It would be totally embarrassing if we got down there and started talking about how terrible Hitler was when it turned out everyone was super into Hitler. It would be like showing up at the annual Larvilkian-B Masquerade Ball not wearing Piltrixian-face. Now put down that rib, we've got an Olympics to dominate."

"Right," King Moho said. He traded a nervous glance with Zzarvon. "And refresh my memory on what events we're going to be dominating?" Their lengthy journey from Hawaii to HAWAll had been spent systematically eliminating events that Larvilkians were physically unable or psychologically unprepared to compete in. They had crossed off nearly half of the available Olympic sports before 9-Krelblax disintegrated the holoscreen generator in a fit of anger.

"Wax-bullet dueling and offshore powerboat racing!" 9-Krelblax said. His moodcore glowed a confident blue as he mimed shooting a pistol with one tentacle and steered an invisible speedboat with another.

"We decided when you drifted off halfway through a shank," Zzarvon informed King Moho.

King Moho smiled, remembering the shank fondly, but his face quickly fell again. "Speedboats and dueling are not Olympic sports," he said.

"Of course they are!" 9-Krelblax scoffed. "Looks like you're not the know-it-all you've made yourself out to be, King Moho. This is why we've got to double check on stuff like Hitler. Tell him, Zzarvon." 9-Krelblax made a firing motion with his invisible gun as he spun the boat's steering wheel, deftly avoiding an obstacle only he could see. He began to hum the theme from a popular Larvilkian holoscreen show called *Speedboat Cop*. It was about a cop who taught proper speedboat safety lessons on the side. The titular Speedboat Cop never actually utilized a speedboat to chase down criminals. He didn't think it was safe to do so, a decision 9-Krelblax vehemently disagreed with. He had written letters to the network. Nevertheless, there wasn't anything better on at the same time, so…

"Wax bullet dueling and offshore powerboat racing *are* actually Olympic events," Zzarvon said, already flinching and pre-shielding his eye antennae. "Or rather, they were. Over a hundred Earth sun cycles ago. At one Olympics. In 1908."

9-Krelblax jerked the imaginary steering wheel hard starboard and nearly fell out of his fantasy boat. His moodcore glowed a furious red.

"Why the hell didn't you tell me that?" he bellowed.

"Well, you just got so excited when we discovered them, talking about how it would be just like all those *Speedboat Cop* scripts you've written in your spare time—"

"Sssh! Zzarvon!" 9-Krelblax's moodcore flushed with embarrassment at the reveal of his secret hobby.

"And you never know, sir," Zzarvon said. "This might be the year they bring them back, along with Indian club swinging, tug of war, and plunge for distance!"

"So, are you guys actually going to come down here, or what?" The two Larvilkians and King Moho turned to look at the *Stupid Butt's* intercom.

"Zzarvon, did you leave the intercom switched on this whole time?" 9-Krelblax asked.

"What? The intercom? No, of course not! Er, I think...." One of Zzarvon's eyes darted to the control panel. His other three stared at 9-Krelblax, hoping the commander wouldn't notice.

"We're not doing any lame old events like rubber bullet dueling or boat racing," the voice on the other end of the intercom informed them.

"Maybe it did get stuck in the on position," Zzarvon admitted as the ship's blinds closed yet again in response to 9-Krelblax's flaring moodcore.

"*Speedboat Cop* sounds really cool, though," the voice said on the other end of the intercom, amidst several audible snickers. "Maybe 'fanfic reading' can be a demonstration sport this year!"

9-Krelblax speed-oozed over to Zzarvon, smacked him on the back of the head with one tentacle and jammed at the intercom control switch with three more. But no matter how many times he pressed the button, there was no burst of static signifying that the transmission had ended, and the indicator light stayed illuminated.

"Come to think of it, Technician Tamblirx did make some adjustments to the PA when you stepped out to use the bathroom," Zzarvon remembered. "He said its giga-cycles didn't have enough pi."

"That doesn't make any sense," 9-Krelblax said. "Look, don't let

Tamblirx near anything important. That hyperwarp clone isn't 100 percent right."

"Who's Tamblirx?" the voice on the other end of the intercom asked. "Speedboat Cop's secret identity?" More snickering.

"Maybe we should just go down there, sir?" Zzarvon suggested.

King Moho nodded his head in agreement. "Intergalactic dominance ain't gonna establish itself, Niner. Plus, we're out of grub." He gestured at the pig carcasses. A faint half-smile inched its way onto the king's face like he was remembering an old friend.

9-Krelblax had imagined a grand, majestic entrance. He'd even picked out a piece of Earth music to accompany it, an imposing composition he'd discovered on the holoscreen called *Also Sprach Zarathrusta*. Currently they were working on an entrance that was less suited to Zarathrusta also spraching, and more suited to Zarathrusta's loser brother Barrythrusta's pants falling down while he was eating a chili dog and wearing a propeller beanie. As he oozed over to the doorway, 9-Krelblax told himself that all this initial incompetence and jackassery would be forgotten once his eyestalks drooped under the weight of dozens of Olympic gold medals.

A cool gust of wind ran up the ramp and through the doorway into the bridge of the *Stupid Butt*. 9-Krelblax shivered, but he wasn't sure if it was because of the wind or anticipation. He looked back at Zzarvon and King Moho and gestured for them to follow. They exchanged a brief, uncertain glance, then shuffled over to stand behind their commander. 9-Krelblax nodded and was about to say a few inspiring words when there was a whooshing sound from the hallway doors and Technician Tamblirx staggered in. The doors were open just long enough for everyone to see a brilliant radioactive green light glowing in the hallway. It had not been there the last time the doors opened.

"Don't mind me!" the duplicate technician announced, his two crossed eyes bobbing up and down. He bent down and picked up a bucket of water that a service bot had left behind the last time it mopped the deck. "Just needed to fetch a wrench!" Tamblirx proclaimed, holding the very obviously not-a-wrench bucket up for all to see. "Now back to work!" The doors opened with a whoosh. Whatever was now glowing in the hall was so bright that 9-Krelblax, Zzarvon, and King Moho all shielded their eyes, but Technician Tamblirx bumbled right through with a smile on his face.

The doors whooshed closed and the glow disappeared. 9-Krelblax lowered the tentacle that he'd thrust across all four of his eyes and collected himself. He would deal with Tamblirx's "repairs" later, assuming said repairs didn't immediately cause his tentacles to fall off as soon as he returned to the ship. Making a mental note to have Zzarvon go first when that time came, 9-Krelblax took a deep breath and slithered down the ramp, out onto the surface of HAWAIl.

eighteen

Kara watched in awed horror as the tentacled, four-eyed, partially glowing mass of Intergalactic StarBarge Commander 9-Krelblax of Larvilkian-B oozed out of the shadows of the *Stupid Butt*. Perhaps humanity's greatest unanswered question—Are we alone in the universe?—now had a definitive answer: We are not, and had been naïve to think so. In the blink of an eye, everything had changed. Suddenly, her grandfather's scheme to rake in easy money by selling illegal drugs seemed unbelievably faraway, small, and petty.

"This is going to be great for business!" Cornelius whispered, leaning in to Kara's ear. "I've got to get a picture of it holding a sign with my website's name on it!"

Kara ignored her grandfather and forced herself to look away from the alien to size up how the rest of the Olympic audience was reacting. They were all predictably gobsmacked except for Goodluck, who continued to plod around the perimeter of HAWAll. The runner was in the zone and appeared not to have noticed the visitors. As he approached the spot on the makeshift track that was near where Cornelius and Kara were standing, he started to sputter broken English at them in between deep breaths. At first Kara had trouble understanding his thick accent, but eventually she made out the two words he was repeating: "How many? How many?"

"What the hell does he want?" Cornelius asked Kara.

"I think he wants to know how many laps he's run," Kara replied.

"So he knows how to pace himself."

"I was supposed to be keeping track of that?" Cornelius asked. Kara shrugged. She figured that the runner had probably put in at least forty or fifty laps in the half hour since he started running, but had no idea of the exact amount.

"How many?" Goodluck insisted over his shoulder.

"We weren't keeping track!" Cornelius yelled back at the runner. "We'll start over at zero right now!"

The runner's rigid shoulders momentarily slumped in dismay as he continued around the island. When Kara turned back to the spaceship, Zzarvon and King Moho had started down the ramp as well. She was surprised to see what appeared to be a human male accompanying the two aliens. She figured he had either been subjected to a fierce round of probing or sold out humanity in order to avoid said probing. Kara was pretty sure she knew what she would pick if faced with that choice, and had no doubt in her mind what Cornelius would do. She narrowed her eyes at the shirtless man, deciding to regard him as a traitor until proven otherwise.

Cornelius, on the other hand, was beaming at him. Before Kara could share her suspicions with her grandfather, he was striding over to the spaceship ramp, a man on a mission.

9-Krelblax spread his tentacles to the sky and surveyed the island, all four of his eyes scanning in a different direction. "Earth humans!" he boomed as his moodcore swirled an awe-inspiring mixture of turquoise and gold. "I am 9-Krelblax of Larvilkian-B! Turn your fawning gaze upon your superiors! We do not come in peace, but rather to conquer! Already one of your planet's leaders has bent his knee to us. Tremble in fear as we present our hostage, Ki—"

"King Moholaiko of Maui!" Cornelius boomed, brushing right past 9-Krelblax. He grabbed King Moho's shoulder while simultaneously seizing his hand and pumping it in an emphatic handshake. "So you saw our ad!" Cornelius beamed at the bewildered king. "Cornelius

Everglades, president of HAWAll. Welcome to my country!"

"Ad?" King Moho asked. He looked past the strange man who was still shaking his hand and his face fell as he gazed at his surroundings. Like most visitors to the country, he found himself in HAWAll against his will. Unlike most visitors, however, his disappointment stemmed not from the country's soul-rending desolation but rather from the fact that there did not appear to be any succulent animals turning on a spit in the immediate vicinity.

"I was hoping it would catch your eye," Cornelius said with a wink as King Moho sniffed the air, just in case there was maybe a secret roasting station suspended somewhere underneath the platform. "I'd love to pick your brain about ruling over an island sometime," Cornelius continued. "I've looked up to the Hawaiian royal cabal ever since I saw a panel about you at the Micronation Conference in Toronto. I know you secret kings don't get all the public glory, but you guys are doing a hell of a job running those eight islands."

"Seven now, actually," Zzarvon interjected.

"What's that?" Cornelius asked. He stopped thrusting King Moho's hand up and down and glanced over at Zzarvon. His eyes went wide as if noticing the two Larvilkians for the first time.

"There's just seven islands now," Zzarvon said, avoiding eye contact and fidgeting. "There was an… an accident."

Cornelius turned back to King Moho. "So, consolidating power, are you?" he said with a wink. "Well, you can count on me as an ally. I'm planning a bit of a 'power consolidation' myself if you get my drift." Cornelius nodded his head twice toward President for Life Makepeace, then dropped the king's hand and turned back to Zzarvon.

"Welcome to Earth, and welcome to HAWAll!" he said, extending his hand. "Please pass along my greetings to your subordinates."

Zzarvon retracted his tentacles. "I don't think I should do that," the navigator said, glancing out of the corner of all four of his eyes at 9-Krelblax.

"Oh thank God!" Cornelius pulled his hand back and gasped in relief. "I was totally bluffing. It would have dissolved my hand, right?

Or turned my arm into a tentacle? Or just given me hundreds of warts?"

Zzarvon looked confused. "No, I just meant that I'm just the navigator..."

Cornelius ignored him. "How about we just do one of these?" He raised his hand to his forehead and gave Zzarvon a casual salute. After a moment of hesitation, Zzarvon returned the gesture with a tentacle. Cornelius continued. "Now I heard your messenger's little announcement when you landed, but you are our guests and we have no quarrel with you. If you need anything else, what say you forego the 'people of Earth, cower in fear' mumbo jumbo and we just talk things out, leader to leader? Sound good?"

"Absolutely!" Zzarvon said with a dopey grin.

"Absolutely not!" 9-Krelblax said, pushing Zzarvon out of the way and stepping in front of Cornelius. "I am the commander of the StarBarge *Stupid Butt* and I reject your hospitality. We are here to prove that Larvilkians are a superior species, here to shame the humans of Earth, here to force you to confront the astronomical scale of your own insignificance! And if you are unwilling, we will not hesitate to destroy not just your planet but your entire solar system with the touch of a button!"

"The *Stupid Butt*?" Cornelius asked. "Did I mishear the name of your shi—"

"You did not mishear the name of my ship!" 9-Krelblax roared.

"How many?" Goodluck gasped as he raced past Cornelius and the Larvilkians.

"Dammit! OK, starting *now*!" Cornelius said. Goodluck emitted a high pitched, whiny sigh that sounded like air escaping out of a balloon and continued on around the island.

Cornelius turned back to 9-Krelblax. "Sorry about that," he said. "You guys landed here just as we were about to start the Olympics. You've probably never heard of it, but it's the world's premiere athletic competition. Every four years we celebrate the pinnacle of human athletic achievement. Really a beacon of hope and inspiration for the entire planet. So if you give me thirty seconds here, we'll get it over with and then we can talk intergalactic business."

"Silence!" 9-Krelblax bellowed. "We know your Olympic Games, and we have traveled a great distance in order to win them!"

"Hell yeah! Go aliens!" yelled Backwards Cap. "Do some gymnastics and shit!" He turned and high fived his friend. Elsewhere on the island, President for Life Makepeace grinned and gave Cornelius a thumbs-up, Kara stood in her track uniform with her arms folded looking impatient, and Henry was slowly getting to his feet despite his wife grabbing his arm and trying to pull him back to a sitting position. The elderly man waited for Goodluck to run past him, then slowly made his way over to the foot of the ramp where Cornelius and 9-Krelblax stood.

"Are you here to trade pins?" Henry whimpered hopefully. "It's a big pastime at the Olympic village. I've got pins from every Olympics from the past sixty years, though I'm a bit short on the '68 Mexico City games. If you have any from that year, I have a very rare Hodori that I'd be willing to—"

"Ugh, that sounds like the most boring hobby in the universe," 9-Krelblax said. "And that includes Piltrixian bird watching."

"Why is that so boring?" Cornelius asked.

"We polluted their planet so much that all the birds went extinct, so the only way to do it is to look at the one dead one they have behind glass in a museum," 9-Krelblax said. "BOR-ing!"

"The embossing on the javelin is the wrong color," Henry continued hopefully.

"My God! Yes, we have a pin, just take it and leave us alone before we die of boredom!" 9-Krelblax said. 9-Krelblax reached out and plucked Zzarvon's navigator pin off of his chest and flipped it to Henry. The old man caught it and held it up to admire with wide eyes. It almost looked like three-fifths of the Olympic rings logo. It would fit in nicely on his duffel bag.

"Hey!" Zzarvon protested. "That was mine!"

"There's an entire sack of them in the storage closet," 9-Krelblax snapped back. "We order them by the gross."

"But I liked that one!" Zzarvon whined.

"So, like I was saying," 9-Krelblax continued. "We intend to compete and win—"

"We have to trade," Henry said, holding out a pin in return. "It's part of the fun." 9-Krelblax looked at the pin as if Henry was insisting he take a dead animal, but Zzarvon oozed over in a flash and snatched it out of the old man's hand.

"Wow, cool!" the navigator said. "A tiger! And would you look at that javelin embossing!" Henry looked very pleased, and when he set off back to the corner of the island where his collection sat, Zzarvon longingly watched him go.

Cornelius opened his mouth to speak, but 9-Krelblax was faster and louder. "We have familiarized ourselves with the traditions of your Olympic Games. And though we will gladly forego the digestive nightmare of corporate-sponsor-provided 'McNuggets' and the casual reproduction that runs rampant in the athlete quarters, we insist on our proper acknowledgment in the ceremony of opening!"

"Well, to be honest, gents," Cornelius said in a "I wish there was something I could do" tone. "The ceremonies just wrapped up. Now, I don't make the rules, but maybe since it's your first Olympics, you'd like to eat some saltines and just observe this go-round? Then come on back in four—"

Cornelius was cut off as 9-Krelblax pulled his communicator out of his pocket, raised it to his mouth and whispered something into it. Almost immediately, the entire country of HAWAII violently shook under their feet. The previously still ocean erupted into whitecapped waves that broke two thirds of the way up the entrance ladder. Goodluck nearly toppled over the edge as he made the southeast turn. Angry seagulls flew into the air squawking from beneath the platform.

"What the hell was that?" Cornelius asked.

"That was a moon 73.7 light years away that I just exploded with a remote triggering device," 9-Krelblax replied, as calmly as if he was remarking on the weather. "Pretty sizeable impact for something so far away, no? I suggest you let us participate in the ceremony."

"Jesus!" Cornelius said, his hands still out to his sides in case the balance of his country shifted again. "Yeah, no problem! We'll re-open the opening ceremony! Just give me one second!" Cornelius took a few unsteady steps, then jogged over to Kara.

"What moon did you explode up there, Niner?" King Moho asked as Cornelius departed.

"Umlaut-R," 9-Krelblax said with a smile.

"The Piltrixian spa moon?" Zzarvon asked, sounding a touch concerned.

"Let's see those idiots get a relaxing lava rock scrub now!" 9-Krelblax cackled. After a few seconds, noting that Zzarvon was not smiling, he stopped laughing. "Oh, relax, Zzarvon! The spa moon is closed on Tuesdays."

"Today is Monday, sir."

"Huh... Well, that's probably their least busy day from a visitor standpoint," 9-Krelblax said.

"Today is actually a planetwide Ribercon-C holiday to commemorate the many who died as a result of the Telegram of Piltrixian Aggression. Tourists undoubtedly flocked to the spa moon to take their minds off the sorrows of the past."

9-Krelblax felt a stabbing in his moodcore. "Dammit, Zzarvon!" he said, clutching at it with several tentacles. "This downer talk isn't good for my mental state before a competition!"

"I'll be quiet, sir," Zzarvon said. He let the mass murder drop and went back to admiring his new pin.

"Yo! Aliens!" Cornelius yelled from over by the governor's mansion. "You got an anthem or anything you want me to play during your introduction?"

"We do!" 9-Krelblax shouted back. He turned to his navigator. "Zzarvon, would you kindly do the honors?" Zzarvon nodded, stashed his pin, and pulled out his communicator.

"Ladies and gentlemen!" Cornelius announced into his megaphone. "We are extremely pleased that the HAWAll games will be the first Olympics to feature athletes from another galaxy! We have a very special act planned that I feel commemorates this monumental moment not just in the history of the games, but in the history of mankind! Gaze if you will at... My slightly bendier than average thumb!"

Cornelius held his right hand up in the air and waggled his thumb forward, backward, side to side, then bent it at the knuckle and started rotating it in circles. Backwards Cap raised his eyebrows and gave a few respectful nods, but other than that, nobody else appeared impressed.

"I'm just saying, this never would have happened if You Know Who were running the show," 9-Krelblax said in a low whisper to King Moho.

"Let it go, Niner," King Moho whispered back.

"It's a good trick," Cornelius grumbled as he lowered his thumb. "You all are just jealous. Anyway, they traveled farther than any of you to be here today, so quit your whining and give it up for 9-Krelblax of Larvilkian-B!"

There was tepid applause from the Olympic attendees as 9-Krelblax oozed forward to the center of the island. The Larvilkian commander raised a tentacle in the air and waved it around. After a few seconds the applause died out. 9-Krelblax continued to wave the tentacle for a bit longer. He looked extremely uncomfortable. He turned two narrowed eyes around to glare at Zzarvon, who was fiddling with his communicator in a panic.

The only sound was the constant plodding of Goodluck's feet around the perimeter of HAWAll.

9-Krelblax let out a nervous cough and stared with his other two eyes at the humans who were now shifting uncomfortably waiting for something to happen. "So..." 9-Krelblax said. He let the statement hang there, piling on the awkwardness as he tried to think of what to say next, before eventually continuing: "Did you ever hear the one about the Piltrixian and the space-llama farmer's dau—"

The bawdy space joke's setup was cut off by a burst of shrill static from the PA on the side of the *Stupid Butt.*

Cornelius, Kara, and the rest of the humans on the island doubled over and covered their ears with their hands. Goodluck did this as he ran; the result was the extremely comical sight of a very skinny man running with his bony elbows jutting out on both sides of his head. Hundreds of seagulls who had just calmed down after the giant waves caused by the exploding spa moon now soared back out into the sky. The blaring noise was droning and atonal, the sound of electronic equipment that was clearly malfunctioning.

And yet, Zzarvon was no longer fiddling with his communicator. The Larvilkian navigator was standing straight up, staring at a point on the distant horizon, silently mouthing along to lyrics that the human ear could not detect. 9-Krelblax was doing the same, with a single tentacle placed respectfully over his patriotic green moodcore. Two of his four eyes appeared to be welling with tears. The seagulls swarmed in the air on the outskirts of the country, their irritated squawking adding to the cacophony.

Without taking her hands off her ears, Kara leaned in to Cornelius. "Grandpa, I think this is their national anthem!" she shouted into his covered ear, hoping he'd be able to hear her over the din.

"This is music?" Cornelius shouted back. "It sounds like an entire planet of robots got their dicks caught in a blender!"

"I'll take your word on that!" Kara yelled. "The seagulls seem to hate it too! It's driving them into a frenzy!"

Cornelius shot the dark swirling cloud of birds a wary look, then turned back to Kara. "I hope it doesn't go on much longer! They'll try to take out its source if it does. If the birds go to war with the aliens, I won't know who to side with! But, Kara! We can't let these aliens win! I've only got one medal, and a country from Earth, a *real* country, needs to win it in order for the UN to recognize HAWAII!"

The Larvilkian "music" had been steadily increasing in volume as the anthem went on, so Kara was mostly reading lips at this point, but she got the gist of what her grandfather was saying. She had no idea how she measured up from an athletic standpoint against the aliens. For all she knew they could sprint at light speed. "What do you think we should do, Grandpa?" she shouted at the top of her lungs, barely able to hear her own words.

"I think we should kill the aliens right now!" Cornelius shouted, just as the anthem cut off and the island was flooded with silence. Everyone looked at Cornelius except for 9-Krelblax who continued to stare straight ahead.

"Uh, that is, we should kill the *concept* of aliens right now!" Cornelius stammered. "It's an offensive term. The Olympics teach us to embrace our differences! After all, we're all the same, aren't we? I mean, sure, some of us have a perfectly normal set of internal organs and others have a weird glowy thing that I assume shows how horny they are, but who's to say that—"

"Would you kindly shut up!" 9-Krelblax hissed as he wheeled around and pointed the tentacle that had been held over his moodcore at Cornelius. "This is the best part!"

Cornelius raised his palms and lowered his head in apology. Then, after 9-Krelblax turned back around and resumed his reverent stance, he looked at Kara. "What the hell?" Cornelius mouthed, cupping a hand to his ear. Kara shrugged. As far as she could tell, there was nothing to hear but an unpleasant ringing in her ears that was certainly a remnant of the deafening first verse of the Larvilkian anthem.

But 9-Krelblax continued standing still, his moodcore glowing brighter and brighter as tears now streamed from all four of his eyes. Kara felt her front teeth begin to vibrate. It was an unpleasant sensation, and Kara was trying to convince herself it was all in her head when the first seagull dropped out of the sky.

The gull plummeted to the surface of the water where it landed with a small splash. Kara didn't even have time to wonder if it was a coincidence before the second one landed a few feet away. She looked up at the avian mass and was stunned to see dozens of dead birds falling every second. There were pops as the heads of some of the birds exploded in midair; others just suffered some sort of immediate cerebral failure. The gull cloud appeared to be raining. At first, small bursts of water shot up out of the ocean as the birds landed, but as more and more of them began to fall, the surface frothed up until it looked like someone had activated the jets in a hot tub.

The tingling in Kara's teeth was definitely not something she was imagining. In fact, it was getting stronger. Kara rubbed her right cheek and wondered if the birds had felt something similar just before their heads started exploding. She looked at the *Stupid Butt* and was amazed to see that the sound coming out of the *Stupid Butt*'s speaker was visible. You couldn't hear it, but it was actually distorting the air like waves of heat coming off of a desert highway. Kara saw no obvious way to stop the music. She could only hope that humans' tolerance for the Larvilkian National Anthem was higher than the birds'.

The birds' tolerance was not high. What remained of the cloud now began to dissipate as the seagulls realized what was happening and started trying to flee the source of their doom. But suddenly—Kara figured it must have been the equivalent of a super high note being belted out—every remaining bird either exploded or simply dropped dead. There was a giant splash as if a party animal made of dead birds had just done a crowd-pleasing cannonball, and then the sky was empty.

The only sound was 9-Krelbalx faintly singing. "Go to Trillig's Bot Repair / for all your service bot needs," he crooned in a wavering voice, clearly choked up. The Larvilkian commander held the final note for a few seconds, then took a deep breath and dragged a tentacle across all four eyes to wipe away tears. He turned to Zzarvon, who was doing the same, and gave his navigator a sad smile and a nod. Then he turned to Kara and Cornelius.

"Well!" 9-Krelblax said with a sniffle. "Shall we get started?"

Cornelius ignored him and walked over to the nearest side of the platform. He looked down at the ocean, where a massive pile of dead birds, feathers, and bird-head goo now floated like a giant, unpleasant raft. "Good lord!" he shouted. "Your anthem took out every single bird!"

9-Krelblax narrowed his eyes. "Some life forms have been known to experience adverse effects. Larvilkian music does tend to use more advanced scales than what is considered musical in other parts of the galaxy. Especially for songs as moving as our national anthem—the traditional concepts of song structure and instrumentation prove inadequate to convey the weighty emotions."

"It sounded like the last line was an advertisement?" Kara asked. "Is there product placement for a robot repair shop in your national anthem?"

"Trillig's Bot Repair signed a very lucrative deal to integrate their branding message into the Larvilkian anthem, so yes, if you wanted to be crass about it, you could say that," 9-Krelblax said, sounding defensive. "But it's better than the original line our founding fathers came up with."

"What was that?" Kara asked.

"It was product placement for a tattoo parlor," 9-Krelblax admitted.

"Fascinating history, really great stuff you guys, but right now we've gotta get those birds out of there," Cornelius said. "Hey! Makepeace!" The President for Life of Warland smiled and waved at Cornelius.

"Get the skimmer and start scooping the birds up!" Cornelius directed. He mimed the gesture of sweeping a bird out of the ocean and dumping it on the platform. Makepeace shot him an A-OK, then went to retrieve the skimmer he'd been fishing with earlier.

"Why do you have to get them out of the water, Grandpa?" Kara asked.

"Look at all that blood and fresh meat!" Cornelius said, gesturing down at the carnage. "Every shark for thirty miles is going to get a whiff and make a beeline for our coast!"

"Ah, that makes sense," Kara said. "You certainly don't want sharks circling the country."

"Don't be naïve, Kara," Cornelius scoffed. "We don't want sharks *at this exact moment*. But a pack of sharks can be extremely handy! Those dead birds are gallons upon gallons of free chum! All we have to do is scoop them out, process them, then wait for the right moment and summon the sharks to do our bidding!"

"I'm sorry I asked," Kara said. From the northern border of HAWAll came the sound of a wet bird hitting rusty metal.

"Enough formality and destruction of avian wildlife!" 9-Krelblax boomed. "The hour of Larvilkian domination is nigh! What is the first event that you have scheduled for us to embarrass you in?"

Cornelius ignored the alien's boastful rhetoric as he kept one eye on Makepeace's skimming effort. The Warlander worked diligently, and there was already a small pile of seagull carcasses on the platform. "Well, before you guys showed up, Kara was about to run the hundred-meter dash."

"I'm afraid that is not an event we are interested in competing in," 9-Krelblax said, his tone indicating that he did not consider the matter up for debate. "Though our physical advantages are myriad, the viscous nature of our forward momentum hinders our sprinting efforts."

"What he means is we ooze," Zzarvon said, oozing up behind 9-Krelblax.

"I prefer my description, but yes," 9-Krelblax agreed.

"Well, you can't force us to cancel an event just because *you* don't think you can win it!" Cornelius protested.

"Of course! We can't force you to do anything," 9-Krelblax said, pulling his communicator out of his thorax pouch. "Maybe we should see what effect blowing up your own moon would have on the tides?"

"No! Dammit, don't blow up the moon!" Cornelius insisted. "We don't have to do a sprint event. There are hundreds more to choose from. How about the mile?"

"How is that any better?" 9-Krelblax asked, sounding disgusted.

"Right! The oozing!" Cornelius said. "Well…" He trailed off, trying to appear deep in thought while subtly looking the Larvilkians up and down trying to size up their physical disadvantages. The key seemed to be to find an event where Kara's chances of victory were all but guaranteed, but one that the Larvilkians would be foolish enough to agree to participate in.

This was going to take a while.

"How many?" a noticeably tired Goodluck panted as he plodded past.

"Dammit!" Cornelius yelled. "OK, for real this time, starting now!"

nineteen

"What about equestrian dressage?" 9-Krelblax suggested.

"Where the hell am I keeping horses?" Cornelius snapped. "Show me the top-secret invisible stable I've got hidden here and you can saddle right up."

Kara rested her head in her hands. They'd been going at it like this for almost an hour. Cornelius would suggest an event and the Larvilkians would nix it because they lacked the proper appendages. Then the Larvilkians would suggest something and Cornelius would veto it because he didn't have the specialized equipment it required, or he was worried that the aliens would kick Kara's ass. Both parties started to take these rejections personally almost immediately, and now tensions were running very high.

"Well excuse me for thinking that you might actually be able to host an Olympic event *here at the Olympics!*" shouted a secretly relieved 9-Krelblax. He'd been terrified of horses ever since he'd seen the first picture of one on the *Stupid Butt*'s holoscreen. The combination of prominent teeth and substantial genital size gave him the willies.

Cornelius sighed, then walked over to King Moho. The king was holding a large poster like a ring girl at a boxing match. Zzarvon had printed off a list of every summer Olympic event. Cornelius pulled the cap off a fat marker and made a big show out of scratching off "dressage." This poster now consisted mostly of strikethroughs.

They had eliminated weightlifting events because Cornelius claimed he'd seen a nature special once that talked about how an octopus was pound for pound one of the strongest creatures on the planet, and now he assumed that this applied to every creature with tentacles. 9-Krelblax found this assumption kind of racist, but it was the sort of racism that he was OK with because it made him look good.

Swimming was out because the Larvilkians protested that as an alien species, they had a deadly allergic reaction to water. Kara pointed out that this obviously wasn't true, because if so, they'd made a terrible tactical error coming to a planet that was over 70 percent covered in water, plus the atmosphere was partially water vapor. 9-Krelblax admitted he'd been lying, and just didn't want to get in because the water looked pretty chilly. Kara had to agree with him.

All the team sports were crossed out because Cornelius didn't trust the people he'd tricked and sort of imprisoned to give it their all for their country. Balance beam was out because they didn't have a balance beam. Cycling was out because they didn't have bikes. Pommel horse was eliminated for the same reason as those other two, but not before 9-Krelblax embarrassed himself by asking if anyone else was uncomfortable around the genitalia of what he didn't realize was an inanimate piece of gymnastics equipment.

They'd also crossed off the floor exercise, hurdles, judo, archery, steeplechase, and canoe sprint. All the while, President for Life Makepeace continued to scoop seagulls out of the water; Goodluck's increasingly exhausted race around the border of HAWAII began to resemble a one-man forced march; Mac and Backwards Cap shot Cornelius a middle finger every time he glanced in their direction; and Henry and his wife respectively stared and glared at the new pin he'd obtained.

Cornelius chewed the end of the marker and stared at the list King Moho held as he pondered his next move. "Let's see... How about... the modern pentathlon?"

9-Krelblax stared back at him in disbelief. After a few seconds, Cornelius's lip began to tremble and he burst out laughing. "You thought I was serious!" he brayed. "You really thought I was suggesting we do a modern pentathlon!"

9-Krelblax broke out in a grin. He spread his tentacles wide. "What can I say? You got me!" For a moment, everyone forgot the tension that had built up over the past hour and had a good laugh at the expense of an event people devote years if not decades of their lives to mastering.

Cornelius reached up and scratched modern pentathlon off the poster. "Even if we wanted to," he chuckled, "It's not like we have any go-karts on the island."

"What's that?" Kara asked. She was actually quite curious to hear which five events her grandfather thought made up the modern pentathlon, but Cornelius ignored her.

"Well, we're running out of options," he said. "You can't wrestle because your gross skin is probably poison to us," he said, crossing out both Greco-Roman and freestyle wrestling.

"Your secretions could be just as poisonous to us!" 9-Krelblax snapped. "Zzarvon! Let one of the two burnouts secrete something on you!"

"Secrete this, pal!" shouted Backwards Cap, flipping 9-Krelblax a double bird.

"Nobody's secreting anything on anybody!" Cornelius shouted. 9-Krelblax shot a tentacle approximation of the middle finger back to the college kids, much to their delight.

"We're not doing platform diving or beach volleyball because every time we've brought up speedos or bikinis, the light in the middle of your navigator's chest gets a little too excited for my tastes."

Zzarvon's moodcore went pale. "I don't know what you're talking about!" he stammered.

"Speedos," Cornelius said, staring straight at Zzarvon.

Zzarvon frantically tried to cover up his moodcore, which began cycling through a variety of bright neon colors.

"Bikinis," Cornelius said.

Zzarvon's moodcore kaleidoscoped through psychedelic patterns, the likes of which even 9-Krelblax had never seen. It was like the moodcore equivalent of a horny cartoon wolf hitting himself on the head with a mallet.

"Yeah, let's go ahead and cross those two out," 9-Krelblax said. He turned two disgusted eyes toward Zzarvon who shrugged two of the tentacles he wasn't currently covering his shame with.

"Well, I don't know what to tell you guys," Cornelius said. "I'm sure as hell not handing my shotgun over to you, so skeet shooting is out. You know what? I think we're just going to have to stick with our original plan. Line it up, Kara, we've got a hundred-meter race to run!"

Kara would have liked nothing more than to dart the length of the island in fifteen seconds and call it a day, but 9-Krelblax was in motion before she could even take her first step toward the starting line.

"One damn second," the Larvilkian leader said. He oozed over to King Moho and leaned in to study the sign intently. "We're sure that cricket is not an option?" he asked with a twinge of hopefulness in his voice.

"Absolutely not." Cornelius's reply was icy and definitive. 9-Krelblax continued to study the poster, each eye scanning a quadrant, hoping there was something he'd missed.

"Wait a second!" he finally said. "What's this one?" He pointed a tentacle at the bottom right corner, where, in between "shot put" and "uneven parallel bars," the name of a forgotten event appeared to have been scrawled in tiny lettering after the initial printing.

Cornelius leaned in to examine it. "Pole vault?" he asked.

"Uh, I think we meant to cross that one off way back at the beginning!" Kara interjected. *Dammit!* she thought. *That sounded way too hasty and unnatural!*

"I don't think we had," 9-Krelblax said. Much to Kara's dismay, he sounded intrigued. "This is a core track and field event, right, Cornelius?"

"Well, I'd consider it more of a 'freak' event than a 'core' event,"

Cornelius said. "We've phased out most of the pole-based events from the games. Nobody really goes walking around with giant poles anymore. But I guess it is still part of the decathlon. But come on now, Niner..."

"9-Krelblax," 9-Krelblax corrected, suddenly all business.

"Sorry, 9-Krelblax," Cornelius said. "But just like the balance beam, we don't have pole vault equipment here either."

"All done!" President for Life Makepeace called out from the other end of HAWAll. "All the birds!"

9-Krelblax pointed at the pool skimmer that Makepeace had been using to retrieve the seagull corpses. "What about that pole?" he asked. "It looks sturdy."

"Very sturdy!" President for Life Makepeace confirmed. He held the skimmer up above his head and flexed it. "Five hundred scoops!"

Kara darted over to her grandfather. She'd borne the disappointment of HAWAll and the sheer insanity of the alien invasion with remarkable cool for a fifteen-year-old. But pole vaulting was a line she was not willing to cross.

"You've got to put a stop to this, Grandpa," she hiss-whispered. "I'm not pole vaulting!"

"What's wrong with pole vaulting?" Cornelius asked. "It seems..." Kara locked eyes with him and Cornelius was unable to finish his sentence. He stammered for about ten seconds, eventually realizing that he would not be able to find the words while looking his granddaughter in the eye. He tore his gaze away, fixed it on a point on the eastern horizon, then tried again. "It seems cool," he said in possibly the least convincing tone a human being had ever used.

"I'm not pole vaulting!" Kara said. "I spent one day training as a backup to the fourth-string pole vaulter. Pole vaulters make the shot put kids look like Johnny Quarterback. People tell jokes in the locker room about the pole vaulters. 'When's the best time to give a pole vaulter bad news?'"

Cornelius pondered this for a moment, then gave up. "When?" he asked.

"When he's finished licking one end of the pole and is turning it around to lick the other end!" Kara said.

"Even though I don't really get it, that's still pretty funny," Cornelius said. But now it was Kara's turn not to listen.

"I'm not pole vaulting!" she said. "Even the frog racers don't want anything to do with the pole vaulters! Tell them it's a no-go!" At this point in time, Kara figured that the complete annihilation of the earth would have a slightly better impact on her social life than word getting out she was pursuing competitive pole vaulting on the international circuit.

Cornelius sized up the fire in Kara's eyes for a few seconds, then nodded. He hadn't known his granddaughter long, but could tell she felt passionate about the subject. He'd put her through a lot over the past few days, but this was a woman speaking to him, not a child, and she'd earned not just his consideration, but his respect. He turned back to 9-Krelblax.

"Can't do it, guys," he said, patting Kara on the shoulder. He shot his granddaughter a warm, reassuring smile. Kara smiled back, but Cornelius wasn't done. "Even if we have a pole we don't have a bar to vault over."

"No! No! That wasn't my concern in the slightest!" Kara started to protest, but King Moho interrupted.

"A bar to vault over?" the King of Maui said, lowering the poster he'd been dutifully holding for the better part of an hour. He had a look in his eye like an old gunslinger who had just strode into a saloon that was being troubled by outlaws. Except he was shirtless with a pronounced gut. "Sounds to me like you're talking about some sort of reverse limbo situation."

"Is that something you'd be able to put together?" 9-Krelblax asked, though the king's tone already let him know the answer.

The king dropped the event poster and let it flutter to the ground. "I've made limbo bars with less," he said. "One time, at the King of Oahu's daughter's wedding, the island vibes were so relaxed that the limbo bar snapped midway through the reception. The entire day would have been ruined, but I managed to fashion one using nothing but two coconuts, some ukulele strings, and the bones from a rack and a half of succulent baby back ribs. We got that bar down to under two feet that night."

"That must have been one hell of a party," Cornelius said.

"Who says it ever ended?" King Moho said, staring off into the distance. He turned to Cornelius and looked him square in the eye. "You give me fifteen minutes and free access to all the raw materials on this platform and you'll get your bar," he said.

Cornelius nodded. King Moho pointed at Zzarvon, then at the *Stupid Butt*. The Larvilkian navigator nodded his understanding, then took off for the ship while King Moho made a beeline for the governor's mansion.

Kara rapidly felt control slipping away from her. "I don't think you've thought this through!" she said to 9-Krelblax. "How are you going to ooze fast enough to build up momentum to vault?"

"Momentum? Don't be foolish! Who needs it when you have all this grippy surface area! I will leverage the pole with absolute precision!" 9-Krelblax flailed several tentacles at Kara and Cornelius. The real answer was that he intended to cheat, but he hoped the Earth humans would buy this explanation.

Desperate, Kara turned to her grandfather. "I spent one day practicing this event! One! You're really going to risk everything you've worked for over the past few decades on someone who's pole vaulted maybe a dozen times?"

Cornelius put both of his hands on Kara's shoulders and looked her in the eye. "Kara," he said. "You're an Everglades. And I believe in you." The real answer was that he too intended to cheat, but he hoped his granddaughter would buy this explanation.

Kara looked at her grandfather. His face wore a firm expression of love and grandfatherly pride. In his eyes, though, Kara saw something else entirely. They weren't stern, or crazy, or confident. They were human. They were vulnerable. But most of all they were pleading. Pleading with her to help him.

Kara looked into those pleading eyes for a few seconds and knew what she had to do. "I'll do it, Grandpa. For you."

Cornelius smiled.

"And for a 25 percent stake in all commerce conducted through HAWAll in perpetuity," Kara continued. "Cash. Not in some garbage trust where I only get it when I turn eighteen or when you die or some other nonsense."

"What in the living hell?" Cornelius roared. "Extortion! Brute extortion! And coming from a limb of my own family tree!"

Kara threw up her hands. "I guess old four eyes here can just compete unopposed then," she said. "May as well just give him the medal now."

Cornelius narrowed his eyes at the hardline negotiating. But a smile, fueled by deep pride in his devious, opportunistic granddaughter, quickly forced its way onto his face.

"Like I said," Cornelius beamed as he embraced Kara. "You're an Everglades!"

There was a loud crash from the governor's mansion. "Everything alright in there?" Cornelius asked as he pulled away from the hug.

"Sorry!" King Moho yelled. "Damn hippo costume scared the hell out of me!"

Cornelius bit his tongue. 9-Krelblax spoke up instead. "Assuming those two idiots are able to construct the reverse limbo vaulting bar, won't we need a mat to cushion our landing?"

"I figure the enormous pile of dead seagulls should be more than adequate," Cornelius said. He pointed at the pile. It was probably fifteen feet in diameter and came up waist high on President for Life Makepeace, who stood next to it surveying his work with pride.

Just then, there was a rustling from a lower layer of the pile. Evidently one of the gulls had survived the anthem and had only been stunned when Makepeace scooped it out of the water. The President of Warland sprang into action, raising the skimmer pole above his head and repeatedly bashing it down in the general area of the pile where the rogue bird had stirred. Eventually the pile grew still, and he lowered the pole and shot Cornelius a thumbs-up and a smile.

"Forty percent," Kara said.

twenty

"I mean, he *just* fished them out of the ocean!" Cornelius shouted into the governor's mansion. "It's like they had a bath. I guarantee you it's the cleanest those filthy scavengers have ever been!"

"It makes my skin crawl just to think about it, Grandpa," Kara replied through the barely ajar door. She was sitting on the floor under the spot where the hammock had been. The governor's mansion, already sparsely outfitted when Kara arrived, had been gutted. King Moho had stripped the place of everything that might possibly be useful in the creation of a pole vault bar. Copper coils from the dorm fridge, the aluminum frame of the whiteboard, dozens of feet of speaker wire from the radio equipment. Even the hammock was being pulled apart so they could utilize individual strands of knit cable. The room looked like it had been ransacked by drug-crazed thieves. Kara found the fact that it had actually been ransacked by budding track-and-field enthusiasts much more disturbing.

Zzarvon had made a similar raid of the *Stupid Butt*, emerging with armfuls of broken furniture and office supplies, some of them glowing. The last time Kara had looked, the navigator and the king were in the process of erecting a ramshackle pole vault bar that was, much to her dismay, directly in front of the seagull pile.

"It'll be like flopping into a big fluffy cloud!" Cornelius said. "Just think of it as the world's biggest feather pillow!"

"Feather pillows don't have beaks!" Kara replied. "And who's ever heard of seagull down? That's disgusting. That's like making a scarf out of rat wool."

"I'm gonna correct you on a few points there, Kara," Cornelius said. "One, feather pillows don't have beaks *anymore* because America has lost her sense of craftsmanship. When honest tradesmen were plucking birds and stuffing pillows by hand instead of a machine run by a four-year-old in some grotesque factory in China, yes, you'd end up with a beak or a foot in your pillow every now and then. My cousins and I would fight over the beak pillow every time we went to our grandmother's house for Thanksgiving. We considered it good luck. And second, rat wool is shaping up to be the third biggest export out of Warland by the year 2038, so I think you should keep your voice down when you're demeaning the future of the textile industry."

Kara did not think that either beak pillows or rat scarves were worth dignifying with a response. She closed her eyes and leaned her head back against the wall of the mansion, trying to relax and failing. A few seconds later she heard the door slowly creak open.

"Come on, stop sulking," Cornelius said. "Verna Dickerson would never have acted this way!"

"Who is Verna Dickerson, Grandpa?" Kara asked, not bothering to open her eyes.

"Who is Verna Dickerson?" Cornelius repeated, trying to sound offended. "Only the greatest pole vaulter of all time! Vaultin' Verna they called her! Rode the rails all over the country doing barnstorming pole vault expeditions. They said she could turn off the lights and pole vault into bed before the room was dark. Took gold in three consecutive Olympics. Course, this was before women had won the right to vault, so they were all nullified. But that didn't stop New Zealand from putting her picture on a bulk-rate postage stamp!"

Kara opened her eyes and looked at her grandfather. "Is any of that true?" she asked.

"Of course not!" Cornelius said. "But you had no idea if it was or wasn't, and that's my point! Nobody gives a damn about pole vaulters! There aren't any who are famous, let alone a household name. But you have a chance to change that!"

Kara looked skeptical. Cornelius soldiered on with his sales pitch. "Look, say there's a baby born today and his parents name him Orville." A horrified expression crossed Kara's face as she imagined a ninety-year-old baby. Cornelius raised his hands in pre-emptive caution. "Purely a hypothetical situation! Don't worry, there's no baby named Orville out there, we can only hope. But my point is: That kid can do absolute jack, just live his life, I dunno, design an app or two, and there's a still decent chance he winds up the third most famous Orville in all of recorded history! And imagine if he actually does something *good*!"

"The bar *is* set pretty low for famous Orvilles," Kara had to concede.

"Exactly! And don't get me started on Ichabods!" Cornelius said, jabbing an excited finger toward his granddaughter. "My point is, pole vaulters are the Orvilles of the athletic world! There are no great pole vault moments in sports history! But if you beat this gross alien guy, after one vault *you're the Top Orville*! Back to the bike shop with you, Wright! Go resemble a dried turnip some more, Redenbacher!"

Cornelius took a few steps toward Kara and extended a hand. "Kara," he said in a calm yet excited voice. "It's time to become the Top Orville."

Kara looked at her grandfather's outstretched hand. It hadn't exactly been the kind of locker room speech that inspires a slow clap in the movies. But it did beat pretty much every speech that the Jefferson track coach had given the team. His speeches had mostly focused on trying to incite the javelin throwers to fight the pole vaulters for the amusement of the rest of the team.

Kara shifted her gaze up to lock eyes with Cornelius. "Forty percent," she reiterated.

"Thirty-five," Cornelius said. His tone was steadfast, and his hand did not waver. Kara still thought she might have the negotiation advantage, seeing as how his decades-long scheme lived or died depending on her participation. Then again, since plotting the demise of those who had wronged him seemed to be the primary motivation behind every action in her grandfather's life, Kara figured she should probably not press her luck any more than she already had by deciding to take a casual summer vacation with him. Kara decided to do whatever it took to stay within his good graces. She decided to become the Top Orville.

"Let's do it," Kara said. She reached out and took her grandfather's hand. Cornelius clasped it and pulled Kara to her feet.

"I knew I could count on you!" he said. Cornelius threw an arm around Kara's shoulders and led her to the door of the governor's mansion. "Now wait until you see what King Moho has done with this reverse limbo apparatus. It seems insulting to call him a party animal, he's more of a party *savant*. Check it—GAHH!"

Cornelius's train of thought was interrupted as he ushered Kara through the door and nearly ran face-first into the back of a hovering Larvilkian.

"Greetings, fellow pole vault competitors!" 9-Krelblax boomed. The commander was suspended in the air a good eight inches off the ground just outside the door of the governor's mansion. He stood with his tentacles akimbo, observing the pole vault bar. His attire was unchanged save for a thick belt he wore around his midsection. There was a low whir as the Larvilkian commander rotated in the air to face them.

"I assume you have been making the final warm-ups just as I have?" 9-Krelblax asked, hovering as if nothing were out of the ordinary. A rectangular device strapped to his belt flashed three lights of various colors. "Every true Olympian has their own method of preparation, be it stretching, listening to inspirational music, or exchanging bodily fluids with a fellow athlete who has already lost their competition and is therefore feeling rather vulnerable. Me, I prefer to treat a competition as just another day. Don't deviate from the routine. Yes, everything's the same as it was before they started building the bar and I went on the ship to prepare. Well, let's get to it, shall we?"

The box on his belt gave off another low whir as 9-Krelblax rotated back around and began to glide through the air toward the pole vault bar. Kara and Cornelius looked at each other, shrugged, then followed after him.

9-Krelblax hovered at about the same rate that a Larvilkian oozed, all the while slowly drifting farther off the ground like a tentacled dirigible. He turned and waved to the gathered spectators. Backwards Cap and Mac waved back, Henry's wife frowned, and Henry appeared too engrossed in deciding where to place his new pin on his satchel to even notice. Goodluck was now lurching around the island, his face pained, his gait zombie-like. Kara figured that it had probably been two hours since he started running, and at an Olympian pace, he was probably close to finishing the grueling length of race he'd prepared for. Nobody seemed to be paying him any attention. Even President for Life Makepeace was staring at the action over by the pole vault bar.

And what a pole vault bar it was!

The pole vault has never been the safest track event. Vaulters start by running at full speed holding a length of pole that is twice their height. As they sprint, they are expected to plant the end of the pole into something called "the box" while they are running. The box is six inches wide. If they somehow manage to accomplish this without impaling themselves, they are immediately catapulted into the air. As they defy gravity, they must twist and contort their body in order to clear the bar, only to release the pole and plummet to the ground. This all takes place in about two seconds. The whole process is rife with opportunities for pulled muscles, broken ribs, and crotch impact. One kid at a Jefferson JV meet even fractured a vertebra, though this had occurred at the same time as the long-jump pit dog-pooping incident and nobody really noticed.

But throughout the history of the sport, it was the inherently difficult act of pole vaulting that had been the primary cause of these injuries, not the actual bar itself. The HAWAIl Olympics evidently intended to change this.

The apparatus that King Moho and Zzarvon had constructed looked like it belonged in a medieval torture chamber *and* like it was a security measure intended to keep people out of said chamber. Two narrow makeshift pillars jutted up out of the surface of HAWAll. A throbbing hum gave the sense that they were being supported by powerful yet unstable Larvilkian magnets. The pillars were formed from metal scraps salvaged from the governor's mansion and the *Stupid Butt*. The scraps appeared to be held in place by hammock thread and dripping florescent green putty. There were also several extension cords knotted around the structure at various points. One of them emitted a brief but furious shower of sparks. About a third of the way down each pillar a service bot was impaled through its center. The bot on the left bleeped and blooped a message that, though unintelligible, suggested to Kara it was not participating in the Olympics voluntarily.

The scent of imminent electrical fire wafted through the ocean air.

The box where Kara would need to plant the end of the pole before vaulting was a jagged old piece of radio equipment that King Moho had ripped the guts out of. The horizontal clearance bar was in no better shape. It rested precariously on top of the two impaled service bots. Kara noted that it was wrapped in various lengths of copper wire. The frayed ends of the wire stuck out every few inches in all directions. But for the life of her, Kara couldn't determine what the bar itself was made of.

"Garbage," King Moho said as if reading her thoughts. The king sidled up next to Kara and Cornelius and pointed up at the bar.

"There's a garbage chute on the *Stupid Butt* that forces out their refuse through a narrow tube," the King of Maui explained. "Now usually that compacted trash gets ejected into an asteroid dump or into the path of peacekeeping satellites owned by something called the Piltrixians?" The king shrugged. "Anyway, it turns out that the tube compresses the refuse into a very usable length of trash. Wrap it up in copper for added stability and there you go! We're ready to limbo! Er, I mean, pole vault!"

King Moho looked very pleased with his creation, even as a different piece of extension cord threw off sparks of its own.

"Well, shall we get started?" 9-Krelblax inquired, trying to look casual as he stretched his tentacles first to the right, then to the left, all the while floating what was now at least a foot and a half off the surface of HAWAll.

"Sure, we can get started," Cornelius replied. He pointed at King Moho, then the pool skimmer. The king walked over to retrieve it as Cornelius continued. "But you obviously can't wear an anti-gravity belt during the event. That would be a massive advantage."

9-Krelblax's moodcore flushed a deep crimson. "Anti-gravity belt!" he roared, rising noticeably into the air. "That's preposterous!"

"You've gradually floated higher and higher ever since we came back outside," Cornelius said as he took the skimmer pole from King Moho. He walked over to stand directly in front of where 9-Krelblax was floating. "I'm directly at eye level with that red light in your chest right... now!" Cornelius squinted as the crimson moodcore drew even with his line of sight, but even as he stood there, it quickly raised above his eyeline. It was as if 9-Krelblax was on an invisible, slow-moving elevator. "And now it's above my head," Cornelius informed 9-Krelblax.

"Unfortunately, it's true," Zzarvon said as he oozed over to the two of them. He looked up at 9-Krelblax. "Everyone can see that you're floating, sir. In fact, you're high enough that your mid-front anus is directly lined up with President Everglades's eyes right now."

"Oh God!" Cornelius said, turning and covering his face with the hand that wasn't holding the skimmer pole.

"Dammit, Zzarvon!" 9-Krelblax shouted. He was rising faster now, and appeared to be unable to stop himself. "It's set too high! It wasn't supposed to kick in until I was actually pole vaulting!"

"I breathed in!" Cornelius wailed. "Through my mouth *and* nose!"

"I'm sorry, sir," Zzarvon said. "Technician Tamblirx tuned the belt up. He assured me it was in full working order. Or at least I thought that's what he said. His muttered ramblings were a touch incoherent."

"That cloned cretin worked on this thing?" 9-Krelblax now sounded more panicked than angry. "I told you not to let him... Oh God, just get me down from here! Help!"

"Press the middle button, sir," Zzarvon said, craning his neck up. 9-Krelblax's entire body was now floating over even Zzarvon's eye antennae. A few more feet and he'd be above the vault bar without the aid of a pole.

9-Krelblax jammed a tentacle at the anti-gravity belt's middle button. There was no noticeable reduction of his altitude. "It's not working, Zzarvon!" he yelped.

"You didn't let me finish," Zzarvon replied. "Push it again."

9-Krelblax tapped the button again. "Still nothing!"

"I still wasn't finished!" Zzarvon replied. "Press it one more time."

"Now why the hell didn't you just say 'press it three times' in the first plaaaaaaa—" 9-Krelblax's sentence went unfinished as he pressed the button a third time and gravity kicked back in. There was a loud *SPLUT* as the Larvilkian commander landed on the surface of HAWAll. His body dispersed outward in a gooey circle, like a water balloon hitting the ground in slow motion. The anti-gravity belt, a communicator, and a ray gun sat in various parts of the puddle that had been 9-Krelblax's body. The only indication that the goo had at one point in time been a Larvilkian were the four eye stalks sticking up out of the center of it. All four of the eyes were narrowed, angry, and looking directly at Zzarvon.

"Is that going to come off?" Cornelius asked Zzarvon. "I've got a thirty-year-old bottle of Windex but nothing else in terms of cleaning supplies." One of the eyes turned to glare at Cornelius.

"He's not dead," Zzarvon said. "The molecules in a Larvilkian's body are not as rigidly attached as those in other life forms. In moments of intense physical stress, our elasticity can be really handy. Look! He's already reverting back to his natural state."

The circle of splattered 9-Krelblax indeed seemed to be pulling inward, and as it did the eyes in the center of the circle began to slowly rise off the platform. The commander's mouth orifice appeared a few seconds later, followed by the rest of his face. As his body continued to reform itself, it appeared that an extremely angry 9-Krelblax was emerging upwards out of the surface of HAWAII.

"What would have happened if he'd landed on one of us?" Kara asked as she watched in horrified wonder.

"That depends," Zzarvon said. "How stable are your molecules?"

"Very?" Kara said, even though she wasn't really sure where a human's molecular stability rated on a universe-wide scale. It didn't seem to matter.

"That wouldn't have been good," Zzarvon said. He thought about it a bit more. "Yeah, that would have been really bad."

The process was gradual at first, but once a majority of 9-Krelblax had re-formed, the speed at which the splattered molecules were pulled inward increased. Before long, there was a satisfying *pop* and 9-Krelblax stood before them looking none the worse, a furious bright-red moodcore the only indication that he'd been a two-dimensional puddle moments before.

"You're not supposed to release the button until you're back on the ground," Zzarvon informed his commander as he bent down to pick up the equipment that had fallen off of 9-Krelblax. "You could have broken the gravity belt. *We* may be made of unstable molecules, but *it's* not. Oh wait, this is the new X-Plus model. It actually is."

Kara initially thought that a final stage of 9-Krelblax's re-forming process was not yet complete, since his entire body appeared to be shaking. He, of course, was simply quivering with rage.

"Go put that damn device back on the ship!" he exploded at Zzarvon. "Someplace where that cloned halfwit from another dimension can't find it!"

"What's that?" Cornelius asked as Zzarvon oozed up the ramp of the *Stupid Butt*. "Cloned halfwit? What's going on in your ship?"

9-Krelblax ignored him. "Give me that pole!" he shouted. He snatched the skimmer from Cornelius. He fumbled with it, gripping it with two, then three, then four tentacles as he tried to manipulate the unwieldy object so that the net end was in the air. Eventually he succeeded in turning it around. Holding the pole at an angle, he looked like he was raising a flag on some intergalactic Iwo Jima—only with a lot more anger and tentacles than the original version.

"What's the all-time record for the pole vault?" 9-Krelblax shouted. Kara and Cornelius looked at each other and shrugged.

"I can tell you the Hawaiian record for limbo is fourteen inches," King Moho offered. "Of course that was at an unsanctioned luau. If we're talking official Hawaiian Limbo Federation records you're looking at fifteen and a half. If that helps."

It didn't help. Fortunately, Zzarvon had reappeared on the *Stupid Butt* ramp and had a communicator accessible. "Sir, it looks like the pole vault world record is a touch over six-point-two meters," he said.

"Ha!" 9-Krelblax scoffed. "Pathetic! I could vanquish it easily on my first try, but that would deprive me of seeing that delusional glimmer of hope in their eyes. Instead, I will start with a warm-up so I can watch their hope wither and die slowly! Set the bar to a still-impressive five meters!"

King Moho looked at Cornelius, who could only shrug. The king walked over to the vault apparatus, where he was joined by Zzarvon. The two of them huddled over a small control pad at the base of the right pole while 9-Krelblax stood by, flexing his grip on the skimmer pole. Zzarvon tapped a few buttons on the control panel, then flicked a lever. There was a shower of sparks from the copper-wrapped trash bar, then slowly, with occasional sparks of their own, the two impaled service bots began to rise. As they slid up the support pillars, they raised the crossbar with them. Eventually they stopped at a height that must have been five meters.

Kara eyed it with a mix of skepticism and nervousness. Admittedly, the pole vault portions of track meets were when she usually opted to go to the bathroom, or hit up the snack bar, or just cast her gaze downward lest anyone cool mistakenly think she was displaying interest in the event. But the few times she'd accidentally glanced at a vault, she'd never seen anyone attempt a height even close to what 9-Krelblax had requested. It looked like he'd be attempting to vault over the backboard of a basketball hoop, with a few extra feet to spare. She didn't think there was a chance in hell he'd be able to do it.

9-Krelblax appeared to agree. For the first time since his body had reformed after his drop from the sky, he was displaying an emotion other than "all-consuming rage." "I said five meters, Zzarvon. How high is that?" 9-Krelblax asked, not bothering to mask his uncertainty.

"That's five meters," Zzarvon said.

"Huh. I could have sworn… Do they not use base twenty-six to measure height?" 9-Krelblax asked.

"They do not, I'm afraid," Zzarvon replied. "They use the primitive base *ten.*" He hit the word ten the way a repulsive wine snob might say "merlot."

"Base ten," 9-Krelblax scoffed. "Good luck extracting the hyper-infinitesimal effect of gravitational pull from structures in theoretical dimensions if you're using base *ten.*" He and Zzarvon chuckled to each other.

"We just want to describe how tall stuff is," Kara said. She felt oddly defensive about the only numerical system she'd ever known.

"Put it at half that height!" 9-Krelblax instructed. King Moho gave a thumbs-up, Zzarvon hit a few buttons, and with a flick of the lever, the sparking service bots creaked their way back down the apparatus until the bar was set at a far more manageable two-and-a-half meters. The two of them took one last look to make sure everything was secure, then joined the other spectators.

9-Krelblax sized up the new challenge. His moodcore glowed a confident dark green. The Larvilkian commander took one last deep breath, flexed his grip on the pole, and began to ooze forward as fast as he could. He was moving with surprisingly fluid grace as he approached the structure, and all of HAWAII watched in amazement as 9-Krelblax lowered the pole with perfect timing, raised into the air, and crashed directly through the trash bar and into the pile of seagulls.

twenty-one

"Hold still," Zzarvon said. "You've still got some feathers stuck to your back."

The Larvilkian navigator plucked at his commander's back as 9-Krelblax rubbed a bruise to the right of his moodcore, where he'd first made impact with the pole vault bar. He was embarrassed and slightly out of breath, but for the most part all that hurt was his pride.

The spirits of everyone else on the island had improved tremendously. The two college students were both still pounding the surface of HAWAII as they howled with laughter. The pole vault bar visibly shook as King Moho struggled not to laugh while he reaffixed it to the apparatus. President for Life Makepeace was imitating 9-Krelblax's graceless flop into the pile of birds over and over again, much to the amusement of Henry. Even the pin collector's wife had briefly cracked a smile. Goodluck proved not too exhausted to bask in the humiliation of others, and gained a spring in his step for a lap or two before reverting back to his previous stance, which resembled less a world-class runner and more someone dying of thirst in the desert.

Kara thought that the alien's crash through the bar was one of the funniest things she'd ever seen and kicked herself for not recording what surely would have been the most viral video of all time. Even so, she had to fight back a slight twinge of sympathy that kept trying to rear its head. The action of pole vaulting was entirely unlike any physical act she'd done in her decade and a half of existence. Even after a day of practicing it, she'd barely felt comfortable with the intricate string of maneuvers a successful vault required. She didn't see how the alien had expected to just pull it off on his first attempt. But at the same time, she found his confidence strangely off-putting. His failure was so total and hilarious that it made her uncertain she'd be able to execute a successful vault of her own.

Cornelius did not seem to harbor any of these misgivings. In fact, he appeared giddy to the point of hubris.

"We've got this bitch in the bag!" he crowed, and did a little jig.

"Grandpa, you've got to stop saying that," Kara hissed. She looked around to see if anyone had heard him this time. 9-Krelblax glared at her, but he'd been shooting the evil eye at everyone since Zzarvon had pulled him out of the seagull pile.

Cornelius gave a whoop and began to dance in a circle around his granddaughter. Kara raised the skimmer straight up in the air and watched the end of it dip. After giving it a thorough wipe down, she'd spent the past few minutes sizing up the pole's feel and flexibility. At the beginning of the season, Jefferson's assistant track coach had made a huge deal out of "getting to know your pole." He'd forced the pole vaulters to carry a pole everywhere they went: home, to class, even in the locker room shower, until the fifteen-foot carbon rod felt like a natural extension of their bodies. Not surprisingly, this did not help the pole vaulters' reputations. In fact, the policy had been responsible for one car crash, blamed for two more, and even though the first ever shower-blinding incident at Jefferson was still technically "under investigation," everyone knew a pole was responsible.

The pool skimmer felt more like an invasive growth than it did a natural extension of Kara's body, but she did think she understood its physics a bit better than she had a few minutes ago. She waited for Cornelius to dance underneath the drooping end, then lowered it to the surface of HAWAII.

"What should our strategy be, Grandpa?" Kara asked.

Cornelius performed a little finale of toe tapping and jazz hands, then beamed at Kara. "What do you mean, strategy?" he asked, beaming. "Get over the bar! There's no chance that oaf is going to make it over. All you need is one successful attempt!"

"Yeah, but it's not as easy as you make it sound," Kara said. "A vault is a series of dozens of unnatural movements happening simultaneously. And you don't have time to think about any of them, you've got to perform them instinctively. To do this successfully requires every part of the human body dancing together in a delicate ballet, Grandpa!"

"The bar's ready again!" King Moho yelled.

"Set it to double where 9-Krelblax had it!" Cornelius immediately shouted back.

"No!" Kara shook her head and the pole at her grandfather. "Did you hear anything I just said? This is very difficult and I'm bad at it! I'm not attempting a world-class height right out of the gate!"

Cornelius sighed in dismay, his enthusiasm briefly derailed. "Fine," he muttered. "Hey, Moho! Ixnay on the doubling! Put it back down where it was!"

"Roger that!" King Moho shouted back. Cornelius smiled at Kara, and she was about to return the olive branch when she heard a horrible screeching sound from the direction of the pole vault setup. Kara turned around to see a shower of sparks shooting out from each support pillar, as well as the copper-coated main bar.

"Whoa!" King Moho shouted as he covered his head with his hands. The shower abated as the upward-moving service bots slowly came to a halt. Then, with another screech, a new burst of sparks, and a few puffs of smoke, they began to lower the bar again.

"Guess you shouldn't try to get them to reverse directions until they're done moving!" King Moho said, patting out a spark that had landed on his belly. "Pew! That smells awful! You sure those things are gonna hold out for two more rounds, Zzarvon?"

"Oh, they'll hold out," Zzarvon said, dropping the last feather he'd plucked from 9-Krelblax to the ground. "That electrical fire smell is just the service bots' way of protesting that we impaled them. Ungrateful little bastards. You employ them for years, *at a time of very high galaxy-wide unemployment numbers!*" He pointedly shouted the last part of his sentence toward the pole vault apparatus. "And all you get is sass and lip and smells that you probably shouldn't breathe too much of—seriously, turn away from them, everyone! Breathe from the other direction!"

Kara, King Moho, and Cornelius all obeyed Zzarvon's suggestion and turned away from the apparatus as the service bots lowered the bar to the requested height.

"So those bots are intelligent?" Kara asked.

"Oh, very," Zzarvon said. "Feel the hell out of pain, too! Yep, they're miserable right now. Probably wish they were back on the ship unclogging toilets *but that's not going to happen!*" Zzarvon again directed the second part of his sentence toward the apparatus.

The service bots emitted a series of synchronized bloops that were all too familiar to Kara. Through sheer cosmic coincidence, the series of tones was the exact same as the sounds the slot machine game on her mom's first cell phone had made when you won. Kara had played the game endlessly in the backseat of the car as a child and the sound triggered a profound sense of happy nostalgia. She remarked as much to Zzarvon.

"That was them begging to be put out of their misery, pleading for quick and efficient assisted suicide," Zzarvon replied. "And to that I say *fat chance, losers!*"

Kara had pretty much prohibited her conscience from wrestling with the dozens of ethical dilemmas she had been presented with ever since her grandfather reappeared in her life. It was tied up in a corner of her mind, wide-eyed and ball-gagged. But now that an intelligent being's right to die was on the table, she decided it was time for The Ol' Sense of Right and Wrong to be boarded up behind a mental brick wall, "Cask of Amontillado"-style. She looked out to sea as two thugs from her reptile brain grabbed her conscience and dragged it off kicking and grunting what were surely muffled pleas for help. Kara fully accepted that her conscience might burst through the wall later in life, bearded, emaciated, and ready to wreak havoc on whatever successful position in life lacking a conscience had elevated her to. But as she gripped the pole, she had to admit it was a lot easier to focus on sports when you didn't give a damn about anything in life that was actually important.

"Are you ready?" Cornelius asked.

Kara narrowed her eyes at the pole vault apparatus and lifted the skimmer into the air. "I do not accept that robots can feel pain," she replied through gritted teeth.

"Uh… OK?" Cornelius said. "Is that like an 'Eye of the Tiger' kind of thing?"

In response, Kara emitted a primal bellow, and took off sprinting at full speed toward the bar. Her focus was entire. The bar was all she saw, but it wasn't even the bar as it existed in real life. It was like a simple line drawing of the bar, reduced to its purest form: an obstacle to be conquered. And each step that brought her closer to it also brought her closer to an understanding of the physics of the act she was about to perform. Velocity, force, acceleration, torque, friction; she was master of them all as they danced, intertwined in front of her eyes. As Kara lowered the pole in a single fluid movement, it occurred to her that the act of pole vaulting was simpler than she'd ever thought possible. And not only that, it was kind of beautiful.

"Miss!" shouted 9-Krelblax.

The swirling, beautiful physics immediately reverted back to a motionless pile of dead seagulls. Kara's first thought was how sweaty her palms were, but before she could act on this, the tip of the pole touched the surface of HAWAIl, and she found herself leaning back and raising up into the air.

The ride was brief. It turns out that advanced physical maneuvers involving a pole depend on more than just understanding torque. You actually have to have muscles that are prepared to do stuff. Kara kicked maybe a half a second too late and held onto the pole for what was probably just a blink of an eye too long, but by the time she realized she'd made either mistake she had already crashed to the ground well over two feet in front of the bar she'd been attempting to clear.

Kara landed on her left shoulder; her hip hit the ground a moment later. She sputtered out a ragged breath and immediately wheezed in another one. The pole sprung up in the air with a comical *BOI-OI-OI-OI-OING* before landing next to her. Kara was on her feet and striding toward 9-Krelblax before it stopped wobbling.

"That's bullshit!" she yelled, pointing at the Larvilkian commander. There was a brief moment where she processed that she was physically unharmed after what could have been a serious tumble. That was good news and all, but the relief was vastly overshadowed by her aggrieved sense of sportsmanship, plus the knowledge that she could have been playing dirty from the beginning if this was how it was going to be.

9-Krelblax threw up some tentacles in a "who, me?" gesture and looked around trying to feign innocence. Kara continued toward him with an accusatory finger outstretched, but quickly realized she had no real plan for once she got within a few feet. Jabbing him in the chest like a baseball manager would an umpire was certainly out. Poking a Larvilkian wasn't something she wanted to do even before she learned they had a front anus, perhaps several of them dispersed all over their bodies. Kara slowed her progress and took a few deep breaths. As she stared straight into 9-Krelblax's second and third eyes, Kara reminded herself that she still had two vaults left. That would be plenty of opportunity to exact revenge on the alien creep. And if she was somehow unable to do that, well then she'd jam the skimmer pole into one of his front anuses.

"Your turn," Kara said. She forced a tight smile onto her face and wondered how on earth the real Olympians who had obsessively trained for their entire lives could possibly tolerate each other's presence for more than a few seconds. She'd been an Olympian in the loosest sense of the word for less than half an hour and she wanted her opponent dead, or at least to get bronze. Hiring thugs to bash a rival's knee with a lead pipe should be the *rule* in the quest to be the greatest in the world, not some weird exception with a hilarious name from the mid-nineties.

9-Krelblax smirked at Kara, then pointed at the skimmer pole. Zzarvon dutifully oozed over to retrieve it.

"I guess it *is* my turn," 9-Krelblax announced to nobody in particular. "Say, King Moholaiko, why don't we lower that by, say, half a meter? No reason to overexert myself if the competition…" 9-Krelblax turned his first eye toward Kara. "Isn't up for it." The Larvilkian's tone was haughty, but Kara was paying more attention to the glowing light of his moodcore, which was a faint baby blue. Kara knew an unconfident color when she saw one. Advantage: Everglades, she thought.

Zzarvon oozed back with the pole and handed it over to 9-Krelblax, who snatched it away with four tentacles. As he stood there working his grip on the pole, Kara retreated back to her grandfather, who had stood by observing silently during her unfortunate first attempt.

Cornelius didn't say anything as she came to a stop in front of him. But as Kara turned to face the pole vault apparatus, he reached out and squeezed her shoulder, the one she'd come down hard on. To Kara, nothing more needed to be said.

Well, maybe one more thing. "Do we need to sign anything regarding the 35 percent, or is an oral agreement going to be sufficient as we move forward?" she asked, still staring straight ahead.

Kara heard her grandfather suck in a little bit of air through his teeth, and his grip on her shoulder briefly tightened. But he quickly relaxed it, and gave her shoulder a few pats. "We're good," Cornelius said. "Just get over that bar, and we're good."

There was a horrible sound of metal twisting as the service bots slid into place half a meter down the pole vault apparatus and then silence. Every eye on the island was on 9-Krelblax.

The Larvilkian captain did not perform well under pressure.

As soon as he began to slither-sprint toward the bar, Kara knew something was wrong. She couldn't exactly put her finger on it. To be honest, watching a Larvilkian attempt an athletic feat gave you the sense that many things were wrong. Jiggling, flailing, and secreting were not typically things one observed at elite athletic competitions. But then again, his first attempt had been full of these graceless maneuvers too. No, it was something else.

It must be something about his posture. Or maybe he was taking a slightly different approach angle? Kara was frustrated that she wasn't able to pinpoint it, but she was also excited that she at least noticed something had changed. She let herself imagine a scenario in which she could sense that something was off about a Jefferson athlete during a track meet. After hours of poring over video footage, the coach would detect a subtle, microscopic mechanical flaw that, once corrected, could elevate Jefferson athletics to the next level. "I don't know how you sensed that, Kara," the coach would say at the awards banquet. "But we owe this state championship to your keen eagle eye."

"Sir, you're holding the pole backwards!" Zzarvon shrieked, jolting Kara out of her fantasy. 9-Krelblax was nearing the bar and lowering the skimmer, which was indeed, turned around so that the end with the net on it was rapidly approaching the ground. Kara decided to hold off on composing her awards-ceremony speech until she was able to recognize important details like "sole piece of equipment required by an event pointing in the completely wrong direction."

Zzarvon's warning came too late, and 9-Krelblax was unable to stop his momentum. He attempted to vault his sizeable body into the air off of the cheap plastic frame of the skimmer net, which immediately fractured into dozens of splinters the moment the commander pressed down on it.

Instead of sticking in the box and acting as a fulcrum, the end of the pole skittered along the surface of HAWAll. 9-Krelblax clutched onto it for dear life as he hurtled forward, like a blind man who had accidentally wandered onto an ice rink futilely trying to steady himself with his cane. 9-Krelblax emitted a garbled cry of fury mixed with despair as he slumped forward at an angle that was clearly not going to sustain itself once the pole lost the ability to support him, which it did as soon as it skewered the first dead seagull and lodged itself deep within the pile.

Over the past three seconds, 9-Krelblax had kept moving when he expected to stop, and now he found himself stopping when he'd hoped more than anything he would keep moving. An experienced pole vaulter, had they found themselves in 9-Krelblax's position, would have abandoned their attempt, flopped forward onto the safety of the pile of birds or the gym mat, then left the sport to wander the remote corners of the earth because obviously, as a worldwide laughingstock, they couldn't continue pole vaulting anymore.

9-Krelblax on the other hand, decided to go for it. With a gurgled grunt, he pushed off the ground. The pole, currently wedged three feet deep in a pile of waterfowl, did not provide much leverage. It was just enough, however, to raise 9-Krelblax to head-bonking level on the pole vault bar, which, as luck would have it, he was directly underneath.

The Larvilkian commander's head slammed into the bar, causing it to emit a blinding shower of sparks. Three of 9-Krelblax's eye antennae reflexively retracted themselves all the way into his head, but the fourth one snagged on the bar as it retreated, and ended up wrapped around the bar like a monkey's prehensile tail. For a brief moment, the entire mass of 9-Krelblax hung by one eye stalk from the pole vault apparatus. The eye blinked once at the gathered spectators. Then there was simultaneously a zapping sound, another shower of sparks, and a Larvilkian yelp of pain as 9-Krelblax came crashing to the ground. Somehow, he landed upright, but the bar had also come detached and wasn't far behind. It hit him on the head again, and 9-Krelblax toppled forward into the seagull pile once more, this time possibly unconscious.

The whole thing took place in maybe five seconds, but the sheer, ecstatic joy that coursed through Kara's body felt like the kind of energy you could use to found several major religions and maybe a few more weird, unpopular ones. Her eyes had seen the glory. It was like that video she'd seen of the little boy kicking the clown in the crotch, but on a euphoric, cosmic level. It was as if the concept of failure had amassed a physical presence, been handed a pole, and told to compete in the Olympics. Nobody had ever been as bad at anything as 9-Krelblax was at pole vaulting.

Which made the fact that he successfully cleared the bar in his third and final attempt all the more devastating.

But before that happened, Kara had to vault again and before *that* there was a substantial break. During this break, the bar was fixed, wildly overpriced saltines were sold to spectators, and 9-Krelblax was verified to in fact be alive.

King Moho was left to repair the apparatus on his own while Zzarvon attended to his commander. The King of Maui reached out and gave the bar a few tentative taps with the back of his fingers. When there were no sparks or electrocutions forthcoming, he picked it up and waited for Zzarvon to get out of the way before he reaffixed it to the service bot mounts.

"Frankly, I don't see why anyone would want to go *over* a limbo bar," King Moho murmured to himself. "It just really seems like it's missing the point."

Zzarvon was rooting through the bird pile with eight tentacles at once, tossing aside the seagulls that covered his commander. As the birds were removed one by one, the dazed form of 9-Krelblax was gradually revealed. The combination of Larvilkian ooze and plumage was not a good one. 9-Krelblax looked like a colonial tax collector who had been tarred and feathered with some sort of radioactive slime instead of tar.

"Are you OK, sir?" Zzarvon asked. 9-Krelblax's eyes all appeared to be focused at different depths and he emitted a weak cough which resulted in several feathers being expelled from his mouth. Zzarvon tossed aside a few more birds, then reached down with every visible tentacle and hoisted his commander out of the bird pile. 9-Krelblax wobbled back and forth. His moodcore appeared to have been extinguished. Observing the patchy coating of sickly feathers from a healthy distance, Kara wondered how closely 9-Krelblax resembled her grandfather's Egbert the Eagle costume.

"Better pluck that chicken before his next attempt!" King Moho roared. "Having wings to flap has gotta be an unfair advantage!" He raised the bar and jammed it into place. The service bots emitted a brief, shrill whine.

"Don't listen to him, sir," Zzarvon whispered. "The patches that aren't swarming with avian lice look very regal." As he led 9-Krelblax to an unoccupied area of HAWAll and again began pulling feathers off him, the faintest hint of furious red began to shine from the commander's moodcore.

"Let's talk strategy," Cornelius said, beckoning Kara closer. She leaned in and glanced around conspiratorially to make sure nobody would overhear whatever devious plan her grandfather was about to unveil.

"Just get over the goddamn bar," Cornelius instructed.

Kara blinked a couple times as she awaited further instruction.

"The...bar..." Cornelius slowly reiterated, in the way you might give directions to a taxi driver in a country where you hadn't bothered to learn a single word of the language. He turned and pointed with an exaggerated stabbing motion in case he wasn't making himself clear. "You pole vault over it!" Cornelius smiled a big fake grin and nodded encouragement.

"Keep the motivational speeches coming, Coach!" Kara scoffed. "Don't bother mentioning any sick kids you want me to bring home the gold for, I've got all the motivation I need!"

Kara was familiar with lousy speeches. Once the Jefferson track coach had been dismissed after a sophomore pole vaulter took a javelin in the thigh, his assistant had taken over locker room speech duty. His speeches usually focused on the fact that he was obligated to be there by virtue of an extremely unusual plea bargain. "The end of this sentence will coincide with the ninety second mark of this court-mandated instructional lecture, thereby fulfilling the letter of the law right... now!" he'd conclude. Cornelius's speeches were somehow even worse.

"I shouldn't have to motivate you!" Cornelius responded. "This is the Olympics! You should be fired up!"

"It's 'kind of' the Olympics!" Kara retorted. "I guess I'm just 'kind of' fired up!"

King Moho walked past the squabbling family members and shook his head. "Really seems like just going *under* the bar would solve a lot of your problems," he muttered.

"Go to hell!" Kara and Cornelius shot back simultaneously. King Moho threw up both his hands in a defensive "I'm just saying" gesture. Kara glared at the King as he shuffled off to join the other spectators, then turned her steely gaze back to her grandfather. The unsolicited advice had once again united the Everglades.

"Just get over the goddamn bar," Kara said, locking eyes with her grandfather.

Cornelius nodded. "Just get over the goddamn bar."

Kara did not get over the goddamn bar.

Her approach was textbook, her plant flawless, and with the proper end of the pole once again facing downward, Kara thrust herself into the air and arched her back in a glorious, fluid display of athleticism. Everyone in attendance watched in silent reverence.

Then the very tip of her left shoe clipped the bar as she fell past. The glancing nudge was just enough to push it free from the hold of the service bots, and as Kara landed gracefully in the bird pile, the bar simultaneously clanked down on the surface of HAWAII.

There was a groan of disappointment from the spectators. *At least they're on my side*, Kara thought. Then the groan continued, gradually shifting upward in pitch and Kara realized that it was not coming from the audience, but rather the pile of seagulls. Pressure from Kara's body was causing them to expel whatever gasses had been inside their body at the time of death, and they were now emerging in one slow, collective wheeze. Flat on her back, Kara's body sunk lower and lower. She squeezed her eyes shut and for a moment it felt like she was lying on a slowly deflating air mattress. It was almost peaceful.

Then a seagull's beak poked her in the butt and Kara burst out of the bird pile so quickly that everyone watching later agreed she seemed to defy physics.

"Dammit!" Kara yelled, rubbing her left cheek.

"Dammit!" Cornelius yelled, hurling a packet of saltines to the ground.

"Booya!" shouted Backwards Cap. He exchanged a high five with his buddy.

Cornelius glared at him. "Traitor!" he shouted.

Backwards Cap shrugged. "No offense to your granddaughter, man, but my allegiance to green trumps the red, white, and blue!"

9-Krelblax and Zzarvon smiled at each other.

"Uh, by green I didn't mean you guys," Backwards Cap corrected. The Larvilkians' faces fell. "Our money is green too," Backwards Cap informed them.

There was an awkward silence. "I meant the money," Backwards Cap said trying to make himself clear. The Larvilkians did not respond.

"I am only cheering for you because if you win I earn a lot of money!" Backwards Cap explained. "Money is what we use as our primary system of commerce!" 9-Krelblax and Zzarvon blinked all eight of their eyes simultaneously.

"The thought of making physical contact with your slimy bodies disgusts me!" Backwards Cap continued.

"Jesus, dude!" his buddy Mac blurted as both Larvilkian moodcores lit up bright red.

"It just came out!" Backwards Cap protested. "Tell me you're not thinking the same thing!" He looked around at his fellow captives/spectators. Henry's wife nodded vigorously in agreement.

A furious 9-Krelblax began to ooze toward where Kara and Cornelius were standing. Zzarvon retrieved the pole and hurried after him. When 9-Krelblax reached what had generally been agreed upon as the starting line, he turned around and stared at the pole vault bar. As Zzarvon approached, 9-Krelblax wordlessly extended a tentacle. Zzarvon passed the pole off to him without any acknowledgement from his commander. As 9-Krelblax continued to focus on the obstacle in front of him, Zzarvon slunk back to stand next to Kara and Cornelius.

"Are you OK?" he asked Kara. With a discreet lower tentacle, he pointed at her rear.

Kara felt her cheeks go a little flush. "I'm fine," she said. "It was more of a surprise than anything. Those beaks are pretty sharp."

Zzarvon smiled. "That's good," he said. The Larvilkian navigator leaned in a bit closer and whispered. "9-Krelblax got poked in the butt too." He suppressed a giggle and Kara raised a hand to her mouth in an attempt to do the same.

"Several of his butts, actually!" Zzarvon continued, a little louder. "Front *and* back!"

"Can we *please* stop discussing what has or has not poked which of my butts!" 9-Krelblax shouted without turning around.

Kara and Zzarvon snorted with laughter and even Cornelius, facing the distinct prospect of having to bankroll a quarter of a million dollars' worth of hookers for an idiot college student, let loose a little chuckle.

9-Krelblax pushed it all from his mind. With methodical care he held the pole out in front of his body and stared at the bar as if lining up a shot through a gun sight. Then slowly, one by one, he began to extend his tentacles and wrap them around the pole.

There was an old saying on Larvilkian-B: "An idle tentacle is a Piltrixian's greatest ally." Throughout his life 9-Krelblax had heard it used in many different situations. When he worked a summer job at the intergalactic carnival, his boss had bleated it whenever he spotted a lollygagging employee who could have been sweeping up peanut shells. A cult leader had repurposed the saying to advocate a series of terror raids on the Piltrixians' home planet of Ribercon-C and eventually get elected Secretary of War. An energy-drink company had used the slogan in a popular series of ads which, now that 9-Krelblax thought about it, were soon enough after the Secretary of War's conviction for sleeping with an underage Piltrixian refugee to be in extremely poor taste.

"An idle tentacle is a Piltrixian's greatest ally." 9-Krelblax had heard the words repeated so many times, and seen them printed endlessly on bumper stickers and t-shirts and protest signs outside the Secretary of War's many suspicious mistrials and eventual public execution that they had long ceased to have any actual meaning. But all of a sudden they resonated loudly in his mind, imbued with a sudden importance.

"Not a single idle tentacle," 9-Krelblax said to himself. Larvilkians possessed a dozen reserve tentacles that remained retracted internally until a moment of great importance required the use of them. Nine out of ten times these moments ended up being weird sex things. 9-Krelblax concentrated deeply and one by one the reserve tentacles began to pop out of his sides and wrap around the pole. Now, with twelve extra primary points of contact, each of them containing multiple sub-levels of suction cups and feelers, the skimmer pole bent and flexed however he desired it. It might as well be an extension of his own body. Why had he not utilized all his tentacles earlier?

"Holy shit, that's revolting!" he heard Backwards Cap exclaim. "It looks like he's banging the pole twenty different ways!"

9-Krelblax turned three of his eyes to glare at the crowd. Backwards Cap threw up two defensive palms. "Don't get me wrong, I'm pulling for you!" he said. He clenched one hand into a fist of solidarity. "Go aliens!"

"It's OK, sir." The reassuring voice belonged to Zzarvon. 9-Krelblax kept one disapproving eye focused on Backwards Cap but turned his other eyes around to look at his navigator.

"You look fine," Zzarvon continued. "Just get over the bar. None of them need to know that several of those reserve tentacles are technically just extremely prolapsed front anuses—"

"Dammit, Zzarvon!" 9-Krelblax shouted. Amidst the titters from the crowd, 9-Krelblax turned all four of his eyes back to the pole vault bar. He flexed all of his tentacles/prolapses, and the subservience of the pole he felt in response filled him with confidence. He began to ooze toward the bar.

They say all folk wisdom has its roots in reality. The nautical legends of beautiful mermaids were very likely just manatees viewed through the eyes of desperately horny sailors. Throwing salt over your shoulder for good luck originated with horny brothel customers as an early attempt to combat the ravages of syphilis. The idea that an apple a day keeps the doctor away was introduced after the first efforts of apple growers to sell their harvest as horniness-increasing wonder-fruit proved unsuccessful. Perhaps the saying should actually be that all folk wisdom has its roots in horniness.

It's probably best not to think about how horniness factored into a piece of folk wisdom that had to do with underutilized tentacles. Not while still processing all those front anuses. What's important is that leaving no tentacle idle did indeed provide 9-Krelblax the strength and finesse he needed to manipulate himself up and over the bar. After he planted its end in the box, the pole bent back toward his launching point in a perfect U. Then as 9-Krelblax soared into the air, the pole quickly straightened, raising him to the point where all 9-Krelblax had to do was let go of the pole and gracefully drop down on the other side of the bar.

Twenty-six tentacles, however, proved way too many to release in the split-second window traditionally utilized by successful pole vaulters. 9-Krelblax managed to free three of them. The tentacles pulled away from the pole, their suction cups making satisfying popping sounds, but the other twenty-three remained firmly attached. If you'd managed to snap a picture at the exact right moment, it would have looked like the pole stood straight up in the air, a horizontal 9-Krelblax floating above it like a defective balloon in a Thanksgiving Day parade that was about to have its permit revoked.

In real time, however, that moment of ethereal, floating grace never existed. The pole simply whipped 9-Krelblax over the bar and into the bird pit with the lighting fast snap of a triggered mouse trap. One moment the pole bent in an upside down U one way, then, a garbled Larvilkian obscenity and an unpleasant sounding thud later, it was facing the other. The path that 9-Krelblax and the pole traced looked like something that Sesame Street might use to teach children how to write a lowercase "m."

When he landed deep in the bird pile, still gripping the pole with nine-tenths of his tentacles, there was a brief moment of stillness. But quickly, the taut pole began to quiver. There were loud pops as 9-Krelblax desperately tried to free his remaining tentacles, but he wasn't fast enough. The planted end of the pole sprung free from the box and shot upright. Everyone held their breath as it swayed back and forth, back and forth. Eventually, the broad path that the untethered end of the pole was tracing through the sky narrowed and finally, after what seemed like an eternity to everyone watching but was probably less than five seconds from start to finish, it stopped wobbling and stood straight up, jutting out of the pile of dead birds like the unadorned flag pole the country of HAWAll deserved.

The trash bar did not move a single inch.

Zzarvon and Backwards Cap let out yelps of glee. In response, an eye antennae shot up from the middle of the bird pile. The eye darted around, trying to get its bearings. Eventually, it located the pole vault bar. After a few seconds, when its dazed owner eventually realized that the bar remained securely in place, the eye went wide, and there was a triumphant cry from inside the pile of dead birds. Moments later, 9-Krelblax burst out of the pile, bellowing like a victorious gladiator.

The Larvilkian commander's moodcore shone a brilliant, pulsing emerald green. He thrust the pole toward the sky and held it aloft, while simultaneously flexing his free tentacles. He looked like he was posing for a painting of himself straddling the corpse of a dragon he had slain.

The fact that elite college high jumpers would have easily cleared the bar he just vaulted over *without* a pole did not dampen 9-Krelblax's spirits. Nor would he have cared if you informed him that most pole vault apparatuses at the high school level would have to be specially modified to allow a bar setting as low as two meters. As you would assume of someone who picked up intergalactic refuse for a living, triumphs in 9-Krelblax's life had been few and far between. But all that had changed. He was about to become an Olympic champion. He suspected that if they could see him now, both his father and Hitler would be very proud.

9-Krelblax spiked the pole to the ground and oozed out of the bird pile. Zzarvon, King Moho, Backwards Cap, and President for Life Makepeace all approached him to offer their congratulations from varying degrees of proximity.

Kara looked at her grandfather. Cornelius was staring at the celebration with mild amusement. She found this surprising, given that a scheme of his thirty years in the making might have just unraveled in the blink of an antenna-attached eye. She waited for him to say something, but Cornelius just stood there, occasionally pulling in a deep breath and exhaling wearily. The thought entered Kara's head that human beings would be a lot easier to read if they had moodcores like the Larvilkians. She wondered what color her grandfather's would be at the moment.

9-Krelblax started to do a little victory dance. Kara thought that it looked like he was being attacked by an entire colony of stinging insects, but the commander was apparently sincere in his efforts. When King Moho and President for Life Makepeace started to clap along, it only seemed to encourage him to ramp it up, and she thought it might be a good time to divert her grandfather's attention.

"Well, I guess I've got one more chance!" Kara said, trying to sound optimistic. Cornelius continued to stare at the celebration. Kara tried again. "I mean, it ain't over til it's over, right?" Nothing.

"Hey!" Kara shouted. "Earth to Grandpa!" Cornelius finally snapped his gaze away from the gyrating alien and looked over at his granddaughter. "We can still win! Aren't you going to give me a pep talk? A little 'Get over the goddamn bar, Orville!' Something like that?" Kara asked. Her grandfather's earlier motivational speeches had not exactly been goosebump-inducing. They were more likely to produce a slight itch, maybe a dryish tongue at best. But at least they had let her know he was in her corner.

Cornelius smiled and shook his head. He started to walk toward his beloved South (actually West) Coast, and after a few steps, stopped and beckoned Kara. Kara gave the pole vault apparatus one more look, then followed after him.

Cornelius didn't speak until they were just a few feet from the edge of the platform. The sun sparkled on the surface of the calm sea. As they came to a halt, the faintest breeze kicked up, and Kara felt the salty ocean spray mist her face and neck.

"It's beautiful, isn't it?" Cornelius remarked. Kara didn't think she needed to reply. She just looked at her grandfather and nodded her head.

"I'm glad I got to share it with you," Cornelius said, tearing his attention away from the water to look at his granddaughter. He smiled. "No matter what happens, these past few days have been very special to me. I'm grateful to finally have you in my life."

"I'm grateful for that too, Grandpa," Kara said. She smiled back at him.

Just then, there was a loud rushing sound from the ocean. Kara and Cornelius both looked back out to sea in time to see a whale that had surfaced less than a quarter mile off the coast of HAWAll. It shot a jet of water out of its blowhole, and as the water fell back to the ocean, it caught the sunlight, making a thousand little rainbows that hung in the sky for a split second before they disappeared forever.

"That's the first whale I've seen from HAWAll in over thirty years," Cornelius said, his voice low with wonder. He turned to look at Kara, his face lighting up with a smile. "I'd say that is a pretty damn solid good-luck sign before your final jump, wouldn't you?"

Kara, still wide-eyed from witnessing such a beautiful act of nature, smiled and nodded. She was about to respond, "I'll say!" when there was a loud *thwump* behind her.

Cornelius's face fell as he looked over Kara's shoulder, and Kara turned to see what had happened. Goodluck, the Warland runner who had by this point undoubtedly put in two-and-a-half, maybe three marathons, had finally reached his limit. He had collapsed facedown, exhausted and dehydrated, ten feet from where Kara and Cornelius stood. His right leg twitched a couple times, and then he was still.

"That's probably not as good a sign," Cornelius said. He reached out and took Kara's hand, then pulled her away from Goodluck, just in case.

"Do you think he needs a doctor?" Kara asked.

"Yep!" Cornelius replied, hastening his pace. Kara took one more glance over her shoulder, then lengthened her stride as well.

"You didn't mean a single thing you said back there, did you Grandpa?" she asked.

"Not a word!" Cornelius said, not bothering to slow down or look at her. "If you fail right now it will ruin my life's work. In fact, you'll probably never see me again. But that doesn't mean I won't hold a grudge! Hey, King Moho!" Cornelius snapped his fingers to get the king's attention. "Let's have the pole!"

Kara had figured as much, so she wasn't super let down. But she had one more question. "And the whale?"

"See them all the time," Cornelius said. King Moho approached and Cornelius reached out and took the pole from him. Over by the bird pile, 9-Krelblax had stopped dancing and was looking in their direction. Streaks of red were starting to creep into the bright green of his moodcore. Cornelius waved King Moho away, then turned and offered the pole to Kara.

"Sometimes there were so many of them I started calling in tips to Russian whalers," Cornelius added. "Gotta pay the bills somehow. Now let's quit messing around. Stick this jump and we'll both earn a lot of money."

Kara grabbed the pole. Against her better judgment, she turned to look back at where the whale had surfaced. There was no sign of the majestic creature, but as she looked on, a sinister boat with a large gun mounted on the bow sped across the horizon. When Kara turned her attention back to the island, she was all business.

"Raise the bar an inch!" she called out to nobody in particular. "Let's do this!"

"What's going on here?" 9-Krelblax demanded as he oozed up to where Cornelius and Kara were standing. Zzarvon followed behind him. Whatever joy 9-Krelblax had derived from his successful vault seemed to have disappeared. He now seemed concerned and flustered.

"She gets a third attempt, too, you idiot," Cornelius said. "If she completes a vault that is higher than yours, she wins and you lose. Pretty simple."

9-Krelblax looked horrified. "But, I thought..." he stammered. "First one to... and they were the... dammit!" He glanced back at Zzarvon, desperate to find a way to blame the misunderstanding on the navigator. Zzarvon simply shrugged.

"Afraid that's not how it works here on Earth," Cornelius explained, refusing to look at 9-Krelblax or mask his disinterested contempt. "We good, Moho?"

King Moho looked up at the service bots and the bar then gave Cornelius a thumbs-up. Cornelius raised a thumb of his own, then ignoring 9-Krelblax's sputtered protests, turned to Kara. He gripped both of her shoulders and looked her in the eye. "You can do this," Cornelius said. He nodded once for emphasis then walked away to join the other spectators.

It wasn't much in the way of inspiration, but it was technically true, and that was enough to renew Kara's confidence. She'd had her warm-ups, the bar was set laughably low, and besides, it was just a stupid scam. Her grandfather could come up with another one if need be. It wasn't like the fate of the planet hung in the balance or anything.

"If you vault over that bar, I'll blow up your planet!" 9-Krelblax shrieked. Kara looked back at the Larvilkian leader. All four of his eyes were wide and angry, and his crimson moodcore was as bright as she'd ever seen it. 9-Krelblax grasped at his side and grimaced. Clearly, the lead in a two-person pole vault competition was something he desperately did not wish to relinquish.

"He's bluffing!" Kara heard her grandfather yell. Fearing an extended, playground-esque battle of "nuh-uh!" vs "yuh-huh!" between her grandfather and the Larvilkians, she decided to just go for it.

Kara looked straight ahead and took a deep breath. Then she raised the pole and began to sprint across the surface of HAWAIl. When she was three steps out, Kara lowered the pole into the box. She felt it stick, and as the pole began to bend, she kicked her legs out and soared into the air. When the pole reached its full vertical extension, she let go, and instincts took over. Kara cleared the bar with several inches to spare.

9-Krelblax was not bluffing. Exactly five minutes after Kara landed in the pile of seagulls, he blew up the earth.

twenty-two

The *Stupid Butt*'s missile struck the HAWAII governor's mansion and detonated with the force of two million atomic bombs. The good news was that none of the seven billion people on the planet suffered. The bad news was that they were immediately rendered into fine particles of space dust along with every animal, car, phone, and ironic t-shirt. The final conscious thought for a shockingly high percentage of the population was a vague sort of worry that some form of entertainment they had yet to view might somehow be "spoiled" for them.

On the bridge of the *Stupid Butt*, 9-Krelblax popped a bottle of Piltrixian champagne.

"Who's in second place now?" he cackled, flailing his tentacles at the observation window where seconds earlier there had been a blue planet. "Guess I showed you the true meaning of faster, higher, and stronger!" he ranted. "Now, you enjoy the ultimate closing ceremony—death! The five rings of your pathetic Olympic logo no longer represent five continents, they now represent Larvilkian greatness! And Larvilkian dominance! And Larvilkian cunning! And Larvilkian—oh crap, the champagne's bubbling over!"

9-Krelblax raised the bottle to his orifice and attempted to slurp some of the foam that was spewing out the mouth of the bottle, but it was coming way too fast. Champagne dripped down the side of the bottle and onto the floor. What little made it into 9-Krelblax's mouth was extremely fizzy and room temperature. The warm foam made him sneeze into the bottle, which only resulted in more foam spraying everywhere. Splatters struck the observation window and ran down in streaks over the view of the former planet.

"Why is this so warm?" 9-Krelblax demanded. "It's disgusting!"

"Sorry, sir," Zzarvon apologized. "We didn't anticipate breaking it out any time soon. We'll keep a bottle on ice going forward."

"Damn straight we will," 9-Krelblax said. He took another, longer, more controlled sip of the warm champagne.

Zzarvon observed his commander with concern from what he'd decided was a safe distance. 9-Krelblax's moodcore glowed bright green, but a trained eye could detect a sickly yellowish tint to it. It had only grown more pronounced since Kara beat him in the pole vault. There was something about the way he'd coldly pushed a button to execute an entire planet that worried Zzarvon.

"Are you feeling OK, sir?" Zzarvon asked, not moving any closer to 9-Krelblax. "You physically overexerted yourself in an unfamiliar atmosphere. Perhaps you ought to lie down to re-acclimate?"

"Nonsense!" 9-Krelblax said, waving a dismissive tentacle and tilting back the champagne bottle for another swig. "This is my time to celebrate! If the first-place pole vaulter is unable to fulfill his or her duties, second place assumes the title! I'm the best in the entire galaxy, Zzarvon! The entire universe even! Get my father on the communicator. The president needs to know he's not the only one in the family who's achieved intergalactic greatness. Oh, and I should probably tell him that any rumors he hears about me blowing up an entire populated planet are true as well."

Zzarvon didn't think that Olympic medals worked the same way as beauty pageant titles, but that wasn't his biggest concern at the moment. "I'll call your father, sir," he said. "But are you sure you want to tell him you blew up Earth?"

"Of course!" 9-Krelblax scoffed. "He'll be happy to hear that Larvilkian greatness has conquered yet another foe! Why would he not want to hear that news?"

"Well, it's just that…" Zzarvon turned his second eye to the observation window and gazed at Earth. It had decreased in size a bit as the *Stupid Butt* traveled farther away, but it was still very much intact as a planet. Zzarvon gazed longingly at the shapes of the seven Hawaiian islands, and though tiny HAWAll was not visible from space, he could still approximate where it was in relation to the United Kingdom. He sized 9-Krelblax up with his other three eyes.

"What are you seeing right now, sir?" Zzarvon asked. "Out the observation window."

"My ultimate triumph!" 9-Krelblax responded, tilting the champagne bottle back again.

"Sure, sure, nobody's questioning your triumph," Zzarvon placated him. "But your triumph was destroying Earth? In that it is no longer floating there in front of us? At all?"

Now it was 9-Krelblax's turn to look at someone askance. "What the hell do you mean?" he asked, narrowing all four of his eyes. "Of course it's no longer floating… Oh, I get it." The commander rolled his middle two eyes. "Sure, if you want to be pedantic about it, Zzarvon, it's still floating in front of us."

Zzarvon sighed in relief.

"It's just in trillions of fine dust particles," 9-Krelblax continued. Zzarvon's sigh of relief turned to one of exasperation. "Not sure why you want to parse semantics at a time of celebration, but if you don't feel like joining in, why don't you make yourself useful and towel the champagne off the observation window. I'm calling my dad."

Zzarvon didn't know what else he could do. He walked over to a closet, opened it up, and fished through a pile of junk until he found a cleanish rag. The whole time he kept one eye trained on his potentially unstable commander, and another on Earth. He blinked the earthbound eye a couple times, just to make sure there wasn't anything about its continued existence he was missing.

Meanwhile, 9-Krelblax set the champagne bottle down, fished out his communicator, and started shouting instructions at it. "Initiate LightYearLink with my father!" He paused, listening to a voice on the other end. "No, that's *me*. You know what, just take that entry out of my address book, will you?"

Zzarvon quietly slunk across the bridge, still careful to give 9-Krelblax a wide berth. He approached the part of the observation window where the champagne had hit and raised the rag to start wiping the residue off, but what he saw quickly made a few window streaks seem wildly unimportant.

Where Earth had been just seconds before, there was only a giant cloud of dust. Zzarvon turned around. 9-Krelblax was standing directly behind him, maybe ten feet away from the window. "No, I'll be reversing the charges," 9-Krelblax said. He looked at Zzarvon and grinned.

Zzarvon turned back around and gazed out at the remains of Earth. He hadn't seen much of the planet, but he had enjoyed the parts he experienced. He had thought that it might be a fun place to revisit someday. Plus, his new friend King Moho was still down there. He might have appreciated not dying. The other humans had been alright, Zzarvon thought. Certainly nobody had done anything that warranted their race's utter destruction. Now, all that was left of their planet was a cloud of dust, and even that was expanding. Soon there would be no trace of—

"Wait a second," Zzarvon muttered to himself. He leaned his antennae in as close to the window as they could get. The dust cloud that had been Earth was indeed expanding, but there was something very strange about it. There seemed to be a distinct border to the cloud. Zzarvon trained his eyes on a particular patch of dust. He watched as it slowly floated away from the center of the cloud that had once been Earth, but all of a sudden, it disappeared from sight, the way the sun might pass behind a cloud. It was as if the dust had vanished behind some sort of invisible wall.

"Hey, Dad!" 9-Krelblax was saying into his communicator. "Guess what? No, it's not about trash, don't hang up!"

Zzarvon had no idea what the hell he was looking at, but as he kept watching it, he saw that the invisible border seemed to stretch all the way around the dust cloud. As the dust floated away into space, it eventually reached a place where it became impossible to see. It was as if Zzarvon was looking into a microscope, and an amoeba had floated out of the viewing plane. A microscope or...

"Or a hole!" Zzarvon whispered to himself.

"Keep it down, Zzarvon!" 9-Krelblax shouted. "No, sorry, Dad, not you. But yeah, guess what? No, I just said it's *not* about trash!"

Keeping his gaze locked on the spot where Earth used to be, Zzarvon slowly oozed to the left. And sure enough, as he moved, a familiar blue sphere emerged from behind whatever it was that had been blocking it from sight. After a couple feet Zzarvon could see half the Earth and half the dust cloud, and once he'd moved ten feet, the entire Earth was back in his field of vision. The dust cloud, on the other hand, was nowhere to be seen.

Zzarvon shuffled back to his original spot, and, sure enough, the visual phenomenon repeated itself. The Earth slid behind the dust as if it were being eclipsed by an alternate vision of itself.

"I'm technically the best pole vaulter in the galaxy, Dad!" 9-Krelblax announced. "What's that? Why did I say 'technically'? I don't think I did! What's that? I definitely did? Well, I didn't mean anything by it! Well, it was the only planet in the galaxy where they have pole vaulting, so it does so apply. Why did I say 'was'? Well, that's the other thing I'm calling about..."

Zzarvon oozed over to 9-Krelblax, stuck out a tentacle, and hit the END CALL button on his communicator. There was a click as the LightYearLink with the president dropped off.

"What the hell!" 9-Krelblax shouted. "I hadn't arranged for him to reverse the charges yet! That's going to cost a fortune!"

"You need to see this, sir," Zzarvon said. He steeled himself to be slapped or disintegrated, but 9-Krelblax was clearly so surprised by Zzarvon's audacity that he did not respond at all. Zzarvon oozed halfway back to the window, then turned and gestured for 9-Krelblax to follow.

9-Krelblax oozed over, still in shock. Zzarvon pointed a tentacle at the dust cloud. 9-Krelblax looked at it, then turned to his navigator. "I know!" he said. "It's beautiful! I still don't understand why you had to—"

Zzarvon beckoned 9-Krelblax to follow him, and slid down the same stretch of the bridge he'd covered earlier. 9-Krelblax sighed, but eventually followed, glaring at Zzarvon the entire way. When he reached the point where Zzarvon had stopped, he threw up his tentacles in exasperation.

"What the hell is this follow the leader nonsense?" 9-Krelblax shouted. "You're ruining my celebration!" Zzarvon reached out with a few tentacles and spun 9-Krelblax so that he was once again looking out the window. When the Larvilkian commander saw what his navigator wanted him to see, his moodcore turned an icy grey and he emitted a low groan.

"Earth is still there!" Zzarvon said, not bothering to mask his delight. He pranced back down the bridge to the spot where the Earth disappeared and waved for 9-Krelblax to follow. The commander stood frozen for a second looking at the planet he thought he'd destroyed. Then he slumped forward and slithered over to where Zzarvon was standing.

"It must have gone through a wormhole!" Zzarvon said, pointing at the exploded Earth. "The missile opened up a tear in space and destroyed a parallel-dimension Earth! From this exact angle you can see into the wormhole, but from just a few feet in any other direction, it's invisible!" Zzarvon breathed a sigh of relief. "I'm so happy that you're not crazy, sir! You really had me worried for a second there!"

9-Krelblax gulped. He too was grateful that he was not crazy. A few seconds ago he'd been having serious doubts. But his relief quickly began to turn to confused anger. A wormhole? How the hell had this happened?

There was a whoosh from behind them as the doors to the bridge opened. "Welcome back, sirs!" a voice proclaimed, a little too enthusiastically.

9-Krelblax and Zzarvon turned around. Standing behind them, his eyes crossed and his antennae drooping, was Technician Tamblirx. The duplicate had a makeshift tool belt strapped around his waist. Several of the pouches attached to the belt were glowing, some were rustling suspiciously, and one was doing both. His droopy eye was now severely bloodshot.

Zzarvon and 9-Krelblax exchanged a look as the technician hitched up his belt and oozed into the center of the bridge. "My, fixing things and regular maintenance certainly does make me thirsty!" Tamblirx proclaimed. "Just the normal thirst of a normal Larvilkian that I shall now quench!"

Tamblirx picked up the discarded bottle of champagne and smiled far too wide a smile at 9-Krelblax and Zzarvon. Then, he suddenly tilted the bottle to his right and poured champagne all over the floor for about five seconds until he righted it.

"Ahhhhh!" Tamblirx sighed, smacking his orifice as if satisfied. "That hits the spot, doesn't it? Well, there's plenty more repairs for me, your real ship's technician, to do!" He began to ooze away, but 9-Krelblax called out.

"Wait a second!"

Tamblirx stopped and turned around. A few seconds later, he realized his eyes were not facing 9-Krelblax and he rotated them around as well. The droopy, bloodshot eye was the last to turn around, and it was now actively oozing a slimy pus.

"What repairs did you make while we were down on HAWAll?" 9-Krelblax asked, suddenly very suspicious.

"Oh, a whole bunch of little things here and there," Tamblirx said. "I fixed a leak in the shower. Replaced a light diode that was out in the hallway. Refined the hyperwarp using advanced theoretical physics calculations and then integrated it into our defense system. Oiled that sticky 'door close' button."

9-Krelblax and Zzarvon shared another concerned look. "What was that third one?" 9-Krelblax asked.

"Oh, just some improvements to the hyperwarp that I'd been meaning to integrate for a long time, since this version of me has definitely been the technician here for a long time. Anyway, I improved the efficiency of the hyperwarp by overclocking it to a degree previously thought impossible: infinity plus one! It turns out, all it needed was some imaginary equations that I invented! They were fairly simple once I realized all you had to do was use numbers that don't exist. I don't know why nobody's thought of doing that before."

"Because that sounds dangerous as hell!" 9-Krelblax shouted at Tamblirx. "Our hyperwarp was already wildly unstable!"

"And then I got bored so I replaced the current defense system with an experimental one controlled by the hyperwarp!" Tamblirx smiled a vacant smile at this memory, but it quickly left his face. "I just remembered that I shocked myself pretty badly hooking the hyperwarp up to the missiles. No wonder I feel light-headed!" And with that, the technician's eye antennae drooped down even farther, and his entire body lilted to the left, then abruptly changed course as he collapsed facedown in the puddle of champagne he'd spilled on the ground.

"That bozo ran amok 'fixing things' while I was competing in the Olympics!" 9-Krelblax yelled. "We're lucky we didn't explode the minute we came back on board!"

"It did sound like he made some questionable choices, sir," Zzarvon said. He was secretly disappointed that none of those choices had resulted in a new roast pig. Accidents like that were the type of malfunction he could get behind. "But it does explain what might have happened with the missile?"

Zzarvon and 9-Krelblax looked out into space again. Now that they knew what they were looking at, it was actually kind of easy to see the boundary of the wormhole that contained the destroyed Earth.

"So when I hit the button to fire the missile, Tamblirx's 'improvements' caused the hyperwarp to kick in?" 9-Krelblax asked, trying to make sense of the situation as he spoke.

"I think so," Zzarvon replied. "And with the hyperwarp cranked up to infinity plus one, it was strong enough to tear a hole in time and explode an Earth in an alternate dimension. Which is what we're seeing when we stare into the wormhole."

"We should probably stop staring into the wormhole, right?" 9-Krelblax asked.

"I think that would probably be wise from a health standpoint, yeah," Zzarvon agreed. "Let's not stand too close to Tamblirx either. I'm thinking he just hit the expiration date for an unstable alternate-dimension hyperwarp duplicate." Both Larvilkians quickly slid over a few feet so that the regular, non-destroyed Earth was visible again. They both ignored the gurgles of the unconscious or maybe dying technician behind them.

"It makes a lot of sense in retrospect," Zzarvon said. 9-Krelblax narrowed a single eye at him. "Well, not all of it," Zzarvon corrected himself. "But did you really think that missile you fired was that powerful, sir? Powerful enough to explode the entire Earth? We're a StarBarge! We don't carry that kind of weaponry. Those missiles are designed for breaking up pieces of trash that are too large for us to fit on board. The last time we used them was on a couch. It took three of those missiles just to break it in half. Without the hyperwarp powering it, I don't think that missile could have even taken out the bird pile on HAWAll."

"I guess you're right, Zzarvon," 9-Krelblax admitted. "I was like a nine out of ten on the pissed off scale when we got back on the ship. I'm sure if I had been thinking clearly I would have realized that."

Zzarvon wondered how the billions of dead people on the alternate-dimension Earth would have felt if they knew their planet might have been spared if 9-Krelblax had merely been an *eight* out of ten. He kept this thought to himself. Instead he opted to offer some encouragement.

"You know, sir, seven billion people dead in an alternate dimension is a pretty substantial number. That's over a hundred thousand times more people than Hitler killed." 9-Krelblax's moodcore sparked at the mention of his Earthling idol. "Plus," Zzarvon added. "Hitler only *oversaw* an Olympics. He never won second place in one."

"Hey, you're right, Zzarvon!" 9-Krelblax smiled and puffed his chest out. "I guess you could say I'm better than Hitler! Bet there aren't a lot of people who can make that claim!"

"I bet there aren't!" Zzarvon smiled.

A light began to blink on 9-Krelblax's communicator and it gave off a shrill series of beeps. 9-Krelblax glanced at it.

"Ah crap, it's my dad," he said. "At least he's paying for it this time. I've gotta take this."

"Of course, sir!" Zzarvon replied. "But before you do, what should our next agenda item be? We had a service request from the Chartex system. They've evidently got over two hundred expired barrels of glue that they need hauled off. There's also the second moon of Mille-Gree-7. They are approaching what they described as 'Peak Diaper.' That sounds pretty serious. There's also a pizzeria near Cassiopeia that needs a couch removed from the alley behind their store. Hope we still have a few missiles left if we're going to tackle that—"

9-Krelblax cut Zzarvon off with the wave of a tentacle. A few days ago the mention of trash and trash-related service requests would have rendered him a sulking wreck. But right now he looked like he couldn't care less about the refuse of the galaxy or what the hell 'Peak Diaper' could possibly mean. Zzarvon had to avert his gaze from the brilliant shade of green shining from 9-Krelblax's moodcore.

"There's another Olympics in four years, right?" 9-Krelblax asked. Zzarvon nodded. "Well, I think we've got some training to do!" 9-Krelblax exclaimed.

"Yes, sir!" Zzarvon replied. His moodcore lit up a bright green to match his commander's, and both men found themselves thinking of the extremely patriotic part of their national anthem, the part that had killed all those seagulls during the opening ceremony.

9-Krelblax reached down, clicked a button on his communicator, and began to speak. "Where were we, Dad? Oh yeah, I was telling you how I technically exploded an entire planet. What do I mean by 'technically'? Nothing. I think you misheard me."

Zzarvon smiled at his commander, the second best pole vaulter in the entire universe. He'd never seen him this proud before. He oozed over to the navigation console, reached out a tentacle, and activated the holoscreen.

"Anyway, it had over seven billion people on it." 9-Krelblax was beaming. "You know that's over a hundred thousand times more people than—that's right, than Hitler! You've heard of him?"

Four years seems like an awful long time to wait until the next Olympics, Zzarvon thought to himself as he reached out and turned a dial. *If I set the hyperwarp juuuust right, I bet we could be there in a few hours…*

twenty-three

"You could have at least polished it," Kara said. "The sun barely glints off it at all! See?" She pointed her Olympic gold medal at the airplane window and tilted it back and forth.

"Ow!" yelped Cornelius as the sun hit the medal and reflected directly into his eyes. Still gripping his Bloody Mary, he raised his hand to shade his face. "It actually seems pretty damn shiny already, Kara. You can polish it when we get home but for now, cut that out! Until the plane hits eighty miles per hour, they can still legally throw you out the emergency exit. Trust me."

Kara smiled and pulled the medal back from the window. She raised it to eye level and inspected it for what was probably the thirtieth time since Cornelius had hung it around her neck back on HAWAII. She had never been a big jewelry person, but was beginning to see the appeal. The medal had real weight to it. On one side it had the iconic five ring Olympic logo. The other side had some garbage about the triple jump, but Cornelius had promised that once they were back in America they'd get it re-engraved to indicate that it had been awarded for pole vault. A *real* Olympic event, in her opinion.

Kara Everglades had no idea that she had exploded in an alternate dimension roughly five hours ago. There had been a bright flash of light in the sky roughly a minute after the *Stupid Butt* took off, but, obviously, the annihilation the Larvilkians promised had never happened. As far as Kara was concerned, 9-Krelblax's threats were as empty as his trophy case.

In the aisle seat next to Kara, Cornelius downed his Bloody Mary and gestured at the first class cabin flight attendant for another quick one before they took off. Across the aisle, King Moho sat with a napkin tied around his neck, ready to feast on the suckling pig he had somehow managed to track down in a remote subsection of Terminal X.

The flight attendant set down a Bloody Mary in front of Cornelius, and handed King Moho a can of beer, since the pig was taking up every inch of his tray table.

"You're going to have to stow that tray before takeoff, sir," she informed the king of Maui.

"The hell?" King Moho said through a mouthful of succulent pork. "I've still got all this pig left!"

"You'll have to stow your pig as well." The flight attendant was smiling, but the pure contempt in her voice was at a level usually reserved for chastising someone who had shown up to their kid's Little League game drunk and exposed themselves to the umpire to protest a called third strike.

"Do you know who I'm with?" King Moho demanded. He pointed a greasy drumstick across the aisle. "That's Kara Everglades, Olympic gold medalist."

"I don't think pigs are supposed to have drumsticks, your highness," Kara said. King Moho raised an eyebrow, then pulled the drumstick back for closer inspection.

"I'll be damned," he said. He turned it over a couple times, then shrugged and took a huge bite.

"I'm well aware of Ms. Everglades's... *achievements*," the flight attendant seethed. "Her grandfather's as well. They've been all over the news, as I'm sure you're aware. My brother has been waking up at three a.m. every day for the last four years to train for rowing in this year's Olympics. Everyone in our hometown chipped in to send him to Hawaii, which is where he and the rest of his team are currently sitting in a hotel across the street from an empty stadium, wondering how to get the last half decade of their lives back."

The flight attendant briefly pulled back her cheeks in a tight, reptilian smile. "You know, I used to think Vietnam was our country's greatest shame," she said. "But now I'm not so sure."

Kara found herself wondering what the woman's moodcore might look like if she were a Larvilkian. She thought there was a good chance it might just be a holographic projection of vultures picking at a dead horse.

"Unfortunately, sir," the attendant concluded, "we're not able to make exceptions. Even for world-class athletes and their entourages. You'll have to stow the pig."

When the attendant had moved on down the aisle, King Moho leaned over to Kara. "Did you hear that?" he giggled, unable to contain his glee. "She knows who you are! You're famous!"

Kara had known that encounters like this were inevitable ever since she stepped out of Terminal X and into the normal part of Heathrow. A row of reporters and cameramen had been waiting there. They stood at the boundary of Terminal X as if possessed by the unspoken fear that crossing over might suddenly age them seventy years in the blink of an eye. They shouted questions, snapped camera flashes, and thrust microphones just far enough to not breach the invisible border between terminals.

They wanted a piece of everyone in the motley group of Olympic spectators, participants, masterminds, and hostages. Some had been more obliging than others.

Cornelius had prepped for the occasion by donning a t-shirt and baseball cap bearing the name of his new online pill depot: http://iPills.HAWAll.gov

"Remember, those aren't *i*'s! Those are *l*'s!" he crowed like a carnival barker.

"So the address is L-P-L-L-L-S dot Hawaii dot gov?" a reporter from CNN asked. "Can we get that up on the lower third?"

"No, dammit, it's…"

"No, I think the *l*'s in pills are actually *i*'s," said someone from MSNBC. "Get the social intern to tweet that address!" she yelled to some miserable idiot who was evidently tasked with managing shit like that.

"No! Jesus, no!" Cornelius said, waving his hands. "iPills where the *l*'s are *i*'s is NOT a site you want your kids going to. Someone has been squatting on that site for years, and if you go to it you will see that I do *not* mean squatting figuratively. The *i*'s are *l*'s in the HAWAll domain. Those are the only fake letters! It's not that confusing, people!"

During the extreme confusion that followed, reporters from lesser networks shouted a variety of questions at the other people who had been on the island, the eyewitnesses to what the press had quickly deemed Vaultgate. Cornelius did not care for the name and tried to interject that it should be called ipillsdotHAWAlldotgovgate but by then it was too late. The media jackals had descended.

"Is it true that Warland is in the running to host the 2034 Winter Games?"

"What happened to the hippo costume?"

"People have been speculating, was it a 'poop over the side' type of situation, or what?"

"President for Life Makepeace, is that guy dead?"

"Sir, can you please put that pin away? Because none of us are interested in it. At all. See, your wife is nodding."

"What would the Larvilkians think of the massive amount of online fan art that depicts 9-Krelblax and Zzarvon kissing?"

"King Moho, were you relieved when the aliens stopped probing you?"

King Moho had nearly choked on a piece of pig. "What? No!" he sputtered. "You've got it all wrong!"

"King... wished... for probings... to continue," the reporter scribbled.

But for every reporter who was happy to interview a witness, and there were many of them—the "HAWAll Seven," as they were dubbed, would dominate the "you're probably asleep already" slot on the late night talk show circuit for the next month—there were three more who wanted to talk to the star of the games. Kara found herself surrounded by a wall of microphones and camera flashes. Every now and then she could actually make out a question in the cacophony.

"Is it true you were pole vaulting before you could walk?"

"Kara, has pole vault legend Verna Dickerson reached out to congratulate you yet?"

"If I get you a pole, will you vault over that Sbarro right now?"

"Where will you visit first, the White House or Disneyland?"

"When reached for comment, your father just said, 'Can't talk, last chance for some sweet, sweet action.' Any idea what he meant by that?"

"Have you received any endorsement deals from pole companies or any pole-related industries in general?"

"How did you decide to dedicate your life to pole vaulting instead of one of the good sports?"

Though she'd stared down the threat of alien annihilation hours earlier, Kara found the media horde somewhat daunting at first. But once she overcame the instinct to be polite and started selectively ignoring the uglier reporters, she quickly grew comfortable with the barrage of shouted questions and started having fun with it.

"The way I see it is, you grab a pole, and you vault. It's not rocket science. In fact, the guy I beat literally had a rocket, so maybe pole vaulting is harder! Next question! He wants to make a biopic? I dunno, didn't his last movie only make like four hundred million bucks? What's that? Slime? No, I was extremely careful to wipe down the pole. *Extremely*. That stuff smelled like batteries that a sick cat peed on."

But just when she'd really been getting into the groove, winking, and pointing finger guns, and calling reporters "baby," Cornelius sidled up beside her, announced that they had to get to their flight, and whisked her away.

"The *i*'s are *l*'s!" he called over his shoulder as they made their exit. "Twenty percent off your first order when you use coupon code POLEVAULT. We ship in old Amazon boxes so you can order without fear of nosy neighbors!"

That was when they'd parted ways with everyone. President for Life Makepeace waved as he paid for a SmartCarte machine that he planned to use to wheel Goodluck to their plane. Mac, per his arrangement with Cornelius, was staring into a news camera and describing the wild time he'd had with all the readily available drugs, hookers, and favorable-odds gambling that HAWAll had to offer. Backwards Cap had stayed on as steward of the island in order to work off the debt he owed to Cornelius as a result of Kara's successful jump. Cornelius had assured him that at the very least, the non-prostitute vices his friend was currently extolling would actually be arriving on HAWAll within a week, and ordered him to not go crazy from isolation in the meantime. Also, Cornelius told him, he would cut his dick off if he tried any funny business.

The last of the HAWAll Seven Kara saw was Henry. He was standing outside the circle of reporters, holding his bag covered with Olympic pins. Every now and then he'd adjust the Larvilkian navigator pin that he had attached to a prominent spot near the zipper. When she took her final glance over her shoulder, Kara could have sworn she saw the pin pulsing a faint green light.

Now that she was seated in first class and about to take off, the whole experience seemed far away and surreal. Kara could only imagine that the crowd waiting for them when they touched down in America would dwarf the hastily assembled pool of reporters in Heathrow. She hoped that the crowd's vibe would be more "beating those alien assholes was really impressive" and less of the "I see humanity at its absolute nadir on a daily basis and yet *you* stand out as someone ultra-worthy of my scorn" attitude the flight attendant had given her. Kara thought she would try to glint an extra bright ray of sunshine into that witch's eyes when she came by with the pretzels.

Cornelius was flipping through a complimentary copy of *USA Today* when he nearly choked on his Bloody Mary. Kara turned toward the sputtering to make sure he was OK. Cornelius nodded that he'd be fine and thrust the paper over Kara's lap, toward the other side of the aisle.

King Moho was carefully stashing his pig in the overhead bin, but after Cornelius gave his backside a few whacks with the paper, he decided it was secure enough, shut the compartment door, and turned around.

"What is it?" King Moho asked. He took the paper, then looked to where Cornelius was pointing. Kara craned her neck into the aisle to see as well.

"Hawaii: It's Not a Shitty Platform" the ad's headline screamed in thirty-six point font. It took up a quarter of page A-2, and had been paid for by the Hawaii Board of Tourism. Below the giant headline, it listed the many things that tourists needed to keep an eye out for in order to make sure they were actually booking a trip to the island paradise and not to the site of Vaultgate.

"They've gone rogue!" King Moho said, his eyes wide. He looked at Cornelius. "The other six kings must have approved this while I was off the grid. You know I'd never say this about you, Corny. 'A fourth-world country?' That's insulting and uncalled for! I'll have a word with them as soon as I get back."

"Now, now," Cornelius said. "Let's not act hastily. They've probably got this ad running in every major newspaper and magazine! Think of the publicity! Plus: 'The world's first fourth-world country.'" Cornelius spread his hands out as he envisioned that motto printed on a banner that stretched the length of HAWAII. "I kind of like the sound of that. There's a lot to be said for being first! Right, Kara?" Cornelius pointed at the gold medal.

King Moho still looked somewhat chagrined at the actions of his fellow cabal members, but handed the paper back and plopped down in his seat. The flight attendant came by to gather up what remained of the drinks, and shot Kara a bitter look. Kara stuck out her tongue, and giggled when the woman nearly dropped the drinks in surprise. When the flight attendant turned her back, Kara looked over at Cornelius, who was smiling proudly.

Once the flight attendant had retreated to the front of the cabin, Cornelius reached into his pocket. He produced two airline bottles of vodka that he'd smuggled aboard or maybe stolen from the drink cart and offered one to Kara. She checked over her shoulder instinctively, then looked back at Cornelius.

"You did a great job out there, Kara," Cornelius said as the plane pulled back from the jet bridge.

"Thanks," Kara said as she took the vodka bottle. She stared at it, turning it over in her hands a couple times while she decided what to say next. Finally she looked up at Cornelius. "I'm glad you turned out not to be dead, Grandpa."

"That's the nicest thing anyone's ever said to me," Cornelius said. From the way he smiled, Kara knew it was true. As the plane began to taxi, she unscrewed the cap from the vodka and dropped it to the floor.

"Do you have enough of those to share?" King Moho asked from across the aisle.

"No!" Kara and Cornelius said in unison, not bothering to even look at him. The plane's engines began to rumble, and as it picked up speed, Kara and Cornelius Everglades clinked their vodka bottles together. They tilted them back as the jet's nose lifted off the ground, and by the time the vodka was nothing but a burn in their throats, the plane was airborne, heading toward America with the newest Olympic champion on board.

Kara felt the warmth run down her chest, and once she realized she wasn't going to throw up, she actually thought she kind of enjoyed it. She knew it wasn't possible for the vodka to get her drunk so quickly, but all of a sudden Kara felt like she needed to tell her grandfather how much he meant to her. How much this experience had meant to her. How much she loved him.

"Grandpa..." Kara started. "I just wanted to say..." Kara paused, but Cornelius looked at her as if he knew what was coming. He patted Kara's hand and nodded for her to continue.

Kara took a deep breath and started again. "I just wanted to say that..."

There was a ding from the overhead sound system. Kara hopped over Cornelius and was in the aisle before he even had his seatbelt unbuckled. As she reached out for the handle of the lavatory door, she glanced back at her grandfather, who was frozen halfway out of his seat with his hands on the armrests. Kara smiled and winked, then darted into the bathroom, and slammed the door shut.

"Son of a bitch!" Cornelius Everglades shouted. There was a sliding noise, then a click. A green light turned red as "Vacant" flipped to "Occupied."

The pole vault champion of the entire universe leaned her head back against a wad of toilet paper, closed her eyes, and began to dream about her next adventure.

epilogue

It was a cloudless night and the surface of HAWAll glistened underneath a full moon. Forty feet below, water lapped at the barnacle-encrusted pillars that supported the former naval fort. The bottom of the rusty ladder disappeared below the black surface of the ocean. There had not been a boat tied to it for five days now, but one would come soon, bearing drugs, and booze, and hookers, and then everything would be OK.

That was what Backwards Cap told himself as he dangled his legs off the edge of the country and watched the moon rise.

He thought he would probably have a beer first. Just crack it open and take a big, long pull, as much as he could at once. Maybe he'd finish the whole can in one sip? It would taste so good after nothing but bottled water. Then he'd smoke a joint. Really relax.

After all, he'd earned it! He'd spent the past five days working his ass off. Getting rid of the seagull pile had been priority number one. That had gone right off the side, piece of cake. Dismantling the pole vault bar had taken a bit more time. Sure, you could have just pushed that into the sea as well, but who knew? Some of that stuff could come in handy down the line. The dismantled apparatus was now stacked with precision on the southwest corner of HAWAll.

Yes, a joint would be well deserved. Then maybe another beer. Or a shot of bourbon! Backwards Cap licked his lips at the thought. Back on the mainland, he'd never been particular about his liquor. The cheaper the better. But this might be the occasion for something nice, something from the top shelf.

He'd worked up quite a thirst scrubbing the surface of HAWAIl. On his hands with a hard bristled brush, it took him a day and a half, sun up to sun down, to tackle the entire platform. But the improvement was marked. And after he finished, he decided to do it again, to see if he could beat his personal best. The second time he finished in under nine hours. The third time was even faster, fourth and fifth exponentially so. After the sixth the country looked good enough to eat off, and so he did, a celebratory feast of a single saltine. Then he scrubbed the entire country, corner to corner.

Backwards Cap couldn't recall the last time he had slept.

After the bourbon, he'd introduce himself to the hookers. After all, that's why he was here! "Welcome to HAWAIl!" he'd say. "I cleaned the place myself. Would you like to see my mansion? Saltine?"

Hey, that sounded like a grand idea! Backwards Cap turned the saltine sleeve upside down and shook it until a cracker fell out onto the surface of HAWAIl. It was the last cracker in the sleeve. He leaned over and picked the saltine up with his teeth. Clean enough to eat off of! As he straightened up and started chewing, he crumpled the sleeve into a ball. He would hang onto it until the boat came.

"Or you could throw it over the edge!"

Backwards Cap snapped his head around. There was nobody there, of course. It hadn't even really been a voice he'd heard. More of a physical sensation.

"Go on!" the sensation reiterated. "Just toss it over! Who cares? This is *your* island!"

Backwards Cap looked at the crumpled wrapper for a few seconds. Ever since he was old enough to know right from wrong, it had been drilled into him that littering was bad. But those had been the rules of the mainland. Of his old life.

He tossed the crumpled cellophane sleeve into the night air. It fell slowly, like a tiny parachute, dancing in the updrafts and unpredictable wind currents that swirled around the country. Eventually it landed without a splash and disappeared from sight.

"Didn't that feel good?"

It seemed crazy but it was almost as if the sensation was emanating from a filling in one of his molars. Backwards Cap reached up and rubbed at the side of his jaw. He didn't detect anything out of the ordinary. But then again, it was hard to feel anything through the paw.

He dropped the paw into his lap. It was probably nothing. But the nothing was happening a lot more frequently.

Backwards Cap swung his feet back and forth, fascinated by the way the moonlight glinted off his claws. The night was windy and brisk, he probably should have been chilly. But he'd felt nothing but warmth ever since he first put the costume on three days ago. Warmth and an impending sense that wrongs would soon be righted.

"Have you considered a killing spree?" came the weird, internalized voice from one of his back teeth.

Backwards Cap never really had. But that was back on the mainland. His old life.

He'd put the costume on as a goof. Just to see what it felt like to clean the island dressed as a hippo.

"I'm a jackrabbit!" his filling had insisted, punctuating its point with a streak of pain that stabbed into his gums. Backwards Cap had mumbled an apology, but it had gone unaccepted. Backwards Cap didn't want to offend the sensation any further. Backwards Cap was worried what would happen if he took the costume off.

"I can help you show them all," his filling insisted. "But I need to be complete."

Backwards Cap knew what this meant, and it was a step he had been resisting. But he was weak now. Weak and tired and hungry. All he wanted was a beer and a shot and a joint and then to show a hooker his mansion. He realized that his right hand—his right *paw*—was reaching up toward his head. He tried to stop it, but it kept moving. He tried to reach over and grab it with his left paw, but it was as if it were numb.

The paw grabbed the brim of his cap and pulled it off his head. Backwards Cap watched as if observing himself in a dream as the paw held the cap out in front of him, offering him what he realized was one last look. Then the paw tucked the cap to his chest and flung it into the air like a frisbee. The cap traced a lilting path down through the night, eventually crossing beneath the platform and disappearing from sight before it hit the water.

"Complete me," his filling intoned.

Backwards Cap got to his feet, his feet which were no longer his own. He was moving slowly, soporifically, yet at the same time it felt as if he'd stood up too fast and blood was rushing to his head. But he moved onward. He didn't have a choice. The toenails clacked on the brilliant, clean surface of HAWAII. Backwards Cap was suddenly gripped by an unknowable horror about their origin, and his jaw began to tremble.

The governor's mansion loomed, a crooked tombstone on the horizon.

Backwards Cap pushed in the door. Jeff the Jackrabbit's head sat in the center of the floor. Backwards Cap shuffled over to it, sleepwalking while awake. When one of the toenails touched the head, he stopped moving. There was only one more step, one thing left to do.

"Don't even think about it," his filling cautioned. Backwards Cap had no idea what it was talking about, but then he did. He could just hurl himself off the platform. He could be done with this. The costume had read his mind before he even had the idea.

"Complete me."

The memory hit Backwards Cap so hard that he was jolted back a step. His family was leaving the Little League field as the sun set on a beautiful summer day. He was eating a pouch of fruit snacks and drinking an ice cold Gatorade and they were the same delicious vague fruity flavor. That day, he had hit a home run and made a diving catch in the field, and when they got to the car, his proud father asked him if he wanted to ride up in the front seat. He'd buckled the seat belt and rolled the window down. When the car pulled out onto the road, a rush of air hit his face, and he closed his eyes and took a deep breath. From the back seat, Backwards Cap's little brother asked if he could see the game ball the coach had given him, and when Backwards Cap turned around to hand it to him, he'd seen his mother smiling at him. She looked radiant.

It was the happiest Backwards Cap had ever been.

He blinked twice and shook his head and realized he'd been standing in front of the head for hours. He turned around. Through the door of the governor's mansion, the moon was at its apex, a tiny version of itself compared to earlier that night. Backwards Cap reached up and touched his jaw. There was no pain, no voices. Whatever sensation, whatever urging he had felt earlier had been nothing but his imagination. Severe malnutrition combined with licking the platform probably hadn't helped either.

"Jesus," Backwards Cap muttered, as he reached up and ruffled his matted hair with the gross costume paw. His longings for vice and debauchery had vanished. When Cornelius returned to the island, he could keep the booze and the weed and the hookers. All Backwards Cap wanted now was a big, heaping plate of his mother's pesto linguini.

But first he had to get the hell out of the idiotic mascot costume. Backwards Cap didn't know why he had put it on in the first place. Even though it was obviously not possessed or evil, the thing totally gave him the creeps. Plus it was itchy as hell. He stepped into the doorway of the governor's mansion, pulled both his arms out of the holes of the costume's arms, and lowered Jeff's torso until it was sitting on the ground.

Backwards Cap took a deep breath of the fresh sea air. It had been a crazy week. His parents would certainly enjoy hearing about it, maybe with a few details about his motivation for coming to the island omitted. He'd tell them over dinner. Maybe Mom would even make her garlic bread. He wondered if the game ball was still on the bookshelf in his bedroom.

He raised his right leg out of the costume, then his left. It slumped to the ground, empty, formless. Backwards Cap chuckled. After a solid ten hours of sleep, it would all seem like a distant dream. The thought made him yawn, and he stretched, relishing how tired he felt. He turned back into the governor's mansion with his arms still raised above his head. A good night's sleep would solve everything.

That was when Jeff winked.

There was a brief, piercing scream as the moon began to set over HAWAIl.

July 27, 2014 — January 26, 2016
San Diego, California
Burlington, Vermont

Acknowledgments

Lauren, your keen eye and patience made this possible, but the sound of your laugh as you read it made this worth it.

Adam Koford, thank you for once again creating a cover that I will be thrilled to have people judge this book by.

Though writing a novel is just about the most solitary exercise one can undertake, this book would have been impossible without two groups of people. So, to the creators who shaped my sense of humor and my desire and confidence to share it with other people, and to the people who were willing to read what I had to say, (if you've come this far then, yeah, I mean you): thank you.

About The Author

Conor Lastowka lives in Burlington, Vermont with his wife Lauren. He works as a Senior Writer - Producer at RiffTrax.com.

This is his second novel.

Also by Conor Lastowka

Gone Whalin'

[Citation Needed]: The Best of Wikipedia's Worst Writing

[Citation Needed] 2: The Needening: More of The Best of Wikipedia's Worst Writing

372 Pages We'll Never Get Back podcast

Made in the USA
San Bernardino, CA
20 July 2018